"LOOPY AND ENJOYABLE . . . OFFBEAT AND
ORIGINAL . . . BREEZY AND ENTERTAINING . . .
sheer zestful storytelling energy . . . a novel that breaks all
the rules."   —*Boston Globe*

"AN 800-POUND GORILLA OF A HORROR NOVEL
. . . WILD, IMAGINATIVE . . . POWERFUL,
UNPREDICTABLE."   —*Kirkus Reviews*

"A MORPHINE NIGHTMARE WITH YOUR EYES
GLUED OPEN. DON'T READ THIS BOOK ALONE
IN BED."   —David B. Feinberg, author of *Eighty-Sixed*

"A BRILLIANT TALE . . . Gannett has boldly entered
the horror genre with total ingenuity. . . . Readers will be
terrified and amazed at the same time."   —*Associated Press*

"GRABS YOU BY THE SNOUT AND WON'T LET GO.
. . . Any writer who gives the horror genre such a rude
spanking is worth watching."   —*Details*

LEWIS GANNETT was born in Washington, D.C., grew up
in Europe, went to Harvard and Massachusetts Institute of
Technology, dropped out to become a waiter, then started
writing. This is his first novel.

Lewis Gannett

THE LIVING ONE

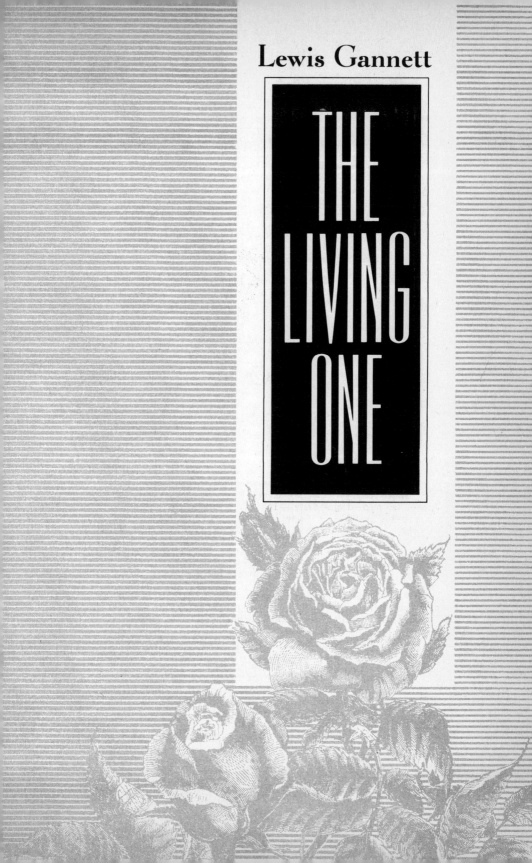

PLUME
Published by the Penguin Group
Penguin Books USA Inc., 375 Hudson Street,
New York, New York 10014, U.S.A.
Penguin Books Ltd, 27 Wrights Lane, London W8 5TZ, England
Penguin Books Australia Ltd, Ringwood, Victoria, Australia
Penguin Books Canada Ltd, 10 Alcorn Avenue,
Toronto, Ontario, Canada M4V 3B2
Penguin Books (N.Z.) Ltd, 182–190 Wairau Road, Auckland 10, New Zealand

Penguin Books Ltd, Registered Offices: Harmondsworth, Middlesex, England

Published by Plume, an imprint of Dutton Signet,
a division of Penguin Books USA Inc.
This is an authorized reprint of a hardcover published by Random House, Inc.

First Plume Printing, February, 1994
10 9 8 7 6 5 4 3 2 1

LIBRARY OF CONGRESS CATALOGING-IN-PUBLICATION DATA
Gannett, Lewis.
    The living one / Lewis Gannett.
        p.   cm.
    ISBN 0-452-27134-7
    1. Fathers and sons—United States—Fiction.   2. Problem families—
United States—Fiction.   3. Teenage boys—United States—Fiction.
4. Gay men—United States—Fiction.   I. Title.
[PS3557.A517L58   1993b]
813′.54—dc20   93–37205
                                                                            CIP

Printed in the United States of America
Original hardcover design by J. K. Lambert

PUBLISHER'S NOTE
This is a work of fiction. Names, characters, places, and incidents either
are the product of the author's imagination or are used fictitiously, and
any resemblance to actual persons, living or dead, events, or locales is
entirely coincidental.

To
Matt Foley, Geofrey Graff,
Mark Harrington, Christopher Ladd,
and Dennis Schmeichler

"Maybe the Grislies know."

—S.M.

Acknowledgments

Good can be found in the world; in of all places, Manhattan. The names are Abby Thomas, Jess Taylor, and Jon Karp.

At Darhansoff & Verrill, Abby is a book agent who won't quit. For two years she didn't quit this book, despite odds, and editors, telling her she should. Thank you, Abby.

Jess goes back to the beginning. There was, then, the problem of a typewriter. Jess said, "No problem." Since that time he has said what's wrong and what's right, and I've listened, mulishly on occasion, always with helpless respect. This work is very much the better for it. Thank you, Jess.

Jon is the editor who finally stuck out his neck. His attention to detail, his vision and sheer energy, were maddening; inspiring, and just what was needed, too. Thank you, Jon.

Thanks to Art Cohen for his help with computers, for his wisdom about many other mysteries as well, and most of all for being an excellent friend.

Thanks to Will Aitkin, Larry Christy, Seth Flicker, Charlotte Kahn, Gerald Peary, Christopher Sawyer-Lauçanno, Theo Theoharis, and John White for their generous criticism, support, and advice.

Finally, thanks to Mom, now deceased, and to Dad, for everything.

INTRODUCTION

When we first examined the material from which these pages took form, our intention was to write a straightforward narrative account. We had acquired a great deal of evidence—documents, videotapes, audiotapes—concerning Malcolm and Torrance Spoor. We had gathered additional evidence concerning individuals who were involved with them. Thus armed, we set out to write a history of what these people did to each other.

After extensive sifting and transcribing, however, we decided—or, more accurately, discovered—that before us lay the makings of a kind of collage; which, edited, could tell the story not in our words, but almost entirely in those of the participants themselves.

We pared, we cut, we spliced. The approach was fruitful. What emerged is, to our knowledge, as factual an account as can be given of the saga of Malcolm and Torrance.

The Editors

The Living One

Note from Torrance Spoor
to a Friend, Ricky

January 2nd

Ricky,

I have to show you something. It's a letter from my father. I got it today, here, at school.

You know I'm leaving soon to live with him. Now I'm glad it's only until summer. You will see why when you read his letter.

Don't show it to anybody. Don't say *anything*. Just put it back in the locker after you read it. And make sure the lock catches.

Talk to you later. Ricky, keep your mouth shut.

T.

Letter from Malcolm Spoor
to His Son, Torrance

THE VILLA SPOOR / BANGKOK

Christmas Eve

My Dear Boy Torrance,

I will be coming to the United States in early January to discuss with you certain family matters of great consequence.

I regret we've not seen each other these last ten years. Do you know how important you are to me? You couldn't. I must tell you, Torrance, your importance is growing.

It is time to make some major rearrangements.

The gloriously misspelled letters from La Jolla come so unoften, alas. I do not hold any grudge on that account. Your reticence is natural. We never developed the intimacy you enjoy with that re-markable woman, your mother (she is, I trust, well?). But I have marvelous plans for you and me, Son, splendid are the plans that I have.

We will spend a few months together!

If the idea of reunion does not make you happy, let me say this, you will be very glad indeed when you see what's in store. At the same time, I am sorry to say, you are due for a number of shocks. I urge you to read this in a private place.

The following is frightening, and must be kept absolutely confidential. You will have trouble believing it. You will not, in fact, believe it. One day, however - I assure you of this - not only will you believe me; even more frightening, Torrance, you will understand me.

Read on with an open mind, please. Your father, darling child, soon will lose his!

I will be insane before the next year is finished.

I hesitate to tell you this, my blackest secret. For I make it yours, your own awful secret as well; and I feel too freshly the haunt of a very old suffering.

Our family, you see, has a history of madness. It is a history extending beyond seven centuries. It is, Torrance, a Curse.

For more than seven hundred years, not one of our male forebears has lived past the age of fifty. Worse, many of our paternals took their own lives; or were murdered; or were executed; or otherwise met horrid deaths. Worst, they all died insane.

And Torrance, perhaps you are aware of a curious Spoor knack. We almost invariably produce only one male child per generation. Our name persists despite daunting odds.

We dangle from one of history's more fragile threads.

I must admit that until recently, I've felt exempt. When Father told me what I now tell you - nearly thirty years ago to the day, on a sunny, warm afternoon - I dismissed it as ludicrous nonsense. And when, seven months later, he shot himself, I still could not bring myself to believe a similar fate could possibly await me. My denial was final, quite complete.

Father, I rationalized, was the victim of a self-fulfilling morbidity. In the midst of his illness he had to have sought solace from a fantasy of doom; it was beyond his control, there was nothing he could do, his very provenance was deadly - a logic designed to prove, I was sure, that it wasn't he putting the gun in his mouth, this was an act of the primordial ooze!

That was my theory.

I never told you much about your grandfather. Nor did he tell me much about mine - until that afternoon, seven months before the gun rang out. I'd known about the Spoor lifespan. We've been prominent in business affairs all along, despite our limited longevity; and there were records lying around, biographies, some medical studies - I'd seen them, even read a few. But at the age of seventeen I, like all teenagers, was convinced of my own immortality. Ancestral case histories could not damp my expectations. I was young, do you understand? - only a year older than you are now! And that, dear boy, is so very young . . . Oh, I grow weepy . . .

Forgive me, the page is splotched. And Pip cannot retype, it's too desperately sensitive.

I was meaning to say it is time for you, too, to try - to understand. Perhaps I can help; perhaps by telling the story, Torrance, of how I came to face facts.

Last Easter, I felt the first chill.

I was strolling through the garden with Pip, dear old Pip. He's a marvelous man, please try to disregard Floria's defamations, not a word is true. Your mother, gifted in so many ways, wasn't quite able to forgive - but never mind. We were strolling, stout-hearted Pip and I, with the dogs. Do you remember my dogs? I'm sure Floria does. (She hated them.)

But as I was saying, Pip and the dogs and I were taking our ritual morning stroll. The flowers were blooming, they do that relentlessly here. The bees were humming, the light's clear slant was just beginning to mottle, with heat, and I paused to enjoy the sight of a simply tremendous sepia-tinted rose.

The entire universe seemed captive within those delicately spiraling folds. I stooped to get a whiff of the musk. And why not? It was a perfectly ordinary thing to do, sniffing a rose. People sniff roses all over the world. Roses were created for sniffing, weren't they? Of course!

But face-to-face, as it were, with this rose, I was overcome. I saw a dance. The petals, very slowly at first, were moving. They were circling, rank by rank, 'round and 'round.

I felt such a delight, I could not move. I was gazing at infinitude. And then the gyre grew! The outer petals broadened, their ring, wheeling, steadily expanded, and the inner petals flushed forth revealing countless more rings within, all of them swelling and turning, turning, turning - ever more distantly, to vertiginous *depths.*

Odd, eh? Oh yes. Because suddenly, I fell in! Into a vortex of rose!

Needless to say, I was alarmed. Something was seriously wrong - Pip, the garden, the villa - all were gone! In fact I was trapped, the thing was *sucking me in*! I seemed to flail in a revolving nightmare, the petals flattening as though by centrifugal force, or was it I who was spinning? - down and down, down and *down,* to the point of a monstrous hollow cone, the whirl a blur, in the center a brilliant spark rushing right at me!

Then the true horror began.

All motion stopped. I was suspended in a vast and indefinite sepia murk. The spark was still there, floating diamond-bright below; it began to mutate, Torrance. It acquired dimension, form, became a kind of fuzzy, then extremely vivid, tableau.

I saw my mother lying on white sheets splattered with red, holding a newborn child; and the child was me - mewling, ghastily.

If this seems mad, it is. The birth, *my* birth, reversed before my very eyes!

A limp umbilicus lay in the blood on the bed. Like a snake come alive it went to my belly. It bit the stump from which it had been severed. I beheld this feeling icy fear.

Red wet and placental junk sprang from the sheets in supernatural attack on the infant, and not only on him, on Mother; the besliming baby was wracking itself in, Mother convulsing the while, resorbing - or the baby, mantling, was a parasite, implacable and alien, *invading.* I watched as every last recomposing tissue streamed between her legs, and she was screaming, there was no sound but she screamed, her agony so keen, her midsection all the while remounting!

Shocking, eh? You've no idea!

Eventually, very pregnant, Mother lay sweating, merely sweating, very quietly, on immaculate linen.

I tried to break the spell but could do nothing. The surrounding space was darkening. I sensed a swirl, there seemed to be a breeze. Mother slept, directly below. And she was slimming. The child-mound shrank. A long time passed and she was a beautiful young woman - nude, every now and again moving a limb, the lips pursed sweetly. She seemed fulfilled, she was lovely.

But then she once again grew sweaty.

And a naked man materialized beside her.

He also was sleeping. I recognized him. He was Father! The man was Father as he had been in his twenties - strong, Torrance, handsome, virile.

Mother and Father caressed. They murmured into each other's crooked arms. Then they were gasping and I knew what would happen, he entered her; and they both - soundless - were shouting, their almost instant ecstasy wild, painful, shocking to see, the sequence all wrong, *reversed*! I was a voyeur, I hated it and watched it powerlessly, without any means to stop the act, to prevent what I knew without the faintest doubt was my own conception - the beginning, yes, of me.

Then they were smiling, kissing, she stroked him, he had his tongue to her breast. After an eternity their fevers devolved. Mother sighed. She slumped. She slept. Sweatless, they both slept. Then, she *disappeared.*

Father remained.

He became younger. His face turned softer. His waist drew in and the bones grew sleeker; the chest, arms and stomach spangled muscle more transparently; the thighs slimmed, and he turned and I saw dimples pooling at the bottom of his back, sinews twitching over ribs; he tossed, tossed more, his sleep was fitful, coltish, and suddenly he flipped and the penis was trembling airborne over the navel - its slit-mouth greedily snatching at slag, at puddles arcing from the sheets, from a pond in the cavity below his throat, the swollen organ was *swallowing down sap* - unassisted, Torrance, the hands weren't on it (please do not let your mother see any of this).

He became even younger. The narrowing torso shed every trace of hair, beard filmed to nothing on his cheeks; the lashes densed, he was a boy, fifteen, fourteen, thirteen, twelve . . .

The genitals regressed, hands and feet diminished, puberty was a wind blowing backward, soon he was ten, nine, eight . . .

I saw where this was going! I gagged, I struggled, I wanted out and screamed for Pip, he had to be somewhere above, but there *was no above* - no help was there that could come.

The child was dwindling to infancy. His mother appeared just as I was certain she would; she dandled Baby, she cooed, it was sickening . . .

Suddenly she fell back and the thick water, half-dried, spread all over. There was the umbilicus reviving, snaking through muck, it was happening again!

But this, Torrance, was just the beginning. It happened again; and again; and yet again and again - so many times I lost count, each cycle a generational crux, each putting remoter progenitors on terrible display. The activities were always the same - birth, intercourse, semen-spilt boy whisked to the womb - but with endless variations, unfolding back, back through time, an obscene family tree *in vivo.*

Here is more evidence for my madness. I began to enjoy it.

I thought I was benefiting from some kind of cosmic instruction. Well, I was learning a great deal. And I grew accustomed to everything being backward, the very exactitude made this easy; I was thinking, Why not? Why can't reality run in both directions? Perhaps it does! I became convinced it does, our one-way sense of time is a halfwit hallucination . . .

I relaxed. Somehow - still bobbing, as I was, mid-murk - I settled down. I even wished for a cigarette, and aperitifs.

As my mood changed, the spectacle changed. The enveloping space showed surfaces, wispy ones; and there were dioramas spreading across, scenes of various kinds, that seemed to appear in tandem with the events on the bed. I was getting contextual cues, the big picture if you will, a kind of running background travelogue.

I saw sweeping views of the 17th, then 16th, then 15th, then 14th centuries - the 19th & 18th already having fast-rewound; I was seeing the baronial and increasingly savage circumstances of our Spoorish past.

We were, I gathered, pitiless. Then again, so were all lords of great feudal keeps. What other sensibility could dwell behind battled walls? Could plant the approaches with impaling stakes, discharge latrines into the moats, put "murder-holes" in ceilings through which to shoot flaming arrows and dump boiling oil if, God help them all, the gates were breached?

In those times, a castle's every surface was made to drain blood.

But Spoors were worse than most. Our enemies were more afraid than were the enemies of others. The grisly instruments racked on great halls' walls gave us more joy, more fiendish joy by far. Knights riding through our villages didn't care if they crushed scuttling children. We took what we wanted and sneered at the entrails. Then we ate the entrails.

And I was agog.

The misdeeds fascinated me. Perhaps because of the "happy endings"; there was a lot of miraculous salvation. Bearded men spat guts that became viscera restored, knives came from wounds and the gashes sealed up, horses trotted backward and trammeled children sprang away, boiling oil disobeyed gravity, as did oceanic quantities of gore.

But Torrance, I saw aspects of a gentler life. Afternoon aeries, for example; places to wrestle and game. During times of peace, when our soldiers farmed, the upper galleries were home to bird and breeze only. Archers weren't there cranking crossbows and shouting, greasing the air with their battle leather and blocking light from slits. So the sun, unshy, put fingers in nooks - probing for youths at play, for laughter echoing from the shadows.

Does this interest you? I should think it might. I'm dallying, I suppose; but you can't imagine how difficult - oh, enough, I'll get right to it.

Late in the thirteenth century, I witnessed disaster.

This was hallucination, mind you, somewhere inside a large sepia rose. I'm not writing history here, these ramblings obviously are diseased. But believe it, I describe what I saw and felt.

Gundulf, Baron Speour, was murdering his family.

That is, unmurdering; he was restoring the heads of his wife and seven children with mighty battle-ax unwhacks.

What drove him to this? Gundulf was handsome and blond, and pleasantly disposed; or had been, I should say, when younger. That I learned, in time. His crime is a mystery. Yet it happened:

Unwhack, unwhack, *unwhack went the ax,* vacuuming blood by the gallon from the floor of a cellar! Gundulf stood raging over his wife and the little ones, six girls and a boy. The poor things were prostrate on damp earth, inhaling screams the moment they regained their heads.

For many minutes Gundulf strode about babbling, hefting his ax and laughing demonically. He enjoyed their terror, their palsy enthralled him!

But then began a curious chase. Gundulf executed sudden high-speed retreats. He retreated, flailing, from back-scurrying offspring and wife. The pursuit boiled up stairs and through halls in ever-widening circles - vassals and servants must have fled, no one else was there to intervene or gape, very wisely I suppose. This pandemonium continued for some time. Tables and chairs and pots unsplintered at raving Gundulf's every swipe. Why the recapitees didn't run for the forest I cannot guess, maybe they thought they had strength in numbers, how foolish. I'd have jumped for the moat, no matter how thick its sewage!

Eventually the bizarre hunt stopped.

Scenes of mad misery followed. All wrong in soul and heart, Gundulf slouched about wearing tattered battlegear; that he'd not shed, apparently, for a very long time. And he was obsessed with what seemed to be souvenirs. They were a bunch of shriveled, dead flowers. His mania for these flowers was frightening. He had a dog, too. A tremendous dog it was, a war hound, quite fearful, really. It had attached itself to Gundulf, this hound - somehow attached itself. Dead flowers, a dog, these were the root of his malady. For he would clutch that horrid bouquet, and berate, so it seemed, that dog, all the while banging his head on a wall! Then he would bang harder and wail unearthly laments, and everyone, not least the dog, would cower!

Little surprise, then, that the household was overjoyed when he backed through the gate and, forlornly holding his flowers, hobbled off into the distance without once looking over his shoulder to see where he was going.

Nor did the dog, which trotted alongside. Backward. A curious sight, indeed.

With flowers, with dog, he continued this trek. Others joined him. Soon, many had joined him, and a bedraggled army was marching, hundreds of weary legs forcing one step behind another. Corpses resurrected from the road, horses for the lucky. These troops, evidently, were defeated. They were returning to the scene of some terrible debacle.

Then I saw it. The year was 1271. That I knew to be fact; I'd been familiar with the event in question since school, you see.

Gundulf was the survivor of a great military ordeal: the siege and surrender of Krak des Chevaliers.

Likely you haven't studied the Crusades. La Jollans, I imagine, do not learn historical facts. This, Torrance, is a fact: Krak was immense.

In the thirteenth century it controlled a gap in the mountains between Syria's main desert and the coast. It was a vital Crusader castle; twelve Muslim sieges had failed to take it. The fortifications were intricate, advanced. Krak was considered impenetrable.

Its garrison was a melange of European misfits. Knights, mercenaries, clerics, they were there for the usual reasons, rank plunder, chiefly. Gundulf arrived late, however. Indeed he witnessed the death of all Crusades, for Krak's defenders were the last of their kind ever to hold sway in those holy deserts.

A fiery-eyed sultan named Baybars decided that he, too, would have a crack at Krak. He besieged the castle, with a masterful, some said devilish, cunning. And he took it!

You imagine, perhaps, a bloody swarm. Heads hurtling by the hundreds to their Christian necks?

Ah, no. On the contrary, Baybars permitted an evacuation. And very strange, I must say, that was. But I can attest to the sultan's mercy. For I watched Gundulf and company undo their exit. Horses backshoved carts under ramparts, enormous ramparts, *breached ramparts,* bristling with thousands upon thousands of jeering Muslims!

Here my story heaves into shame. Gundulf, you see, wasn't a hero. In actuality, he was a traitor.

And Torrance, his traitorousness Cursed us.

Of that I am certain. For I saw it. He betrayed his fellow knights, and I saw why, why he did this. But I am not prepared to discuss it, now.

No, not now. I will leave you in suspense as to what happened between Baybars and Gundulf in the castle of Krak.

I'll say this much, however. The bed, still floating below, enlarged. On it were Gundulf and Baybars; also on it was the dog. The hound, my boy, the war hound, was on that bed. And it was watching. And the whole ensemble seemed to jelly, even billow, quite strangely - for the bed was strewn with masses of petals. It was buried under a profusion of soft floral petals, Torrance. Need I specify what color?

And in this unholy bower . . .

Make of it what you will. A tryst occurred in the castle of Krak.

A tryst, Torrance, unholy! Consummated with sepia-fleshed fervor!

———

Now we move forward. Very rapidly. We skip over certain events; events that halted the backflow of the spectacle, indeed sent it roaring to the present like a tsunami deflecting from shore and racing out to sea.

With triple the force.

Does this happen? It did in the rose. The laws of physics are different in the rose:

Gundulf's ragged army ran from Krak's gate, hellbent for Europe. Most dropped dead along the way but that didn't stop the others. They ran, this was a nonstop marathon, intercontinental, at full sprint speed.

Then Gundulf was on his own, streaking straight through France with the dog and the flowers - and yes they were roses, Torrance, *roses* - and when he got to the place we had in Normandy he instantly murdered the family.

Whack-whack *whack* whack-whack!!!

He screamed at the full moon for a few split seconds, then got rid of the bodies - wolves devoured them in the forest! Chomp! Eaten and digested in one fell chomp!

Then he flew on his horse to the closest village and grabbed a girl who bore his son: the first Spoor born after the Change.

In a trice the boy was fifteen, and Gundulf killed himself and the boy was the baron. This continued. The fast-forward was death in staccato, mostly suicide, always before the baron was fifty.

These premature ends tore through the centuries.

They ripped up time as though ripping up flimsy pieces of paper!

All the way to Father putting the bullet through his brain and then I was staring at . . .

Yes, Torrance! Yes. Yes.

Christmas Day

I have deliberated the wisdom of mailing this and have concluded it is my duty to do so.

Pip is supervising the roast of an imported French goose. Geese are scarce in Thailand. French geese are. But we always obtain them at Christmastime. And we serve them very rare, of course; with Sauce Cilantro; which isn't in the least bit scarce in Thailand. I am sick of cilantro, in fact. But Pip is fond of the perfumy stuff. And I do humor him.

Because he humors me.

I hope festivities in La Jolla are in order. They must be, your mother is in charge.

Now then. I woke up, babbling, from the Voyage to the Bottom of the Rose. Everyone was most concerned; I had been out for hours. I woke up in the old nursery of the villa here, surrounded by legions of grimacing doctors. That I woke up babbling was considered a very good sign. But what do they know?

Nothing.

Within minutes I'd ordered everyone out. I had to think. And I did think, very deeply; for months. While I convalesced. Slowly.

I now know the futility, of convalescence. And I have made a decision.

Torrance, I have directed my financial assistants to arrange the complete and irrevocable transfer of all of my considerable assets. To you.

The process is complex. It requires that we spend some time near certain financial institutions. I have chosen a site in Massachusetts, north of Boston, by the sea. Our stay there need not be more than a few months.

Actually, our stay need not be more than a week. But for the reasons I have discussed, you must realize we should spend more than a week together.

I have arranged for your enrollment in a school in the town, a public school, I hope you won't mind. Public schools are fun. Don't you think? I am sorry if it bothers you, but the little time I will have with you precludes the possibility of involvement with all those activities that do happen in private schools, especially in boarding schools, the worst things go on there. I have been of the opinion for years that such environments are unhealthy for boys of your age.

You will attend an ordinary public school, a "high school."

My legal help have discussed the matter with your mother's legal help and everyone is in agreement that no one has any choice but to do exactly what I have outlined. What I have outlined happens to be central to the divorce settlement that took you away from me in the first place. I foresaw the eventual necessity of getting you back, even if only for a short while.

All parents have rights. And my rights, Torrance, are very well protected.

Pip will collect you and accompany you to Boston, wherefrom you and he will proceed by automobile to our - house. Our home.

There I will be waiting with open arms.

Do not be afraid.

You are, I know, friskily athletic, so I've arranged for facilities. You shall not lack for workouts. The more grueling the better, yes? Good for the soul, all that. Wonderful tonic.

This has been an ordeal. I must point something out - you soon will have resources to acquire the very best medical help on the planet. Should you so desire.

Torrance, whether or not you wish it, you will understand.

I anticipate with great impatience putting my eyes on you.

Until then I remain,

Your devoted Father,
Malcolm,
BARON SPOOR

Letter from Torrance Spoor
to a Friend, Ricky

Sunday

Hey Ricky,

Here I am looking at the Atlantic Ocean from my father's giant mental hospital. That he calls a house.

I got here day before yesterday. This place is wild. So is Dad. Pip, too, and the dogs, wow. My Dad has these things he calls dogs that - no shit, man. They are strange.

I know you have to be kind of worried. That letter Dad wrote me. A total FREAK. Yeah, we laughed. My Dad the Baron. Who says he's going to kill himself and make me rich. Who dives into history in a rose, all because of his Curse - is he on drugs or what? (Do not tell anybody. If you told I will break your legs, you promised. Ok?)

Anyway don't worry. Things are fine I guess. But you have to keep all this secret too. It's weirder than we thought to tell the truth. You know the last time I saw him, I was six? And I remembered he was kind of cool. Guess what, he is. Kind of. He dresses cool. Like a movie star who had a nervous breakdown. And lives in fantasy now, or something, he wears silk suits. All different colors, like

black, and pink. And the way he talks - the dude is high class. Sometimes funny too, he says these things that seem like jokes. About
what a "sad world we live in," stuff like that. The way his lawyers
had to fight with Mom's lawyers for years, just so he could see me,
and have a real family relationship. Right! Then I remember what
kind of world he lives in. All over the place, in foreign countries,
with this guy Pip at his side. I can't figure out if Pip is supposed to
be a guard or a butler or a slave or sex maniac, like Mom thinks, or
what. (She calls and sounds so nervous, she thinks Dad is - you
know, evil. Mom, the worry nut.)

But Pip is more like Tonto in the Lone Ranger far as I can tell.
Faithful Sidekick shit. He works out with me in the gym, that is cool.
Ricky, we have a gym. And a pool! Heated, way too hot matter of
fact, but at least I can swim. Makes me miss La Jolla though. All the
fun times we had on the team. And everything.

So it is kind of unusual here. A crazy adventure just like we
thought. My visit with Dad the Baron. Who falls down roses into the
Crusades, where nobles eat the guts of victims. And do seriously
strange things on beds, sepia flowers all over, with the War Hound
- watching!

Watching what? Baybars and Gundulf doing kinky stuff, ha ha ha.
(I am not laughing.) Hey, I have to tell you something. This is weird.
Dad sort of "sings." To himself. Ricky, he sings to himself. When he
thinks I can't hear. And it does not sound like singing. It sounds like
screaming if you ask me. And not just to himself, to the dogs too -
he screams at his dogs! Did you ever hear of insane barons who
scream at dogs? Does that remind you of anything? (Like maybe his
letter?)

Oh well. He is wacked out. But get this. His dogs, they kind of look
like - this will make your day. What do war hounds look like? Really,
think about it. Big, very big, over two hundred pounds, with rust-
brown fur. They never bark. They seem like they think? And, can't
forget this: red eyes!

No shit. Hey, Dad is such a nut. Don't tell anybody, I am serious.
It is embarassing you know. He makes up stories, about a Curse,
and a War Hound, and then he has these dogs - for what? I think he
likes to scare the hell out of people. Like me, his own son he wants
to have a real relationship with. Sure. He is just too rich, and mentally ill. He plays games in his own creepy world. Probably he is
lonely and wants attention (that's what I told Mom last time she
called. She laughed. Nervously though.)

But I almost never see him. Except at dinner. Which is barftime for me, you should see the things they eat. He makes Pip serve these disgusting - I can't even talk about it. Anyway you would not believe it.

Not any of it. Like what happened today. There is this building away from the house, Dad calls it the gazebo. To me it seems like a pirate lookout, cause of the hill this place is on, you can see the ocean for miles. It is round, the gazebo, with a pointy roof, but the sides are open, with rails to lean on, and benches inside. So today, I was there, and I found an old wood box, under the benches. It had carving on it, and a key sticking out, from a silver lock. So I said, wow - treasure! Dumb, right? Who would leave treasure lying around, even at a place like this? But I opened it, and inside, wrapped with velvet cloth, there was a *pistol*. Like it was meant for a duel or something. It's old, and small, but the thing is really nice, it works for sure. A box of bullets too. So what the fuck? Target practice! Some time when Dad and Pip are not around, they might not want me to have a gun, even though Mom lets me at home. I wonder who it belonged to, what they used it for. And why they hid it?

Man I wish you could be here. I should take pictures and mail you some. This place, I have not checked out even half. It is so big.

First of all, the ocean. From my room I see everything. There is a long, long hill going down to these cliffs. And then, the ocean. I feel like I am in a lighthouse up here. There are other hills too, behind us, covered with forest. The whole place sticks out into the water. Around the house are fields and garden - grass in summer, right now it's frozen. Out my windows I see the cliffs. They are high, about three hundred feet! You can't see the surf unless you go to the edge and look straight down. Even then the waves look tiny, so do the rocks, but they are giant. Surfing, forget it. Bad news if a boat got wrecked there. In my room I am so far up I can't hear it. I just see the waves crawling in, slow motion, from the big cold sky.

Beautiful. But it is winter. And this is not California.

Hot in here though, Dad keeps the heat on full blast. What a strange guy. I knew he must be crazy from Mom's stories. She warned me, I told you. Then I got the letter. Freaked me so much I didn't show it to her (another reason you have to keep your mouth shut). All the stuff about Dad killing himself. I mean - a joke. Who could write something like that?

I have to stop him. If he is serious. He is sick, man. So this is not a lot of fun. Just have to play it really cool, and see what happens. I miss you. I miss LJ. I even miss Mom, though she bothers me a lot. All the reasons you know about too much.

Tomorrow I start school. Thank God, I want to be around normal people. There is a swim team too. So maybe it will be ok.

Take it easy.

Your Best Friend,
T.

P.S. I was kind of joking about the dogs. They aren't that bad - they follow me wherever I go. When I hike in the woods, or stare at the surf under the cliffs. Almost like they want to protect me. Like I am the most important guy in the world. Cool, right? Watch it, dudes. I got my dogs!

Sort of weird. Hey, have to go. Talk to you soon, ok?

The Diary
of Sheila Massif: I

What a crew. They came in with wet hair combed and faces shining, from gym I guessed but they said "fizz-ed" when I asked. This is great. The class is right after gym. What do they do there—trampolines, a pool? The school is huge. I got lost effortlessly today just walking around.

Our room is big too, for eleven students. The windows need washing; plastic chairs clash with antique wood desks. The kids were scattered all over, which was awkward at first. But the space is good. I like it.

Anyway we lucked out with the timing of gym. They'll be less tense and readier to concentrate. And it's true, more in touch with their feelings. I shouldn't have told them that, though. That boy said: "Uh-oh, psycho-lingo."

And some of them laughed! Especially the beefy kid in the back. I was nonplussed for a second. Then I announced, "My name is Sheila. Your names I'll know pretty soon. Welcome to class."

Not one said a word. I walked around the room, wondering why they touch their faces with hands or pens or anything at all—one girl pressed chewing gum on her forehead. Is she retarded?

"Writing," I said finally, "or what we call 'creative' writing, requires that we know our feelings. Which isn't easy, given the culture we live in, because our culture is obsessed with the mystery of feelings—are they really there, if so where, what words should label them? It's a culture that reveals emotional uncertainty by the very fact of its use of the strangest kinds of, yes, 'psycho-lingo'—what is your name, young man?"

"Torrance," he said. He's a calm child, about sixteen, black hair. Green eyes, intelligent mouth—capable of saying anything, I should have known, that mouth. And a little fierce. Calm but fierce, odd. Maybe his parents are therapists.

I walked at him and said, "Torrance, you seem to be familiar with lingo. Tell me—are you in touch with your feelings?"

"Yes," he replied. "To tell you the truth, I touch them all the time."

Giggles: the girls think he's cute. He is. Someday he'll be a knock-out hunk. He's just a babe to these eyes, but I'm not sixteen, thank God. I asked, "What do your feelings feel like when you touch them, Torrance?"

The room went quiet. He was studying long, pale fingers. "Well, they feel warm," he said. "Matter of fact, they feel pretty hot!"

"Do they?" I said.

"And," he added thoughtfully, "smooth."

"No kidding," I said. The beefy kid in the back snickered. I ignored this and said, "What else, Torrance?"

"Don't think I better say anymore," he said, grinning pinkly. He was embarrassed, I realized. But it didn't bother him a lot. He seemed to enjoy the fact he was blushing. I should have stopped it right there. I didn't, though, I wasn't sure what he had on his mind and I wanted to know.

"That's all you have to say about your feelings?" I said, returning to my desk under the blackboard.

"Maybe," Beefy called out, "they feel hot and *juicy*."

Give me a break, I thought. "Feelings" had taken on a whole new meaning, suddenly. Torrance stared at Beefy. "Juicy?" he said, glancing at his hands and looking shocked. Then he exclaimed, with the wounded dignity juveniles feel, "How do you know, you never felt my deep personal feelings!"

A couple of boys guffawed. The fattest girl turned red. The one who'd adorned her forehead with gum was blankly rechewing; that blankness meant something terrible. This had to be dealt with. "Torrance," I inquired, "how did your emotions develop such interesting anatomy?"

There was an explosive silence. The room was about to erupt. "His emotions," Beefy whispered, "are transsexual."

"Yeah," Torrance declared. "I'm *transemotional.* I guess." Fingers splayed over lips and eyes tragic, he then moaned, "But how could you understand? I just know you never will . . ."

They screamed.

Wow, I thought. The boy is a find. "That's right, Torrance!" I cried. "You just can't help it!" The students, expecting maybe anger, quieted. But I said, "And that's why you're in this class, believe it or not, that's why you're all here, because you are, I'll borrow the word, 'transemotionals.' That means you're here because you're smart, because you're expressive, because above all you have active imaginations, and, not least, because the authorities—I don't know who they are, but you probably do!—because the higher-ups around here have decided that all these qualities make you subjects for an experiment called Learning How To Write."

"Really creatively," said the fattest girl, wanting to be helpful.

"Yes," I said, staring at this one.

"You just used seven 'becauses,' " a girl with red pigtails accused.

"I did?" I said. Beefy yawned. Gum Chewer, blank as ever, freshened her gob with a few quick chews. The rest stared into space. It was time to grab them by the necks. I said ominously, "Now I'll get to the point. The point is, we're dealing with dynamite."

I felt like a cop from the bomb squad. I had their attention. "In this class we will deal with dynamite, namely with aspects of ourselves; which we will express through writing, of course, and discussions too." As I talked Gum Chewer repasted her forehead. Maybe she thinks it's voodoo. Yeah, sure, shamanistic, she was starting to really annoy me. "But as I think we just saw, self-expression isn't always easy. Sometimes, in fact, it's a little risky! So let's talk about how we're going to handle it." Gazing at Chewer, I asked, "What does your psychic third eye tell *you*?"

She stared at me—third eye wide open, too—and said, "I think the higher-ups you mentioned will want to know what's going on here, talking about sex and stuff." That stopped me cold. She wasn't finished. "My name is Samantha, by the way. And I wish you would tell us what's on your mind."

Why bother, was my reaction, when your chewing gum's already read it?

I walked to the windows and looked at the parking lot. Piles of snow, dirty, were icebergs in a sea of cars. Might have to talk to Duane about this, I thought. Is she really psychic? That would be a disaster.

Then I remembered that not even Duane can read my mind. But sometimes he seems to come close. And he doesn't blink when he does it; the eyes stay wide open, *just like Samantha's.* God, Sheila —get a grip!

Turning around, I said, "I didn't expect the turn our talk about 'feelings' just took. Neither, I bet, did you." I moved to the desk, sat down, clasped hands. "But you can be sure we'll have more times when even the safest subject turns to dynamite." I cast an eye on Beefy. "Which means we will extend the courtesy of respect. Respect is crucial, class—our success requires that we open, that we reveal, that we express!"

The mood tightened. They were thinking this over. The mood snapped, however, when Red Pigtails exclaimed, "You mean we can't even *criticize*?"

"Your name, please?" I said.

"Rhonda."

I stood and walked at Rhonda. One of these days I'll fill that prescription for glasses. Or contacts, I thought, studying Rhonda; who wears serious glasses. Black-framed, they circle the eyes of a zealot nitpicker. "Good question," I said. "But tell me, what do you mean by 'criticize'?"

"Well," she said, "what if I point out dangling participles and clumsy clauses, or repetitive use of the fricatives, for example . . ."

"Ahem," I said, going back to my chair.

". . . is that 'dynamite'?" Her pout was manic. Not only that, she was ignoring all the yawns and hostile sighs. Evidently the others were up to here with Rhonda. But Rhonda didn't care.

I had to think about this. So I sat down. Yeah, this had to be nipped in the bud. What the hell are the fricatives?

Yow! Pitfalls were getting bigger. It struck me that maybe this project wasn't such a great idea. Deep down, I felt a flash of uselessness. I saw myself in the Chamber again—there I was, slamming hatches and sealing exits. Emergency air was hissing. Ridiculous, I thought. Sheila, you're not doing that anymore! Remember?

Then I wondered what would entertain Duane, if he were here.

Watching this spectacle. He'd tell me to get over it and deal. And, out of nowhere, an idea came floating at me.

I psyched up and proclaimed, "The Japanese did it during World War II!", standing so fast the chair scooted back and crashed.

Watery windowlight jounced off Rhonda's glasses. "Did what?" she demanded. She thought I was insane.

I smacked palms on desk, jutted out jaw. "And today, Rhonda, it's unheard of. Almost unheard of . . ."

"What are you *talking about*?" she wailed.

"Torture, Rhonda." She was saucer-eyed. Air pressure dropped because everybody in the room took deep breaths. I pounded the desk and said, "There's no way, the Geneva Convention forbids it, it's completely indecent to mess with anyone's fricatives! And especially *criticize them!*"

Suddenly my jaw was jutting into a wind tunnel of thunderous clapping. It was so exciting. They were applauding me. I felt like Amelia Earhart, scarf flapping as she flew to Iwo Jima. Wherever it was that she led the armada. The holy war to stamp out critiques of the fricatives . . .

"You're making fun of me!" Rhonda screamed, pigtails lashing at the bedlam. "You don't even know what a fricative *is!*"

Arm raised, I shouted, "Enough! Enough! QUIET!"

"This is unfair," Rhonda yelled, "really unfair!"

"Rhonda," I said sweetly, "I'm so sorry. That *was* unfair." She glared at me. "Of course we will criticize," I went on. "What we won't do is make each other defensive. That's all."

"I wasn't . . ." she said.

"Of course you weren't," I interrupted. "It's just that we need to be careful about using big words. When we are trying to understand each other, Rhonda. And we do want to understand each other, don't we?"

The rest of them enjoyed this. "Ok!" I said. "Now the good news!" Lord, if looks could kill—whatsamatter, Rhonda, nobody shut you up before? "The good news is I've spent a lot of time making class seem dangerous when it isn't, really. If this is understood, we'll move along to the real work, which, boys and girls, is having—fun! Count on it, we're going to have a lot of fun here."

So. That's what happened. A couple close calls, huh, Diary?

Anyway, I stayed clear of the Chamber. The good old Drama Chamber, God love it. But let's not get into that. That, I hope, is history.

The remaining time went quickly. I told them to write down her or his name and a brief "self-description, of what you look like, and maybe a little more about yourselves." Then I told them about their assignment.

"Listen up," I said to the heads bent over the sheets of paper I'd issued, from which in a few minutes I'll glean much information (can't wait to find out how Rhonda did it). Samantha was still scribbling. She'd scribbled a lot as it was. The most avid scribbler, strange. This must happen to blank-eyed gum-blobbed girls; when writing they're wild.

I glanced at the clock. Just over two minutes left. "I want you to imagine," I said, "the person who you would most rather not be." The faces clouded. They were imagining darkly.

"This person can be anybody, someone you know, someone you have read about or have seen on TV, anybody at all—providing it's the one person whose life you most especially would not want to lead."

I wandered around collecting the self-descriptions without looking at them. Torrance turned his over as I approached; it's true, the most outgoing kids are secretly so bashful. "All right, I want you then to pretend that you are that person. Try to *become* the person you have the least desire to be. Ok! Your assignment:

"You will write a few pages self-describing that person. In first-person exposition—you'll be using 'I,' not 'she' or 'he'—got it?

"That's all. Oh, keep in mind the possibility that the person you choose might be quite happy with her/himself despite your own reservations, your subjects don't have to be contemplating suicide or anything."

The bell rang. The whole building started to shudder. My students stood up, reflexively crafting bundles of books and clothes. I, already ready, sheets in hand and tape recorder in jacket turned off, was headed for the door. I didn't want to linger and chitchat or answer questions. I looked back—they were staring. Maybe teachers aren't supposed to make a run for it. Well, what the hell. I'm an unusual teacher.

"See you on Wednesday!" I called out. "And good luck!"

Torrance gave me the nicest little wave.

I lit out of there, got lost, finally found the car. Then I drove back to this frowsy apartment I subletted day before yesterday.

Dear Diary, I'm doing it. I can hardly believe it!

I'm very optimistic. I won't be getting my hands on really hard data, but who needs hard data? There is so much sterility in clinical psych, I'm sick of being a technician, collating statistics, running reliability checks. This is life I'm studying, in the trenches! I think I'll pour a glass of Amazon gewürztraminer from that gallon vat sitting by its lonesome in the fridge.

The kook I got this place from must know a lot about wine.

The Classroom Writing Exercise:
The Self-descriptions of
Samantha Conners, Rhonda
McQuisling
& Torrance Spoor

THE SELF-DESCRIPTION OF SAMANTHA CONNERS

This is Samantha Conners. We're moving fast. Writing, already.

I have gold hair, variable eyes, nose that's too straight, ear lobes that droop, dracula cheek bones, mouth some have described as enigmatic, and a habit of sticking gum on my forehead I developed today to see if that kind of thing annoys you. It does. My "psychic" third eye!

Class was enjoyable. I hope you don't mind me saying that. A word of warning though about Rhonda. Her father, Caspar McQuisling, is vice-principal of school. He's what I meant about "higher-ups"—people who might want to mess with what we do in class. Trouble! Because he's a true believer in Traditional Values—wrath of God, you know, about sex, in any shape, combination and form. And what is there to write about really creatively except sex in every shape, combination and form? Do you agree? I think you might, but don't take it personally, or anything. To me, nothing is more sensible than pornography, but—some people object to that.

Why I don't know, we all know millions of babies are born to unwed teenagers every day, at least thirty million every morning and another fifty million every afternoon, so something is going on out there and everywhere, including here, right? And it must be our duty as Writers to explore it, wouldn't you say?

So my word of advice, if I can presume, is get rid of Rhonda. She'll ruin everything. I am writing fast as I can because you are looking at your watch and also looking pleased with yourself, which I don't blame you for, you made us pay attention, that's not easy around here, but I can tell you're about to make us stop doing this, so—the Rhonda problem. We must find a solution to this glaring problem, she glares good, huh? One more thing. None of us will blab if class gets kind of experimental. I don't know about that Torrance kid, he's new and hasn't passed our tests, so we just have to wait and see. But everybody else is more or less cleared by our security bureau. Except R. McQ.

Ok, time to stop—remember, if he gets any funny ideas Caspar will come down like communists did in Europe before they got kicked out of the palaces, so mum's the word, ok?

Also I just have to ask. Are you really a writing teacher?

(Doesn't make any difference, of course.)

THE SELF-DESCRIPTION OF RHONDA MCQUISLING

My name is Rhonda McQuisling. I have red hair and a clear complexion. My eyes are very clear blue, and I wear glasses. My clothes are neat but not show-offy. Excuse me, that is a careless description. But I will not correct it because I write slowly, which you can see from my flowing penmanship. (People who say things like "pen-womanship" make me grit my teeth.)

Do you remember who I am?

I think you should know that my family raised me to look upon Education with humility, and with awe. We feel, strongly, that moral decay, and lack of reverence for the traditional values, have weakened the backbone of our youth. We have the opinion, hence, that, in many respects, we are a Nation in Decline.

But we have hope, because we cling to sound educational *principals.*

Therefore, I was appaled that you tried to make fun of my concern that, in Writing Class, we hew to the dictates of English usage. I look forward to discussing these problem areas in great detail.

Most sincerely,
Rhonda McQuisling

THE SELF-DESCRIPTION OF TORRANCE SPOOR

I am Torrance. You did not tell us your last name by the way. So I guess we call you Sheela.

Sorry I got carried away. One time in California, that is where I am from, I don't live around here usually, this teacher Mr. Perkins kicked me out because he thought I was making everybody laugh at him. We did laugh at him come to think of it. But I do not want to be disrespectfull to you because you are pretty smart and I loved what you did to that girl with red hair.

So I am new around here just like you. Got to say, I look forward to the class. I never did much of that kind of stuff, I'm more into sports, specially basketball and swimming but I play tennis also, do you play tennis? It's really great. Also I do computer stuff and other electronics. Don't tell anybody, ok? Just kidding.

My Mom gets mad at me when my school work isn't perfect like she wants. Everybody thinks I am a future wizzkid, and she is the leader of the pack that wants to prove the dumb tests mean a lot. So there I am in your class, because of Mom probably and the guidence counceller back home in La Jolla. One more brain scene to make sure I get dropped from fast, that's what I told myself. But now I want to stay and learn. I will try my best.

Torrance Spoor

The Chronicles
of Malcolm Spoor: I

Monday Afternoon

Where are you, my Grislies?

I know you are here. You are waking. You are, you must, it is time.

I've much to show you. It's time!

Mundanely speaking, it's 4:10 in the afternoon. But this isn't so very mundane. My new magic will impress you. Pip is drilling Torrance in the airy attic gym. And I, Grislies, am watching.

Naturally I am. But the method is more modern, now. Amusingly so - for in this bunker, tapping my console, I am a technician of the new breed. An electronic warrior, surrounded by buttons, lights, video screens. Quite the command post, eh? Cameras, open fire!

Wondrous. And what delicate prey, for these machines. Take a look. He is stunning. Grislies, Torrance goes on! And I will be gone, gone, the prospect makes me so happy!

I would howl it out if they weren't one floor above. But they are; and the Drills remain sacred, nothing interrupts, not even my giddiest howls. Look at Pip honing, forcing the sweat - are you not impressed?

Of course you are. This isn't a chink in a moldering court. Cold parapets don't give me these views, who was that one? I remember the Drills long ago. That one, he was something. We had no zoom at the time. Rude scopes and peepholes, musty drapes, even echoes, and dogs, as always the dogs, that was what showed them. I am trying to remember his name, of the one of whom Torrance so reminds me. Wygzifreth, I think? This is dismaying, the mind does flee - would you *talk*?

They are balking. I was afraid of this. Bunny's fault. I do blame you, Bunny. You - make - me - *puke.* You know who I heard say that? Guess!

Jealous, that is all. At any rate, the monitors are a vast improvement. I need not move, my fingers do the skipping - let's see. This button summons gymnasium, in every detail but vapors. There he is toiling, Pip chanting the rhythm, bless you, Pip. Bless you for your perfectionist zeal.

Now, then. A preview of coming attractions. I'll show off, show you what I can do. This one rushes down stairs, through dim passageways, through granite-groined vaults to the pool. Ah! The steamy, galleried pool! Another button dives us - we plunge, Torrance knifing the fizz, off he darts, quicksilver, a dwindling minnow. But he reappears, ghosty and silent. He glides by walleyed - a smartly wigged shark, trailing black tendrils!

He gets out, wet aerodynamo headed for shower. I follow. With a split-second watusi he wrenches off Speedo; my own hips woggle. He soaps all over and I share the lather, he hops foot-to-foot and my ears are draining, he looks in the mirror and I'm self-inspecting! He reaches for a towel and abrasion sears me, he pulls on briefs and elastic snaps me, the cotton soft, brusquely containing; he jogs to the pantry and I gulp his juice, then it's up, up, up to his room, where I sprawl on the bed with the book he's reading!

He doesn't know, of course. Doesn't suspect a thing. Motion detectors guide hidden cameras. Quite artfully hidden, and the house is riddled with them. The entire network is primed for sequence; a few taps at the buttons, and I very nearly become that boy.

But do you Ghastlies understand any of this? Does it bewilder you? Does the magic make you shy? Bunny, where are you? *You* watched TV.

Poor Bunny hated TV. Scared you, didn't it? All that end-of-the-world nonsense, the News. Cringing Bunny. Bad Bunny! Never mind.

So here I am keyboarding, communing or trying to, ogling Torrance's ordeal the while. He is sit-upping on an angled platform, the swift ups weighted at neck, Pip, Gibraltarlike, anchoring ankles. I am sipping sherry and smoking cigars, watching the boy's midriff *turn to steel.*

Is there anything else you would like to know? It has been a long time, hasn't it? Yes, a very long time. What could you want to know?

Housekeeping, perhaps. That might interest you.

This house - an awkward crescent of stone. The center is large by the standards of today. The south wing is smaller. Torrance has that to himself; his pool fills its basement, his gym its attic. A service wing swerves northeast annoyingly. At the end, a carriage house blocks too much view. My new establishment stares at the Atlantic from the top of a promontory, its big left foot thrust into the view.

I loathed the place when I first saw it, last winter. An elderly woman had died. She'd not maintained much of anything for years. The cold rooms reeked of camphor, illness, disgruntled heirs. Lackluster beings had squabbled here. They were from Chicago. The walls held residues of vulgar summers, mercantile souls.

But the property had one conspicuous merit. Pip saw it immediately, of course, he always does: privacy. The terms included an option to buy some land. The entire promontory was for sale, three hundred acres, most of it forest, the rest garden and lawn. From the house, lawn rolls down a great hill to a stretch of cliffs. Cliffs, Grislies. And forest. Perfect for dogs. Perfect for everything. Pip knew I couldn't resist. On the spot he outbid five consortia. They wanted to build "planned communities." A condo vacationland jutting into the sea. A tacky condom on this bold peninsula - do you know what a "condo" is?

You don't know anything!

He had a boat ready. We circumnavigated. I listened to screaming gulls and stared. Waves smashed rocks at the base. The house isn't visible unless one goes quite far out. I drank Pernod while he unpacked lunch. The windows were briny, so I told the boatman to clean them, but the cabin filled with fumes. On deck, the wind was cold. I drank much Pernod, you know how I dislike cold. Clouds moved clumsily, low, leaden. The gulls, louder, were screeching, yes! Then Pip said the woods are full of deer. That did it.

I told him to get rid of the carriage house. He complained. Too much work, it's stone, there isn't time. Where would we garage the cars?

You know Pip. Ever the fussbudget.

I flew back to humid Thailand. He went to work. Remodelers, decorators, furnishers, they came in waves starting early last spring. Now their coffee-stinking Styrofoam is gone. The trucks, ruts, mud, the friends, brazenly picnicking - all that is long gone.

The video specialists came last. From Seoul. I hired them because they do not speak English and their carpenters and painters are very skilled. The ballroom was a kind of gangland barracks. They didn't leave the place, even once, until Pip bused them back to the airport. Thus there is no risk that gossip concerning my network will reach its solitary, unsuspecting star.

Then in December I arrived by chartered boat with the dogs and the plants. It was a lengthy cruise, via Panama. The dogs disliked it. The plants loved it. I broiled in the upper deck's sun, sipping negronis. Crew and girls thought I was crazy. At dinner I showed off spots, declaring they were turning melanomic. That created a stir. How much darker can one get than black mahogany? The girls we dumped in Nassau. They were disappointed, particularly three very big ones I picked up in the islands - without Pip's help, mind you, oh I had a ball. It was exhausting. I was a teenager again, insatiable. Wallowing in fat!

The girls weren't quite as amused as I. Oh, they pretended, they squealed as I wallowed, and shuddered very nicely, but they had motives. They wanted to get off in New York. I tried to explain. I was very patient, actually. But their simple minds could not grasp the idea that the United States interferes with the importation of plants and dogs, never mind women, thumping belowdecks undocumented. That suety Stella even threatened me. Then I had a word with the dogs.

They were delighted to disembark in Nassau.

After six weeks of that I am glad to be here. The house is tolerable. It is peaceful, steady, the grounds don't heave when storms come lashing. There is a marvelous topiary below the library terrace, geometrically iced at the moment. Elsewhere the shrubberies have a gnarled attitude, of bereavement I would say, suggesting a landscape from which obelisks and mausolea have mysteriously vanished. Pennants flutter, dogs roam about eating deer when I let them. They eat other things, too. There was a sad incident, recently. A pair of youthful trespassers - did you notice?

I thought it would rouse you. Even excite you. The local police were excited, at least. They were here. They searched, and found nothing, despite tramping the forest the better part of two days. The dogs are clever, eh? And the forest is hilly, it is deep, too, I was sure a hunt would excite you. Do you not miss the dogs? Have you no urge to sniff and stalk with them, to prey? The drive zigzags through wooded gloom, Grislies, to the wall that cuts us off from the mainland. I should think you'd enjoy such a playground. A tame variation, no?

Oh, yes. On ancient themes.

I hope you are pleased. I am trying, to please you. Come on, wake up! You are here, all of you are, even Bunny, I know it - I taste your creeping deadness, coming to life!

Grislies, I ask you respectfully - can we have a talk?

The Diary
of Sheila Massif: II

This dump is so beige. It's a studio apartment in a complex of studio apartments, all of which are unbelievably *beige*. The complex is located on a highway. Across the highway is a shopping mall. A pedestrian ramp connects the complex to the mall. How nice. We studio dwellers can dash right over without dodging the incredible four-lane traffic.

I'm beginning to get it. This isn't the serene countryside. I thought it would be, but it isn't. Why did I have the idea it would be? I know why. Because of all the serene countryside you go through to get here. All the open fields, and estates. Plutocrats live around here. People with land. I'm in the middle of the latifundia district but my dump borders a highway full of trucks and cars. It's night, so there is a nightmare of lights. The window in my living nook frames it. The bottom edge is the highway whoosh. Above that is the mall parking lot, which looks like a giant airport at war. What am I doing here?

Oh, yeah. I moved to a rustic New England town to teach writing to adolescents. Knapsacks and bandannas and everything, and robust sexuality. Maybe even yodeling. Perfect material for my thesis. My brilliant thesis on sexual identity. But instead of yodelers, what do I find?

A girl who puts gum on her forehead. A psychic girl. A girl who wrote in her self-description, "By the way, are you really a writing teacher?"

Diary, I'm making it a bigger deal than I should. But this kind of reaction has been a lifelong issue. It's why I'm here to begin with, right? To teach myself to be fearless and bold. I want to be fearless and bold—no more Drama Chamber!

And I've tried to get a grip. Really. For example, I made a list. I took inventory of my concerns and wrote them all down. It's supposed to be a "centering" tactic. Helpful for taking charge of your life:

1. Claustrophobic apartment.
2. Enormous shopping mall across the highway.
3. Inadequate food.
4. No food.
5. Ringing telephone.
6. Impulses to go for drives through the serene countryside.
7. Feelings of being anxious.
8. My history of feeling anxious.
9. Fantasies of living forever in my peaceful Drama Chamber.
10. Needs to be safe, and out of reach!
11. Fears of suffocation in the airless Chamber.
12. This studio apartment is very beige.
13. It's a bundle of tiny beige nooks that add up to a tiny beige *nothing*.
14. What about Caspar McQuisling?
15. If Samantha knows what she's talking about, sexuality frightens him.
16. In fact, it terrifies him.
17. This caused Rhonda's many serious problems.
18. Samantha's right. Traditional Values will ruin everything.
19. Career anxiety.
20. Freud felt such anxieties. When he created psychoanalysis.
21. He likened himself to a Spanish conquistador. That's why he was able to venture forth so boldly; but he definitely felt many anxieties as he swashbuckled along, conquering.

22. Fear of failure. And maybe, fear of success.
23. It's fear of success—I'm a quick study at things like teaching writing.
24. That kid Torrance didn't describe himself. The nerve!
25. At least he didn't call me a fake.
26. What I really want is to get rid of the Drama Chamber.
27. I'm starving.
28. There's a Burger King in the booming mall.
29. I think I just centered myself.

———

Then I thought about it. How does Samantha know I'm not a teacher?

How does she know I'm interested in sexuality? Maybe she even knows I'm supposed to be an expert. Or will be, if I ever get my PHD, write the thesis. If I ever contribute to the field of gender boundary development.

But maybe it's screwed. Because she obviously *knows*. Gum or no gum, she must be psychic. She's worse than Duane!

———

That reminds me. Duane called, late this afternoon. We had an intense little talk. He wants to see me. Why I'm not sure, but I felt some of that old zing, over the phone. I guess he's driving up on Thursday. Fun? Probably. I think I miss Duane to tell the truth.

Anyway, I can ask him about Samantha.

Duane Allbright's
Confidential Reports: I

Monday Night

MEMO: CODE DA/PERSONAL///ACCESS/NONE

This afternoon I had the oddest phone conversation with Sheila.

I was at the Lab, listening to the director in the staff meeting—as usual he's upset with the findings, last week's trials aren't panning out, big surprise—when she hit me. Out of the clear blue.

This has happened before. I haven't written it up, however. My relationship with Sheila is private. And I aim to keep it that way, because the Lab would be intrigued. A little too intrigued. The last thing I need is Sheila being dragged in here, making a racket about hocus-pocus. She doesn't buy even the idea of psi research. Actually, she thinks I'm a kook.

Even so, we're attuned. She doesn't feel it. She doesn't feel it at all, in terms of psi. But I do.

In fact, the woman hits me stronger than anything I have experienced. It's been going on for about two years. Usually it happens when she's in trouble. I can feel it—her panic, her mood swings—from hundreds of miles away.

On top of that, she's a relayer. She picks up psi traces, all manner of traces, and relays them, completely unconsciously—to me. This stuff is vaguer than the mood swings. But it's fascinating. It's also the reason she likely would be recruited into the Program, with or without her cooperation. As far as talent goes, it's fairly rare.

So there I am at the meeting, director's complaining, why can't we nail down evidence, the funders are getting edgy, blah, blah, blah, the usual crap, when suddenly—as if to remind me psi is real and worth pursuing—she hits. A triple-A panic hit, to be exact.

My mood improved. Not that I enjoy Sheila's panics. The woman gets herself worked up. Sometimes, in fact, she worries me. But it was fun to sit there staring at the director and Cunif and Schmidtt —the three of them so gung-ho and earnest, not a trace of talent between them—feeling undeniable evidence the Holy Grail exists.

What to do with it, there's the problem. One of these days I'll quit. Then they can fuss on forever, without me yawning at their grand designs. What I did with that particular hit was keep my mouth shut for the rest of the meeting.

I called Sheila soon as I got back to my office. Sure enough, she was in a state. The new job she took is a little high-stress. She's afraid the kids can tell she isn't a real teacher. She even thinks one of them might be psychic. I nearly laughed. Sheila, the great skeptic, undone by a teenage mindreader!

But I didn't laugh. Because after talking with her for a few minutes, I started to feel something extremely strange.

It was a relay. Sheila's never relayed to me over the phone. Before today, she hasn't. I didn't even know it was possible. Getting relay from her always required physical proximity, usually touching, preferably intimate touching, to be candid—there's another reason I don't talk about Sheila at the Lab. The psi connection with her gets personal.

Not surprisingly, then, the relay was weak. Coming as it was from many miles away, over the phone. But the fact I got it at all means the source isn't weak. On the contrary. The source must be strong.

Very strong. Apart from the typical sensation of heat—I got a good little blast of that—I don't have the faintest conception of its characteristics, of what it could possibly be. One thing, though, is obvious. Sheila has stumbled into something big.

The Lab has me locked straight through Wednesday. So I'm driving up on Thursday. To find out what, exactly, this thing is.

The Chronicles
of Malcolm Spoor: II

Tuesday Morning

The dogs caught a deer this morning. Torrance was taking a walk, and saw it happen. Will that do him good?

How about you? The kill didn't liven you? Bunny, you at least must be here. Won't you stir, wake the others?

Perhaps they resent my spyroom. Rather too spectral, is it, Grislies, these flickering screens - even for the likes of you? Perhaps you don't understand it, eh? And that is why you hold back.

No matter. Eventually, they will adjust. Meantime, I will proceed. There is business to consider.

The schedule. Those people.

A week from now comes the first of three sets. Automobiles will nose past the gates and up the drive, will crunch the forecourt's gravel bearing sober, plain, dark-suited men. My accountants.

They will glance at an honor guard sitting on the lawn's frozen edge. The red-eyed beasts will flash tongues around jaws, smelling money in the laptops and attaché cases - sleeker than the valises of yore, but so much richer. Yes, you Fools. Try to guess what a laptop is! If you are listening. Or reading these green electric words. I don't really care if you are not. This is for me, isn't it?

Why, yes. It is.

The men will hurry inside. Several hours later, they will leave.

A few days after come the bankers. They look much like their number-crunching cousins, but pudgier, usually. The dogs will taste fat marbling the breeze. They will whine. The bankers, buttocks wobbling, will lunge for the door. The morning will pass slowly. Then they will get the hell out.

Two or three days later it's the lawyers. Jauntier than accountants and bankers, they'll wave and call to the dogs, who will pant smoke on the chill gray air - at flanneled lunchmeat, packaged to go, in loud suspenders and tasseled shoes. Chomp, chomp.

Pip will lead them to the library. I like looking at the topiary and the water from it, the east wall is a row of French doors; besides, I've four cameras in there. I want everything taped. The way Torrance looks at them, the way they look back. Do you think me too prudent?

Times have changed, you know. I want you to pay attention!

They will sit, they will make envious jokes about furniture and views. Then they'll take a drink from formal Pip, cross and recross legs, fiddle with the oafish tassels.

I'll enter. They'll stand, bologna hands extending. I will decline.

I then put my signature to many stiff pieces of paper. They will cough at the endless nib-scratchings, bow heads in contemplation of dynamic neckties. Cuffs and fingernails will receive obsessive scrutiny. Tiny snags will be found, fascinating irregularities.

And at some point, inevitably, drinks will slurp. This proves élan, verve, for slurping is virile. "Doers" do it, do it smugly, and these lawyers are the very worst of the doers. At barbecues, they tell foolish jokes. Then they backslap and laugh, raising bottles to swig beer direct - and the mouths carburet air! They lengthily suck *air* with the beer, fine-tuning loud gurgles as the heads toss back, eyes bulging skyward in moron glee!

Just as likely to do it with vodka or sherry. My nib will rip parchment mid-scratch. Pip, gravid, will confiscate glasses, murmuring words like these: "The baron does not tolerate that sound." To which I would have him add, "This way to larder, the other scullions are supping."

My lawyers won't be led to greasier quarters, alas. They have become so consequential. They uncap fat pens, and - lick them.

But not till the high point, no, no. They must wait for the climax.

No doubt he will be lurking in a distant corner, reading; or be upstairs, keyboarding fresh trash for that class. I will ring him. He will put homework aside and yawn nervously, I can see it. Then he will descend, come through the doors, blink, and approach.

They'll swallow hard at the sight.

How should he dress? In matters of attire I haven't been offering guidance, with Torrance there is no need, but for this occasion?

A Speedo? The livid turquoise one. His legs pour out like exotic fauna - twins, very pale, fleet things of the forest. Perhaps I will time everything for immediate post-swim. He could come in dripping!

Too extreme. Even for me. "Gentlemen," I will say, "meet my heir."

I will wave Torrance to the escritoire. He will sit, profile lawyer-wards, misunderstanding their embarrassment; uncertain now as to etiquette, they will be standing with armthrusts aborted, remembering too late for dignity their earlier gaffe. Torrance, taking the path of least resistance, simply will avoid their eyes.

I, hot-faced, will be sipping sherry. Noiselessly.

Is drama called for? Those plangent rituals - we used to have hordes on hand to banquet and revel and, most of all, scheme. Abdication realigned the cosmos, naturally. Or not so; many held the Infernal One responsible, why else would a lord renounce power, land and treasure, cut short his rule? And if the Devil's talons were in it, who could know who was coveting what?

Plotters skulked, but yes. Yet always did the cunning prevail. We course forward with the relentless slide of a river. Or a snake.

I think it best we sign the documents without fanfare.

Torrance will be very rich.

He'll be unable to grasp the extent. To him the stack of paper will seem unreal, another incomprehensible whim. The lawyers will be befuddled, they always are, now it's the nitrites they reek of; nor will Pip understand, these days we can't let him. But why should anyone understand? Some things should not trouble the ignorant. They have "no need to know," as the military say; that is a good twentieth-century term, no *need,* so blatant, so pious. "Sorry, you simply don't need to know."

Truly, it is bliss. None of them needs to know anything except that Torrance has joined the leisure class and I am out of my mind.

Everyone will sign, even Pip, he can witness. Then at last he will eject them. That is all there is to it.

Today's procedural brevities are another improvement the nostalgists underrate. Modern legal work is so efficient. It doesn't rank with Speedos, of course, but the law, too, can be a kind of instant undressing - very convenient if you are in the mood.

I am in the mood. I will divest myself of all earthly possessions, including the body. I've had it with stale flesh, this slum address; I'm in decline, the site of terrible decay, my habits as entrenched as cockroaches or rats - nicotine, drugs, I'm a sleaze pharmacy in here, tawdrier than a crack house. The roof is leaky and the wiring erratic. The floorboards and banisters creak. My plumbing is *shot,* I've no central heating, termites gnaw the rafters where bats loosely flit. It is high time, therefore, to self-condemn. Bring on the demolition crew, the place is infested!

Well? No comments?

In a few weeks; I cannot hurry. Two or three weeks is all. Torrance must be ready, so must I; and so must you, since you obviously aren't now.

And there is Pip - oh, he will find a place in the sun, somewhere. Torrance will provide for him. Yes, Torrance will do that. Put him in the kennels, the silly galoot.

Until then he will continue to drive Torrance to school every morning and pick him up promptly every afternoon. The boy will stay clear of all distractions. He must concentrate on his body, on subtle enhancements, the last-minute minor honings. It is important he go to bed exhausted. I am pleased he thinks this is some kind of camp. That is exactly what it is: boot camp. Pip is the domineering Master Sergeant. The boy is our fresh-faced trainee, ardently attaining pure goals; he cannot contaminate his quest with even the thought of sex. I, the strict Commandant, forbid it—

Wait a second. What is going on - Pip is——

Chasing Torrance to the pool?

They are whooping it up to the pool!

Pip knows better, he does not join us in the pool! Look at him, he thinks he is sixteen! Such a sport, belly-flopping -

He is polluting the pool!

I cannot stand it. Torrance, he makes friends. They are *buddies.* And I am jealous, wretchedly jealous, I abhor camaraderie, any form of goo-goo bonhomie, it makes me sick in the stomach. Just nauseated——

But it's worse. Oh, I smell it.

Time to face the issue head-on. I have been avoiding it, since last night, avoiding it. Fine, Pip, frolic. Plash away. Could be you are doing a service. For I must think this through - I will not be meddled with!

Grislies, listen. This is important.

That teacher. Torrance has a crush on her. After one day in class, it was all he could talk about last night at dinner. I reviewed the tape and was shocked. It is so obvious. Then I checked his computer and read notes he made about class - a highly irregular class; but that wasn't all, he has something locked up in there! And what could this be? Homework? If it is homework, why did he code the computer so I cannot get it?

Hiding something from me. Incredible.

I most certainly will find out what. But not by asking. I mustn't let him know that I know he has a need for - privacy. Privacy doesn't exist here. Not for him, and he cannot know.

I overreact. But there is something odd about this woman. Torrance and the girl Samantha think so, I listened to them discuss it on the phone. And after seeing those notes in that computer that dares keep something from me, I quite agree. But it's not simply that this Sheila is "faking it." That is what they said - and it thrills them, how very boring.

No, there is more. I feel it. I taste it. I smell it. I cannot get rid of this perplexing *flavor*. It comes from Torrance like rancid vanilla. No, Grislies - I'm inventing. I wish it were rancid vanilla. It isn't, it's more beguiling. More dangerous. Something about Sheila is - dangerous.

I feel a foreboding. Torrance is enthusiastic, how could one teacher do it? That class got him going, and others too, the phone hasn't stopped ringing. Those cheap boys and girls want to be friends with him———

I can deal with it. We've dealt with worse, haven't we? Look at Pip. Going orca in the pool. Forgetting what he is. What we have made him all this time.

They are swimming. Torrance can't hear me now. I can howl, howl to the dogs. I am happy, you know. Did you hear that, Bunny? So very happy, to be killing myself.

Truly, I am.

Torrance Spoor's "Note to Me"

Tuesday Evening

Kind of weird doing this but I think I better. This is to me. A note to me. Cause I been thinking, but God. I'm freaking.

Bunny - what is bunny? And the dogs. The fucking dogs. How come I don't tell somebody? Like Mom, right. Almost makes me laugh.

Dad has this office. On the second floor, that he won't let me in. He doesn't even let me see in, one time I was walking by and he waited until I was down the hall before he opened the door. He stays in there for hours. Working, he says, but he will not say on what. So, sometimes I go by. To check it out. And I hear him doing it. The screaming. Or "singing." Or whatever, it sounds so twisted. It has to be really loud, too - the walls are thick. He does it to himself, like he is in his own world, where it is ok to scream, or sing - to yourself! Or to something. Because last night, it sounded like "bunny." And it did not seem he thinks this bunny is cool. At all. I even heard him scream: "Bunny, I hate you!" Is that unusual, or what? If I told Ricky he would laugh his head off.

But the dogs. They are worse.

Today this happened: I saw them kill a deer. Not just kill, they ate it. And I saw it. Really gross. They sliced open the stomach and everything fell out in two seconds, I could not believe it. Five of them the teeth like knives - these things are dogs, right? What the fuck. The deer runs so scared right across the field. I am walking around, after working out, as usual wondering what I am doing at this place, really spacy like I always am, in this home for the mentally ill, thinking why am I here - waiting for Dad to kill himself, or what? - and then this deer comes running over the field fifty feet away. And after it, the dogs. Two of them. Only two. Only two, that's funny. The things are huge. They run totally silent, tongues hanging, the *red eyes*. Then three more came out of the woods. They stood still in the sun, staring at the deer. When it saw them it almost fell down! It froze, like it could not believe what it was seeing. Me neither. The way the dogs were staring, eyes really red, the eyes like, controlling it - it *couldn't move*.

Then the two running behind caught up, and the deer fucking squirted shit! Making this horrible noise. Cause they had teeth in the belly, slicing, guts flop, the deer kicking on the ground making the worst sound, it happened in four seconds, over, there's the blood. Right in the early morning. In the peaceful daytime, the breeze was blowing, branches moving in the sun - then this scene. I lost it. Threw up. Cause it's just lying there, legs spazzing, while they gobble its guts. So gross. Really gross. Worst thing I ever saw. The deer's eyes were *wide*. And the weirdest thing was the silence. The dogs - the deer was croking, like gargling, but the dogs - spooky, they didn't make any noise. Just the faces in the stomach, eating. Like they were eating carefully. With fucking table manners or something. Even the trees stopped moving, like they were watching too. Even the ants in the grass were watching - the weirdest thing, everything stopped. So nature, the clouds, me, could watch. Watch them doing it. Death of a deer. This beautiful animal running so scared, then they get in and it's kicking out guts and blood all over the grass, sick fuckers.

No wonder Mom is a basket case about dogs.

These things. Never heard of this kind of dog. And I know they like - this is stupid, hard to believe - it's like they talk to Dad. Mentally. I feel this feeling, I really think they read his mind, when he "sings" at them. The screaming shit that totally freaks me because their eyes get redder, and he is screaming, so he is - he must be.

Insane. He is. Because he never says anything to them. Just the screaming when he thinks I can't hear. I never heard him say one word to those dogs, in the usual way people talk to dogs or any pet, they don't even have names - I asked Pip, What are their names? And he said with this expression coming on his face, "They do not have names, Torrance. They never had names." But they look at Dad like they know what he is thinking, right? Too much. Am I going nuts or what?

Should I talk to somebody? Who?

The Diary
of Sheila Massif: III

Wednesday Afternoon

Whirlwind!

Back in the nooks. Sunk deep in beige, trying to catch up. Except for Torrance, who behaved oddly today, class went really well.

To my amazement. Last you saw, Diary, I was a wreck. The McQuislings were going to intercept me at school. "Your romp," they were going to say, "is over." I was a day-glo paranoid. It was Samantha, of course. What am I, transparent? How does she know? Do they all know?

But today's class provided an outlet for stress. Not one, except Rhonda, had completed the homework. So I stomped them. I made them think I might even throw them through the window—Berserko Woman!

Rhonda sat there staring smugly. She thought she was so much safer than the others. Then her father, Caspar himself, came in at the height of the tirade, and I roared, "Who are you, get out!"

He gasped, "Why, I'm Caspar McQuisling, and I heard some commotion and just thought I'd check in . . ." A complete milquetoast, Caspar McMilque!

He'd been snooping, obviously. But so what? His lips were jabbering and his hands flabbergasting when I, Thatcherlike, the incensed Prime Minister of Inexcusably Late Homework, declared, "It's a sad day when students come to class unprepared, without any evidence they know the meaning of hard work—I will speak with you about this later, but if you will excuse me I am *not through with them, yet, sir.*"

So what can I say? My life is transformed. The audience I granted Dr. McQuisling later on was a juntalike meeting of the minds. We discussed laxity, flab, sloth, spinelessness and slippage. Students must work, work, work, otherwise where will the nation be? We'll be just another offshore drilling platform belonging to the greedy Japanese! But that will change, because of the fearless new breed of teachers like me. He said this, a sincere catch in his voice. He also said he is pleased that Rhonda will benefit from my inspirational right-mindedness, did I know she "is my daughter and one of the very best students in the school?"

I said, "Why, no, how nice, but please understand that my students must start at zero and *work* their way up. Painstakingly."

He said, "Of course." He is whispery and urgent. His glasses circle furtive blue eyes. His suit is generic gray. No chin; turkeylike jowls. Eighteen long hairs lie glued to the top of his head. The jowls shake as he nods it. They were shaking hard as he heard me say, "I can't tell you how delighted I am that we see eye to eye. But if you will excuse me I must go now, because I really have a tremendous amount of work to do."

So much for Caspar McQuisling. Rhonda is just another inmate in Stalag Massif. Nobody escapes and lives. Get back to work!

I think I'm a real teacher. But how am I going to live up to this?

Then there's Torrance. He added a twist, today.

The kid could be a problem. After class, he gave me a picture of a dog. A big, vicious-looking dog. I was somewhat disturbed, considering his earlier behavior, during the exercise. Which reminds me, I have to get that down, too. That exercise went so well. Diary, I introduced my students to a whole new way of reading. I told them about reading with the body.

———

I was glad I'd planned something fun, because after the yelling fit, I faced the problem of making them not hate me. In a way, the fit was helpful, actually. They were cowed, and did exactly what I told them to do.

I told them to drag desks and chairs to the front of the room. That accomplished, I lowered the blinds and turned off the lights. Then I told them to lie down in a big circle on the floor, and to close their eyes.

They thought this was very weird. But they obeyed.

I told them to let their minds go blank and to breathe from their stomachs. They obeyed.

I sat on the floor in the middle of the circle looking at eleven pairs of shoes and decided they had to come off and the heads had to point in instead of out, and they obeyed, some of them by this time giggling a little.

Eleven heads then ringed me, eleven prone bodies stretching out in different shapes and sizes into the dimness. I was the hub and they were the spokes, but if this wheel had a rim it wouldn't have rolled; the fattest girl, Wendy, is much too short.

The result? They couldn't see me, even if they'd opened their eyes. I was sitting directly behind their heads. I got on my hands and knees and crawled around to make sure the eyes were closed. Torrance was fluttering long black lashes. "Close 'em up," I growled as though issuing orders from a police helicopter eight inches above his face and he winked, then obeyed, and I glanced and saw the hard-on in his loose antique trousers: stiffening right at me. Uh-oh. Doesn't he wear underwear? Yow! I crawled away to my throne the hub, from the safety of which I said melodiously, slowly, hypnotically:

"Think of a nap. You are falling asleep. And you're dreaming; let's say you're dreaming about climbing stairs. And suddenly, you miss your step. What happens? You're in bed, not climbing stairs, but as you feel yourself missing that step, you twitch. You twitch because you feel a space where the step should have been, so the twitch is a spasm of trying to balance, and maybe you wake, feeling foolish— but at the same time you're glad you didn't really slip, you can still feel that slip, the alarming space under your foot, and what does this mean?

"It means your body thinks.

"Your body is part of your mind and it *thinks*." Torrance's especially. It's thinking hard—why can't he reach in and *pull down the tent*? "And I want to suggest that because your body thinks, it also reads. What I mean is this: just as when, drifting off to sleep, you can feel an unexpected space that causes you to twitch, so it is sometimes when you read. A set of images makes a surprise, an amazing surprise, and you feel as though you are falling into that surprise; and if you pay close attention to these kinds of surprises you will realize you are reading not only with your head but also with your body, everywhere, all over, in your knees, your neck, your chest," your big-top pole, the boy was beginning to piss me off.

"Now I'm going to read a passage from Gustave Flaubert. I want you to relax into the story, into the images the story conjures up. While you do that, your mission—the point of this exercise—is to find out where the images are. Where are they? In your heads? On the insides of your foreheads? Or are they sometimes in your bodies, in your hands or feet or stomachs?" It occurred to me that this talk of body parts might be doing Torrance no good. I was worried someone would open eyes and see it. Then I decided to totally ignore him.

I read several pages of Flaubert, giving them, I hoped, a number of kinesthetic surprises. Torrance, thank God, deflated. The beefy boy, Alex, fell asleep; but Samantha twitched violently when I got to the famous line, *"It was like an apparition."* The apparition being something in a dark doorway on a sun-drenched boat, the reader not knowing what it is and therefore tumbling right into that doorway, right into the embrace, it turns out, of the ripe Madame Arnoux.

Samantha thought it was going to be the ripe embrace of Frankenstein. She said so later, in the discussion.

It was a good discussion. We got up, opened blinds, dragged chairs into a circle, and argued about the location of images. There was a fifty-fifty split. Half thought the images were only in their heads, the others thought they felt them elsewhere as well, and Torrance, who could have tipped the tie, said nothing. I gave him no clue I'd noticed his erection. When I asked him to speak up and vote he shook his head, then said, "To me everything was invisible. No images at all." The way he said this disturbed me. Either he was playing games or has a problem. Maybe he blocked out the experience. But I doubt that, the way he winked—the boy doesn't just have a problem, he is one, he has the hots for me!

Anyway, I introduced them to the idea of thinking with the body. So the exercise was fine, basically. Except Torrance's body should keep some of its thoughts to itself. Well. He's a kid. These things happen.

The episode wouldn't really concern me if he hadn't proceeded to hand me a photo of a large, savage-looking dog. The boy rushed up after the bell rang. When I took the photo he blurted, "Keep this. Can't talk now but I want to later, ok?" Then he rushed off. Is something wrong with this kid?

———

It's later, getting dark. The doorbell just rang. It was a neighbor. An odd but kindly neighbor. He wanted to say hello. I said, "Hello," then told him I'm up to my neck in important research. He said, "I see," and bowed. He's big and bald and formal, but he smiles a lot. It was awkward. His name is Pip. When he said it he looked flustered, very strange.

Probably he's harmless. I need dinner. Think I'll go to the mall and get something. I hope I don't run into that guy.

The Chronicles
of Malcolm Spoor: III

Wednesday Night

How amusing. I am in my control room, spyscreens ablaze. And I cannot stop smirking.

But he shouldn't have told her his name. Pip can do very good work. But he is stupid. No, he's an idiot savant - brilliant in some ways, doglike in all others.

After chastising him for the pool incident yesterday, I ordered him to break into the woman's apartment and photograph *everything*.

That he did, this evening. Which brought me a good many photographs, tonight. On this I yield - Pip knows how to take pictures and develop and print them, quickly and exquisitely, in color.

Her cubbyhole is a sty. The kennels are neater than that apartment. Newspapers lie fallen where she reads them. Clothes lie strewn where she jumps out of them. She does not wash dishes. She lives like a drug addict alcoholic. Perhaps she is a drug addict alcoholic. And to such a person we entrust our young? What has happened to the country? I nearly choked looking at those photos. Tears ran down my face, so hard was I laughing. What a tramp, what a wench this woman is! She dresses well, at least; she fancies herself a vixen I'd say, but the bathroom is disastrous and the shoes in the closet all seem single, it's a tarty coven of spinsters in there. How old is she, seventeen? Pip must have been shaking; he becomes so extremely upset in the presence of mess. And this is just the surface. Underneath she is even more chaotic. How could I have thought her dangerous?

Her flavor is less dangerous than melted sorbet. Do you agree?

Oh, *never mind*.

A horrid little cubbyhole, that's her domicile, but she keeps a diary. Pip found it. In it is a total of three entries, all recent. He also found eleven samples of student writing. I have read and reread his reproductions of this heady literature. And I cannot stop *smirking*.

I know you are keeping track of this. If you insist on lying low, I don't give a damn. Vile Bunny, ugly Bunny, I hope you never come back. Like the others, you are dead. There, I said it, dead, dead, *dead!* Ha, ha. Sad Bunny, dead Bunny! Ha-ha-HA!

The point is, the trollop has inspired me. Now I want to write. I yearn to join the ranks of the "really creative" - are you dumbfounded? Just thinking about it makes my blood run cold. Enthralling. Sheila has acquired a new student: me. So fuck off!

I smirked at Torrance straight through dinner tonight. At Pip, too, as he served us sweetbreads in cream with shiitakes, morels and pleurotes.

"You're in a good mood," Torrance said as he eyed his steaming dinner. "What are these things?"

Three cameras tracked his entry into the dining salon. I mashed the remote the moment I heard him come loping.

"Glands," I said in response to his question.

"You gotta be shitting me," he said, aghast. He rubbed his nose for emphasis. Such a beautiful nose. Pale, shapely, flaring with horror at glandular steam.

"I do not shit you. Pip, do I shit him?"

"You do not," Pip said, standing with the chafing dish in his hands.

"I can't eat - *glands* - what do these glands do?"

"They are thymus organs, crucial for the production of antibodies in the - body. All bodies need antibodies, even yours does, am I right, Pip?"

"UGGGHHO-YUCKK-*YECCCH!*" Torrance shouted.

"These are not human glands," Pip said, "they are veal glands, but you are right, even Torrance's body . . ." He couldn't finish the sentence; so dismayed was he that Torrance was spurning his cuisine, the fragrant lobes nestled on my plate and on Torrance's plate and in the silver dish he was continuing to hold, mournfully now; as though it contained the shattered remains of a prized pet.

"I do not shit!" I said smirkingly. Neither disputed this statement. "Please take away Torrance's sweetbreads, Pip; Torrance, what would you like to have for dinner instead? The chef and his entire staff of mechanical assistants wish to know your whim."

"*BLTs,*" Torrance declared, standing, "and I'll make 'em 'cause I can't stand that bacon stuff you use - sorry, Pip. I'm really sorry, I appreciate all the work you put into these glands but man, I never even heard of people eating - thymus - and what's that, some kind of *node*?" He was jabbing his fork at a plump morel.

As he spoke, #2 zoomed. Torrance's waist plays best to #2. It's because of the position of his chair. He will stand, wanting to leave, but will wait for permission, arms crossed on his chest. Then, as he gets impatient, he'll slowly shift weight from one sneaker to the other, angling hip this way, then that, dipping rib cage that way, then this, flesh going concave in one side and snug at the other, then snug at one and concave in the other, thus tilting the waist - so captivatingly that, on-screen, I see afterglows. Perfect ellipsoids, tilting! I can't stare while he's doing it, of course. He would resent open scrutiny. He might make a point of sitting dead still in his chair wearing drab baggy clothes, shoulders hunched. We do not want that. Uggghho-yuckk-yeccch, as Torrance would say.

But #2 gets it all. #1, meantime, gets buttock-flex. One curve then the other pressing harder, in tandem with his pitch and yaw.

Tonight, however, he was very impatient; unsheathing shoulder blades, he hugged elbows on the top of his chair. It's the food. He's getting annoyed. #3, which never leaves his head, never if possible leaves his face, recorded an emerald scowl. Torrance was about to take a stand. How marvelous; I design our menus to provoke such moods, for the benefit of hungry cameras. So far he has rejected shad roe, sautéed kidneys, brains in *beurre noir,* and gamy venison carpaccio. If Pip weren't so masterful a cook, so proud of his productions, and so inherently doglike, he would accuse me of tormenting the boy. As it is, he thinks I am trying to broaden Torrance's palate, and hasn't seemed to have made a connection between the cameras and our boy-gagging dinners - bow-wow-wow.

"Torrance," I said, "you look as though you have something important to say. If you do, please say it."

"Yes," Torrance said, fingers clutched to the elbows and chin gouging an arm, "I do. I don't think it's funny that you try to make me eat brains and fish eggs and raw deer and *glands*. I respect the fact that you and Pip are gourmets who travel around the world looking for strange things to eat. But I am a normal American and I can't eat inner organs. So I need some say about dinnertime, and I'm glad to make my own food anyway, because I really don't understand why Pip has to do all the work if you are such, uh, close friends, you know."

"Thank you," Pip said stiffly, putting inner organs on the sideboard.

"You're welcome," Torrance said, still staring at me.

"I do not think your difficulty with our meals is funny, Torrance," I said, attempting not to smirk. "I have various items of business on my mind that happen to amuse me, you see."

"That's a good sign," Torrance said. "You haven't been very amused since I got here, by anything that I can tell."

"Your father doesn't get amused these days." Pip sighed. He sat down and tasted sweetbreads in the discreet manner he long ago was forced to adopt as habit. "Why don't you tell us about it, Malcolm?"

"No," I said.

"If it's private," Torrance said hopefully, "I'll go make some BLTs."

"There's regular bacon in the second refrigerator," Pip said.

"I know," Torrance said.

"A growing boy must eat, eat, eat," I said broadly. "Torrance, of course you may go prepare those luscious BLTs. When you have prepared them, all seven of them I imagine, you will, however, consume them in my presence, in here or in the library, I might by then be there; I would like to discuss something with you, and no, it does not concern the amusing business that has been distracting me. No, what I wish to discuss is rather serious. It concerns school. Specifically, your writing class."

"Really?" Torrance said. "What about it?"

"When you have made mountainous BLTs, Torrance, then we discuss."

"Ok," Torrance said, leaving. He looked shaken.

I promptly smirked at Pip.

"Good stuff?" he whispered.

"Good stuff," I replied. "Did you read the diary?"

"I didn't even try."

"Yes, that's no surprise." I'd needed time to decipher the floral but epileptic script. "She is conducting research into adolescent sex."

"You are joking."

"I do not shit. For a thesis on 'gender boundary.' Whatever that is, she makes her students lie on the classroom floor while she reads Flaubert - which, she claims, teaches them to 'think with the body.' These academics are so decadent now."

"Reminds me of us."

"Of course. But she doesn't have money, and is worried her superiors will think she doesn't adhere to traditional values - whatever they are! She is so insecure she even has something she calls her drama chamber. Where she goes to hide, apparently."

"What?" Pip said, shocked. "I didn't see any . . ."

"It's imaginary, mental. The sort of thing addled therapists invent. Deeply foolish *lingo,* Pip. And she thinks Torrance is cute."

"Aha. Bad."

"Perhaps. Anyone would think Torrance is cute. However, when he was on the floor, she noticed that the boy's body was 'thinking hard' - quite visibly, and personally, you see. I gather she was impressed."

"Really?" Pip gasped. "But - you seem excited."

"I'm pleased, yes. That my son should be so red-blooded."

"Good," Pip declared. "You haven't been yourself for a long time."

"You ain't seen nothin' yet," I drawled. And he hasn't!

"You never explain anything," he complained. "And you call me a dog."

"Don't start!"

"I just want to know what you're doing. With Sheila."

"We will have a little fun, with her. What does she look like?"

"She is pretty. But not big."

"Not for me, then?"

"No. Not big enough. Not for you."

A shame, eh? Grislies, how can I find suitable ladies, ladies with heft, in this land of the obsessively scrawny?

———

Torrance came into the library carrying a platterful of the disgusting sandwiches and a half gallon of milk. I was on my second cognac.

"You drink a lot," he said.

I beamed at him.

Torrance's most laudable characteristic, apart from his appearance, is the way he disposes of food. One is almost unaware he is eating, or drinking. This is exceptional; particularly since he puts away several times his body weight daily. He sat on the floor not far from the fire, poured a glass of milk and drank half of it with two soundless gulps. Admirable. He said, pointedly, "You had something you said you wanted to talk about."

"Yes," I said. I wore a brocaded Thai smoking gown and, of course, was smoking, deep within the blinkering wings of a wingback chair; Torrance, cross-legged on the carpet twelve feet away, had chosen center stage of my limited field of view. The boy is bold when he sets his mind to it.

"But," he said, "I think we should talk about why I am here, and why you wrote me that crazy letter."

We hadn't discussed the letter. Not since his arrival, shortly after which he'd said, "You need help, Dad, that letter was a joke or a cry for . . ."

To which I'd said curtly, "You will understand. But not now."

"When?" he'd asked.

"Later," I'd said.

So he was determined that "later" be now. Why? He might suspect I've tried to burgle his computer. Which I have, without success, the files are protected rather cleverly. Even Pip is stymied. But this line of reasoning assumes the files contain material worthy of counterattack - and there is no evidence they do. Intuition, however, leaves little room for doubt.

I've an idea who the subject of his first homework assignment is; the person whom he "most especially would not want to be." If I am right, how diverting. But not smirkably so, it's too poignant, and there is very little in this world I would classify as *poignant*.

I said, "I am your father. Isn't that reason enough for you to be here? Torrance, do sons not live from time to time with their fathers?"

"Cut the crap," he said. "You're up to something."

Shades of Floria! "Of course I am," I said.

"Now we're talking," he said, and another BLT was gone. His eyes were flashing and his lip on the next one glistened like gravlax.

I said, "I am up to a something that will make you rich. And that is all, I'm not up to much more now, as I near the end, my end - my passing."

"Bullshit," he said.

"The accountants will be here in a few weeks," I said. "I hope you will take an interest."

"Yeah, yeah, yeah."

"Suit yourself. Money, in large enough amounts, has a way of handling itself, you need not take any interest at all. Other than accrual."

"I don't care about it."

"But that is precisely the point, you see, you don't have to care about it. It cares about you."

"*You* don't."

"Ah! Cruel child!" I poured more cognac. "Torrance, I care profoundly. I am in the process of 'taking very good care of' you, as they say. Why would I do that if I were uncaring?"

"That is what I do not know."

"I also care, deeply, about your education."

"This is a first. Why?"

"Your enthusiasm, Torrance, the élan with which you speak of writing, of that class, of that teacher, a youngish woman; you have mentioned her any number of times. The experience is stimulating you."

"This is what you wanted to talk about?"

"Of course. I sense a sea change in the wellsprings of your creativity, if you will pardon metaphorical sweet mixing with brine. Unlike you, I am not inclined to the written word."

"Coulda fooled me. That *letter*."

"The product of a diseased and desperate mind, Torrance."

"Yeah, you keep saying that. What makes you think I'm creative or want to write? I just like that class, and I also like being with people my own age, which I need to discuss if your diseased mind doesn't mind. Don't get upset, Dad, but this suicide shit is a game, right? I mean, Pip laughed when I told him. Kind of weirdly, though."

"You told Pip."

"Yeah. He's the only one who's close to you, and then there's me. Somebody has to take responsibility. If even half of what you say is true."

I gazed at him, feeling an unpleasant shock of affection. He is disconcertingly adorable. "Torrance," I said, "your concern moves me. In the deepest part of my being, such as it is. Thank you. Now, as to people your own age. I was getting to that topic myself."

He sat very erect, his mouth open, tongue alert. All my danger signals were blinking. But I said, "I was thinking it would be nice if you invited your writing class, including the teacher, of course, here; for a swim in the pool. Pip could barbecue. On a Saturday or Sunday afternoon."

"What?" he gasped.

"Why not?" I asked, swirling contents of snifter. "You think I do not care about you. But you know in your heart that naturally I do. And here is evidence, I desire to meet the teacher you like so much, for the ordinary reasons any good parent would have. I am curious. I want to know who the human beings are who have custody of your mental advancement. At least who one of them is, we can't have the whole school here . . ."

"We could," he pointed out.

"Yes, but no," I said, "there are limits, the nervous drain, and so on. Well! What do you say?"

He seemed annoyed. Then he said, "It would be embarrassing."

"Why? We three are not the Nuclear Family?"

"No, no," he said, blushing, "not that, who cares if you're gay, and Pip's a great guy - uh - and so are you; but this place is, uh . . ."

Again I suppressed my smirk. Pip and I - "gay." Strange to say, I felt an impulse to disabuse him of that long charade. But who knows what he might blurt to its principal beneficiary, his mother? Not that she'd believe a word. Nor that it makes the slightest difference. I said, "Torrance, do you worry about what people think of where you happen to live?"

"I guess I shouldn't," he said, gnashing inaudibly into a BLT.

"Very good, then, it's decided. Bring it up with Teacher on Friday, you have one of those classes then. It's the, what, third one, is it not?"

"How'd you know that?"

"Because you've been talking about it since the first one. Which was day before yesterday, Torrance. You think I am deaf, child?"

———

A miscalculation, perhaps. Perhaps not. I must enjoy myself in these days of wane. Before I kill myself? I will have some fun, before killing myself, I deserve that, no?

There is more practical benefit as well. I will tape the voices and faces and movements of the children. Samantha, in particular, interests me. And Rhonda. Yes, Rhonda is very valuable.

What could Sheila be stumbling into? The woman may be ready for a permanent vacation in her drama chamber.

Pip will bug the classroom. He will not let Torrance out of his sight. Unless, of course, the boy is in mine.

Torrance Spoor's Homework; Letter from Torrance Spoor to Sheila Massif

TORRANCE'S HOMEWORK

Wednesday Night

Writing Class
Torrance Spoor

THE SCREAMER

My name is The Screamer and I'm a scary guy.

You never heard of me. I keep my life private. But I am unbeliev-ably rich. Also, I am crazy.

I sing to myself when nobody else is around. It sounds like scream-ing. Like the screaming ladies do in foreign countries when their man died or a earthquake just destroyed everything: grief stricken. But full of glee sometimes too, like it tortures me, to be so sad and happy at the same time.

So I call myself "The Screamer."

I live in the jungle, in a huge house with my dogs and my faithful servant Kip, who follows orders and nods his head like a Kung Foo rip-your-guts-out-Artist.

Speaking of guts, I eat a rich diet of animal guts that Kip cooks with tons of heavy cream and butter and fine spices that Americans would barf up in about two seconds if they ate it, which they would not since it is totally horrible.

My dogs don't eat this stuff but they look like they do. They eat normal dog food that gets delivered by truck every week, since I have twelve of the monsters. Each one eats a whole garbage can of Alpo every day. And even though they are monsters, with huge jaws, they gobble their food quietly - they are high class dogs. The kennel is in the basement, with private doors, so they can come and go to the jungle when they want, and do seriously strange things out there, like eat, and I am not kidding: Zebras.

Lucky thing, the doors are electric. I keep them locked when friends come to visit. I like to scare the hell out of most people. But not everybody.

My dogs have red eyes, by the way. They are great for hunting. They zap animals - making them so scared, they can't run! They just stare back, waiting to get their guts ripped out! And I notice that when I sing, the eyes turn redder. I don't even have to tell these dogs what to do. If I go for a walk they pose really nobly on the cliffs, and I smile at them, but do not say a word:

I think they can read my mind.

This must be why they don't have names. No names for these dogs - if they read my mind, see, I never have to call them, right? Wild!

Kip cleans out their kennel. He does everything around here as a matter of fact: cleans, cooks, drives the truck and the car, and he brings the groceries from the most expensive stores that sell raw guts in the tiny village. You never saw anybody more loyal than Kip. He never complains except when I'm not around. Then he does, but cheerfully. He has amnesia. He was in a war and a bomb exploded too close to his head. So now he can't remember anything about his past and his whole life is completely pledged to me, The Screamer.

This is convenient, because I make him perform acts that I will not describe at the moment since they are kind of personal.

But it is great to have somebody around who does anything I say. Like train the local children to be fit. Kip loves doing that. The kids get all sweaty when he leads the vigorous drills. And they sort of appreciate the chance to get into very fine shape. Also, I give them money. Dump trucks full of money pull into the yard and they practically choke to death under the piles of cruddy hundred dollar bills.

I come from a family that is so old in history that maybe that is why I went crazy. My ancestors were kind of cruel. They went on Crusades and I think the experience had a bad effect. Too much

killing and harsh sex probably. So now, I have to admit, I am thinking of committing suicide.

Which is not such a bad idea.

And if this seems too macabre to be true, think again. You would
be amazed by all the activities I keep busy with behind locked doors.
You would not believe it. I can hardly believe it myself. But it is true.
I am one crazy and scary gentleman. Of course, I'm pretty slick,
being so rich.

I'm even kind of handsome. In a jet set boozy way. I forgot to
mention: I drink like a fish.

LETTER FROM TORRANCE SPOOR TO SHEILA MASSIF

Wednesday Night

Dear Sheela,

Class was very cool today. The stuff about "reading with your
body," that is pretty interesting. Sorry if I did not seem like I was
paying attention.

Also, I am sorry my homework is late. Honest, I did not know it
was supposed to be ready. Anyway I just finished it and you will get
it Friday.

But I wish it was now. So you could get this tonight. I have something to tell you. I feel I should explain why I gave you that picture.

I know it seemed weird. Coming up to you and giving you a picture
of a dog. Pretty wild dog, right? Does it look like a normal dog to
you? It might be hard to tell how creepy it is, from a picture. But I
would appreciate hearing what you think.

My reason I should talk about in private. I need to talk to somebody soon. Please do not get ideas I am a little out of it, from my
homework, or from this letter. All I can say is, I'm in a strange
situation. A lot stranger than the homework. And I'm getting nervous about it. So nervous, I have started to lie to my mother, who
lives in California, about how bad it is right now. She is the only one
who might believe me, though. But she worries so much, she might
have a heart attack or something if she knew what is happening. So
I am having a hard time figuring out what to do.

I really hope we can talk about this.

Torrance Spoor

The Diary
of Sheila Massif: IV

Thursday Evening

Duane visited today. It was nice, all told, but slightly strange, as usual. He's developed a funny interest in Torrance. For some reason, the picture of the dog really grabbed him.

It's silly. But disturbing, too, he seems serious about the Torrance thing. I just wish it made sense. Duane's psychic trip always baffled me. I think it always will.

———

He came in at nine looking sleepy. We kissed and I liked it. Then he sniffed around the nooks, eyebrows raised. As if he were intrigued. I thought he'd laugh, but he didn't. That turned me on.

By 11:00 we'd fucked three times. And it was great. He does something to me. We go somewhere together. We fly away. Nobody else does that and I'd like to know why, because Duane, after all, is a kook. A kook and a hick, but he has that bod. That fuzzy hair on his chest, he's my fleecy hick with the golden dick. God, you'd think I'm in love.

So it was terrific. It was fun to be reminded of why we were crazy about each other; of the way it used to be, before we decided we can't stand each other. I mean, I'm a scientist, a professional researcher, at least, which he isn't. Anyway, that's ancient history.

We went out to lunch at Mr. T's Mexican Cuisine, situated conveniently in the booming mall, not far from that other standby, the Burger King. But Mr. T's serves cocktails. We stared at each other's frozen margaritas and got off to a good start discussing the condoms we hadn't used.

"I've been celibate," he said. "Have you?"

"No," I lied.

"You're lying," he said. "And why are you taping this?"

"I'm sorry about that," I lied. "I should have told you. I tape everything now. I'm writing a detailed case history of my disturbing life."

"Can I read it?"

"Of course not. You know how you get with jealous rage."

He smiled and said, "You're high-strung. I felt it on the phone."

"Now you do psychic readings over the phone?"

The smile turned into a yawn and when he was finished with that he said his work is going well, how about mine?

I told him everything. Everything except the basic reason I'm here is to teach myself to be brave, and face the real world. I'm not ready to tell him or anyone else about my problem area—my Drama Chamber. Anyway he probably knows about it. He's Psychic Duane.

He listened to an hour's worth in his lazy, blinking, patient way. He doubts Samantha is psychic. I should keep the research to myself, be low-key. People are too messed up with their own strange stories to notice or care about mine. Soft-pedal the sex angle, that's all. Keep the tape recorder hidden, nobody will get around to suspecting anything. He's so sensible. Nothing shocks him. As to whether I'll succeed in mining thesis material, who knows? Maybe. Maybe not. Life goes on.

This is why I dumped him. He's too *blasé.*

Or why he dumped me. I tried to talk about it but he wouldn't accuse or make claims or anything. If only he weren't so much fun in bed. Duane, sexual genius, addictive substance of flesh.

We went back to the apartment and had more of it. Later, he was lying in the bed nook, smoking, he still smokes, while I was making lemonade, and he said, "You know, somebody besides you has been here."

"Yeah," I said. "You."

"No," he said. Heeby-jeeby-creepy-heepy. The offhand way he

was so sure meant he wasn't kidding. But I've never bought the psychic mumbo jumbo; more or less, never.

"Taking pictures," he said.

"Prove it," I said, approaching with lemonade and otherwise naked.

He, naked, furry, the fine hair catching rays from the window, was looking at two small objects. Batteries. "You use these for anything?" he said. "They were on the floor. I stepped on 'em."

"They give you spooky vibes?" I asked, drinking lemonade and thinking, Huh—where did those things come from, anyway?

"No," he said. "But maybe, spooky."

" 'No, but maybe,' there's something about being psychic, Duane, that resists the issue of proof . . ."

"Yeah," he said. "Like studies of teen sexuality derived from samples of creative writing. Let's not get hung up on proof, it's counterproductive. Somebody was here taking pictures, and that person used these batteries to do it, and left them behind, by accident, probably."

I said, "Describe the shadowy snapshotter. When did it do it and why?"

He said he can't tell what the person looks like. But he insisted somebody took pictures of things that belong to me. The batteries are the kind professionals use for flashes. Do I know photographers with flashes?

No. I don't. For some reason I thought of Torrance's cock. Battery-powered? I hadn't told Duane about yesterday's Erection Incident.

He said, "What are you thinking about?"

"Can't you tell?" I said. He looked at me and didn't blink. Unusual, for him. It means, "Talk."

So I briefed him on Torrance. He's fiercely calm, and transemotional, and doesn't experience any mental imagery at all, and has an out-of-control penis, which is flattering, I guess, because it pointed at me, but is inappropriate, all things considered, to say the least.

He said, "Holy shit," and lit another cigarette.

"What?" I said. I thought this was funny. "Resentful, Duane?"

He didn't answer. And he wasn't blinking. "There's another thing," I said, to pass the time. "He gave me a picture. Of a dog."

"Where is it?" Duane said.

I had to think about that. "Out in my car," I said.

Duane was looking at me strangely. "Please get it," he said.

He'd listened all day to me. So I got it. And I swear, when I handed it over, Duane turned pale. "Did he tell you anything about this?" he asked.

"No. Duane, what's the matter?"

He ignored me. I touched him, and he trembled. This was getting odd. "What else can you tell me about this kid?" he asked.

"Nothing. Except that he's very attractive. The girls adore him."

"What's his last name?"

I had to check the self-description. Duane grabbed it out of my hands, and scowled at it. Then he muttered, "Sheila—that kid is connected."

"Yeah?" I said. "What's he connected to, Duane?"

"To something," Duane replied. "And, *to you*."

"No kidding," I said. "It's called a crush."

"Maybe," he said. "But that's not what I'm talking about . . ."

"Duane," I said firmly, "you're mumbo jumboing! Stop it!"

He did. He snapped out of it. Actually, what he said was, "Ah, I don't know," lighting yet another cigarette. But he asked if I had Torrance's address. I found the packet the secretary gave me at school. The address is a postbox number on a Mace Lane. I asked Duane what he's going to do with it. "I don't," he said, "have any idea."

We took showers and went for a drive. It was rush hour around the booming mall. Fifteen minutes to get through one light. I made small talk but he wouldn't play. He kept fiddling with his scraggly mustache. Finally he said, "Something's going on."

I said, "Shut up. We are going for a peaceful drive through the serene countryside." We looked at the traffic and laughed.

So it was a pleasant visit. We had dinner at a quaint country inn that belongs to one of the more reputable international chains. Over mineral water—he wouldn't have wine—we agreed our fling is over. Out of bed we're miles apart. He's a psychic nut and I'm a psychologist; he's working on a secret project somewhere in Cambridge and I'm in the boonies mapping adolescent gender. The contrast got us giggling.

"I'll be in touch," he said when he dropped me off.

I miss him, to be honest. He's fun. He's nice. And we fly away—why does that have to be so rare? Why do good lays have to be so rare? But why do they have to be such cuckoo-birds? Which Duane, of course, is. Photographers. Connections. A dog. Torrance. It's making me dizzy. Torrance is just a normal, oversexed kid.

Duane Allbright's
Confidential Reports: II

CODE: DA/PERSONAL///ACCESS/NONE
REPORT: VISIT WITH SHEILA

I'm at the Lab, trying to make sense of what happened tonight. Something bizarre is going on. More than bizarre. So much more, to hell with procedure. I'm keeping this to myself.

Whatever it is, it's nothing obvious. It's shielded. Heavily. And it's dynamic, not static—it shifts. Slippery's the word that comes to mind. Big, too. How big? Hell, gut feel says this thing's chartless.

Cunif would have a cow. They'd all have cows. One big moo, that's what we'd have here. But that, comrades, can wait.

———

Tuesday last, 1530 approx., I experienced a moderate ideation, PSI-DEFINITE. Object: Sheila Massif. Content of ideation: Sheila in distress.

Recently she took a teaching job up north. It's a gamble. The circumstances, for her, are trouble. So I figured she had a problem, and phoned her. We spoke briefly, discussed me visiting, agreed I should.

I didn't reveal my reason. Talking with her, I was hit by the oddest thing I ever felt over the phone. The oddest thing ever, because it wasn't Sheila. It was something she was relaying.

Sheila, as I mentioned in my first report on this subject, is a powerful relayer. She picks up traces, and relays them; she relays to me, and probably can do the same with other Psi, although I know of no such cases. She is completely unconscious of these abilities. A psychologist, academically oriented, she is skeptical, even hostile, about the idea of psi phenomena. (Key point, however: at some level, her mind must be aware.)

It will come as no surprise to personnel who read this report that I never before have experienced psi-relay during a telephone conversation.

I concluded the source of the relay must be unusual, and strong. Hence the decision to visit Sheila.

——

I arrived at 0930 this morning. I'd puzzled over the above all the way up. Had wondered if I'm losing my touch.

Then I walked in and kissed her. The relay was there. It was as vague as it had been on the phone, but it hit me the moment my lips touched hers—a bang, that's an understatement. I didn't tell her about it.

I should mention, Sheila and I have carried on an affair for just over two years. It's been fun, mostly; the nature of our attunement renders us almost irresistible to each other, sexually speaking. But again, she isn't aware of the psi aspect. She thinks we "click."

The relationship is germane due to this fact: sex with Sheila enhances my receptivity to her relay powers.

Today, that proved useful. Traces, strong ones, were all over her apartment. They were peculiar. They were hard to read; definitely not something I'd sensed before. The gut feel was: alien.

Naturally I was excited. Unaware of the undercurrents, Sheila was too. I have to say, it's a shame this woman resists knowing her talent. She can do so much with it.

At any rate, in bed, where we spent most of the day, she relayed the traces. Actually she did more than that. She magnified them.

I explored them. I should mention something. When I get in deep with Sheila, it often feels like an exploration. In a sense, it's an out-of-body experience. Part of me is making love. Another part detaches, and goes looking around. It's like prospecting. Sheila is the detector, so to speak, through which traces show up, almost like glows.

Her apartment, I learned, was full of glows. What they mean, I don't know. The nature of the Entity—for lack of a better term—is plain weird. It seems crazy, but I can't fret now. It's what I read. It's what I felt.

First, it's part animal. It's a person, that was clear; some kind of person, anyway, who carries psi. But, it is animal psi. Needless to say I was shocked. The very concept of animal psi is outrageous. I've never felt, or heard of, anything like it.

Second, I got hit with some kind of odor. It was faint but ubiquitous, the odor was all over that apartment. This doesn't make sense. But nothing about this makes sense. So I may as well say it: the odor seemed almost like a psi perfume. The odor, it's perfumy. Sort of sweet. Sort of floral.

Those were the basic characteristics. I read more, though. I learned the Entity had been there twice.

The first time was brief. A faint burn at the door was all I got. I asked Sheila if she'd had any visitors. She had. It turned out she'd met this thing. A man had come by. He's around forty-five, big, bald, formal, smiles a lot. The name: Pip. He'd claimed to be a neighbor saying hello. She thought he was odd, but harmless. We'll see.

Because the second time he was there, she wasn't. He broke in. I deduce this, can't figure it any other way. For one thing, she didn't know. But she relayed the traces. No images, not even vague ones, but I did get an impression of sequence. This sequence seemed methodical. The Entity Pip had left traces everywhere, even in the closets.

Then, in the mid-afternoon, getting out of bed the side Sheila doesn't, I stepped on some batteries. The kind photographers use. They didn't belong there, I knew that right away. They bothered me. I picked them up, got back in bed.

I had a feeling Pip had used them. I puzzled over that, tried to relate it to the impression of sequence. Then it hit me: Pip took pictures. He shot the place, systematically, top to bottom.

Why would a bizarre creature, the likes of which I'd never imagined, take pictures of Sheila's apartment?

Knowing she would pooh-pooh me, I told her a bit about this, and asked her to focus on the idea of a photographer, just to see what she might pick up. She pooh-poohed, all right; but proceeded to talk about a student named Torrance Spoor.

I had a hunch her doing that wasn't an accident. She thinks this boy has a crush on her. He'd given her, she went on to say, a photo of a dog. I asked to see it. It amazed me. The dog amazed me.

What struck me were the eyes. They're pink. Staring at them, I got hit, hard. So hard, at first I had no idea what the hit was. Then I knew what it was. It was fear.

Those eyes scared me. I must have gasped; I did something of the sort, because Sheila was looking at me strangely. I said, "Tell me more about the kid who gave you this picture."

The only useful thing she had was the address.

———

We ate out. Later, after dropping her off, I stopped at the mall and bought a map. Then I went for a late-night drive.

Torrance Spoor's address is a postbox number on a road called Mace Lane. It's a lonely road, near the ocean; which I couldn't see due to the dark, and woods that pressed in close. For quite a stretch, trees screen a tall brick wall. In the middle of that, brick towers hold a gate.

The gate wasn't lit. Using my flashlight, I saw it's iron, and heavy, the old-fashioned kind with two swinging sides. Fretwork spelled a word in the crest. I made out "MACE." On one of the towers, a brassy thing caught my flash. It was a postbox cover. The number matched the one Sheila had given me.

Maybe he lives here, I thought, because he works here. Then I thought, No. He lives here because he lives here. He's rich.

I pulled the car back a little, turned off the lights. My eyes adjusted; gradually, the sky showed stars. The gate gleamed in the black. What, I wondered, is behind it?

Heater blasting, it was cold out, I sat there for maybe half an hour. I'd experienced two pretty intense things at Sheila's. A human with animal psi; a snapshot of chilling animal eyes. It was farfetched to think they aren't related. What's happening in that gigantic estate?

Bright light hit the gate and my reverie skidded. It came from floods set in the towers. I heard a metallic click, then a creak, and saw the gate shudder. It was opening. Across my rearview mirror, beams chased shadows; a car was approaching. That gate, I thought, may be old, but it's remote controllable. Should I get out of here? Or wait, and see what happens?

I waited. A Land-Rover pulled up beside me. The gate lights glared in its windows. I rolled down my window. Then one of the Rover's slid down, and at the wheel I saw a large, bald man.

I held up my map and said, "I'm lost."

The man stared at me. I got a sharp jolt of psi—the same sweet-smelling, half-animal psi I'd sensed at Sheila's. I was looking at Pip.

It seemed he felt me feeling that. His stare hardened. "What do you want?" he asked. "Directions?"

"Please," I said.

He sighed, then pointed the way I hadn't come. "Down the road a half-mile, on the right. It's easy to miss at night, it's just a path through the forest. I think the others are already hiding there."

Astonished, I said, "Huh."

He said, "I haven't seen you before. But my employer is aware of you people, we feel for you, of course. Tell us if there is anything we can do." His window slid shut. He drove through the gate, which closed on his taillights disappearing up a long, dark drive.

———

Keeping my lights off, I headed, slowly, down the road. He was right about the turn. It's a barely visible gap in trees. The wall turns there too, it makes a right angle from the road and runs on through. That path, I thought, doesn't go into the grounds.

I debated driving versus walking. Driving seemed safer. But walking might provide more information. I got out of the car, locked it and walked.

The woods were dead dark. I walked and walked, using my flash, which worried me. Anyone down there would see it. Outlandish scenarios went through my mind. Pip, and his employer, "feel for you people"—what does that mean? They're psychically on the lookout? They're sympathetic? Both meanings spooked me. I imagined a cabal—people who are attracted to what's going on in that estate, who gather outside it, secretly, at night . . .

I heard a twig snap, off in the black, to my right. I froze; and noticed that the wall stopped, just ahead. A chain-link fence continued from it through the woods. On the other side of the fence was a big murky space, few trees. Was something there? I put out my flash.

Instantly, a light fixed on me. A voice yelled, "Halt!"

Other lights got me. More voices shouted. I stood still, illuminated like a statue. The lights began to move. Behind them, people were coming around trees. They walked at me. As they got closer I saw they were men in hunting jackets, carrying rifles pointed not far away.

"What," one of them called out, "do we have here?"

"Hands up!" another one snapped. I put them up.

"Drop it!" another one said. He meant the flash. I dropped it.

There were four of them. They ringed me, faces distorting over their flashes. The heaviest said, "Explain yourself."

"This is a mistake," was all I could say.

"You're out for a walk, buddy?" the man behind me asked. He poked my back with his rifle. "Why'd you come here?"

"I was curious," I said.

"Curious," a bearded guy snorted. "Curious about what?"

"Maybe what happened to the bodies, huh?" the heaviest suggested.

"Bodies?" I asked.

"You did it, didn't you?" the one behind me shouted, poking again.

"I don't know," I said, "what you are referring to."

"Kind of strange you're here, then," the fourth man said. This fellow seemed calmer than the others. I smelled beer. I realized they were scared.

"The whole situation is kind of strange," I said. They couldn't disagree. "You guys are looking for somebody. It isn't me. I got lost on Mace Lane, see, and pulled over by the gate there to look at a map. A bald man showed up and asked if I wanted directions. When I said yes, he told me to come down here. I guess he thought I'm one of you. But I had the impression he was talking about a party. Something interesting, anyway. I'm sorry."

"Some party," the heavy man muttered. "Where you from?"

"Cambridge."

"Figures," the one behind me said. "You say Pip knows we're here?"

"Yes. He said if he can be of help, let him know."

"How does he know we're here?" the bearded one wondered.

"Cops," the calm man said. "The cops think he's God." I wanted to ask why, but didn't. "You have ID?" he then asked.

I gave it to him. He wrote down my name and address. They were relaxing. I said, "Can you tell me what's going on?"

The man behind me came around and put his flash in my eyes. He wants to remember my face, I thought. "This here," he said, "is what you call a lover lane." I nodded. "Three weeks ago tonight, my daughter came here with her boyfriend. They parked by that fence." He swept the fence with his flash, and shivered. They all shivered. Then I did, too. "They parked right there, buddy. And then—they disappeared."

"A friend found the car," the calm one said. "But no kids."

"They vanished," the bearded one put in. "Volunteers searched. The police searched, everywhere. Not a trace. Nothing."

I was staring at the fence. A bad feeling had come over me. It was a feeling of being watched. "Did the police," I asked, gesturing at the fence as casually as I could, "look in there?"

"Oh, yes. Yes, indeed," the father affirmed. "For two days solid. It's real nice in there, a big meadow. The kids like to climb the fence and run around, you see."

"Not anymore," the heavy one said.

"That bald man helped out?" I asked, still looking at the fence.

"Why you want to know?" the father inquired.

I shrugged. "The way he seemed concerned about you all, I suppose."

"Pip cooperated," the calm one grunted. "He supplied the beer."

"Better get going, mister," the father said. "This is a stakeout."

I didn't want to leave. Something, I now was convinced, was watching us through the fence. And that thing felt—awful. It felt hungry; it felt curious; it felt *animal.* I turned, making as if to walk back to the road, and said, "I wish you luck."

They did what I wanted them to do. They turned with me, putting their backs to the fence. The beams from their flashes lowered; behind them, the darkness deepened. I pretended to have one last thing to say, and gazed at the black beyond. Wondering what the last thing I had to say was, I saw something.

Behind the fence, close to the ground, red sparks were glowing. I blinked, stared harder. They were still there. Two bright red sparks.

Then I smelled them. They smelled animal. They smelled *floral.*

What I had to say was, "Gentlemen, this scares me shitless."

My sincerity was clear. It impressed those guys. But they didn't know why.

The sparks went out. Feeling weak, I made a little wave, and walked down the path.

I figured the men were safe. Whatever those sparks were, they were pure psi, extremely powerful psi. Nothing that powerful wants attention.

It's getting too much attention already. I reached the car, got in and sat.

The smell stayed with me. I tried to analyze it. What killed me most was, it smelled just like Pip.

Letter from Torrance Spoor
to His Mother, Floria Shade

Thursday Night

Dear Mom,

I been here a week and nothing terrible is happening. Thanks for the calls, I like hearing your voice too, but you do not have to worry so much. Everything is fine. Really!

I just worked out with Pip. He is a fitness freak like me and guess what? He's an all right guy.

But you are right, Mom, Dad is a weird dude. I never have to see him though, except at dinner when I try to be polite about what they eat: GUCK! You did not warn me about the food, you know. I am laughing, I can't believe what Pip makes for dinner. I think they are torturing me or something.

Did you know Spoors go back in time all the way to the Crusades and we - I guess it is "we," my name is Spoor - were dangerous nobles who ate the guts of victims? (This must be why Dad makes Pip cook those things.) Dad still is a noble. A "baron," that is embarassing. Did he ever tell you about Gundulf and Baybars? And a castle called Krak, with flowers and a War Hound, and - pretty kinky! Mom, you would not like it.

Anyway, Dad and Pip and I live in a humungo edifice (Thesaurus Button - slick!) that is 70 times too big for just three people. I remember us being rich when I was little and hey - your pretty rich, compared to the usual world, but Dad - he is filthy, filthy *loaded,* and the place here proves it. It has two elevators, and tons of remote control stuff for the music system and even some of the windows, Dad is like a kid with toys. All the electronics are new, too. He will not let me see half the stuff he has here. He says it is security. But I think he just likes to play with his toys.

Guess what? He says he is giving everything away. Mom, this is sort of hard to believe. Take a deep breath, Mom. Sit down: he says he is giving everything he owns to me.

He told me this a while back in a letter I got at school and did not tell you about because it seemed sort of disturbed and I could not believe anything it said at all, you might of flipped if you saw it.

But everything is turning out ok, so do not worry, but I get the feeling Dad might be a little depressed, the letter he sent me - it was long - went into a few areas. That seemed kind of gloomy.

Did you know a lot of Spoors offed themselves before they turned fifty? Anyway. Dad is kind of kickass sometimes. I think he likes to shake people up. You warned me about that.

Basically, he has a sense of humor that is macabre (wow! ugly-looking word, right?) So he is a little scary, Mom. But not in any way you do not know about already. I think. Did he use to "sing" by the way? He sings to himself sometimes. When he thinks I am too far away to hear. Kind of like screaming, weird. He screams at this thing "bunny." Maybe his mind is a little unstable. There is no bunny here, or anything. Unless he hides it. He might, he has these locked up rooms.

But if you ask me it sounds like bunny is supposed to be a person. Who bothers him a lot. Who he likes to tease - you know, make fun of. Does that sound like mental illness? Maybe it's just a game he plays in his head. And he is not really, really, crazy. Or anything.

Oh well. I wanted to ask if he ever told you about the bunny. If there might be something to explain this. And I can't figure out why he keeps talking about people coming here to dump his money all over me. Sometimes I feel like I'm being strangled - ALLGHSSH!! Just kidding.

If he gives me all that money what is going to stop me from becoming a skinny boozing pill-popper just like him? With eyes that make crows drop dead out of the sky at 500 feet? I never saw him do that but I would not be surprised. Oh and the dogs - but forget it, you hate big dogs. His dogs are ok. Sort of. But if I get rich, then would I need cow-size dogs with red eyes? They have these eyes that make other animals do really strange things. Like deer - the eyes make deer totally helpless. Even though the dogs seem like they want to rip them apart, and gobble them!

Sorry, you should not worry about stuff like that. But one thing I do not get, is - Mom, when you were with Dad, did the dogs have names? Pip says "they never had names." Dad has these pets, that he spends a lot of time with, and - they do not have names? I asked Pip why. He said he does not know. Then tonight, we were working out, I asked him again. He said: "Maybe because they had so many." I asked, so many what? He said: "Names." I said, Wait a second. They do not have names - because they had so many? If they had so many, how come now, they do not have names at all?

He got nervous. I guess he does not like to talk about it. Weird.

To tell you the truth the dogs look like they could eat cars off the road if they ever got out. But I keep my mind off all this stuff with the workouts with Pip. He is huge, strong as a elephant. And he is bald, but he giggles - he thinks I am funny. At least we have something in common, staying in shape, and I am learning a lot because he used to be a Green Beret, did you know that? His little finger could crunch a skull, SPLISH! Except he had memory loss from the war he was in. Bad amnesia. I wonder what he and Dad do for, you know, kicks? (Uh-oh)

Pip takes pictures too, he has a darkroom in the basement next to the secret rooms. Dad keeps those rooms locked up. And he stays in them for hours. To tell you the truth I think he has problems. He looks at me funny. I think he hates being old and likes me being young, so when he looks at me he sees himself when he was young. So when Pip takes pictures of me - like, when we work out - Dad looks at them to think of the past (God his past gives me the creeps.) Maybe that is why Dad is so depressed, he hates thinking of death and being old. The reason he has to make me be here - parents like to see their kids as the future, right, it proves everything does not just stop when you die? But also I think he is jealous. Hey, are you jealous of me being young? No way! And I hate it when Pip takes pictures. But Pip is ok, he smiles a lot.

Seven days, come and gone, wham. I almost did not notice I am like a prisoner - Dad does not let me go out. Pip takes me to school and picks me up after. We go shopping and then come here. I have a million new clothes but nowhere to go. Except this big place. Behind the house are really spooky tall bushes that people must of worked on with clippers for years because they make a giant maze four times the length of a tennis court. Dad calls it the "towpeeary." A little kid could get totally lost in there - the bushes are five feet high and frozen solid. I tried crawling around inside and it freaked me since the maze just keeps going, sometimes with dead ends and you do not know where you are. Reminds me of being here in general.

Guess I'll print this up now, and homework too - I am doing great writing homework - and put them in envelopes so Dad will not look (I get the feeling he is nosy).

Time for gym again. Yeah: the gym. Just for me. And Pip. Strange!

Love, Torrance

P.S. HELP!!
  (just kidding)
    (but not really)

The Diary
of Sheila Massif: V

I'm bored with my nooks of beige. It's Friday night and I want to go out! To the world of fine dining, of discotheques, of intimate tête-à-têtes. To the world of deeply masculine single men and their tasteful apartments! I deserve to get a piece of that great big throbbing world. Why? Because I've concluded the first week of my daring experiment. I wrapped up with style—triumphing over hesitation and doubt, and lingering dread of the Chamber.

Another spectacular class. Today was #3. In which, due to my newfound confidence, we progressed from reading with the body, to: writing with the body! My students, I think, will benefit. I mean, this isn't just a selfish thing I'm doing. It's not just gathering data. Because they're learning amazing things about reading and writing. I'm amazed myself—about the mind/body connection, actually it's like therapy, really. I even told them, as much as I thought they can handle, about the psychology of visual thinking. About theories of creativity—like Einstein's claim that when he did his deepest thinking, he "thought with his body." He felt "kinesthetic pulses" all over his body, when he dreamed up relativity and stuff. Ok, my students aren't Einsteins, and neither am I, and I don't know much about these pulses he felt, but it's on the right track. Because I want the kids to feel their bodies when they write. To pay attention to what they physically *feel*. They'll be more in touch, which will help them write, of course, but even better I'll get insights—the psychophysical self-conceptions!

I'm convinced this will work out. My thesis will be groundbreaking. Anyway, the whole project is becoming a lot of fun. The only thing is Torrance. Who, unfortunately, is a big thing. Christ, what a scene that was. His condition—whatever it is—appears to be worsening. In fact, he really shook me up.

However, most of them were fine today. Even Rhonda was fascinated. The Einstein stuff really got her. Samantha too, they both took plenty of notes, it made me feel so good. The crackdown on Wednesday paid off, I guess. The assignments were ready. All eleven were piled on my desk when I came into the classroom.

I glanced at them when I got back here. Tomorrow I'll make profiles. Read them carefully, compare them to the self-descriptions, checklist traits, code for locus of control, try to dream up interpretive schema. Suddenly this seems like much too much work.

Then there's Torrance. That kid needs help. The boy is disturbed, he really is a Problem. He mixed up his homework with something else, a letter to his mother. It shocked me. There were these sentences about her "not having to worry"; it isn't homework, it's actually a letter to *his mother*. Which I don't especially want to read. I'm concerned he might have done it on purpose, and I am not his mother. But this isn't all. There's more.

Today. After class. He came up to me again right after the bell rang. This time, he didn't give me a picture of a dog; no, this time he said we have to talk. I said, Fine. Thinking he'd want to get hormonal confusion off his chest, or something, after the display of Wednesday. So I waved him to a chair, ejected the other lingerers —that took a minute—and closed the door.

Then he said, very seriously, that he'd like to invite me and the students to his house for a swim. Day after tomorrow. Sunday.

I nearly laughed. A swim. I shot a look at his pants. They were another pair of antique trousers, dark gray, tight at the waist, pleated and baggy there on down, narrowing to crisp cuffs above expensive Italian-looking shoes. The boy has nice clothes. I caught myself thinking he probably looks even better in a swimsuit—the kid is well-built. Albeit slimly. But these are not issues teachers should dwell on. I was thinking up a way to decline when he said, "I'm desperate."

"That's terrible," I said. "Why?"

"And it's not sex even though it probably seemed like that when —uh—on the floor, last class, you probably saw . . ."

"Yes," I said carefully. "Don't worry, Torrance. These things happen. If it's not a big deal for you—well, I tell you what. It isn't for me."

"Yeah," he said vaguely. As if he hadn't heard me. "It's—I'm unbelievably lonely."

"You are? Torrance, everybody feels lonely from time to time. That's perfectly normal." He was staring at me as if I was speaking Latvian. So I changed the subject. "Why don't you tell me about the dog? You said you wanted to talk about that, didn't you?"

"Sheila," he said, "I'm so scared." Suddenly, he looked it. What, I wondered, is going on?

"Huh," I said. "I think you better talk."

"Thanks," he said. He was trembling.

In the hall, beyond the closed door, I heard kids gathering for the room's next class. This was going to have to be quick.

"My dad," Torrance whispered, "is crazy." He gestured at the pile of homework on the desk. "I wrote you a note about it."

"Ok," I said. Not then knowing the "note" is a letter to his mother. Which I still haven't read. God, do I ever hope it wasn't on purpose.

"He has these dogs," Torrance continued. "The picture is of just one of them. He has twelve."

"That's a lot of dogs," I said.

"They have red eyes!" he exclaimed. "Eyes that hypnotize deer! You should have seen the beautiful deer—they used their eyes to freak it out, and then they *ate it*!"

"Really?" I said. "How awful."

"And Sheila—this is weird—I think they read my father's mind."

"No kidding," I said.

"See . . ." Torrance was having trouble talking. I was having trouble thinking. Because he then said, "I'm scared, see, there might really be some kind of curse. Like, on my family . . ." He trailed off, staring at the floor.

"Don't stop now," I said, glancing at my watch.

"Because my dad—he screams. He screams at this bunny, and, and . . ."

"Does the bunny annoy him?" I asked gravely.

"I think so," Torrance replied, mind elsewhere. "Yeah, the bunny bothers him, I think. But see—there is no bunny . . ."

"That's a shame," I said. "No bunny. Maybe the dogs ate it, too?"

"This is hard to explain!" he blurted. "You think I'm crazy!"

I smiled at him. "No I don't. I'm just having trouble understanding you. That's all. Look, Torrance. Maybe you should go to the guidance department—for some counseling."

He shuddered.

"Maybe it's not such a bad idea," I insisted. "I think I'm out of my depth, kid. Don't get me wrong. I'd like to help."

He didn't look as if he believed me. In fact, he looked as if he'd just decided the conversation was hopeless. "You're all dressed up today," he said sulkily. "How come?"

What could I say to this loony kid? I thought about it. And ended up saying, "I tend to get dressed up when I feel lonely and scared." His eyes narrowed. "Teaching," I confided, "intimidates me. So today I figured I'd put everybody on the defensive by looking like the self-confident vamp I'm not." I was wearing the crimson dress that matches the heels and, yes, the jangly bracelets. "But look at you," I went on, waving an arm to clatter home the point, "you're decked-out too. Maybe for the same reason, huh?"

"*No,*" he said. "I just don't have anything else to do."

"Listen. I don't know what's going on with you. It sounds like trouble. But whatever it is, we can't go on talking here, there's another class out in the hall waiting to come in . . ."

He grabbed my knee and yelled, "I am not making it up!"

I thought about telling him to take his hands off my knee. But there was a pleading in his eyes, and I didn't; though I should have. What I did was pat him on the shoulder. Reassuringly, I thought. Big mistake. He jumped up and grabbed my shoulders, hard.

"Wait a second," I gasped, aware of all the people behind the door. Luckily, there isn't a window in that door.

"I need to talk to somebody so bad," he hissed. I thought I saw an erection. Maybe I didn't. Maybe in the panic of the situation I imagined it. Whatever, I was suddenly angry.

Someone knocked on the door. "Let go of me," I said.

He went limp. I, too, was limp. He sat on the floor, then fell on his back. "Sorry," he mumbled. "Really, I am sorry . . ."

"Yeah," I said. It was hideous—he was lying on the floor, *shaking*. This had to be fixed. Fast. I leaned over him and snapped, "Let me tell you something. At your age, things can be rough. I know, I went through it myself." He looked up, and the look was doubtful. "But I'm here to tell you, things work out."

He looked more doubtful. "Maybe," he mumbled, "they won't."

"Listen to me—you're finding out all kinds of things about yourself, about your body, about sex, right? And it's a real discovery, so it can be confusing, right? I mean, for me, at your age, I felt I had a responsibility to clear everything up right away. To invent myself immediately! Which, believe me, turned out to be pretty dumb. Torrance, you have your whole life before you. My advice is this: take it slow."

"You don't have any idea what you're talking about," he said, sitting up and rubbing his face. He seemed badly embarrassed.

"I see," I said. "Look, you have a crush on me, right? You have an eveready flashlight in your pocket and that's ok. But romance is out, Torrance. And swimming is out, flashlights and water don't mix, kid, not when I'm a teacher and you are my student."

His face went cold. The coldness hid tense and feverish calculations. He said, "I need someone I can trust." Then he said, "I know you have your own stuff to take care of, you put on a big act. But guess what? I also got trouble. And I betcha mine's a bitchload *worse.*"

He stood, and walked to the door. "Wait," I said.

"Some people," he sneered, "see a dick getting hard and they think it's helpless love. But you know, sometimes a dick getting hard is just a dick getting hard!" He opened the door, shoved into the crowd, and slammed the door behind him.

I thought: Freud once said the same thing about cigars.

The door banged open and a soft dense thing flew at me and landed on my desk. It was a large rose, in bad shape, molting. An odd color—light red-brown. He was scowling at me. All around him, kids were staring. At this point I was utterly scandalized. I said, "A token of your esteem?"

"No," he yelled, "it's *evidence,*" and he slammed the door.

In the hall, there was commotion.

I tossed the rose in my purse, put on my coat, gathered the homework, marched to the door, opened it, and said, briskly, "Excuse me!" The crowd parted. A large woman I'd never seen before was inspecting me. A colleague, I assumed, whose class was delayed. Wondering how much she had heard, I was thankful the coat covered my dress and bracelets; the outfit now seemed total Jezebel. I nodded, briskly, at my colleague.

"Trouble?" she asked.

"Disposed of!" I heard myself proclaiming in a loud, clear voice.

"Oh, good," she clucked sympathetically.

"Nothing to worry about," I said. And added, "Well, you know, these things happen."

"Yes," she agreed with gusto, "they *do*." She winked at me, and I loved her. "All right everybody," she then bellowed, "what do you think this is, get in there!" There was sudden, massive shuffling. I winked at my colleague and marched briskly down the hall.

In the car, I sat for a while, thinking. That poor kid. What on earth is going on? Whatever it is, he's a troubled young man. I debated informing the guidance department. But with what spin? Was his lunge at me sexual—or some other act of desperation?

Unsure if I had let him down, I ripped open his homework envelope. And saw, at the top of the page, "Dear Mom." Of all things, a letter to his mother! Which was supposed to be a note about his father—who has twelve red-eyed dogs, and, if I heard right, screams at bunnies.

Yow! You, I told myself, are getting in too far. I was so alarmed I didn't even read his letter. I crammed it back in the envelope. Now it's stacked with real homework in the nook.

———

So. That's the Torrance Problem. Doubt nags me. Am I letting him down? What if he's a potential teen suicide and I'm ignoring the danger signs? Maybe a rose is a danger sign. I don't want to, but I will read his letter. And try to not become too annoyed with the possibility he thinks I'm his mother.

Which makes me wonder—if there was a real mix-up, where did the homework go? And the note to me? To his mother?

Meantime, it's Friday night. The night which leads to the throbbing world of sensual single men who naturally hanker for the likes of me. I'm not up for it. I'm worried about a beautiful boy who probably is out of his mind. All right, all right. I'll read it.

———

Holy shit. Holy shit, dear Diary. "Pip." A photographer: *Pip.* That guy takes pictures of Torrance!

Jesus Christ!
Oh my God. There's the phone.
It's Duane. I gotta go.

The Secret Journal
of Torrance Spoor's
Secret War: I

Friday Night

Fuck Sheela!

Get serious time. I am freaking.

This is my Secret Journal. I know Dad can't get it, I read the manual seven times and this is under "Lock Control" for sure. Die, Pervert!

Yeah, do it, see if I care and why should I, I'll be rich, unless you are lying you asshole CREEP. I am really, really, really - MAD.

This is WAR. It started this morning, at eight-fifteen to be exact, I was coming back from the pool. No! The WAR started before I even got here to Baron FUCKFACE'S HELLHOLE. But I did not know it. But now: I DO.

Wait till Mom finds out. She will rip his head off. And karate-smush Pip, SMUSH!!! Too bad, Pip. Cause you are in it, big time.

This happened: after swimming I took a different way than usual. I went by the secret room across from the darkroom. Think you got secrets, Dad? Now I do.

Pip was in the darkroom. He goes there after workouts to make pictures of me. Pictures - crazy! Scary. I am so scared.

He did not see me cause he was printing, the black door was shut. And I saw that across the hall, another door was open. The door to one of the secret rooms, one of the most secret, I never saw that door open before. But I know they use it - the lock and the door are new, anyway I can tell from the floor. Lots of stuff, like dirt, goes in and out of there.

A bright pink light was shining from it. So, I looked.

Unbelievable. A big room full of flowers. *Roses.*

Rows and rows of roses, all the same color, and I looked up the word "sepia" back in California, sepia. Sick. Millions of sick sepia roses growing in rows of pots on long tables under bright pink hitek lights. A robot machine was watering and spraying them, it moves on a rail that drops from the ceiling. Up one row, down the next, automatic.

That was when I heard it: above my head.

Clicks. Little funny clicks. They were familiar, cause I been hearing them since I got here - but they are really, really soft. So I been hearing these clicks underneath the regular sounds, but didn't know it, until I heard these louder clicks today, and looked up, and saw it:

The camera. Clicking.

It was clicking because it was moving. And it was moving because it was watching the robot sprayer moving. And its clicks were loud, I realized, really quickly, staring at this camera, because it is not *hidden.*

And the reason it's not, is because it's in a locked up room.

That I'm not supposed to see.

I thought: if I go into that room, the camera will see me. Which means Dad might see me. If the camera has an alarm that says something besides the robot is moving.

But the important thing - the clicks. It was really clear, like a religious bomb, like a "apparition" according to Sheela, in a church when God talks to the Sinner and the Sinner understands like in a movie, and there is music, really sacred, and I was not a Sinner or anything but I understood:

This house is full of hidden cameras.

Everywhere. Softly, softly, softly clicking while the things they are watching are moving. And the thing they are watching is *me.*

So I told myself: Get out of here. FAST.

But first I picked up a dead rose on the floor that I did not have to reach too far to get. Then I ran away, the rose in my towel and I remembered: I dripped. And what could I do about that?

I thought: Pip is printing, it will be dried up by the time he comes out. I hope. I got back to the regular way I take to my room and tried to be really normal. And I listened.

They were there. Clicks. I heard the clicks. Behind mirrors. Behind screens. In decoration things and woodwork and bricks: clicks. So soft I thought: you are making this up! And I was careful not to look. If he was watching he would see me *looking into cameras*.

The worst ones are in my room. No, the worst ones are in my *bathroom*. And the dressingroom. All those new clothes and me checking out how slick I look: click-click-SICK.

I almost can't hear them. Almost. They are like muskitos hickupping. Tiny. But they are there. I know, they happen when I move. If I lie still, no clicks. Cause the camera is already on me. Watching.

This means I am my own father's PORNAGRAPHY STAR.

Some of the things he must of SEEN ME DO.

I'm so mad I want to cry. I better not, he is watching - but I can make something up. If he asks. A sad story I'm writing. Makes me cry, Dad. A really sad story. MOTHERFUCKER! But he won't ask. Cause he doesn't want me to know he is watching.

He is, all right. I feel it now. But no way he has a camera on the screen, I checked it through. So he will not get this: THE SECRET JOURNAL OF MY SECRET WAR.

"Revenge Is A Dish That Is Best When You Serve It Cold." Dorky Walter Shade says that saying. Does anybody know I might be in danger here? Mom! How can this happen? But if she knew - she would die. Heartattack: DEAD.

———

Dad says I'll understand the crazy stuff in that letter he sent me. Gundulf and Baybars and what they did on the bed, the flowers and the war hound - he said it was watching. What was it watching? Now I find the cameras. What does that mean? It means Dad is watching. I feel like there are secret eyes all over the house!

His shit is turning out real. First, the dogs. If somebody asked what a war hound looks like, it's them, those things are war hounds from hell and that is no joke. And now, the roses. They are sepia. Like blood that has dried - that's what made his letter dive back into history, all the suicide shit and the killing. So I have to wonder what is happening.

I will find out. Cause this is WAR. I talked to Sheela hoping I could get her to join. But she has problems. Anyway, why would she believe me?

UNBELIEVABLE. If Dad wants to kill himself, why spend the time on cameras? If he's not sticking around, why? Who will watch?

Maybe he isn't the one who he plans will die.

It could be me. And he's making tapes so I will not be totally gone. Too crazy. I'm glad I found that gun. I might need it? What the fuck. I have bad dreams. I dream he is eating me. Like, the worst idea I ever heard, but I dream it. So is Dad going to eat me? I'm scared. And it's kind of dumb, but what bothers me the most is:

He must of seen I am gay.

The Chronicles
of Malcolm Spoor: IV

Friday Night

I have installed a portrait gallery here in my spyroom. Of you, my dear Grislies. Yes, of you.

Not everyone is displayed. To nail you all to these walls, I would be obliged to have crates flown from England, and France. Even then, a number would be missing, no? Oh yes. Lost, lost forever, some of you are; in terms of portraiture, at least. Which is just as well.

The whole lot nailed up, let's agree, could be disquieting.

In any case, there isn't room. This chamber cannot accomodate the acreage of oil, the tonnage of gilt, stored in those dusty crates. So I have settled for something rather less formal, Grislies.

I hope you won't find my method offensive. It is, I fear, a touch iconoclastic. You see, I have ripped you from books. And I have torn you from magazines, bound sets mostly, oh they were moldy. In short, I have done something sublime on your behalf. I have vandalized the library.

Thus do I honor you. A kind of shrine, this is, to my wretched and ghastly Grislies. It reminds me, I must say, of Torrance's room - of the way he has Teen Idols tacked up, helter-skelter, to keep him company. Any comments? No? Are you not, in some sense, idols - here to keep me company?

To be sure, the comparison quickly breaks down. Nonetheless, I have made an effort to include you. To encourage you to make your presence felt. To speak to me, that is - yes, to *speak to me*!

Will it never end? This silence. Look at poor Bunny - staring, inert, from his mug shot.

Yes, Bunny. Your mug shot. On the front page of a newspaper, a yellowed scandal sheet, in fact. You do remember, don't you, your scandal? That sensation of yours? Your arrest, Bunny - your notorious trial?

How could you possibly forget?

I am glad, by the way, to have you, too, nailed to the wall. Despite your jaundiced pallor. Because even if you continue to refuse to speak, I can remind myself that you are, at least, listening. And I know you are - do not pretend you are not!

I want you to listen carefully, please. All of you, please listen, I must confide something. Torrance smells strange. Very strange.

Just look at the monitors. He is so terribly upset!

It has to do with hearing me howl, evidently. At you, Bunny. Oh yes, at you; he told Sheila this. So you see, you see how you torment me.

However, I fear the cause may be something else as well. What? What could it be? Love? Lust? Sheila, perhaps?

A splendid creature, Sheila. Pip must photograph the woman, from a distance, with a powerful zoom lens. I am intrigued. She seems to have rejected Torrance. What can such a person be like, one who rejects Torrance?

He was indiscreet, again. Possibly it was the same indiscretion as Wednesday. I should have been listening, Wednesday. But I couldn't have; the classroom wasn't then bugged. Today, however, it was bugged. And I, along with the other students, learned about the role "kinesthetic images" play in the process of writing.

How does she invent this drivel? Writers feel images in their bodies? She claims Einstein did his deepest thinking via "kinesthetic pulses" he felt in his body. Rubbish. He'd never have come up with relativity if he'd relied on that scrawny body. No, Einstein obviously thought with his hair. Kinesthetic pulses in the hair. That is why his hair stood on end, from too much thinking, the electric pulses, I am annoyed I cannot raise my hand and participate in class. We are learning so much about the importance of feeling one's body as one writes. Oh yes, *feeling* it, Grislies.

A shame you can't feel your bodies, eh? You don't have bodies, do you? Think of what happened to your poor abused bodies. The things you did - so terribly self-destructive!

Where was I? Torrance's chat with Sheila. A private chat. A touchy little talk. No one was there except the boy, she, and, electronically, me. Sheila seems convinced Torrance desires her. Perhaps he does. But if he does, I am afraid it is because he is desperate to get his mind off boys.

So desperate. Just look at those angry tears!

A pity I cannot read his mind. But then, I have other plans for his mind. The real pity is that I cannot read his computer. But I have plans for his computer, too. Careful plans. Unlike Pip, I am tremendously careful. At least, I am trying. But if Torrance has heard me howl - why haven't I known of this blatant eavesdropping? Too much drinking, no doubt. And the black moods that overcome me. How can I watch the boy every minute? I simply cannot. The eyestrain, the fatigue, make it impossible; the drinking, too, which is entirely your fault, of course. What was I thinking?

Torrance smells strange. And it cannot simply be due to hearing me howl. Nor due to thinking I am insane, that he has known for weeks. No, it is something new. And the plants are upset, I would even say withdrawn - this is all very sudden, and recent.

Therefore I must analyze. I must deduce, from facts I know to be true. And I must join these facts in a way that will explain his reasons for having words with Sheila; because if I cannot explain those reasons, I will be worried, and there is nothing I hate more than *worry*.

The facts: Torrance is bisexual. At least bisexual. This I know from the La Jolla agents. And more recently, from studying him.

Torrance furthermore has a mother who is terrified he is homosexual. This I know from the agents, from my own experience with Floria, and hers with me; I nearly destroyed that woman. She simply could not cope. But I couldn't go on either, feigning lust, when she was too petite. Too scrawny, she doesn't weigh enough - no thighs, nothing. So it was convenient she began to think I like men. Which she thought anyway, because of Pip, the naïve fool. She couldn't understand Pip at all. Then again - who could?

But from my point of view, the marriage was a success. It pro-

duced Torrance. That was all I wanted. In this day and age, however, my wants, and my needs, create repercussions; one of which
is Floria's belief I am wicked, a terrible role model, an influence
Torrance must elude at all costs, a man whose motivations are in-
explicably but certainly dire. A fact!

Surmise: Torrance has compelling reasons to maintain a façade
of heterosexuality. Floria has brainwashed him for years: "You do
not want to be like your father." That's almost funny.

In any case: Fact: Torrance has intensely homosexual fantasies.

I know this is fact. I watch him, when he is alone, in his room.
Does he suspect? He couldn't. Autoerotically he isn't inhibited, he
is utterly unstinting, he never would do what he does if he thought I
were watching. The poor boy. No other outlet; workouts with Pip,
but that doesn't count when one lives head-to-toe in a body so exquisitely built for fun. And why would he lock the doors? Why keep
his disgusting pornography collection in a triple-locked suitcase? He
is clever with machines. He would find the cameras, and destroy
them, if he had any inkling.

So he doesn't suspect. That is a fact.

Surmise: Torrance has heterosexual fantasies. This I surmise
from the fact that a portion of his porno collection consists of girlie
magazines. I am so pleased. Of course, the young do experiment. He
may turn to girls, even big ones, perhaps. Wishful thinking, Grislies?
Is it even possible? Or is that body of his irrevocably - fixated? Lust,
I have heard, is now considered chemical, a question of enzymes, or
some such thing, that defy the mind. Disturbing, no? Considering
what he had going with that La Jolla youth, Ricky - oh, never mind.
It upsets me.

But, Fact: Wednesday, Sheila beheld Torrance in a state of viru-
lent maleness. This they discussed today. The flashlight, sometimes
a dick getting hard is just a dick getting hard; that happens to be a
fact. His needs no reason at all. It simply hardens. While he is
cleaning his room, or watching TV; when he puts on socks. What
reason could there be for that?

Surmise: The flashlight resulted from too much thinking with his
body.

Surmise: Torrance is so lustful his body doesn't think, it acts.

Surmise: Torrance is confused. He needs someone with whom he
can talk.

Fact: That person is not me.

Of course it cannot be me. I am his father. Fathers do not discuss sex with sons. Fathers like me do not, because mothers like Floria will do anything to prevent it. It is equally true mothers like Floria do not discuss sex with sons like Torrance, the sons will do anything to prevent it.

Surmise: This leaves Sheila. Sheila is the perfect person with whom Torrance might think he could talk. He might not want to tell her about the entire scope of his attractions. Then again, he might. Sheila has the distinction of being neither Floria nor me; but she is an adult, and has flair, she is knowing in the ways of the world. Conceivably she could be willing to introduce Torrance to some of those worldly ways. Or so Torrance might have thought. She is, after all, an expert on the mental ways of the body.

Fact: Sheila is nervous about Torrance's body. She tiptoed carefully today, uttering clichés. You need not "invent yourself," not "immediately," "plenty of time to invent," and so on. Well, yes. But of course. Quite true; another fact, in fact. An interesting fact. Rather too interesting, at the moment, eh, Grislies?

Because that is what you are, no? Inventions? Botched inventions? And am I not, myself, precisely that disaster? Sad, so sad. But hope does spring eternal, no? Oh yes. Because things will be different, this time - oh yes, we will *invent,* this time. Wait, and see.

Surmise: Sheila may have wanted to assault the boy in class. But appearances concern her. After the McQuisling scare, brought on by Samantha.

Surmise: Torrance stormed out of the classroom thinking Sheila had turned a cold shoulder. That she couldn't care less.

Final Surmise: This is why, now keyboarding, *he cries.*

That explains everything. Why he told Sheila he is "so scared"; why he told her he needs someone he "can trust." The boy is a madhouse, and the one person in whom he thought he could confide sends him packing!

Marvelous. I can stop worrying, Grislies. I can stop worrying he knows about us. Sheila refuses to help; this torment on the monitor is due to her scorn. That's it, her scorn.

So he doesn't know.

He cannot know about us. Of course not. But he smells as though he knows. But how could he? It is much too early for him to understand!

The very idea is absurd. So shut up! Don't start!

Why, then, do I still feel worry? What was the "evidence" he showed her? The "token of esteem" about which she inquired so unenthusiastically?

Above all, why are the plants so upset? What is it?

———

Yes. I'm worried. And the Grislies aren't with me, they haven't come. I was afraid of that; well of course, I've ignored them for years.

But I acquired this property, didn't I? I gave them the hunt, I gave them deer. Yet they did not come. Then I went further, the dogs devoured trespassers, I thought human blood would rouse them. But even that produced nothing, they *did not come* - and village idiots stand vigil in the night, attracting things. That feverish little man who tasted the dog.

Now I ransack the library, rip apart books, nail up pathetic pictures, and still the Grislies do not come! Why? Oh, I am *worried*. I cannot think. I tell them to shut up. But I haven't heard even a peep.

Not the faintest peep out of any of them. They cannot do this. It is insane, what they are doing. It's Bunny's fault, not mine, but they are making me pay - I need something extremely strong.

———

That's better. I was just thinking, perhaps what I feel is a twinge -

Again? No. No, no, I groan. No, never again!

But this absurd Age of Consciousness, has touched even me. Everyone has rights. No one is on earth simply to be used. That is the modern fancy. It's the modern hypocrisy. Use or be used remains the Golden Rule!

But now we try to conceal it. And I go with the flow. I conceal, ever more elaborately, I am thoroughly modern. And so I keep Torrance under a microscope. I learn all his ways, his joys, his passions and habits, and, at the moment, his raging pain - his lovely "inventions," as Sheila, oddly apt, would say. And if there is any twinge——

Speak to me! Please, the plants are upset. They are losing confidence, you Fools, can't you see I need help? Can't you see I'm not well? Badly invented, I suppose, is that it - Bunny, have you nothing to say? About what you did to me?

I am so tired. So angry.

Duane Allbright's
Audiocassette Notes: I

Friday Night

A Baron. The Director and Cunif would laugh themselves sick. For about twelve seconds. For as long as it would take to see the reality, which wouldn't be long. Then they'd order up men with guns. Claus Schmidtt in the lead, wearing his purple hat.

I'm packing bags as I tape this. It's time to break loose. Time to say bye to those people.

Torrance wrote a letter to his mother. But his mother didn't get it, Sheila did. That's not all she got. Torrance gave her a rose, too.

It clobbered me. The rose stank of the smell. Call it the "Odor"—that sweet psi Odor poured from my phone.

This was an hour ago. Sheila hit me, so I called her—I knew something had happened. It was the letter. It had upset her. She read it to me twice and I sat here amazed, that letter is full of outrageous stuff. For example, Torrance's father, the Baron, owns dogs. Twelve of them. The kid says they have red eyes and are scary as hell. I believe that. Red eyes looked me over last night, through the Baron's fence. They scared me good.

Torrance wrote about other fun details. But I couldn't concentrate on them, because while Sheila was reading the Odor hit, and started to heat. That really surprised me. I had no idea where it was coming from.

Then she mentioned the rose. I asked her to hold it. When she did, my phone wasn't a phone. It was a burning perfume factory.

I thought I'd overload. I didn't, and that's the strangest. I do not know how to say this. The Odor felt—curious. It felt curious about *me*. It seemed to be—probing me?

What I'm saying is, I think the Odor is *sentient*.

———

Comes from a rose. Where did Torrance find this rose? Sheila doesn't know. All she knows is, the kid said it's "evidence." Well it is.

There's more. Later, at my suggestion, she called him, and talked to his father instead.

She was worrying Torrance might be suicidal. That I doubt, but I said call him, offer support. A gamble. I wanted to see what would happen. What happened was, I got hit by a ton of bricks. I had an extreme, almost a religious, need to call her. When I did, it came through so powerful. She relayed the father. And I felt it, he's it. He's the center of the whole thing. He's some kind of monster Psi. He's *huge.*

This bears on Sheila's crush theory. A crush Torrance may have, but there's a more interesting explanation for his attraction to her, if that's what it is. Due to his father, I assume, the boy is supercharged with psi. And like anything supercharged, he's a potential. He's a flow waiting to happen. It's like he's giving off sparks. Then Sheila, excellent relayer, walks smack into him. She gets a job, there he is—and the flow starts to move.

That's what hit me on Monday. It's what got me into this, when she relayed something strange over the phone. I think it's also why Pip took pictures of her apartment. The Baron must have sensed Sheila's a relayer. He wanted to check her out, maybe shield the flow, contain anything she was getting from Torrance. If I were him, that's the first thing I'd do.

But it prompts a thousand urgent questions. One question, however, looms large. Why is it so sloppy?

For example, why did Pip leave batteries on Sheila's floor? Leaving them there was a mistake. It's evidence. Then there's the rose, that's ultrahot evidence. Whatever the Baron has going with Torrance, with Pip and the dogs, and especially with the Odor—he isn't shielding it well. In fact, his shield's leaking like crazy. Why?

It just doesn't make sense. If there's anything that doesn't leak—or shouldn't, if it wants to survive—it's a source of monster psi. I conclude that for the Baron, something unusual is happening.

Then there are the unstable states of mind Torrance describes. They suggest flux. Maybe major flux.

I think I've bumped into a very rare moment.

Duane calm down. You are packing bags and getting out. In the morning, I wish it were now, but I have things to take care of. For one thing, my Lab computer. References to Sheila, the reports I wrote getting into this, they have to disappear. Also I should research this guy. Try to find him, anything remotely like him, in the Lab's database, I have to do that before saying bye. Time to stop this. I have to get out clean, as clean as I can. I have so much to do.

The Diary
of Sheila Massif: VI

Hang Tough, Stay Cool, Admit *Nothing*.

That's what I'll do. I have to get to the bottom of this.

Duane's being very heepy-creepy about the whole business. He's on his way here now. "Go to sleep," he said, "I'll be there by ten." That was last night on the phone.

Sleep? I tossed and turned all night. Yesterday, Torrance had a breakdown after class. I tried to get a grip on what he was saying, but couldn't. Now I've read his letter to his mother five times and still don't have a grip, but obviously something's going on. Ok, what is this?

Who knows? I don't. Torrance doesn't. Duane doesn't either, but he's making it all seem so much worse. The way he had to hear everything last night. The rose, the letter, the crazy father—but especially the rose. We're in the middle of this crisis, and Duane plays psychic with a dead *rose*.

Something Is Going On:

Wednesday: A big bald guy named Pip comes to the door. A "neighbor." He smiled a lot and left.

Thursday: Duane's in the sleeping nook looking at batteries, saying somebody took pictures of this place; and "Torrance is connected."

Yesterday: Torrance's letter to his mother is in the homework envelope and, among other things, I learn a "Pip" works for his father, and takes pictures, and develops them, and is big, and bald, and *smiles a lot.*

Then Duane calls, just as I'm starting to get nervous. The obvious was hitting. Pip could have read you, Diary. And if he did, he found out about the thesis, about me being a teacher, the Chamber— everything!

Meantime Torrance gives me a dog portrait that makes Duane look ill, and his letter tells me his father, supposedly a baron, really does own a dozen red-eyed dogs—that are barely restrained from eating cars off roads!

So I'm interested. What are these men doing, if Pip took pictures? What on earth are they doing to Torrance?

I might find out. Last night, I called Torrance's house. Duane suggested it. He said to relax and "Do it. Call the boy and tell him you feel bad about the talk after class. Say you're willing to talk more if he wants. Be there for Torrance, calmly and confidently."

And why should I commit this dangerous act?

"Sheila," he said, "he's in trouble."

"How do you know that, Duane?" I was staring at the falling-apart thing he was making me hold in my hand. "Because of the rose?"

He didn't say a word. And I could almost feel him *feeling it.* Then finally he said, "Yeah. The kid's on to something."

Weirdly enough, I think he might be right. What kind of a baron would own twelve spooky dogs, and rail against a nonexistent bunny?

The answer is, a strange baron. When I called he answered the phone:

"Hello?"

"Is Torrance Spoor there?" I said it very calmly.

"Why yes. He is."

"This is Sheila Massif. I teach at Torrance's school. He's one of my students and I would like to discuss homework with that young man."

"How marvelous," this creep said, "that you take such an interest, Miss Massif. Or is it Mrs. Massif?" His voice scared the shit out of me: courteous, Old World, slurry—he sounded drunk—but deadly. Yow!

"Ms. Massif," I said, "will do."

"I am Malcolm Spoor, Torrance's father. Torrance has told me so much about you. Your class excites him."

Tell me about it. "That's nice. Very nice."

"You must be an exciting teacher, Ms. Massif."

"Well, thank you. May I speak with Torrance, please?"

"That won't be necessary."

"Excuse me?" I said.

"I beg your pardon," he said. "What I meant to say is this, that it won't be necessary for you to speak with Torrance tonight, Ms. Massif, if you would be so gracious as to accept my invitation to dinner—tomorrow night—and I do hope you will come. Oh you must, we dine rather well here. I would have the opportunity to meet you, and learn more about you and your exciting class, and of course we all could discuss Torrance's homework! That would be grand, don't you think? Please say yes. Oh, do."

By the time he finished I was sweating. That *voice.* I wanted to ask, Will Pip be there too? I didn't say that. I didn't know what to say. This man with eyes that make crows drop dead out of the sky, probably right onto my dinner plate, wanted me to come "dine."

"Ms. Massif? Are you there?"

"Yes," I said. "I'm checking my engagement diary" (SHIT!) "and it appears, Mr. Spoor, well . . ."

"Nonsense!" he screamed, no it wasn't really a scream. More like a shout. A deadly shout. "Ms. Massif, nothing could engage you more entertainingly than dinner at my house, I promise you that. If you have other engagements in your engagement diary, you must immediately cross them out and write in 'Dinner chez Spoor,' and make this notation: 'Pip will be by at seven-thirty with the car.' Oh, what fun. You won't regret it . . ."

"Who," I said very calmly, "is Pip?"

"Why, Ms. Massif," the man said, "you have met him."

"I have?" I said very calmly.

"Of course! He came by your house, just a few days ago . . ."

"Uh . . ." I said, "yes! A man did come by, a 'Pip.' But he said he's a neighbor, Mr. Spoor. Are you and Pip and Torrance my neighbors? I'm a little confused. I mean, I can walk right over if you . . ."

"Oh, he was lying, Ms. Massif. Pip lies through his teeth. I've tried so hard to get him to stop but he *won't.*"

"No kidding," I said.

"Devotion," the man was saying, "does odd things to people. And Pip is so very devoted."

"Perhaps you could explain, Mr. Spoor."

"Call me Malcolm. Would you?"

"Sure. Malcolm. Call me Sheila, that's very nice . . ."

"Splendid! Now, about Pip and his awful lies, and the devotion that makes him lie so much, I will explain that tomorrow night—it's quite simple, Pip is Torrance's bodyguard, you see, and he does go overboard. I owe you an apology for that. But surely my apology is best delivered over aperitifs, before dinner—Pip is an extremely talented chef, you know."

The room was spinning. Beigely.

"Well," I said, "I guess I really can't refuse, Mr. Spoor . . ."

"Of course you cannot. I am enthralled. Dear old 'Mr. Overboard' —ha, ha!—he's harmless!—will be by at seven-thirty to pick you up."

"Thank you," I said.

"Good-bye, Sheila," he said, and hung up.

I stared at the phone, wondering if I should call Duane to tell him about this stunning new development: "Dinner chez Spoor." The phone is beige, too. I expected it to ring—can't Duane feel the stunning new development? The phone didn't ring. I ran out over the ramp to the mall to buy cigarettes. While buying them I had a vision of Pip breaking into the apartment. So I ran back over the ramp, feet thudding, ramp clanging, and barged in murderously, and no one was here, but: the *phone rang.*

I jumped out of my skin.

It was Duane again. Of course. I told him about the new development. "Pip lies through his teeth," "Dinner chez Spoor," etc.

"All the more reason for me to come up tomorrow," Duane said.

"Are you thinking of going to dinner?" I asked. "That's not a bad idea. In fact, it's a good . . ."

"No," he said sleepily. "But I'll be around. We'll talk when you get back. Sheila, go to bed."

We said good-bye and I was alone with Diary and scenarios of ruin. What if Pip did read the Diary—or even took pictures of it? Is Torrance's father outraged by my plans to analyze gender boundaries? Will he make a stink at school? But he seems too crazy to care about stuff like that. He's threatening to kill himself, for crying out loud!

I didn't really sleep. I tried, but couldn't. But Duane's coming. He'll be here in a few minutes. And he'll be mad I didn't sleep. No, he never gets mad. He's too blasé. Blasé Duane.

Thank God for blasé Duane. I'm so tired! But I'm better now. I need you, Diary. You make me feel better than the Chamber. You're much nicer than the Chamber, you poor thing. Snoops flashing all over you.

Jesus. It's snowing.

The Secret Journal
of Torrance Spoor's
Secret War: II

Saturday Morning

I heard it last night on TV: snow. When I woke up early they were saying: big one. Then Pip tells me Sheela is coming over to eat. Tonight. Why? Pip does not know. Dad wants to meet her or something. Ok. I think about it. And I get an idea. Now the TV is saying: blizzard. Great. God is on my side.

It is 9:17 Saturday morning, snowing hard. And I have a Plan.

I told Pip I'm in charge of dinner. He said Dad said it's all right. Thank you, Dad.

Soon we go shopping. I wanted to go by myself but Pip won't let me. He says Dad won't let me. I might get abducted. Sure! Ok. No problem, Dad. Are you watching? Guess what? I'm right here and nobody is abducting me. Except you and your PERVERT CAMERAS.

Going to get him.

Normal food tonight. Roast beef, mashed potatoes, gravy. I asked Pip to ask Dad if Sam can come. Dad said no. Anything you want, Dad. No Sam tonight. Too bad.

Seems Pip is going to pick up Sheela at half-past seven. If the snow is heavy it might take time. So it's good I'm cooking, Pip said. He looks at me strange. Guess I look strange too. I am trying not to. He said, "Are you homesick, Torrance?"

And I said: "Yeah." Fuck off, SHITHEAD. "But cooking will make it better," I said. "Normal food, you know. Make me feel right at home."

Pip, my "friend." Thanks for all the concern. DROP DEAD.

I'll do it when he's getting Sheela. It will work. Dorky Walter Shade taught me. He didn't know he did, but he did. The only tricky part is Pip, later. I have another idea for that, though.

When we get back from shopping I do the outside stuff. I'll tell Pip I want to play in the snow. But without the dogs. No dogs, Pip, ok? I want to be really peaceful by myself in the snow. In the blizzard! I'm from California, remember? Snow is really cosmic for people from there. We communicate in private with blizzards, you did not know that?

God I am even smiling. Smiling like a terrorist with poison gas.

Pip will say yes. I am homesick. Torrance needs to be peaceful by himself in the snow. He is from California and this is really meaningful. Maybe the snow will make him think this place is delightful or something.

The dogs have to stay in the kennel. I do not want them looking at me. I think Dad can read their minds - am I going nuts?

Yes. But I have reasons. Dad's letter was full of dogs and roses. Now his house is too. He is becoming a horror, only it's real. I keep thinking I will end up being made into a dish with too much cream and spices. "Torrance is delicious!" he screams at Pip. "The best guts I ever tasted!"

I feel like I'm in a house full of secret eyes. The gun I always keep hidden. He can't know about it. The only good thing about this place is that I found a gun. I am sitting here thinking of using it. Crazy. Totally crazy.

———

Happy like a terrorist. Revenge is a dish best served during a very cold blizzard. I wish Erik could come. But I don't even know him yet. He wouldn't understand anything. Neither would Sam. This I have to do by myself. Oh well. Later for - I just realized something.

Should of thought of that. I can write about Erik. Too bad this is a War Journal. But same difference. Dad - and Mom - could never find out.

Great. Sitting in my bathrobe cause of cameras. If I get up he will see it. I'm trapped. No way Dad can see what I'm writing but even writing his name is like sex, I am done for. I can't even move.

Going to get you, Dad.

They probably work in the dark. Which makes no difference. I never do anything in the dark. But I bet they do, in case I did. They click in the dark, so hey. He must of thought of every angle. Eight cameras between here and the bathroom. Big time investment, of course they see in the dark. In case I was the type who does not like to watch. In the mirrors, Fuckface. You know, you seen everything. Cause *you* are the type that likes to watch!

———

Here I am trapped thinking of Erik when I have work to do. Shopping and stuff. Hey, stupid! Calm down! He IS NOT HERE.

We don't know each other except for the locker room. And practice. We never talk. But we look. We know. We both know enough to know.

He does the same I do at swimteam, and after: he peeks. Then he gets his pants on fast. Or his speedo. (Uh-oh)

And I saw he has the same little (HA) problem that I do (WOW). We can't take showers at the same time at all. We never talk but we agree on that. If he comes in, I go out, he goes out when I come in, and now we kind of look in the eye man-to-man when it happens and one time he *winked.* I laughed. Soft, but so he could hear it. We understand, man-to-man, boy-to-boy, what ever. We both know and agree. It has been going on for the last four swimteam times. Some day we will talk about it. Do something about it! Or I'll lose it, bad. The shower, whew. Couple close calls. The other boys got to be blind. Just like La Jolla. Wonder if he has a boyfriend?

In the pool it's ok. Usually.

He is about one inch shorter than me, 5-8 I guess, he has yellow crew-cut hair, and I saw his weight, 130. He noticed me looking when he was on the scale. That was not cool. I walked by with clothes on and he was naked. Not fair. He frowned! He won sophmore gymnastics medals last year, Sam told me. She said he will win again this year if he competes. He might do swimteam only (dangerous - so what?). He has blue eyes, really blue, big smile. But not for me. Not yet. Too dangerous. We both look totally serious at each other. Almost like we hate each other so our dicks stay under control. But we both *know.* He used to have a girlfriend, Sam said. They broke up. Good. Sam told me everything about Erik. She is jealous. She likes me. I catch her staring all the time. But she likes

Erik too. "A double disaster," she said. We had a private talk. I told her. She is ok. She's cool about the fact I have to get Erik. And funny. She teases me when we sit together way in the corner at lunch. She really makes me laugh. Everybody thinks we are doing it. I don't mind.

After what the counsellor blabbed to Mom in LJ about Ricky. The worst day of my life. Until yesterday.

Mom. She would DIE. If Dad tells her.

I feel him looking at me. So I smile like a terrorist. Bet you can't figure it out, huh, Dad?

Just so happens I have a lot of practice keeping things to myself under a smile. More practice than sports. It comes easy. Too much practice. I get it living with Mom.

Duane Allbright's
Audiocassette Notes: II

Saturday Morning

It's snowing bad. I'm driving through it. I'm leaving Cambridge, the only one on the highway, in a blizzard. The wind is fierce. I can't see ten feet. I swear this car wants to fly right off this road.

Quick getaway here. Thirty miles an hour. Well I didn't rent it, I sort of borrowed it, so I can't complain. No credit cards now, no nothing, just cash. Cold, clean cash.

The lam. I got tunes, mournful hillbilly blues. I got a coolerful of Pepsi. I got seven cartons of smokes. I got clothes. I got snow, lots of snow, but it's ok, because I'm free. What else do I got? Nothing. Except this borrowed car and a mess of cash, and a big old mess of trouble up ahead.

Whole mess of trouble behind, too, but that's where the clean break comes in. I have to sort this out. Get clear, Duane. You have to be clear, clear enough for whoever hears you, if anyone ever does.

———

This is Dr. Duane Allbright. As I tape this I am driving through a snowstorm, headed north, in a stolen automobile.

People are after me. I'm the object of a manhunt. It's a quiet manhunt. Still, it's a hunt. Two hours ago I almost killed a man named Claus Schmidtt. He caught me erasing my computer. He tried to stop me, but didn't succeed. Claus looked so surprised, lying on the linoleum, wearing that hat.

I'll say why I am making this tape. Two reasons. First, I want to put my story in context. Second, I want some record to survive in case I don't. I intend to mail this, along with notes I've already made, to a secure location. Updates will follow.

———

Where to start? Today I resigned from a program conducted at an institute in Cambridge. Not at the institute, exactly; the program is a spinoff, you could say. I don't want to reveal its name. I'll settle for something false, but descriptive. Call it the "Psi Project."

"Psi" is a term for psychic powers. It's what some people call extrasensory perception. The Psi Project experiments with psychic powers. It's sponsored by business interests and the government. It's secret.

Until this morning I was assistant director of lab research. That means I did most of the work. In fact I designed the experiments and ran them. I was underpaid, but didn't mind. To be at the cutting edge of what the Project devoutly calls science was, in general, reward enough for me.

From the beginning of my tenure at this place I was skeptical about its founding premise. The premise holds that psi powers are militarily useful. I always thought that was a crock. But I never revealed my lack of faith in "Psi Wars" to my colleagues—even though a number revealed their own doubts to me. No, I kept my nose clean. I knew what could happen to my control of the work. If a professional ethicist studied my career, and my deceit, the verdict would be uncomplimentary. I couldn't care less.

I'm my own ethicist, an amateur, that's for sure, but I have qualifications. I can balance my qualms. And I don't need expert opinions. Because expert opinions on the ethics of psi do not exist. We're all amateurs with psi. The people who do it don't know where it will lead. The moral issues are mysterious and vast because psi itself is even more mysterious and vast. And the notion that it will win wars or revolutionize espionage is, mostly, a giant joke.

The Project bureaucrats do not get this joke. They are paid to make psi work. To make it real—predictable, reliable, standardizable. But their definition of real has defects. Psi isn't mechanical. It isn't predictable, reliable, standardizable. So, applied to warfare, it could be messy. I know about this. I designed the experiments, and ran them, and I am myself a Psi.

Maybe most important, I am, or was, a recruiter of psi talent.

That means I'm a psi detector. That's my main claim to fame, psi-wise. Except nobody outside the Project is aware of it. And now, I'm outside the Project. So my claim to fame is a little obscure at the moment.

But the fact I can detect psi is why I am driving through a blizzard away from Cambridge, Massachusetts, in a stolen automobile.

I have detected an awesome Psi.

His name is Baron Malcolm Spoor. I want to learn all I can about him. And I don't want the Project involved.

This has meant a career change. I could have kept my job. Or I could have studied the Baron. But not both. If I'd tried to do both, the Project people would've known I'm up to something, and gotten involved. Because in theory, the Baron could be useful. My former bosses would think so. I reckon they'd kill to get their hands on this man. Literally. What I'm saying is, a Psi like the Baron is of interest to a couple different agencies with long, strong arms.

Therefore, I'm vanishing. Tracelessly I hope. So far I've stolen two cars. Probably I'll steal more. I'm wearing gloves, I am serious about what I am doing. I even had to brain the chief of security just to get out of my office. That was an ugly scene, and a very close call.

You might say I'm taking drastic measures. They're not drastic enough. I wish I'd had the nerve to blow up the telephone company's computer center before I left town. I almost did that to destroy records of the calls I've been making to Sheila. Those records, I'm afraid, will be trouble.

I don't know what's in store. I'm not clairvoyant. That sounds like Sheila—she said those very words once, to be sarcastic. The fact is, no one's clairvoyant. Unless it's the Baron. Now that makes me smile. But who knows? The more I think about this man the more I know I know little. He is so much. He has so much in orbit around him that seems entirely unique. I don't usually talk in such sweeping terms. But right now, I have to. The Baron has no counterpart in the historical record of psi.

At least, to the extent I know that record. My research on the Baron so far is sketchy. I did less than an hour's worth this morning, because of leaving Cambridge. Sometime soon I will have to go back there, or somewhere, and spend time in a library. But as far as the

Project's data base is concerned, not only does Baron Malcolm Spoor not exist, nothing like him exists, or ever did.

Which means, very likely, he's dangerous. If you're unique, and uniquely powerful, you need a shield. You need protection from people who might want to get a piece of the action.

Could be, the Baron will decide one of those people is me. But I won't be remotely the menace the Project would be.

Claus Schmidtt is the security chief of that organization. He is large and muscular, and he isn't stupid, not at all, but he looks it, and he also looks mean, especially when he has his purple hat on—then he looks positively vicious. Sounds fun, but isn't. Then there's the Director, he's the boss, and Cunif, she's the overseer from the government agency. These people would feel betrayed if they knew what I'm doing. In fact, they already feel betrayed. I left a resignation letter a couple of hours ago that doesn't say much, and is causing some panic.

So much panic, I almost didn't make it out of there. Cunif came in early. I was in my office erasing my computer, and her computer let her know that, what a disaster. My computer started yelling Stop Stop Stop. Then she sent Schmidtt over, and he, sometimes he behaves strangely, decided to take a peek at me from the hall, through the transom. Dumb move. Because I can feel his hat forty feet away. That's a joke, what I feel is him—but he is that hat. I even told him so once. "Claus," I said, "that hat is you." He didn't smile. He definitely didn't when I jerked open the door, he was standing on a chair, and I kicked it. He fell. Then I brained him with my typewriter. Caught him on the way down. Not too hard, but hard enough. He looked so surprised lying on that shiny linoleum. Out cold. Hat on. On even tighter than usual.

Well I reckon he never thought I could be so mean.

Not sure I did, either. But I had to do it. The Director and Cunif are serious people. They pretty much get away with anything they decide to do, and some of it isn't funny. The reason, however, is: there are people in the government who are very big fans of the occult.

I say occult because it's so stupid. It's hocus-pocus. It's junk, suckers and con men do occult. The point is, these government people, they are suckers. But they're believers. They think tarot cards or astrology might tell us which bunker to bomb to get the next bad dictator. They think maybe we can read enemy minds. Some day, maybe, but I doubt it. Anyway, these guys are gung-ho. That means they don't obey laws. They could decide to get rid of me, no qualms at all.

The reason? They could decide the Baron is a very nice weapon.

Rational people might doubt that idea. Those people should take a look at what they think is rational. The psychology is simple. If we don't do it, somebody else will. From the Project's point of view, that can't happen. And, in theory, they'd have a good reason. Compared to the Baron, they, and all known competitors, are totally primitive.

Take the Project. It has three or four major talents. Not Cunif or the Director, or even Schmidtt—not a bit of psi in any of them, that's how they got to the top. Their positions require stable people. And the psi spies tend to not be stable.

Spies, agents, spooks, call them what you want. These people can do some remarkable things. They can detect psi; namely, know when they're near other people with psi. They can signal each other over distance, send basic emotions, like alarm, fear, elation—when the conditions are right and the emotions are charged, which is hard to control, much less predict. They can read places and objects, what I did at Sheila's, and get impressions—almost always, vague ones. They can make what seem to be lucky guesses, and sometimes aren't. In other words they're good at detective work. They're sort of like human bloodhounds. Except instead of scent, it's psi. The other big difference being that dogs are infinitely better at what they do. This is an analogy I used to think of often. It makes me uncomfortable at the moment.

Because the Baron's dogs, I suspect, have us beat by a mile. And that's just starters. There's Pip, human animal. Then there's the Odor. Whatever it is that comes from the flower, that seems sentient. And, if I'm not deluded, aware of me.

All of this means the Baron has some kind of system under his control. The dogs, the Odor, Pip, they interconnect. Somehow, he communicates with them, I assume through a psi channel—one that really and truly works. That, to be plain, is what we all have been looking for, for a long, long time.

I can't help but laugh. I thought I was smart. I thought I was major talent, working with these earnest jerks, who want to revolutionize espionage, put a lid on the world, all that shit—I was so superior, see? And cynical about it. I had everything figured out, how petty the Lab work is, never mind what it costs, which is millions. Well, it truly is petty. But for reasons different than I thought.

I now realize I am some kind of mongoloid idiot. And I can't express how exciting that is. It opens everything up. Sometimes I think I'm just dreaming this. However, I'm not. I even love snow now. I even love my stolen car! I have to ditch it, it's useless in this weather.

What I'm saying is, the Baron is an opportunity. One that exists nowhere else.

The venture is risky for all the above reasons. I don't know what the Odor wants of me, if anything. I don't know how the Baron will react to me poking around. But I do know that the states of mind Torrance describes may mean the man is open, or even vulnerable. More accessible, at least, than he usually is.

So I have to take advantage.

That's what I aim to do, starting tonight. Because tonight, Sheila is going to his place for dinner.

Memorandum from Miss Cunif
to Claus Schmidtt: I

Saturday Morning

TO: SCHMIDTT
FROM: CUNIF
RE: ALLBRIGHT

Clinic informs me the injury isn't grave. I expect you to report 0600 tomorrow.

This is not the time to review your performance today. I will say, the Director is disappointed. So am I.

But our chief concern is Allbright. You must find him, immediately.

Factors:

1. His memory is photographic.
2. He has had access to all Program files.
3. He erased his computer. Tech is working on salvage. Preliminary assessment: nothing is recoverable.
4. Recently he has been moody, distracted.

5. Blovko checked his apartment. Most belongings remain, personal effects are missing. Departure was made in haste.

It is conceivable he is going through a personal crisis, unrelated to our work. I doubt that. Three other possibilities seem more likely:

1. He is taking his expertise to another organization.
2. He has discovered something he does not want the Program to know about.
3. A combination of -1- and -2-.

Blovko is preparing a report on all known issues, professional and personal, that may bear on his behavior. We are reviewing credit card transactions. We have requested telephone records for the past three years.

See you in the morning.

The Diary
of Sheila Massif: VII

Sunday Afternoon

We've been staring at the snow that's silenced the boom of the mall. Snow has silenced the world. How appropriate. Background hush.

Duane said he won't bother me while I write this. He said to pretend he isn't here. Easier said than done, after last night.

The latest, Diary, is as strange as I hope you will ever get.

———

Yesterday, from the beginning:

Duane arrived at half-past eleven. Blasé as usual, he came in talking about the storm and carrying a large suitcase. The highway was a mess. He couldn't go more than thirty the whole way up. A major blizzard, isn't it something. Then he wanted the rose.

I found it and tossed it at him. He turned away—as if he didn't want me watching—while he put it in a plastic bag and stuffed it in his pocket. That really alarmed me. I don't know why. I felt—sick in my stomach.

"Major blizzard?" I said. "Then dinner's canceled. What a relief."

He swung around and said, "I just acquired a jeep. Four-wheel drive. It has good tires and goes fast, it'll get through anything."

This wasn't the first sign yesterday was going to be a very odd day. But his words and tone put a new gloss on my mood. "Did the jeep," I asked, "come with a St. Bernard? What do you mean, 'get through anything'?"

He said, "I might have to get you out of there."

I said, "Rent a snowmobile. They're much more glamorous for late-night blizzard rescues. Why, by the way, would you have to get me 'out of there'?"

"With the blizzard," he said slowly—and I realized he was working pretty hard at being blasé—"you might be stuck chez Spoor for the night."

"If there's a blizzard, Duane, I don't think I'm going *any-where* . . ." I stopped talking because he was unpacking a funny-looking oversize handgun and large bullet things that didn't really look like bullets. "For the dogs," he explained. "Just in case."

He was polishing my mood to an absolutely brilliant new sheen. I said, "Do you really have to nuke the dogs? That's inhumane!"

"Darts," he said. "Knock 'em out."

"Those things would kill a hippo," I said. "What is *going on*?"

"Something is," he said, producing a hypodermic needle and a small vial that contained cloudy fluid.

"Hold it!" I exclaimed.

"You didn't sleep," he said crossly. "Sheila, you need rest."

"Just shoot me with the gun and get it over with," I quavered, backing away. "I'll die much faster than a hippo and won't feel a *thing* . . ."

Duane smiled at me. Suddenly he didn't seem blasé. I realized something. This is a man with whom I've had great sex, the best sex ever in fact—but who I don't know well. Not at all well. He put down the syringe and lit a cigarette. His moustache scraggily dragon-winged it. His eyes squinted at the dragon's fiery mouth. Smoke billowed. His eyelashes are short and colorless. Who is this man and what does he want?

He said, "You haven't slept. You're a wreck. Do you want to stagger around at that dinner party behaving like a fool?" The way he said "fool" was Southern: "foool." He told me once he's from Memphis, Tennessee. At this point I would have believed he's from Uzbekistan, wherever that is.

I said, "What's that drug? Why do you seem like a spy, Duane?"

He said, "You're in worse shape than I thought." He went to the window that displays the mall, and looked at falling snow. It was falling thickly. "I could answer your questions," he said to the snow. "But now I'm thinking of getting out. You don't trust me. I should leave." He waved an arm. "Make a decision. I can help you. Or I can leave."

"Why," I said, "are you helping me, Duane?"

"Because I'm interested. That's why. But I'm losing interest." He yawned. "Lot of snow. Listen. Let's make a deal. You sleep, then when you wake up and think straight you can decide. I don't care. You can decide to run away like you always do and I won't care. But decide when you can think. Honestly, you have no control. And another thing."

"What, Duane?"

"You're concerned about yourself. How about Torrance?"

He had a point. Craftily made, too—he was being very rude, very male, very irritating, and very effective. I was stumbling down a dark flight of stairs: missing steps, putting feet in black spaces that shouldn't be there, *twitching*. "That drug won't make me an idiot, Duane?"

He smiled. I wanted to hit him. He said, "You'll wake up more clear than if you just came back from the Betty Ford Clinic."

Bastard. I bared my arm and snarled, "Fine. Shove it in and *squirt*."

He did and I fell out of an airplane into an ocean of warm molasses.

———

When I woke up he was towering over me holding a cup. I had a fresh sting in my arm. There was no noise. The quiet was dense. He said, "Drink this." I took the cup and drank. It was cocoa. The nearest window was strangely blank. "Fifteen inches," Duane said, "and rising. The windows froze over. That's ice."

"What time is it?" I said.

"Seven," he said. "Pip called. He left a message on the machine saying he'll be here by seven-thirty. How, I don't know. The roads are closed, nobody can move. But he said he was calling from the highway."

"Dog sled?" I said. I sat up without effort. My mind was the Hall of Mirrors at Versailles: scintillating and very, very long. "If the dogs are cow-size like Torrance wrote his mom," I said, "then the sled must be Santa sleigh-size and they're all Rudolphs, but with red eyes instead of noses."

"Yeah," Duane said. He seemed nervous. "I'm turning on the shower. And I laid out fashion . . . options. On the couch."

He disappeared. For some reason I was in the sleeping nook. He'd drugged me in the living nook, then must've dragged me to the sleeping nook. I glided to living nook, where I saw several outfits arranged on the couch with shoes and hats to match. They looked stunning. I realized I felt *marvelous.* Duane reappeared. The shower was thrumming. "Feel ok?" he asked.

"Honey," I said, "if this is what they did to Betty Ford, book me in at the clinic. For a year. How much do drugs like that cost?"

He said, "Get in the shower, be a good girl," and I didn't even mind. Because suddenly, in the shower, I was a rocket launching. Blast-Off! Full Thrust. Ignite Second Stage. The O-rings are holding. WHEEEEEEEEEEEEEE!

He stuck his head in and said, "Fifteen minutes."

Within twelve I was dry, emolliented, powdered, faintly rouged, lipsticked, mascaraed, perfumed, coiffed, pantied and hosed. The labors, so intensive, stropped my edge. All the waves were in step. I *cohered.*

"Duane," I asked, "does this high have a crash?" I didn't care, just was curious.

"No," he said.

"I love you," I said, "what should I wear?"

The doorbell rang. I went to the door, chained it, jerked it open two chain-taut inches and said, silkily, "Five minutes," and *slammed* it, then splayed myself on it better than Marilyn Monroe and said, "Which one, darling? Which dress?"

"The black one," he said. Thirty seconds later he was zipping me up.

"Your purse," he said, handing it to me.

"Thank you," I whispered. "Tape recorder?"

"In and ready to run, Commander."

"Perfect, extra microcassettes?" I briskly hissed.

"Five, Excellency," he said.

"My *shoes,*" I snapped.

"Right here, Madam, uh, Ambassador," he said.

"The coat?" I said.

"Allow me," he said.

"And the hat!"

"Of course," he said, grabbing it.

"You perform well under pressure, Ensign," I said. "Admiral Zoltran will hear all about it. But where is my ray gun?"

"Huh," he said. "Funny you said that. Here." He pulled out a slim silver flashlight. Gal-size. But heavy.

"Whaddul needatt for?" I said in pidgin Klingonese so Pip wouldn't understand if he had his ear to the door.

"Just a guess," he said, and I nodded and jammed it in my purse.

"Bow and scrape," I commanded. He did. He got on his knees and salaamed. "Ok, ok," I sighed. "Open the air lock, but first give me a hug."

He got up and did. I said in his ear, "I'll be fine."

"I know," he said.

"How long does this last?"

"Hours."

"Just what I wanted to hear. Do I look all right?"

"You look," he said, "like the Supreme Commander of the Solar System." He snuck up to the door and silently unchained it. I, Supreme Commander, positioned my stance to suit my rank. Duane snatched the doorknob and put his back to the wall. The door swung over him like the lid of a sarcophagus. The corridor simultaneously oblonged forth: Pip stood there, framed in the rectangle. In formal clothes, he looked like a diplomat. But he was a diplomat caught off guard. Hands cupped over his nose, eyes bulging, the man was making an explosive "*Kaachew!*"

"Excuse me," he then said, thickly, through the cupped hands.

"Do you need," I asked, "a tissue?"

His eyes, still bulging, were mortified. The hands were staying clapped to the nose. What we have here, I thought, is a predicament. He muttered, moistly, "I am—very embarrassed . . ."

I said, "I'll get a tissue. No, don't come in with that *specimen*—stay out there!" The big bald lug had started to stagger in as if he'd just been shot in the face. The nerve.

"I'm very, very sorry," he said when I came back yanking off a yard of paper towels. He looked about ready to burst into tears.

"Use this," I said. "These things happen. Do I need boots?"

"Oh, no, no," he said, turning away and wiping. Suddenly I saw a strange dignity in the guy. Like he's a real gentleman. But fallen on hard times, and brooding about it. "What shall I do with this, Ma'am?"

"Keep it for the road," I said, closing the door and telepathing, *Bye, Duane.* "You might need it." The road. It was Valley Forge out there. But he'd gotten here somehow.

"This way, please," he said, poise regained. As if taking me to a table in a four-star restaurant.

I clack-clacked my heels down the corridor behind him, noticing that the howling elements had done him no damage. His shoes were patent leather. No hat. The skull and shoes were spotless. Wind was shaking the corridor. The building was groaning. How'd he done it?

He opened a door I'd never seen open before. Cement stairs went down. "I parked," he said, "at the loading dock out back, Ma'am, watch your step, please. It's better this way, oh the weather. I could have parked in front but the *wind.*" I smelled custodial smells and clacked fearlessly down the steps. Alarming spaces did not open up under my heels but I saw mops and industrial cleaner containers and thought: this is a good place for murder.

"Call me Sheila," I said, "and you, of course, are Pip, we've met, you know. How come you're so familiar with the layout, Pip?"

"Why, yes," he said. "We have met! Yes, we did."

He led me past furnaces and water heaters to a biggish dimly lit cement room, the receiving area for the complex of studio apartments, I guessed, and I said, again, "You know your way around."

"It's much better this way," he said. "The wind, it's blowing!"

Right. The wind was blowing. I sized up the available weapons and thought: I'll rip out a water boiler and throw it at him if he tries anything. I'll steam him to death. I'll iron him. He said, "This is fun, isn't it? Well! Are you ready?"

He smiled at me, but gravely. I saw it again: a weird dignity in the guy. We had reached a set of big steel doors on sliders. Somewhere garbage was stinking and I couldn't help but grin back. It was so silly. The paper towels were sticking out of a pocket in his coat. The doors were grinding and razors of frigid air were whipping in around the edges.

"Show me what you got," I said. "The suspense is killing me."

"Ha-ha!" Pip cried. He put one of his meaty palms on a handle and sent the 800-pound door down its rail as if it were a patio screen.

The basementlike air instantly sucked out into an ammonia ice storm on one of Jupiter's moons. The Supreme Commander wasn't ready for this. Try as I did, I couldn't breathe ammonia. The blizzard was one hundred million muscular ghosts who were mad as hell. I couldn't see. I had a hand on my hat. I couldn't see but dead ahead was a brightly blinking UFO. Pip yelled, "Come on!" He took my hand, then put an arm around my waist and *picked me up,* the other hand crashing shut the door, and we plunged into a turbulent cavity under the overhang. He opened something and I saw the fuselage of a very hefty truck stretching away like a Star Wars cruiser into the violence. Then I was swinging up and crawling onto a firm red sofa that turned out to be the seat in the cab. I jackknifed and, in a flash, was sitting. Then he was beside me slamming the door, and the roar of the storm went slack.

"I hope you didn't mind that," he said.

"You," I said, "did the necessary thing, Pip." I was breathing hard. "No, I didn't mind, are we safe now or what?"

"Yes!" he said. "Look at the driffs!"

The driffs. I looked at the drifts. On my side they seemed twenty feet high. "Nice it isn't the other way, Sheila, weeda hadda diggout!" He was speaking pidgin Klingonese. He knew my secret language. I thought: these things happen.

"We still hafta diggout!" I said.

"Easy!" he said, dropping his hand to a lever.

There were many levers and they all were elegant. The appointments of this truckcab had style. My heels were stuck in thick carpet. I looked up and saw an enemy starship warping from hyperspace through the windshield. It was a massive *blade* thing. It was lunging up and down. Blinking lights put red-orange gleams on the wide, sharp, lunging blade.

A plow. We had a bulldozer plow out there. The thing could move.

"Ha-ha!" Pip yowled, jerking the lever. "Oh boy!"

"Oh boy," I said.

"You want a drink?" he said.

"Sure," I said.

"Bar's right behind," he said. "You mix or me?"

"I mix," I said, twisting around and staring at a lovely little bar with thirteen kinds of liquor, seltzer bottles to one side and glasses and a bowl of ice to the other. I said, "Oh boy. What's your poison?"

"Nothing, thanks!"

I said, "No booze? We're on a suicide mission in the Asteroid Belt and you're gonna do it sober?"

"I couldn't," Pip said, "I mean, you know, I just can't. Because . . ." He was pursing his lips, manically.

"Yes?" I said, pouring Chivas. Small glasses. Standards have slipped. But just the thing for dodging asteroids . . .

"Well," he said, grinding gears and heaving us into the savage fracas of the parking lot, "I don't drink because—because, you see, Malcolm does."

"Ah," I said. Made sense. Pip the Co-dependent. Sure. "Tell me about Malcolm, Pip, and tell me all about yourself." The big blade was punching through five- and six-foot drifts and then we were at the street, facing the desolate waste where the mall usually is. No lights except for a yellow traffic signal blinking bravely at us, the sum total of traffic. We jounced past it and plowed into zapping nothingness. "But first," I said, "tell me how you can see. I can't see anything. Can you?"

"Ha-ha!" he said.

And we were off, rolling down the highway, punching through drifts and wind and darkness. The headlight beams preceded us by ten feet or so. Beyond ten feet there could have been anything, an erupting volcano, and I wouldn't have known. But Pip seemed to see. He seemed to know where all the volcanoes in this part of the country are erupting. How? I'm still wondering. I gave him tomato juice and he drank it straight down. He handed back the glass and said, "We'll be there in twenty-five minutes."

I realized he hadn't been answering my questions.

———

I'll take a break. Duane is still staring at the buried mall. No. He's looking at me. I guess he's been looking at me every now and then, as I've been telling you Part I, Diary Dear, of yesterday's—saga.

But just wait till you feel Part II's more ominous scribble across your willing blank pages. Yow! I think Duane's about to say something.

———

This is what he just said: "Sheila. There's something to the Curse. It's real."

The Chronicles
of Malcolm Spoor: V

Sunday Afternoon

My fury: pure.
  You know who this is. Do not trifle with me - speak to me, now!
  I tell you my fury is pure.

—

I will temper it. I must. It will serve my ends.
  I hate worry. I destroy worry. Who is Duane?
  Something ghastly has happened. If necessary, I will destroy them all. First Sheila. Then Pip. Then *Duane.*
  The dogs, they are hungry. They need more fire. More fire for the dogs, Grislies, I will feed them Duane - they will hardly feel it, eh? But still, a snack. His miserable little fire, it will go out! But live on, and on, in the dogs. To serve us. Like countless others, no? The dimwits, who find us. The seekers. Who are attracted, fatally, moths rushing to flame.
  As for Sheila - I will ruin her. Because I might need her. Yes, why not, she is very good. So I think it is time to do some writing. Some

creative writing. I have been anticipating that. We need scandal, scandal for Sheila, yes. Ha. Ha-ha. She will weep!

———

But I am tired. Grislies, I am tired, tired. I need rest. I need death, I do so badly want to finish me. To be done with Malcolm. I tell you, I feel a murderous rage. What a joy, no? The killing of me? I cannot wait. You know the feeling, do you not? You enjoyed killing yourselves, yes? All of you, so eagerly self-destructive, you delighted in it. I, too, will savor that fate. The blissful end of me!

Because - it has become too much. Why am I so shallow? So boring? And I am - I am an old reprobate, that is all. As were you. Look at you, nailed to these walls. You insubstantial drunks. You spectral *sots.* Oh, I shan't heap abuse. You know who this is, speak to me!

———

I am The Living One! Answer me!

———

The dogs are upset. And the plants are furious. I believe the plants are rather *worried,* Grislies. Oh, I don't care! I simply do not care. I am drinking. Drinking Ouzo Extra Fino, for the sheer poison. To face tomorrow. I must talk with Torrance, tomorrow. Today, no, I cannot. But tomorrow, I will put him at ease. I must, he is desperate. He will stay home from school and we will have a Father-Son Talk. There won't be school anyhow. Too much snow. We'll talk. He won't be terrified. Can't have it. Later, yes, but now - no terror.

And the schedule will speed. Speed up. I make phone calls tomorrow. Many phone calls. To London. To New York. To Tokyo. They can bill me. Chartered jets, I don't care! Nor will Torrance.

———

Pip, beseeching, brings food on a tray. Dog. Angry upstart dog!

———

Sheila thinks she is clever. She should stay in her nasty little drama chamber, because she is stupid. But then, everyone is. Except me, and the plants. And you. Wake up!

But I have been thinking - she is good. Good genes. Is she healthy? Do you care? You hate me. But you need me. And I need you. Charming, our mutual discomfort. Suffer!

You know, I would like to say something. Grislies, I crave peace. I believe I should put a stop to all this. Shocking, no? But I must confide something - I would like to be an innocent child. How appealing! Well, isn't it? But it is not possible. Is it?

I really do not speak lightly, of death. I want to die. I am bored. I'm all washed up. I am sick of the Curse!

Ah, I've provoked you. I felt it - *a musty little chancre, bursting!*

Bunny, I exile you. I have had enough. Enough of your pallid, pasty *mug.* So don't you dare make waves. However - I will consent to speak with the others. Any of the others, who will talk? Horrid creatures - *speak to me!* Gainsborough? I see you on the cover of that magazine, every inch the cosmopolite. So languid and debonair you are! I will speak with you, do you hear me? This is The Living One - answer me!

If not Gainsborough, then - who? Francis? You'll do! The Change is coming, you Fools. Don't you want to make your parade? No? But you always have. You did when you were fewer!

The Change is what they live for. They cannot be gone. Where could they go? This silence brings me so low - I believe I am going insane. They can't want that. Can you want me insane, truly insane? Do you want me raving and disrupting? Like Bunny - the last time?

But Sheila is good. Oh yes, yes - yes, please, I beg you, listen——

Black hair. Hazel eyes. Short but shapely. Wonderful cheekbones. Fine skin. Astonishing skin! Legs I would like to inspect more closely. Perfect bones, throughout. I need X-rays. Magnetic resonations, I need a complete medical on this woman. Alluring lips. Very good lips. And teeth. Savagely beautiful teeth. Delicate wrists and ankles. Effortless waist, inherent, she doesn't diet, no need. The breasts: edible. I would eat them. I would enjoy that. Maybe I will!

In fact she is sumptuous. I think she may even be - perfect. Too small for me. Much too small, no bulk, nothing there, like Floria. Like Floria too delicate, but listen: like Floria - perfect, yes?

She carries the Fire! Did you notice? My Lethargies? From the plants, like Floria she attracts it, *did you notice?*

She carries it very well, this is what gave me that odor I called putrid vanilla. But isn't. Her odor is beauteous. Very strong. Very unconscious. One of the best, admit it.

No comments? No comments on Duane? Who stinks! The runt. This is how he smelled me, through Sheila. He is who stared at the dog that night in the woods; the one the villagers almost shot, when they were standing vigil. A shame they didn't, eh? He is puny. Ambitious. Envious. Dimwitted. No mind. Bad flavor. No Fire. Some, but too little. A runt. A runt. Miserable runt - like all the others, who dare come begging, I will feed him to the dogs. I will add one tiny flame more to their fire. To our fiery hoard, Grislies! Does that excite you? No?

No. I am losing control. Never would have thought it. I am lost without you. Lost. I am The Living One - I beseech you——

Gainsborough - are you there? Speak to me. I beg you, speak - Bunny - stay away. The rest of you, please listen: Bunny will kill us all. I tell you he will be the end of us all! You do not believe me? Think back - back to the last time, think of what happened. He nearly finished us, then.

————

Gainsborough, you know what happened the last time. Talk to me, now!

The Diary of
Sheila Massif: VIII

Sunday Evening

Duane just left. He's going to Cambridge "to do some research." On
what? He didn't say. I don't even care.

———

Pip and I were in the truck, plowing through the night. The blizzard
was raging, the Chivas tasted good, Pip wasn't answering questions.

His domed profile was dark. In front, the blade was moving literally tons of snow out of our way. The stuff was creaming under my
window. A public service—nobody else was doing it. Nobody else
was out except for smooth humps of abandoned cars. Why didn't
we stop, look and save?

Because we were going to a dinner party.

We made turns. The roads narrowed. "Pip," I asked about ten
minutes into our ride, "do you have hobbies?"

"A few."

Like photography, maybe? "Like what?"

"Oh, I cook," he said. "But Torrance is cooking tonight."

"I thought you were the master chef," I said.

"Well," he said. "Torrance wanted to cook. Such a good boy."

"You're his bodyguard?" I asked casually.

"Yes!" he said. The dome nodded. "Oh, yes."

But you lie through your teeth, I thought. So how do I know you're not lying now? "Huh," I said. "What's Malcolm doing?"

"He is a private person," Pip said firmly. He'd already said this once. "Very private." That made it three times. I gave up and said:

"What's this truck for, anyway?"

"Jobs around the house. I used it last year to get the place . . ."

I didn't say anything.

"Ready," he said, uncomfortably. "And a course I have to plow the drive." A course he does. "It's long," he added.

"But you don't drink, a course, so does this mean Malcolm shares the chores, Pip, all the while mixing up manhattans and daiquiris?"

"No," he said, "the bar is there just for you, it's not built-in, you know. Malcolm said, 'Get her nice and . . .' "

"Drunk?"

"Warmed up," Pip said reproachfully. "It's cold, you know."

"How thoughtful," I murmured. It wasn't cold in that deluxe truckcab.

"Yes," Pip said hesitantly. "Malcolm is thoughtful."

There! I'd learned something! Suddenly I was supernaturally at peace. Nothing could stop the truck; nothing could stop me. I was on my way to unravel the riddle of Malcolm Spoor. And *I would succeed.* I had the inner potency of a vat of hot chilies. The Drama Chamber wasn't a hiding place. It was a jalapeño reactor, propelling me forward.

When I poured my drink into the ice bucket, Pip didn't notice.

————

The snowfall thinned. The storm seemed about over. We'd been unclogging a tree-lined lane with a high wall running alongside when the truck slowed, and turned. The headlights fell on ornately frosted gates. Emblazoned, they looked like dessert. Pip pressed a button. The frosting shivered off and the gates, shuddering, swung in. Ah! The Secret Kingdom of Spoor! All the amenities, here: *defrostable gates.*

We drove up a winding and forested incline for about ten minutes, maybe a mile. Where were the dogs? I expected the attack any second. Hounds of Hades, in packs.

No dogs.

Then we rounded a curve and there was sudden space. Lots of

space; thickly frosted meadows were rolling. In the distance, there was a brilliant mass of lights. "At last," Pip said.

The lights got bigger and bigger. Yes, a big house. Really big. Stately too, a Home of Distinction, suitable for a school or head-quarters, or raising livestock on floors one and two, and the kids on three; with space left for bowling, and skating, and roller coasters. There were turrets and towers and conical roofs, and spiring brick smokestacks every thirty feet, and stone that banded the brick, and more stone, ever so solidly. This man, I thought, cannot be allowed to get away with this. The ostentation!

We rumbled around, past a side portal that was slightly less monumental than the portico in front. The dimensions seemed to laugh at the snow. But drifts had banked ground-floor windows, had invaded terraces and porches. I felt a deepening distance to the left, and asked Pip, "What's over there?"

"The ocean," he said.

It was misty and dark. We plowed to a building at the end of a long snowduned wing. A wall rattled up, and the blade rose too, saluting the rising wall, and we went in. The wall rattled down behind us. The motor cut. Nature was gone; we were garaged, or hangared. It was brightly lit. Straight ahead was another retractable wall. "Where does that go?" I asked.

"Back lawn," he said, pressing a button. The wall rattled up, revealing a bank of snow that came tumbling inside, and more deep black. "A hill runs down to the cliffwalk."

"I can't see any cliffwalk," I said, opening my door.

He jumped out to help, too chivalrously. But he was weirdly sweet. "Look," he said, taking me beyond the blade. Warm air swam at the night. Frigid air rushed in over tumbled snow. We got to the opening. I stared. It was breathtaking.

Outside, hangar-lit, was a frosted area that disappeared. It jutted out and vanished. Above this, suspended midair, was a strand of lights. I felt dizzy. I realized those lights weren't above us. They were far away, and far, far below. Yes, I thought. A "hill."

"That's the cliffwalk," Pip said. "Those lights run the edge."

I said, "Waste of electricity, isn't it? Pip, if those are cliffs down there, what's right ahead? I mean—does the hill just drop?"

He said, "It's steep along here. Over there it isn't—do you ski?" He was waving his arm to the right. I looked and saw the outlines of a magical floating pagoda. Whatever it was, it too was lit. The thing seemed hangar-level, but a long way off, with a void in between, the hill—my eyes adjusted and I saw that the top of the hill is a crescent. The hangar is on one end, the pagoda on the other, and in between, behind a garden, is the house. I looked at it. The lights were scorching. They lit a rectangular bush, a huge clipped thing, tall, the kind with a maze inside.

But all I could think of was, View. "Gazebo," Pip said, pointing at pagoda. "Nice skiing from there if you're not good. The hill goes down more gentle, then there's a field at the bottom so you can stop." I nodded. I'd been wondering about that, how you can stop. "See, this is a peninsula, then it's the Atlantic—you're looking at Portugal!" He was pleased with that.

"Oh," I said. "Well what are we waiting for? Let's ski to Portugal!"

He laughed. I sighed, and shivered, not wanting to be too bowled over. He flipped a wall switch that brought the wall back down, shutting off Portugal. "This way," he said. "Let's hurry, I am ravenacious."

I wasn't hungry at all. My jalapeño power plant was a long-range supplier. Which was handy, because it took a while to get where we were going. The floors were tiled. Our movements echoed. Storage rooms, mostly empty, lay between us and our destination. There was no chill, anywhere. Malcolm Spoor, I thought, is too much.

We reached pantrylands and butlerplaces. I began to smell kitchenny smells, and thought, This is it. It was:

Bursting into an industrial kitchen, I saw Torrance, white-aproned, in the middle of vast overlapping messes, the boy was *cooking;* he said, quickly and quietly and nervously, "Oh, hi."

And a Creature was rising from a big armchair at the far edges of mess.

Dear Diary, an apparition:

He wore a pale yellow suit, a white shirt, the tie was an odd dark blue; he was tall, and lean. The black hair was slicked back, the eyes were blue, and he was smiling a gentle, rueful smile; very like Montgomery Clift's. He said, "Sheila!"

I swooned. Not really. But sort of. The man was incredibly tanned, incredibly good-looking, and incredibly *sexy.* He had a cigarette in one hand and a glass in the other. He took a puff, exhaled gorgeously, smiled again, waved the glass at Torrance, who seemed sullen and brattish, and said:

"Torrance is preparing a simply magnificent multicourse dinner, may I get you something to drink? Pip, please help Sheila with her coat. There's a good fellow. Oh, my—Sheila, you are devastating."

VA-VOOOOOM. I concealed all symptoms of valve malfunction deep in the jalapeño reactor and strode across the room and stuck out my hand in a businesslike manner and said, "Sheila Massif, pleased to meet you in person."

He shook my hand with a warm, dry, sexy hand with tiny gleaming hairs on long tanned fingers, and said, "I, also, am pleased to meet you, Sheila. In person." His voice was magnetically husky. His eyes sparkled good humor and generosity and wit; and deep, caring intelligence; and nurturant sensitivity; and tender vulnerability.

"Let's see," I said, calculating my first lie, but sparklingly, like those woman who put personals in the backs of cultured magazines, dreaming of men exactly like Malcolm Spoor, "I only had two drinks in that jouncy truck."

"Two?" he said, mock-aghast. "That's horrifying. Pip, what has happened to your manners, get this goddess a drink!"

"Yes, Malcolm," Pip said, lurching away. Torrance, meantime, was sneering. It seemed to me that children should not disrupt the dinner parties of cosmopolitan adults. They do not comport themselves sparklingly. They always sneer. They're selfish. They get in the way!

I did, I'm afraid, think those thoughts.

"Does Pip know what you're drinking?" Malcolm inquired.

"Chivas," Pip said to Torrance, who was helping.

"Good evening, Torrance," I said.

"Hi," he said, staring at me thoughtfully, the sneer fading. For a second he looked desperate. I reminded myself: Something Is Going On.

Pip returned with an undericed highball glass. "That's a good start," I said. "Cheers."

"Cheers!" Malcolm said, and finished off his. "Oh, Pip!" But Pip already was lurching.

Torrance raised a coffee cup and said, snidely, "Cheers."

"A truly world-class chef," Malcolm confided to me, glancing at Torrance, "is like a brain surgeon . . ."

"Yeah," Torrance blurted, "I'm cookin' pig-brains!"

"Ha-ha, Torrance." Malcolm chuckled. "What I mean to say, Sheila, is that such a chef must concentrate, undistracted by chattering spectators. Isn't that so, Torrance?"

"Dad." Torrance sighed explosively. "Get *out,* please."

"You see?" Malcolm beamed at me. "The chef must create unencumbered. Thank you, Pip." He took his drink. I caught a whiff of pricey bourbon. "Therefore, Sheila, I suggest we withdraw. Shall I show you around? Or do you find that tours are tedious?"

"Oh," I said, "infinitely. Tedious."

"Splendid!" Malcolm exclaimed. "I quite agree. We'll move quickly, eyes focused straight ahead and nowhere else, and all will be a mercifully brief blur, until we get someplace where we can sit, and relax."

"Better still," I declared, "Pip should blindfold us, Malcolm, and lead us to that place! We will avoid seeing anything at all!"

He laughed. He seemed to think that was funny. Suddenly, I liked him. I discovered myself liking Malcolm Spoor!

Torrance was glaring.

"Come on." Malcolm laughed. "The Chef is about to throw knives."

He took my arm and we moved through swinging doors into a huge room that turned out to be the antechamber of a huger dining room, off which, through high open doors, were yet huger and stupider and very opulent rooms. My whole apartment would fit into one of those pantries out back, I thought.

"I think he's jealous," Malcolm was saying, "he adores you, you know."

"He's a sweetie," I said. "But he does seem a touch moody tonight." The paintings were hung five-high to the ceilings. Archipelagoes of Rooms glimmered endlessly through Doorways. I felt slightly sick. What is this man doing to me? Why is he attractive? So attractive? What's wrong with him? Something had to be wrong with this guy.

He was much too perfect, and much too *rich.* My Mission was expanding like the War on Drugs. I sensed: quagmire.

"Well I think he's just a bit over his head in there," Malcolm said. "He's trying very hard to impress us, you see."

"I see," I said, glancing at a ballroom that also seemed to be trying very hard to impress, and was doing a pretty good job despite the fact that I had no idea what one does with such a room if the household numbers three, plus dogs. Maybe the dogs waltz. On their hind legs, paws over the partner-dog shoulders, staring into each others' bedroom-red eyes . . .

"It is big," Malcolm was saying, "the house, but it comforts me.

My family goes back, Sheila; and sometimes," he added testily, as if regretfully, "I think I live in the past." We entered a cozy, forty-foot room where sofas, settees and chairs were clustered like families: Mama Sofas, Papa Sofas, Little Sofas. The place where we would sit and relax was a library. The orderly texture of its leather-crammed shelves made me wonder if the books were fake. A fireplace was a towering inferno. A wall of glass doors, dramatically draped, reflected the blaze. Covered with snow, the glass gave off no chill. At the very tops there was evidence of open air; it looked like trucks had backed up and poured cement. "Come," Malcolm said, "let's sit by the fire. 'The storm of the century!' Somebody said that on the news. Enchanting, don't you think?"

"As long as it stays outside," I said. He sat and I sat and the fire said, "It will stay outside." He crossed a well-creased, pale-yellow leg. The sock was the same dark blue as the tie: fifties Kodacolor. This man wore the tints of a stupendously refined Italian or South American whose family "goes back." Goes back to what?

"Tell me, Malcolm," I said, "about your family."

"Don't get me started," he said, laughing. You raised the subject, I thought. He leaned forward and stared at me. He seemed to study my neck, then my hands. He looked at my legs. I began to feel rather closely sized up. This wasn't an unpleasant experience. His gaze shifted to my breasts. I wondered, in the humming Chamber, if I should blush. Should I raise my eyebrows ever so faintly? Or delicately clear my throat? The man's eyes were undressing me. Inside, the drug fizzed. I was flustered; I felt radiantly naked. All this attention for little old me?

"How old are you?" he asked.

What a surprising question. I said, "Twenty-six. And you?"

"Forty-seven," he said. "Much too old."

Much too old? "For what," I said, "could the age of forty-seven be much too old, Malcolm? That's a wonderful age to be."

"You're not drinking," he chided, so I sipped. "Oh, I don't know. I feel old, Sheila. I'm one of those Peter Pans, I suppose. Kicking and screaming at my own fading youth."

Ah yes, I thought. Screaming. "But there's nothing to be done," I said. "This happens. Besides, you seem fit. Do you exercise?"

"Are you joking? I loathe exercise."

"Then how do you do it?" I asked. "You look—thirty-nine. At most."

"Piffle," he said. "I could keel over tomorrow and probably will.

Genes, Sheila, genes are everything. One inherits the ability to maintain the illusion of youth. Does one not? Look at you. You're twenty-six, you say, but you look twenty. It's your genes, my dear. You have good genes."

"Don't be silly," I said. "To me, age twenty is ancient history. A galaxy that's long ago and far away."

He laughed. Oddly. A little creepily. Then he said, "You're only ten years older than Torrance."

"Yes," I said, puzzled.

"Do you find him attractive?"

"In what way," I said, "do you mean?"

"Sexually."

I stared at him. "No," I said.

"Really?" He was frowning.

"He's a boy," I said, alarmed.

"But yes," Malcolm said weirdly. "He's in love with you, Sheila."

"Ridiculous. Sixteen-year-olds don't know what love is."

"But he's homosexual, you see. Sad. My son, Sheila, is gay. I'm feeling . . . Sheila, I'm feeling unwell."

"You are?" I said. This was getting very strange. "What makes you think Torrance is gay?" Torrance? Gay? Uh-uh. No. Not gay.

He said, "His mother, Sheila—to her terrible shock—has caught him *in flagrante.* . . . More than once."

"Huh," I said. "That doesn't have to mean much of anything."

"No," he said morosely. "But, yes. And how I wish he were not! And how I wish I weren't feeling dizzy . . ." He slumped—not, suddenly, looking well. Not at all well. Too much to drink?

"Can I get you something?" I said.

"Torrance," he mumbled, "is gay."

"But if he is," I said, "why would he be in love with me?"

"Because he really . . . duddent wantoo be."

"What?" I said.

"*I* don't wantim tobee—gay! Beeooouuuteefulll boy." He sickly sighed.

"You're looking woozy, Malcolm."

"You could help . . ." he said.

I stared at him.

"You could help . . ." he said again.

I stood up. "Tell me, what do you need, medicine? Malcolm, what is the matter?"

"Don't wantim toobeee . . . gay . . . yoookud . . . helpim." He was about to fall out of his chair. "Juddink," he mumbled, "ov dee boieee yookudalve wid Torrr . . ."

"I beg your pardon?" The man's condition disturbed me. He didn't look like Montgomery Clift any more. He was beginning to look like a drunk George Hamilton—gross. Or a retarded Julio Iglesias—double gross. What on earth was *on his mind*? "I think I better get Pip," I said. "Maybe Pip can help."

"No!" Malcolm Spoor screamed. He smiled at me messily and said, "Shleea, yoo muszt marrreeee my boy Torrrrrr . . ." and he fell. Thunkingly. To the floor. His glass flew from his hand and shattered on the hearth.

His eyes, wide open, were as blank as the snow on the glass doors.

I thought: Why aren't I screaming?

And if I do, would anyone hear?

Malcolm Spoor lay spread-eagled in his expensive pale yellow suit on an expensive Persian carpet, in front of a snap-crackling fire.

And his mouth was guppying.

"Huh!" I said out loud. "An emergency!" I knelt to loosen his tie. He was breathing ok. He'd gotten sick and passed out. Why? A medical problem? He hadn't seemed drunk until about a minute before. People do not become drunk and pass out in one minute. It was a medical problem.

Yes, I was at the scene of a serious medical emergency.

I got up and trotted kitchenward, wondering if Torrance was about to become suddenly rich. At least there was the truck. We could rush the sick man to a hospital . . .

Then the lights went out. All of them. Every single one. Out.

I stopped trotting. I couldn't see anything.

There is darkness and there is darkness, but this was DARKNESS, total, unqualified, absolute *black*. I was in the middle of a huge, stupid, dead-black room. I realized I didn't know where any of the doors were. I was turning around to look for some trace of light, turning here, turning there, and my orientation, in the process, fell apart.

There were no reference points. Nothing! I thought: I should yell. Or scream. But then I thought: flashlight. In my purse. That Duane, psychic Duane, had given me. The ray gun. I needed my ray gun. Because what if I started hearing dogs running around in the darkness? The purse was in the library. But where was that? I said out loud, "Stay calm."

The library wasn't very far away. Malcolm probably was dying there while I stood foolishly paralyzed in inky dark. So I filled my lungs and was about to yell HELP when I saw it: a faint, ruddy flicker.

A dog.

This is hard to swallow now. It damages my self-esteem. At least I am not the only person in the world who is phobic about large dogs; phobic being a polite way to put it.

So I have something in common with Torrance's mother. She, I knew from the misdirected letter, "hates big dogs." Brava! She admits it! I am not alone. But, in that black room, I was alone; alone, that is, with a faint red flicker in the distance that was, of course, the weaving eyes of a large and slavering dog that wanted to *eat me.*

So, I did the natural survivalist thing. I froze. For about twelve minutes. I went deep, deep in the suddenly lifeless Drama Chamber, my hands clapped over my eyes. Trying not to sob. This protects one from dog-attack, of course. If you can't see them, they can't see you. But every time I unclapped my eyes to look, I saw—more red flickers in the distance.

The pack was gloating at me. They could smell my fear!

But no.

The flickers weren't dogs. They were the fire. They were on a shiny lacquered something that was reflecting the library's lively flames.

I got on my hands and knees and crawled for the flicker. I was staying calm. My nuclear tranquility was seeing me through. I had to get that ray gun. I had to get it because I had to vaporize dogs, every one of them, to death. If at all possible, I also had to help Malcolm. But how could I help him if I were being savaged by dogs that definitely were out there somewhere? I praised my cogent thinking as I crawled, over chilly marble and soft carpet, to My Friend Flicker.

On the way I bumped into chairs and tables, I hit horribly plush drapes, and I was hating that house. If the firewood was running low in the library when I got there, I was going to toss in Rembrandts and Goyas and all the Van Goghs. If there were any to be found and I was sure there were.

The firelight got brighter. I stood, and walked around the corner into the library, aching for my purse and the flashlight within, and saw:

That Malcolm was gone.

I screamed.

"Hey!" It came from the dark mass of a couch well away from the fire. "Sheila! Hey, take it easy!"

"Torrance?" I quavered.

"Yeah! Over here! Wow, Dad passed out, Sheila. That's a shame!"

"Torrance," I said, collecting purse and heading for couch, "what is going on? How did you get here?"

"Pip calls it 'Butler's Passage.' Just another way around."

"Where is Pip? Your father might be seriously . . ."

"Nah," Torrance said. I could see him now. He was sitting on the floor, back to the couch, munching an apple. On the couch lay inert Malcolm. "Dad's fine, Sheila." The voice, I realized, was gleeful.

"And Pip?" I said sharply.

"In the basement," Torrance said. "He went down to try to fix the fuses. Ha-ha! The fuses! Ha!" The laughter was barklike.

"What's so funny, Torrance?"

"Everything," he said. "You were just a second ago. When you yelled like a struck pig."

"What is the matter with your father?"

The fire danced in Torrance's eyes. He looked like a young, elated ghoul. "He is resting comfortably. He'll wake up in the morning thinking he drank too much. Again."

"All right, Torrance," I said. "What are you doing?"

"I think," he said, "I'm saving my life."

I sat on an oversize pincushion and said, "Explain."

"No," he said infuriatingly. "I'll show you. As soon as I finish my apple since dinner's, uh, delayed."

"What did you do to your father?"

"Spiked his bottle."

"With what?"

"My step-Dad," he said, "is a doctor. A psychiatrist." I knew it! I knew he grew up with shrinks, from the way he'd said "psycho-lingo" in class and from the way he's fiercely calm. Everything became terribly clear: only the stepson of a psychiatrist could have done this to his father. "He prescribes drugs," Torrance went on. "Lots of 'em. I keep a couple form pads handy. For emergencies"—munch, munch—"like now, Sheila."

"Ok," I said. "I buy it. What about Pip? He'll be coming up any time to throw you to the dogs, Torrance."

"Ha-ha!" Torrance barked. "No. He won't. Sides. The dogs like me."

"Great. That's just great. Just great. What did you do to Pip?"

"The fuse room in the basement has a tricky metal bar in front. It can come swinging down, if it's not latched right. And the door, it's metal, and heavy, it tends to swing closed, see? Then, if the metal bar swings down . . . Clang! Like a jail. Get the picture? Pip goes in the room, the door swings shut, and then, clang. Simple. No way out. Even for Pip. Sheila, the door is solid metal. Like if there was a fire or something."

"Are you sure this is what happened?"

"Positive. I checked. Really quiet. So he doesn't know I know. That would be too bad, if he knew that I know. Or if he knew that *you* know. And you will see why. When I show you—why."

I said, "You think you're going to get away with this?"

"I know I am." He rattled something in his hand. "Lookit. Keys. Upstairs, there are locked-up rooms. These open 'em. All of them, and then you will see."

I sighed. "Torrance, I'm sorry, but we will go downstairs and liberate Pip, and then he, and I, and you will drive your father straight to a hospital. As fast as is safe and possible!"

"You're dreaming," Torrance said.

I turned on the flashlight, directly in his face. He blinked; I said, "I am going to a telephone and *calling the police.*"

"Good luck," he said, a hand shielding his eyes. "The phones don't work too good. As a matter of fact they are totally dead."

"I am on my way to the basement, Torrance."

"Good luck," he said. "The doors to the basement are electric. For security. And now, they are shut. And the electricity is off."

"I am on my way to the truck, Torrance."

"Good luck," he said.

Right. The "electricity is off." And the moving wall of the hangar weighs about forty tons. "You," he said, "are trapped. But it could be worse. At least you are trapped with me." He jerked a thumb over his shoulder at his father. "Not him."

Photocopy Fragment
From Duane Allbright's
Research Findings

Monday Morning

[*Photocopy:*]

[. . .] a dashing roué who won and broke the hearts of a succession of famous society beauties. Some called him decadent. Others called him evil, a gifted tormentor of women. But the preponderance of the evidence indicates his animus was not flesh. Many contemporaries and acquaintances agree that his paramount desire was honorable, quintessentially so: he wanted an heir. A son was what he wanted, a son! This view suggests he divorced wives one through three because they proved to be barren (or he infertile, a possibility that, some observers maintain, very nearly drove him mad).

Wife number four, however, the raven-haired debutante Lolly Gleason, did conceive. She grew heavy with child, to the extreme joy of us all. I must say we also were very relieved.

Disaster ensued, alas. She delivered a stillborn. Two in fact, twins, a boy and a girl.

This was a terrific blow. Perhaps it was the final blow.

He was inconsolable. The fact he had been unable to recoup financial setbacks brought on by the Crash did not help matters. He held title to the ancestral lands, but these for the most part were in German-occupied countries. Indeed, three of the Chateaux served as headquarters for various military officials. By his standards he had become quite poor: utterly *déraciné*. A never-ending source of anguish!

Unkind gossip exacerbated these difficulties throughout the mid-forties. It was the opinion of many in his circles that he had no business being in New York, puttering endlessly with horticulture, dog breeding, spending too much time with that dour valet, Phipps. Why, these scolds demanded, wasn't he at war? Wasn't this his duty? A question of particular honor, given the obligations of his forebears?

Thus it was not only grief, but ostracism too, that drove him from New York in September of 1943. Young wife Lolly did not accompany him on this exile-from-exile. She suffered a nervous collapse and was institutionalized; never, sadly, to recover. (Lolly died brokenhearted at the age of twenty-two, one year later. It is said that toward the end she lapsed into a delusional state concerning her marital fortunes. "Where," she would inquire, "is my darling husband?" The nurses were too kind to tell her what she should have remembered. That she had failed, that he had left her.)

The Baron went abroad, to Central and South America.

He was to spend the last year of his life there looking for a young man whom he had reason to believe might be his own flesh and blood; a "natural" product, he hypothesized, rather bizarrely we all thought, of a brief affair he had had in 1917, at the precocious age of fourteen (the *rascal*), with the daughter of a French diplomat then posted to Lima, and later Tegucigalpa.

The Baron's reasoning did seem strange, quite mad in fact, to his few remaining friends, including, it must be admitted, the author. He had the most evanescent of evidence to justify this search for issue (any male issue at all it seemed would do). The opinion was formed that he finally had lost his mind, out of despair at the prospect of his name's extinction—a noble name, that had endured centuries of tumult only now to disappear, it seemed certain, in the spasm of boorishness we call the Twentieth Century.

There was a method in his madness, of course. We should have known it. Deep down, perhaps, we did (those of us that is who still kept faith, however sorely tried). Indefatigably, the Baron established a number of facts. A bastard boy had been born to Eugenie de Swett, age seventeen, in Tegucigalpa, in 1929 (a very bad year for the Baron in more ways than one, as those unfamiliar with the tragedy shortly shall learn). The child was healthy, and had been given up for adoption (scant surprise), and had been reared gently, or semigently, by the proprietor of a remote estate in the Argentinean Pampas. The Baron furthermore learned that the boy, a handsome creature, resembled him strongly; this he was told by the crone who ran the adoption hostel where the infant languished parentless until the age of two (no doubt to very ill effect).

He immediately flew to Buenos Aires.

What delight he must have felt when his Daimler finally arrived at the estate after a gruelingly dusty four-day journey. For, so the story goes, he beheld, indeed recognized, a lad on horseback, galloping about a distant field; playing high-spirited polo with a gang of local bare-chested bucks.

He knew a Spoor when he saw one. He saw his son.

There was no question. Twenty-four-year-old Felipe de Garanzagga y Krump, né de Swett (in a manner of speaking), was the long-sought answer to his prayers.

Naturally there were legal problems.

Unfortunately, he solved them.

Alas, alas! The ungrateful Felipe was to be his undoing!

This I shall prove in the following, contrary to the findings of what is speciously called "Justice."

Hear me out, all who read what I say.

I say a murderer walks free!

J'Accuse:

Gainsborough, Twenty-fourth Baron Spoor, died by the hand of his son Felipe, now the Wrongful Twenty-fifth; by the hand of a boy whom he rescued from obscurity and made his sole heir; by the hand of a grasping killer known to his knavish intimates and defenders as: Bunny.

From the Author's Foreword to:
Dear Gainsborough—Rascal Baron!
—An Inquiry Into His Curious Death—
By Emil Hoggshead   Published Privately, Palm Beach, 1949

Paydirt. I wasted time last week researching Malcolm. I should have looked at the genealogy instead.

Baron Bunny was Malcolm's father. According to Emil, he shot and killed Malcolm's grandfather, Gainsborough. Murder. Well I bet it was.

I would have photocopied more but the lady behind the desk followed me downstairs to the machine. She told me I couldn't do it because the spine's cracking. A musty book that nobody's ever taken out even once is some kind of treasure. I thought about stealing it after she marched me back up to the reading room that's grand enough to be a railway station. But Widener searches bags. Should have put it in my coat.

Now I'm across the street eating onion rings. In disguise, and nervous about it. Keeping an eye out for Project people, the purple hat. Trying to make sense of what I've dug up.

Funny, the way Spoors die. Even funnier the way they transfer money & property & title right before they kick the bucket. And scary as hell.

For example, the way Emil's friend Gainsborough died, when "Bunny" shot him. That was funny. So did Bunny die funny. He supposedly shot himself at the age of forty-four, orphaning Malcolm. Same with Gainsborough's dad Francis, when a dog spooked his horse and he got trampled to a pulp. Francis was Torrance's great-great-grandfather. And Hippolyte, and Blake and Persiflage and Fennel, all those Barons going back—all the way back, it seems, to a "fair knight" named Gundulf—they all died the weirdest deaths.

Torrance will be the twenty-seventh Baron Spoor. It's a long line. Now that I know about Gainsborough's desperate search for a son, and the obsession Spoors always had with heirs in general, I'm beginning to see Saturday in a different light.

For example, Malcolm's idea that Sheila might make a good mother.

I think Malcolm had more to do with what happened on Saturday than any of us could have imagined. Damn coffee's spilling right out of my cup.

The Diary
of Sheila Massif: IX

Monday Morning

Duane didn't come back from Cambridge last night. He didn't even call. He's being spooky, as usual. More, later, on Duane. I've been thinking it over. He's almost as much of a riddle as Malcolm.

No. I take that back.

———

Torrance and I and drugged Malcolm were in the dark library. The boy finished his apple and threw it at the fire. A long shot, but the core hit a bull's-eye and bright-orange logs sparked and sagged. He stood up.

And I saw a pistol jammed in his waistband.

"You," I said, "are crazy."

He said, "You would be too."

The gun, his earnestness, scared me. Evidently I was the only adult able to exert any influence on this deranged child. I had to use that influence to best advantage. Otherwise, I would go down in history as She Who Bungled It. I stalked to the fire and dragged the heavy screen in place and said, "Honestly! The house could have burned down!"

Torrance laughed.

I looked at him with the far-gazing serenity of the Statue of Liberty and screeched, "You little bastard, I'm going to break your neck!"

That's how I kicked off my coolheaded attempt at crisis control.

He sauntered over. He's bigger than me, or taller, anyway, and he was dressed in jeans and a tie-dyed psychedelic T-shirt. "Where's your apron, Chef?" I snapped, casting an eye at iron fire pokers. I could try bludgeoning him to death, I thought. That would tidy up this mess.

"Sheila," he said, "I think you better calm down. 'Cause if I'm right, you are gonna get shocked pretty soon."

"Fabulous!" I shouted. "I hope I'm electrocuted!"

"Electricity's off," he pointed out. "Let's go upstairs. Ok?"

"Torrance," I said tremulously, "I want to know why you have a gun."

"In case things fell out of my hands," he said, "you know, went cuckoo, like if the drug didn't work and Dad flipped and called in the dogs . . ."

"What?" I said.

"The dogs."

"You said they like you."

"Not when Dad says: 'Eat Torrance.' " He frowned. "That would be bad news, Sheila."

"Yes," I said. "But Dad can't say that now. Can he? No, he's passed out—he can't say 'Eat Torrance' to the dogs . . ." I looked at the situation from all angles. "You better keep the gun. Do you know how to use it?"

"Yes," he said.

"Do you know how to fire it with great speed and accuracy?"

"I was La Jolla champ," he said.

"Excellent," I said. "Just in case 'things fall out of our hands.' Torrance, where are the dogs?"

"You're scareda dogs!" he exclaimed.

"I adore animals," I said.

"You wouldn't adore these animals," he said. "Nope. You wouldn't. They have red eyes and they are—giguntic."

"Ok, ok," I said, "let's change the subject. What is upstairs?"

"*Dogs,*" he growled. "No, they're in the kennels. Locked-up kennels in the basement. But—upstairs?" He shook the clip of keys. "I don't know. Maybe the bunny, huh? Let's find out."

"You mean you went to all this—and—and—you don't even know . . . ?"

He bounded to the distant couch and said to now-snoring Malcolm, "Dear Old Dad! Alas, alas, I know the sucker much too well." Then he stooped and picked up something and came back carrying a small, full backpack.

"What's in that?" I said.

"You'll see," he said. "Come on."

The firelit face was determined. I saw resemblance to his father: a teen Clift, fiercely calm. The shoulders were militant. Psychedelically militant—the T-shirt gave him a savior faire which the apron, earlier, hadn't. He somehow seemed competent. He was fully prepared to shoot vicious, roaming dogs if they chewed their way out of the kennels.

"Come on," he said. "We're wasting time."

"Wait a second," I said, "I've got to change microcassettes." I sat, fumbled open the purse and, under flashlight's white flood, did it. "For a sociology project," I explained, shutting purse and standing. "Let's go."

"I don't even want to know." Torrance sighed. "Follow me."

He turned into the dark. I put my torch on his back and followed. He had a flashlight, too. His beam swept the cavernous spaces ahead, my beam stayed on that molten patch of exploding blue-green. His beam manufactured myriad objets d'art and details of paintings; my beam occasionally dipped to his hard, round butt. By happenstance, of course. The movement.

"Get that off my ass!" he yelled as we were going up the blacked-out main stairs of the Bolshoi Ballet.

"Just keeping you in sight, dumbo," I hissed.

"You like?" he quipped, pausing suddenly to shimmy, expertly.

"Move it, sugar-tush," I grunted, "I'm getting a hard-on."

"Ha-ha!" Torrance shouted, leaping up. "Get used to it, Sheila!"

"Please don't go psycho on me now, Torrance," I panted, stumbling up after him and clutching at the wide marble—banister? What did he mean, "get used to it"?

"Relax," he called over his shoulder from the depths of a landing, "the psycho one's snoring his head off."

I reached the second floor. Torrance was waiting. "Out of shape," he observed. We went down one wide hall, then another. The establishment rambles. And it was cooling. Ghost-white busts on pedestals were watching us closely. They were stoic but disapproving about the coming chill.

"What's the heating bill for this joint?" I asked.

"Trillions," he said. He stopped at a door. We'd passed many doors in that high-ceilinged hallway. I was getting into the spirit of things. I had my mission, too. So what if Commando Boy was calling the shots?

I wanted to know what was in those locked-up rooms.

"Is this going to be kinky?" I said.

"Definitely." He was trying keys. "Dad holes up in here for hours. He calls it his 'office.' I never go in or see in, he makes sure I don't. I don't think he even lets Pip go in . . ." The lock turned. "Stand back," he said. "It might be booby-trapped."

"That's not a kennel by any chance?" I said. "Put the gun in your hand and point it." I was steadfastly floodlighting but the knees felt shaky.

He pulled out the gun; a good move anyway, what if it fired by accident and shot off his tender manhoodisms? Then he turned the knob, stepped aside and kicked. The door swung open. He peered with flash and said, "Another door. But, no lock. This is like Columbo. I'm going in."

"Be careful," I squealed.

"You're such a girl," he said, and edged in and was gone.

I heard a strangulating boyish scream.

"EEEEEEEEK!" I yelled, lungpower fullthrottled. The darkness vibrated, the white busts babbled aristocratic fright. My body fell, the hallway swooped blackly and my flash rolled away, strobing insanely the pedestals and parquet and wall.

"Just kidding," Torrance called. "Come in."

I got up, with flash, and said, "I am going to kill you."

"Sorry," the voice said nervously. "That was mean and Sheila—I'm scared, too, so—I'm sorry. But get in here. You won't believe this."

I went in. Beyond the second door—which obviously is just a screen against the outer door's opening and closing—was a windowless television studio.

The studio is maybe fourteen feet square. My flash and the boy's zigzagged and crossed swords around it. Sixteen monitors, big, make a four-by-four bank in one wall. Facing these monitors is a desk with computer keyboards and headphones on it. Side tables support video equipment, a ton of it, many fancy machines. And there's a shelf filled with videocassette boxes, larger than the usual home-user size.

Finally, nailed to the walls, are a bunch of photographs and reproductions of paintings. The subjects are eccentric, rich-looking men. They appeared to have been ripped from books. More on them, later.

"Torrance," I said, my relief that he hadn't been eaten now curdling my stomach, "your father is a video nut. And why shouldn't he be a video nut?"

He said, "Lock the door, ok?"

"Why?" I said.

"So cameras won't see it's open," he said. "There's knobs on the inside for locking; forget it, I'll do it." He went to the doors.

An antenna stuck out of his backpack. "What's this?" I said, stabbing with torch.

"Power," he said, coming back.

I didn't understand and said so.

He said, "I messed with the power trunk that comes from the road to the house. Today when Pip and me went shopping I made him stop at a couple places, and got this while he stayed in the car. It's just a radio. But it controls another thing I bought that I put on top of the power pole on the road. That thing screws our power, electrically, simple, on-off and now I hope off-on, if the snow didn't crash branches on the line by now. Tomorrow I will climb up the pole again and take the thing off and Dad and Pip will think the blackout was because of the storm, right?"

"Huh," I said. "Why didn't you try turning on power downstairs?"

" 'Cause of cameras." He flashlit the monitors accusingly. "Dad's not a video nut. He's a *snoop* nut. He's got cameras all over this house. And if the power's on, the cameras might be taping everything we been doing."

"It's a security system," I said.

"Yeah!" Torrance said. "Sure it is." He sat next to the backpack and folded his hands and closed his eyes. He was praying. Then he pressed buttons. Little lights blinked. He flipped a switch and pressed buttons as though telegraphing a very short message.

Nothing happened. He muttered, "Fuck."

But then he said, "Oh!" He painted the walls near the door with his flash. The beam hit a wall switch and stopped. "Want to try it?" he asked.

"What the hell," I said. I walked to the switch and slapped. I felt like slapping something . . .

The room blew up with light. Our faces scrunched. "The whole house is on," he said breathlessly. "Wow."

I unlocked the inner door. "No!" he shouted.

I didn't turn around. I didn't want to see him pointing the gun. "You're a genius," I said, hand on the knob. "But I'm not wild about the idea of going to jail." I realized I was furious.

"Please," he said. "Please don't go out." His voice was breaking.

I turned around. Torrance, cross-legged on the floor, torso pitched forward, had a fist pressed to the floor. He'd been pounding. He was shaking. Licks of black hair were quivering.

The gun was on the desk.

I said, "You have ten minutes to prove this is worth it. And put that gun away. I don't want to see it again, all right?"

"Thank you," he moaned. I felt bad. I felt complexly curdled. His hand trembled as he put the gun in the backpack. A second later he was tossing a tube. It was a sheaf of paper, rolled up and rubber-banded. It fell at my feet. "Read that," he said. "Just fast, if you want." He stood. "I have to see how to turn on the system, won't take long." He stared at the shelf that holds videocassettes. "Ten minutes," he muttered, "shit . . ."

I picked up the tube, fribbered off the rubber band. The thing flopped open and I saw these words: "The Villa Spoor. My Dear Boy Torrance . . ."

"A letter," I said.

"From Dad. Hey—*wow.*" He was gesturing at the pictures nailed to the walls.

"Now what?" I asked.

"These guys are all Spoors," he said. "My ancestors. The old barons."

"Yeah?" I said, seeing foppery in the various poses. "So?"

"Dad talks about them in that letter. He said they all killed themselves. Or just died weird deaths. Sheila, he said there's this curse . . ."

"Oh yeah, the curse," I said, peering at a buffoon wearing seventy pounds of frocks and ribbons and feathers. He was sailing his horse over a fence. THE BARON GIVES CHASE, read the caption. "They probably all broke their necks," I said, "foxhunting. What a ridiculous hat."

"If you ask me, it's creepy," Torrance muttered, moving along and squinting at pictures. "Oh my God! Check it out, this one's named—I can't believe it—*Bunny!*" He was gaping at an old tabloid newspaper. It was yellowed and crumbly. The whole paper, thick, was nailed to the wall.

"So he is," I agreed, taking a look. This gentleman seemed to have run afoul of the law. I said, "Bunny's in the can there, Torrance. That's a police mug shot." He looked like a young criminal type. The caption was sensationally worded. "Felipe was his real name," I observed, "so 'Bunny' was his wise-guy nickname, I guess. They got him for . . ."

"Shooting his father," Torrance whispered.

"Don't get any ideas, kid," I said, a little alarmed. "By the way, you now have seven minutes."

"Wait a second! This is like—evidence! Sheila, he's the Bunny!"

"Sure," I said. "Your father must be bothered by it. By Bunny's— I don't know—blotch on your family's escutcheon? Or something."

Torrance scowled at me. I wasn't about to let him make Bunny into a big ordeal. I wanted real dirt, if we could find it. If we couldn't, I wanted to wrap this up fast.

He moved to the desk and started flipping computer switches. The monitors went snowy; scenes from the great outdoors? I sat on the floor and scanned the letter. It is loony and sinister in all kinds of ways. It raves about suicides, and a Curse. But it did not strike me as criminal. I resumed an activity I'd been tending all along—inventing high-tensile alibis.

Meantime the monitors flashed vignettes of the house tour Malcolm and I hadn't taken. New views jerked into the matrix as Torrance pressed buttons. I kept thinking, a security system. Malcolm can afford it. Every mansion needs one. You can't be too careful in this day and age . . .

"There!" Torrance said, shakily triumphant. "The top eight, Sheila."

"Yeah?" I said.

"Left to right," he said, "my bedroom, my bedroom, my bedroom, my dressing room, my dressing room, my bathroom, my bathroom, my *bathroom,* God *damn.*" He was having a fit. "God damn the *fuckface staring at me!*"

Nausea spiraled through my stomach.

Torrance was not fiercely calm. No, I thought, he's all shook up. "How long have you known about that?" I asked.

"Yesterday," he said, "shit, damn, sorry, only yesterday. The cameras, they are hidden, better than the CIA could do, unbelievable how hidden and *covered up* . . ."

"Torrance," I said, "that is extremely strange."

"Yeah," he muttered. "Get a load of this." He was fooling with a computer mouse and buttons. The screens zoomed. Images of his bed enlarged. Images of his tub went blank in the dried-up pond. Images of his toilet hit gleam-rimmed water.

The implications—yes. My curdlings suddenly felt sick. Malcolm, I thought, is a parent with—*no respect for boundaries!* He's the ultimate parental intruder! Yow! It upset me more than I wanted to let on. A *lot* more. I said, lamely, "You keep a neat room."

"I have to clean," he snarled. "Or Pip would, he's a clean-queen. I told him not to feel like he has to come in and clean. But he did anyway. So now *I* clean." He wiped his eyes. "Dad even watches me clean."

"Some parents," I said idiotically, "have a need, uh, to pry . . . Torrance—are you sure you found out about this yesterday?"

"Yeah," he said, incredulous, "you kidding, think I'd still be here? Sheila, I'm getting out."

"Hmmm," I said. "But—how do you know . . . ahem. How do you know how to work those controls? Don't get me wrong . . ."

"User friendly," he sneered. "Dad isn't hi-tech trained. The buttons and functions are marked, look, labels. He's got buttons for the pool, for the changing room and shower at the pool, buttons for everything, for the dining room, the gym upstairs, all the places I do things. Don't you see? This is to get me. This whole house is to spy on me, Sheila, God damn him . . ."

"That might be going a little far," I said. There had to be some other reason for this setup. "Security, Torrance, is a legitimate . . ."

"Bullshit!" he said. "Bullshit," he repeated more quietly, moving to the videocassettes. "Ha! Lookit this. I can prove it, look."

I looked. The gray plastic boxes were labeled. And on most of the labels was a "T"; a T, followed by a dash and a second word: T-Dinner, T-Gym, T-Swim, T-Room, T-Bath, T-Dress; and: T-Sex.

I thought: Tyrannosaurus Sex. T-Sex?

There were three or four boxes for each category except one, the T-Sex one. "I'll ice-pickim to death," Torrance whispered. "Now."

"Please don't do that," I said.

"Then I'm leaving here with you."

"Oh, Torrance," I said. "I don't know . . ."

"How much I gotta prove? How much? The guy's sick. He could do anything. Anything!"

"Maybe he's making home movies because he'll miss you," I said. I didn't believe that. Why did I say it?

"Of me taking shits? And then there's the rose room." He darted to the desk, stared, and pushed a button. A greenhouse filled a screen. "Crazy," he said, glowering at what looked like roses: many, many roses. "He's crazy. You have to read the letter. Did you read it?"

Sensory overload. I didn't have anything to say.

"You gotta read it!" he yelled. He went to the shelf and extracted T-Sex. "And what do you think *this* is?"

I shrugged. Malcolm was beginning to frighten me badly. "Torrance," I said, "telephone your mother and tell her to take you away from here . . ."

"No, I can't!" he said, dropping the videocassette. It slapped the floor. The sound punctuated his exclamation. He stared at the gray box, distraught; and stammered, "He'd blackmail me—for sure."

"Oh my God," I said, "you poor kid, what on earth, blackmail you, look, you're upset but you're going to ex . . ." I stopped talking because the word "blackmail" was spinning, vividly, up and down my spine.

"What's the matter?" Torrance said, watching me move to the desk.

"I have to check, uh, something," I said, opening drawers. They were empty. Torrance paced back and forth, hugging himself, chewing his lips. I opened the big lower-right drawer, and gasped.

My handwriting was dancing on a large photograph.

"What is it?" Torrance sad.

"I just got fried," I said. I reached in, felt deeply for the bottom, and lifted the stack. The heavy, tall stack. A quick fan across the desk confirmed it: Malcolm's henchman Pip had taken pictures of my apartment. Of every square inch, of cooking utensils, makeup, shoes, the works; including, of course, the Diary. Monday and Wednesday: down to the very last word.

"Pip took those," Torrance said.

"My privacy," I said, "like yours, Torrance, you may or may not want to take comfort from this" —I took a deep breath—"has been *trampled,*" I screamed. "Where's the ice pick? Holy *shit!*"

"That's your place?" Torrance asked, shoving into my shoulder, a hot ear microwaving my neck. "Wow—it's a mess."

"Get away!" I shouted.

He got away, rubbing his ear. "I wonder why?"

"Blackmail," I snapped.

Torrance stared at me. I stared at him. We both saw sweat. "That makes two of us," he said. "What's your secret?"

"None of your business," I spat. "What's yours?" Nausea had liquefied my stomach. He looked at me; and said:

"Forget it. You even got a tape machine going. I don't trust you. I don't trust anybody, not nobody! You freak when you see he's spying on you. You don't care that he spies on me. You don't care that he has eight cameras watching me when I'm supposed to be alone in my own room and bathroom. All you care about is that he spies on you. And I am so wicked *scared* . . ."

I was, too. Then I remembered. Part of this mission was supposed to be looking out for Torrance. I walked to him and said, "I'm sorry." And I hugged him.

His heart thumped through the T-shirt. My heart thumped back. He hugged me and we stood there, hugging, for a whole minute. His head fell on my shoulder. My neck got wet. I felt my own tears slipping on his chest. Inside, I welled what I'd been trying not to well, a maternal affection for this kid; I'd been so angry that he'd been needing me; now I understood how much he needed me, or someone, and I was the only one; I suddenly felt willing; even though I am not his mother; nor the teenage girl against whose hip his stiffening cock should have been pressing; but I didn't care. This wasn't sex. It was solidarity. If he couldn't help getting hard, so what? Plastering bodies with me would get any boy hard. I whispered, "Steady as she goes, kiddo, we'll deal with it." He sighed. I whispered, "And your father for some reason thinks you're gay."

He said to my collarbone, "I am."

I said to his fuzzy-wuzzy cheek, "You're kidding."

He sighed into my hair. "No, I'm not."

I said, "Torrance . . ."

He said, "I don't know what is the matter with me with you. I never had sex with a girl in my life."

"Huh," I said, astounded, and strangely relieved, and mildly annoyed, but most of all I was astounded. The hugging got slippier. The hardness against my hip got harder.

"Think I should try?" he asked.

"Well, sure, I mean, I guess, you should," I said, noticing that I was patting his oddly sexy back and then noticing that he was kissing my neck. "Torrance," I said, "stop."

"Ok," he said. We held each others' elbows, leaned back and gazed. His wet eyes met mine. "That's my secret, Sheila," he said. "If my mother found out she'd die."

I squeezed an elbow and disengaged. "Gay kids," I said, "always think their mothers will die. But you might not be gay. Ever think of that?"

He wiped his eyes and crossed arms over that crisp, solid chest. The bulge down his leg didn't look gay to me. He saw me staring and laughed. "Nice, huh?" he inquired.

"Torrance," I said, "what you do with it counts most."

"Yeah," he said, "I know." He glanced at the cassette on the floor.

My God, I thought, leaning on the desk and crossing my arms. Both of us had arms crossed. Not a good sign, I thought. "What could your father have taped," I asked, "that your mother wouldn't want to see? I mean—is that the blackmail material? Or what?"

"Could be," he said, shuddering. "I get horny. I get off by myself. I do things . . . she wouldn't wanta see. Yeah: She'd freak."

"But," I said, "how would she . . . know? I mean, how could she tell?"

"Remember the first class?" he said. He was suddenly pink. "If girls can—uh, you know, uh, guys can, too." He frowned. "Kind of personal. Never thought I'd talk about this with anybody like a teacher. He looked away. "Mom would croak."

"Hmmmm . . ." I said. "You, uh, mean?"

"Yeah!" he blurted. "It's, like, normal! Except, Mom doesn't—"

"I hope you 'play safe,' as they say," I admonished, feeling fifty years old.

"While I'm getting off by myself?" he asked pointedly. "Listen. I know about sex, Sheila. I even got rubbers on me right now."

That's when I started feeling it. And smelling it—perfume. Where did it come from? The drug?

He winked. Then he said, "So what're we gonna do?"

"I don't really know," I said nervously, arms still crossed. His were, too. It meant something, this barricading of the chests.

"What's your blackmail problem?" he said. "Maybe I can help."

Fiercely calm Torrance, back again. It hit me: He's a sexpot; he's heterosexually virgin, but eager; he's very, very attractive; and we are masters of this blizzard-bound mansion, where secrets everywhere lie hidden, waiting for us, that lusty duo, Tom Swift and Nancy Drew. We didn't know what we were doing. But we were doing it.

"I'm not a teacher," I said. "I'm pretending to be one so I can gather data about sexual identity, Torrance. The terrible part is that I intend to get that data by asking my students to write about their fantasies. Not flat out directly, but still—it's a big no-no. At any school I can think of. Especially one with a Caspar McQuisling. It's all in my Diary."

"Aha," Torrance said. "That's great."

"It is?" I said.

"Yeah," he said. " 'Sexual identity,' that's cool." He sighed. "Kids should write about stuff like that . . ."

"Not going to happen," I said. "Not in my class, anyway."

We looked at each other. Then we looked at the videocassette on the floor, then at the stack of photos on the desk.

"Let's take it down to the fire," he said.

"What if he has copies?" I said, feeling doomed; and triply doomed because I couldn't stop looking for signs of disengorgement. There were no such signs. "Or if he has the negatives hidden somewhere?"

"I'm burning that tape no matter what," he said. "Can I kiss you now?"

"What?" I said.

He blushed. "I can't help it," he announced, glancing at his leg. "Sorry." The look he then gave me slayed me. The eyes were very green. They were serious. They were seriously sexy.

I cleared my throat and remarked, "You're kind of young."

"Try me," he said, uncrossing his arms. He leaned back, shoulders against the wall. The T-shirt hoisted. His navel stared. Jeans rimmed his waist, sagging slightly. The band of his underwear was flat on his stomach. His hands were splayed on the wall and his cock pressed through the denim like a piece of pipe. I looked him in the eyes. They were open, curious, frank.

I said, "Can we make sure your father hasn't revived?"

He knew what the question meant. It meant: "Let's get naked."

"Yeah!" he said, face flooding excitement. "Check him out on his own fucking system!" He stood straight, body taut—his whole body was suddenly *electroplated*. I trembled. No resistance: He was galvanic force.

"Ok," I said.

The grin blinded me. He flashed to the desk, bent over a keyboard, rapidly tapped it. I wrapped my arms around him. He yelped, then shoved his butt in my stomach. I wondered how many men, boys have felt this. Who cares? Woman Gonna Get That Butt—Now. It's the drug, I thought. The drug has put me *in heat.* My face was squashing into his back. My hand was reaching into his jeans. He moaned. He groaned. I heard him say, "Sheila, Dad's still out but somebody else is down there, *looking at him.*"

I jerked my nose from his back and craned around his goose-pimpling arm.

The miniature man in the monitor, examining Malcolm, was Duane.

"Duane," I said. "He's looking for me. He's ok. He might even know what to do." I'd nearly fainted, but was rallying. I was, as a matter of fact, unbuttoning the fly. Torrance said, "Whew." Then he said, "He'll never find us, let's do it."

I slid down, dragging jeans to his knees. His ass was green. Green underwear, smelling sweet like a field of warm summer flowers. I ripped it down: the ass of an angel. He whirled and his cock whoppered my face. His hands were in my hair, tugging. He was saying, "Wait, wait." His pubic hair is black. His cock is pink and the veins aren't blue, they're dense, buried cords. A pearl glistened. Cyclops, I thought. The pearl was an inch away: glistening, unsafe. I said, "I put condoms on with my mouth." He grunted a laugh. His jeans and underwear tangled his ankles. The thighs were pale. I squeezed one. The hard muscles were hot. "In my wallet," he said. "In my pants." I found it, tore foil, and did it. The rubbered Cyclops gorged me. Tasting latex fire, I thought of Malcolm: marry Torrance? How silly. Let's fuck.

He helped me undress and we went to work.

For a novice he was amazingly good. Then again, he wasn't really a novice. This, I told myself, is suicidal. But the tiny, hard nipples, the straining taper of his body, the green dare in his eyes as his lips dangled spit to my face, hot strands deliberately and deliciously painting my face—was just too . . . much . . . fun.

I had an exciting little fantasy—his ancestors are watching!

We were out of control when we heard the knock on the door.

Oh, God. This is the bad part. Diary, we heard loud knocks on the door. It took a few minutes to get our wits in order.

It took two or three very long minutes, because he discovered that the condom had broken.

Duane Allbright's
On-site Read: I

Monday Afternoon

I'm at a motel. The cheapest, lowest in town.

The last couple days seem like months. I read him and could not make sense. Then I went to Cambridge and looked up the genealogy. It still didn't make sense. But the trouble is—it does.

I think I know what he's doing.

———

I'll back up. Torrance booby-trapped the dinner. A neat scheme, but dumb. He thought he'd show Sheila what a pervert Dad is. The boy has no idea. I'm worried. There he was helpless, drug cold. I could have put an end to it. I didn't. Maybe because the rest of it was watching. All of it, watching me. Waiting to see what I'd do. I did nothing. I was just too dumbfounded.

———

Best place to start is the letter. The Baron wrote Torrance a letter, from Thailand, where he usually lives. "The Villa Spoor." It's in Bangkok. Why live there? Could be people there don't pay attention to strange rich foreigners.

In the letter he tells the boy about a family "Curse." The Spoors, he claims, have a long history of tragic early death. This claim has many strange aspects. One of them is, it's true.

Understandably, the letter made Torrance nervous. Nobody likes the idea of a terrible family curse. Especially if it strikes in the form of insane suicide, as Malcolm suggests. Well, about ten days ago, Torrance arrived at the palace here for a visit. It wasn't long before he became more nervous. Then, last Friday, he got really upset. He discovered something: his father has a downright unhealthy obsession with him.

So he took action. He's a smart kid. He even set up a cover story. What he couldn't know is, his father has ways to see through almost anything. For example, the roses. I knew the one Sheila got from Torrance is trouble. That rose is one of the hottest things I ever felt. But I wasn't prepared at all for what I found at the Baron's.

———

Rose in my pocket, I arrived about midway through.

I knew the way, having been to Mace Lane before; but I'd planted a transponder on Sheila in case the blizzard threw me off. I didn't need it. Pip, who seems to be the Baron's one and only goon, picked her up in a snow-plowing truck, and I followed the tracks. That truck paved the way, lucky thing too, the snow was deep. It was kind of magical. Gliding along a nice packed path, all alone in a storm. Nobody else, going anywhere else, able to move. Just me on my path.

I kept way back. Didn't want Pip to see my lights.

Then I had to stop. The path went under the gate on Mace Lane, sure enough. But the gate was closed. I jumped out, checked it. It was locked solid. Fancy new hardware, no way to pick it.

That's when I got hit. The storm was easing. I was standing at the gate, the sky was opening, the wind was dropping. And in my pocket, the rose started to heat. My first impulse was to toss it in the jeep. I had to figure it was telling somebody, or something, that I was preparing to snoop. Then I decided, what the hell. Probably it's wise to assume the someone, the something, will know about me anyway; which proved correct. I stood still for a minute, thinking this over. And suddenly, flowing at me through the rose, there it was, angry, in the distance: the burn.

A massive burn. An out-of-control burn, in the middle of a dying storm. The rose was like a satellite, beaming images at me: images of something large.

Huge. However, it felt funny. It felt—sick. A sensation, I'll say that. Call it Hurricane Sick, seen from three hundred miles up.

At this point, though, compared to later, it wasn't so much. It was mostly just dogs. Worried dogs.

I was scared, of course. The dogs weren't of a friendly disposition. They knew I was there. And they felt me feeling them—they knew I knew they were there. They also knew I knew something else. What they wanted to do if I climbed their gate.

I climbed it. Then I stood still for a minute, ready to jump back on and over. I had to see how they'd react. Soon, I felt the hate. Then I felt it getting purer—pure waves of animal frustration.

This sounds more heroic than it was. I wasn't about to go in there and be pet food, that's not my kind of end of story. I had a hunch the dogs couldn't get me. If they could have, they wouldn't have been that frustrated. So something was wrong.

It turned out, what was wrong was the Baron. Torrance had drugged him. He was completely unconscious, which meant he couldn't release the dogs from the cages; as far as they were concerned, things were out of control. Then they felt me at the gate. That's when they would have gnawed steel if they could have, or whatever the kennels are made of, not wood, I reckon.

I started walking up and they just had a fit.

It took me a while to get there. The Baron's place resembles a public park. His road forks, more than once, and it's hilly, which meant the truck path stayed useful. My talent isn't good for that kind of navigation. The burn was growing, getting more and more intense; but psi, even monster psi, isn't a beacon I can follow. It's not a signal like that at all. It's more like an air-raid siren. Telling you to get cover, fast.

My flash was next to useless. The beam just went off into the snow and the black. All I saw were silvery white sweeps, sharp glimmers, black.

Then suddenly, finally, rising beyond the path, there was the house. It was dead dark. That really surprised me. Not one light was on, anywhere.

However—I am having trouble even saying this—it seemed to glow.

This wasn't visible in the regular sense. And it was faint. But I swear, the glow was the smell of the roses. It was the Odor, *glowing*. Glowing out the windows and in the walls themselves, the place was lit up like a dream monument: one big pile of flickering sepia stone.

As I stared, my pants suddenly seemed on fire. It was the rose. I pulled out the plastic bag, dropped it quick. Then, aloud, I said, "Hi."

The glow disappeared. It extinguished, *just like that.*

———

That meant something. I think it meant, "Get lost."

So this was different from the time on the phone. The Odor, the glow, whatever, it wasn't open. It wasn't curious. It seemed more like it was plain shocked. Shocked I was there at all, never mind saying Hi.

I thought about turning back. But Sheila was inside. I picked up the plastic bag. It was cool; I pocketed it. My flash bounced off glass doors. Wading through snow at them, I made a telltale mess, but at this point that didn't seem important. The first door I tried opened. Which struck me as odd, until I remembered. Usually, the dogs aren't trapped.

I was in a gigantic room. The ballroom, I found out later. Sponder told me Sheila was upstairs. Psi told me Malcolm wasn't with her. But psi couldn't pinpoint where he was. Then I thought of using the dogs, and it worked. The things went wilder and wilder the closer I got.

I found him on a couch in a ground-floor room with the only light so far, a dying-down fire. He was snoring, feebly.

The man is handsome in a Madame Tussaud waxlike way. His appearance didn't interest me much. Looks and psi don't correlate at all. One of his arms dangled to the carpet. I said to myself, maybe you shouldn't do what you're thinking.

I sat down and did it anyway. I took off a boot, and the socks, then lay down and touched the palm of his finger-curled hand, very lightly, with my toes. My toes conduct the best. I don't know why. But they do.

The rose I'd put on the carpet. I had an idea it might do something bad, like explode. The precaution soon seemed sensible. Because the instant I touched that man's hand, my foot burned. It literally felt as if it was burning up. I couldn't have kept it there long.

But I didn't need to. Almost immediately, two realities took hold. Coming through as separate but interconnected, they gave me more than I could handle. Call them Reality Number One and Reality Number Two.

Number One: I learned Malcolm is old. Incomprehensibly old. Everything is old, in a sense, but Malcolm is not old in that sense.

He, himself, is somehow old, somehow *very* old. Maybe even centuries old.

The fact was obvious. Completely impossible, of course. But obvious.

People might wonder how such a thing could be so obvious. I'll try to explain. When I do a read, I often get a feeling of dropping through space. This comes through my toes: I feel like I'm falling. It's the first thing that hits, and it sets the tone, because the "space," call it a kind of inner space, is the subject's psychic construct of his life.

Think of being in an elevator that's plunging to the basement. It's plunging because the cable has snapped. This is sort of analogous, but usually without the panic that would go with a situation like that. I say usually, because sometimes there is a lot of panic—it depends on what has happened in the person's life. Ok, the cable has snapped. The elevator is plunging from the top of the building past all the floors to the basement, and it's a glass elevator, so I can see some of what's whizzing by. Not "see," really—"feel" is more like it. So I'm falling down, down, down, and pretty soon I hit the basement, which—so to speak—is where the subject was born. The older the person, therefore, the longer the plunge. This, like I say, is fairly routine. It's a typical first impression I get when reading a subject, especially a Psi. Most especially, a powerful Psi.

With the Baron the plunge kept on going. The elevator fell and didn't stop. It kept going. And going, and going.

It was still going when I broke the connection. Unbelievable.

And yes, I felt a great deal of panic. Riding that elevator wasn't pleasant at all. This brings me to the second Reality:

Malcolm is a drunk. He's a voluptuary, a compulsive stimulation-craver. The punishment he takes is unreal. It was unbearable, in fact; I couldn't tolerate it. I had to remove my foot. That foot was in pain. So was the rest of me. I sat, in the dark, in a state of shock.

I was outraged. This Psi is a cosmic freak, a cosmic wastrel! I don't know how to describe this—he's a skyscraper of sickness, and the basement's in China. I decided the man has deep and awful trouble. There must be something foul at the bottom of Malcolm Spoor.

I didn't find out what it is. The fall down his shaft was a howling blur, anyway I don't think I even got close to bottom. Putting on socks, lacing my boot, it occurred to me his power may be too strong. So strong, he needs to cut it, dull it, do anything to not feel it intact. I was trying to think up reasons for his self-abuse. They didn't ring true.

But another thought made sense. Maybe Malcolm's problems were the reason I wasn't dead. Not a bad situation for me, but for him—I wondered if his powers might somehow be jammed.

That depressed me, thinking about jammed power.

Then the lights came on. Suddenly I felt less depressed. It hit me: This situation is an advantage. Use it.

I decided to go upstairs and find out what Sheila was doing. All along I'd been getting flashes. She'd been vibrating utter fear. Now, though, she was vibrating utter sex.

The sponder, it's a wristwatch, took me straight to them. They thought I did it psychically. I didn't dispel that idea. I needed cooperation, and the spook factor could only add to my authority.

But while I was zeroing in, they were carrying on. It seemed like a foolish thing to be doing. We had to find out as much as possible, as unobtrusively as possible. Nothing else mattered. And here the boy was fucking Sheila. Vigorously, too, I could feel it. This irritated me. In fact it bothered me a lot, because Sheila was loving it. So I knocked, loudly.

Long wait. Then the door opened. There was Sheila, standing in a vestibule, another door open behind her. She looked deathly. I hugged her. She wriggled, didn't want it, but I kissed her. I heard the boy say, *"Shit."* I nearly yelled at him, but didn't, because I was hitting hard.

It came from all sides, and made me afraid. I realized this place is crucial to Malcolm. Crucial to the Odor too, because I could smell it, feel it. The Odor was in the room. And it was shuddering. It seemed to be shuddering with some awful pleasure—that seemed erotic, the Odor felt orgasmic, like it had *gotten off.* In my pocket, the rose was heating. And suddenly I was sensing, in too much detail, what Sheila and Torrance had done in there: eyes locked, spit dangling, the young dick deep singing its song . . .

It passed. I found myself hugging Sheila, too tightly, in the entrance to a quiet, dimly lit room. The boy, shirtless and nervous, was staring at us from behind a desk.

Keep moving, Duane, I told myself. I let go of Sheila, went in, looked to my left, and saw a bank of glowing video monitors.

My neck hairs were prickling. I sat on the desk and stared. I could not take my eyes off those lit-up screens.

They radiated. They radiated the Baron's impossible ancient psi. I thought: cameras. He sits in here and watches. I knew what he watches. I looked at Torrance. He was putting on his shirt, trying to stay calm and collected. Trying to be brave. I thought: Being brave here is hopeless.

I saw the boy in a blue-gray flicker of video hell. I saw his father watching day by day from that secret hell. Watching feverishly. Watching hungrily, inspecting the boy's body, so clean, strong. I said to myself, Whew. And wondered: What is this, with the Odor and Malcolm? Rank voyeurism? Or something worse?

I said to Sheila, "Talk to me."

They both babbled. They pointed at the monitors, at tapes on a shelf, at photos of her diary. All that was insignificant. I told them to shut up and think. They did. Then Sheila started on Malcolm.

Just as the drug was putting him under, he'd spoken incoherently. He had said something about Sheila marrying Torrance. That mystified me. It seemed so off the wall. Did he say why? I asked. She replied, it had to do with "good genes." Go on, I told her. She said this: Malcolm was excited about the baby boy she and Torrance might have.

Torrance mumbled, "Dad's crazy." He was staring at a picture that was tacked to the wall. I went over, took a look. It was of Felipe "Bunny" Spoor. A dazed young man, he was in a newspaper photo nearly fifty years old. The news, headlined boldly, was his shocking arrest. The charge: murder. The victim: his father, Gainsborough Spoor. Who, I then saw, was also tacked to the wall, right next door. He was brandishing a glass of champagne from the cover of a magazine. As if that, too, had been big news, a caption said: TOASTING THE NEW YEAR, GAINSBOROUGH, BARON SPOOR, PREDICTS IT WILL BE: "TOO DULL TO SURVIVE!"

I checked the dates. Gainsborough hadn't survived it. According to the paper, he was shot dead one month later. Allegedly by Bunny.

There were fifteen or so other pictures tacked around the room, all of various Spoor barons. I realized they were bothering me terribly.

Sheila and Torrance meantime were talking. He remarked, " 'Too dull to survive' sounds like something Dad would say."

The oddest thought swam through my head: He did say that.

I spoke to the boy directly for the first time. "Torrance, your father claims there is a curse on your family. What is this curse?"

He frowned at me. He was wondering what I was doing in his

house, interrupting his booby trap, interrupting a good time with Sheila. He asked her, "Is he really ok?"

Without conviction, Sheila said, "Yes."

Torrance shrugged, and waved at the pictures. "Dad said all those guys died weird deaths. Yeah, because of a curse."

I asked, "Did he say how the curse works?"

"He just said it drove them crazy. So bad, I guess they felt they had to do stuff like commit suicide. And now it's the same with him!"

"The same with him?" I asked.

"Yes. The same thing, over and over, and now it's him."

"This has been going on for a while?"

The reply chilled me. "Dad said the curse is old. Centuries old."

I thought: Your father is, too. But it is impossible for a man to be centuries old. Or is it?

An idea was starting to take shape deep in my mind. I didn't have a clue what it was. But I knew I didn't like this idea. And I could feel it coming at me—squirming, slowly, to the surface.

I said to the boy, "The notion of a curse is scary. But try to focus for a minute. The 'Bunny' your father talks to. You figure it's that picture of Bunny Spoor?"

"What else?" he replied. He thought for a moment. "Maybe he hallucinates and thinks the picture can hear him. Because it sounds like he's trying to talk to somebody who really is here."

"Somebody," I said, "who really is here?" The idea I didn't like was coming closer.

The boy muttered, "Maybe—like a ghost."

Sheila said, "Torrance, that's silly. Dead is dead, people who die are gone. No ghost can really be here." Then she added, in her most no-nonsense voice, "Malcolm obviously is talking to himself."

Talking to himself?

My mysterious idea sank deeper. It was swimming away.

I looked at the pictures of the barons. An eerie thought hit me: They don't want me to know what that idea is. They almost seemed to be saying, "We're here, buddy. So *get out.*"

A fanciful thought, sure. Or maybe it wasn't. I sensed hostility in that room. I wondered if it had anything to do with what I'd felt when I first entered; if it had anything to do with the Odor. I definitely had experienced that, at least. Something evilly prurient.

The Odor, I decided, is the direction to go. I asked Torrance, "Where did you get the rose you threw at Sheila?"

He went to a computer console on the desk, and tapped buttons. There are sixteen monitors in that video room, four-by-four. It's an impressive display. It was even more impressive when I saw sixteen identical images of a room full of roses. On long tables, under grow lights, were hundreds, maybe over a thousand, pots of plants—every last one of them blooming sepia roses.

"Creepy," Torrance said.

I couldn't disagree. Nothing, however, was hitting me. That made me uneasy. Those roses, I figured, have to be the source of the Odor. And I'm getting nothing at all?

As I stood there staring, Torrance poked me with a sheaf of papers. It was the letter from his father. It had been lying on the desk all along, but that was the first I'd noticed it, or even known of its existence. Torrance said, "Check it out. Dad claims a sepia rose did something weird to him last year. He said he fell *into it*—and it was like history went backward. Like a movie going backward, he saw the history of the Spoors, all the way back in time to a guy named Gundulf, who went on Crusades . . ."

"Gundulf is here," Sheila said.

That made me jump. I thought she meant he had suddenly materialized. But she was gesturing at a picture on the wall. "No shit," the boy exclaimed, going to look.

"Fine print," she said, "fancy lettering, and the text is Old French. But I think that word is Gundulf."

I didn't need to see if she was right. The monitors had just told me she was. Or at least that she'd touched some kind of nerve. For a split second, the sixteen patches of sepia on the screens seemed to swell, and darken.

She and Torrance didn't see this. It happened so fast, I wasn't sure I had, either—partly because the roses then looked exactly the way they had before. However, my scalp was tingling. *Something had happened.*

I asked Torrance, "Where is that room?"

"In the basement," he replied. "That's where the kennels are, too."

I looked at the console he had used to put the roses on-screen. The system is sophisticated. But the Baron, I thought, might not be; the controls are labeled so simply, a child could use them. One array is marked with Ts, meaning Torrance, I figured. Other arrays are marked with words indicating various areas of the house: library,

dining room, pool, a mess of different places. One of which says:
Plants.

There are four buttons marked Plants. I pushed them. Nothing
happened. The screens blinked, with each push, but the image
didn't change.

Torrance watched me do this. "You've been there?" I asked, waving at the screens. "That's where you got the rose?"

He said, "I was coming back from swimming. The doors down
there are always locked, Dad does not want me in those rooms at
all. But yesterday, one of them was open. I guess Pip forgot to lock
it. Usually I go a different way, so maybe he didn't think I would see
it, but I did. And I looked. There they were—millions of sepia roses.
But what really got me was the camera. I heard it clicking. I looked
up and saw this clicking camera, that was not hidden . . ."

"Not hidden," I said, "because you aren't supposed to go in
there?" Torrance nodded. "Did you, in fact, go in there?"

"No. I was afraid the camera would see me. I just reached in a
little, to get the rose."

Pointing at the Plant buttons on the console, I asked, "What about
the other cameras?"

He said, "I tried those buttons. They don't work. So there might
be only one camera. I didn't see any others when I was there."

"But," I said, "you didn't go in. Could you see the whole room?"

The kid frowned at the monitors. "No," he said. "All I saw is what
we see now. A bunch of bushes, tons of flowers . . ."

"Looks like a big room," I said. "Looks like it goes back a way."
The angle of view was tilted downward in such a fashion that the
opposite wall wasn't visible. Besides which, the grow lights, suspended from the ceiling, pretty much filled the top part of the image.
In the bottom part were the ends of four metal tables, evidently long
—the aisles between them stretched off into vanishing points. The
points they vanished into were sepia gloom.

Sheila said, "You think something is behind them?"

The three of us stood still a moment, staring at the mass of leaves
and flowers, receding into the back of that room. "I'd like to find
out," I said. "How do you get there?" I asked the boy.

"Elevator's the easiest," he said. "End of the hall. It's all locked
up. But, I have Dad's keys."

Duane Allbright's
On-site Read: II

Monday Afternoon

They were glad I told them to stay in the studio. Torrance, especially, was relieved to see me go. He didn't know what to think of
me, and probably wanted to ask Sheila questions. Anyway, they had
some cleaning up to do. Not just of themselves; of the studio, too.
The reason for that I'll get to later.

The boy had started to give me directions, then stopped and drew
a map. I was grateful for it when the elevator opened at basement
level. It isn't a basement down there. It's a catacomb. And it's
vast.

I had my flash, but didn't need it. The passages, stone-floored,
were lit. And they were fairly clean. However, the spaces were big
enough, and irregular enough, to hold plenty of murk. The kind of
place rats love, I thought. Maybe, I then thought, the dogs scare off
things like rats. I hadn't asked Torrance to mark the kennels on his
map. Which was too bad, because the dogs were getting irritated,
again. I felt it, through the rose, in the elevator.

They were hitting hard. But I had no idea where they were. I realized: Duane, you better not open the wrong door. You do, they might be crafty. Crafty enough not to make the faintest sound. That would be unfortunate for you.

Straight ahead, the map told me, left, a right, down this corridor, down that one, count the doors, the third door down, opposite the darkroom, which isn't locked—I would know I'd found the right door, if it was directly across from the darkroom. I found the dark-room. A bunch of pictures of Torrance, in color, were pegged like laundry on strings. In his gym clothes, he looked healthy, alert, fit. So fit. I wondered what he and Sheila might be doing, upstairs. I couldn't feel a thing.

Forget it, I decided. No big deal. I went across the hall and fumbled with the keys for a couple of minutes.

Finally the door opened, and there they were. The roses. In the flesh, so to speak. The scent was a caustic wind. And although nothing physical happened, I felt a kind of rustle. A stir. As if I had entered a church—a crowded, silent church, in which the worshipers, all at once, were aware of the intruder. And were turning around, slowly, to face him.

That was impressive. But it was a fleeting impression. It went away.

I looked up. Sure enough, there was the camera. Not clicking. Not moving. The place was dead silent.

I moved forward, and heard clicks. The camera was picking me up. I waved at it, thinking Sheila and Torrance might be reassured. If they were watching.

I myself was nervous. The physical presence of the roses was overwhelming. As was their scent—a keener, sweeter smell than what I called the Odor, but otherwise identical. These things, I kept thinking, have psi. That means they somehow are sentient. Which probably means they are watching me. Somehow, these things *think*.

I peered down an aisle. I saw what looked like a tapestry, hanging on the far wall of the room.

Not wanting to get close—the aisles are narrow, and I may as well admit this, I had absurd ideas, of thorny branches lashing out—I went to my left, and found a wider passage, along the wall. I quickly walked down it.

At the back of the room is an open area, carpeted with plain industrial carpet, in the middle of which, set against the end wall, is a platform. Carpeted all over, on top, on the sides, this platform is maybe nine feet by eleven, about two feet high. A tapestry, the same width, eleven feet, hangs over it on the wall. Looking at the tapestry, I thought, "backdrop." Faded, buff color, not much different a color than the wall itself, the tapestry is an intricate design. Its motif: roses. Spiky, medieval-looking roses.

To its immediate right, dropping from a hole in the ceiling, is a long, thick cord, heavily tasseled at the end. This looked to me like a slapstick prop. Adding to the stagelike effect are three cameras, mounted in the ceiling, pointing—left, right and center—at the platform.

The arrangement is simple, even austere. It seemed functional. But what, I wondered, is its function? Amateur theatricals? I stared at the roses. What are they—the audience?

Whatever the Baron uses it for, I thought, he wants the proceedings taped. Why, then, don't the buttons in the studio work? I thought: Maybe the proceedings haven't happened yet. So he hasn't used those cameras yet, and they aren't turned on. Maybe they've never been turned on. But what will they be looking at, when they are turned on?

I jumped onto the platform. It isn't hollow; landing, I made a muffled thud. The thing is solidly built. I turned to the roses, raised my arms, and resisted an urge to recite *Hamlet*.

At the moment of resisting that urge, I became aware of a kind of hum. It wasn't an ordinary sound. I listened carefully, and realized it wasn't a sound at all. It was a force—low, muted, powerful—that seemed to be vibrating. In the air, in the sepia-hued light, it was vibrating all over, in my boots, in the platform, and, especially, in my pocket. It bothered me. I sensed a disturbance—a *shift*. I looked at the roses. The bushes, the branches, the blooms, were totally still. However, they weren't. They, too, seemed to be vibrating. I blinked, looked away, looked back. They were absolutely still. But —they weren't. Without moving, they seemed to be *shuddering*.

How can anything shudder—if it isn't moving?

I thought: Those things are trying to hide their power. And they are not succeeding.

Then I had another thought, a strong thought, that was nauseating. The roses can't hide their power. Not for very long, they can't; because they are much too powerful. But they're trying—and the effort is *pissing them off*.

And I saw it, felt it: I am in a room full of psi plutonium.

It's shielded, I realized. It's massively shielded, the psi equivalent of seven feet of lead. But even a seven-foot shield can't contain that power. Nothing can contain that power.

Onstage, I felt weak. Everything was shuddering.

Suddenly, it stopped.

I sat down. After a bit, I felt better. I took the plastic bag from my pocket, stared at the decomposing thing within. It had gone cold. I repocketed it, awed. I'd known the rose was potent. I'd known it was associated with the Odor. But I hadn't known I'd been walking around with a specimen of something so extremely big, *in my pocket.*

Numbed, I sat there, thinking. Simple things attracted my eye, like the nap of the carpet. A draft was cooling my legs and butt. The tapestry was touching my shoulder. I ran a hand over it. It was thick, heavy, stiff. I looked at it closely, saw it was finely woven, and very old.

The roses in the design—interlocking, spiky, ornate—seemed alive. I slid backward, stage right, to get a fuller look. Something bumped my back. I almost shouted.

It was the cord, dangling from the ceiling—swaying a bit from the bump. I heard a distant whine that sounded mechanical. What the hell was that? Then I had a fright—the tapestry was going up.

It went up maybe a couple of inches, and stopped. The whine stopped, too. The tapestry, I realized, is attached to a hoist. For some reason, it can be raised. I looked at the ceiling, and saw in it, flush with the wall, the slot into which the tapestry retracts. Along my legs, the draft had gotten stronger. It was coming from behind the tapestry. There was a space in back of there, maybe a large space. The draft was cool. And it smelled of something. It smelled musty.

The whine sounded a second time. The tapestry lowered. The draft ebbed, and the room was dreadfully silent.

I tugged the cord. I did it gently, thinking of how softly I'd bumped it. A moment later, the whine sounded, and the tapestry went up. This time, it went up four inches before it stopped. The draft came through, stronger, mustier. My heart was pounding. Under the tapestry, and almost its length, was a four-inch-high strip of inky black. I thought of sticking my hand in, to see if I could feel anything—there wasn't a wall there, that was for sure—and my heart pounded harder.

I flattened myself on the platform, cheek plunked to the carpet, and tried to look in. All I saw was inky black.

The whine sounded. Once again, the tapestry lowered. It dropped to the carpet in front of my face. I tapped it. The whole expanse was rigid. This thing, I thought, is almost like a moving wall. And it's designed to drive people crazy.

I jerked on the cord, hard.

Up, up the tapestry went. The first thing I saw was a heavy iron bar, black, horizontal, about seven inches above the platform. It ran the length of the space that was being revealed, into vertical grooves in walls on either side. Then, seven inches later, there was a second bar. Seeing this, I thought: That's a barricade. And it, too, can be raised.

Then I saw the first red spark.

I scooted back. I did that instantly.

I wanted to look away. But I couldn't. In fact, I suddenly couldn't move at all. Up, up the tapestry went, and I saw the second red spark. Then the third, the fourth, then there were nine, twenty, and more—red sparks burning, burning brilliantly, burning into me from the inky black.

They were eyes.

I heard the hum again, vibrating behind me—not a sound, a sensation richer, sweeter than sound. It was the roses, humming. They were singing, humming, louder, louder . . .

One of them poked its head through the bars. The eyes, closer, stabbed me. Another one stuck its head out, eyes stabbing, then all twelve heads were out, straining through the bars, eyes stabbing. . . .

It paralyzed me. Every muscle in my body wanted to get off that platform. But it was as if the eyes, working collectively, had sunk hooks in my brain. They were irresistible. Staring, I felt the fascination of a trapped prey. Of a prey beyond hope—I was certain they were about to devour me.

But how could they? The bars were holding them back. In a frantic corner of my mind I thought, They can't get through!

A few moments passed. I began to understand my fear.

The eyes were swelling. They seemed to grow, and bloat. Then they bloomed. In the centers, purple dots appeared. The dots became bigger, brighter. They became bigger, bigger, and they *opened.* They were purple holes, deep, that glowed. Something bad was in them. Something hot, and roiling.

Something like lava.

The holes deepened. They glowed hotter, tunnels to a terrible place, a place I did not want to go. They widened, widened more, and then, they unified. They merged, into a single glowing hole.

My peripheral vision was gone. All I could see was a kind of chasm —purplish, fiery, it dropped away, below me. Everything else had disappeared. The heads, the bars, the whole room had vanished. Feeling alone, I thought an awful thought: That chasm is alive. And it's hungry.

Staring at this, I heard, reverberating all around, a rumbling but harmonious roar. It seemed familiar. It was strangely beautiful, too. Then I felt its focus. The harmony was focusing on my body, on a specific place, on my groin. It ignited and I knew what it was. I must have screamed. In my pocket, in the plastic bag, there could have been a white-hot coal. I thought, No. Please, No. But—it is. It's them, the roses. They are unleashed, now. And they are pouring through the rose in my pocket.

I felt a probing. The rose, molten, was spreading. Its force entered me. It was puncturing, pushing in, and suddenly, with a rapid intelligence, its force was coursing throughout my body. I realized it wanted something. It was looking for something. Then I knew what it wanted; it was curling, greedily, around my mind.

Like a vise, the rose fastened. It began to pull. I felt a kind of psychic rip. I thought, It's tearing my mind. The purplish chasm before me deepened. The roiling energy in it became clearer, and so, too, did my fate, for I saw what was in there, in that chasm, in that fiery caldera sprung from the eyes of the dogs:

It was their living, burning psi. And it wanted me. When the rose pries loose my mind, I thought, that hole will consume me. Nothing I can do will stop it. I am prey, I am helpless, my psi is *about to be eaten.*

Then came the most horrifying realization of all.

Like a hellish smell, torment was rising. Deep in the dogs, there was a fire, an inferno, of suffering. Of pain. And I saw what it is that fuels those dogs. They are a furnace prison—in which the prisoners are burning.

An enslavement! A cauldron, derived from people! I thought, I'm about to become fuel. My body, mind torn out, will die. But my psi will live on, burning there. Trapped with others, maybe many others, in that conflagration. To give the dogs power. To give power to the Baron!

An extreme terror overcame me. I had to get away.

I flailed, I writhed, I screamed, NO!

I fought the rose, I did all I could to get away. And inside, something snapped. Something *broke off.* Which was wonderful; because it was rushing, with tremendous speed, up, up and away.

All around, rage exploded. The roar of the roses intensified, it became a shriek. I rushed up, away, faster, faster.

I wondered, What's happening? How am I escaping? Where am I going? I'm rushing up, up, up—but, to *where?*

Then the coldness, the emptiness was all around—vast, silent— and I realized:

I am zooming into the sky.

———

In the sky, floating, I thought: How amazing. I have just been—
Scared out of my body.

———

I saw the Baron's snow-covered peninsula, far below, glimmering ghostily in the sea. I saw the house, the hill, the cliffs, I even saw the surf, a phosphorescent rim on the shore. My body, I thought, is lying in the basement of that mansion, so arrogant on its hill, above those cliffs; my poor body is lying more and more lifelessly, down there in that basement—because it is empty, so very empty of me.

I knew I should try to go back. But the idea was impossible even to think. It meant returning to the eyes. It meant the purple chasm, the furnace prison, all those others who were burning in the dogs.

Burning in a hell of psi.

The thought of being there was completely impossible to think.

But then I wondered: If not back to my body, where will I go? Where can I go? And I knew, suddenly, I was going nowhere. Bodiless, I was going to die.

I floated. I floated. I floated . . .

Things were getting dimmer . . .

Then she touched me.

She was calling my name. Doing so, she was reaching up, up into the sky—and *touching* me.

I could hear it, too, her calling my name. She was calling, shouting, louder, and louder: "Duane! Duane! DUANE! *DUANE!*"

It drew me. The calls were rearranging me, changing me; they were rearranging my float, my fading float, my dissipation in the sky. Like a delicate cyclone, I was swirling; then, like a tornado, I was funneling; I was funneling, down, down, and then touching, touching *down,* into her arms; and finally, I was there.

I had touched down.

———

When I opened my eyes, Sheila was leaning into my face, and she was still shouting: "Duane! Duane!"

She saw my eyes open, stopped shouting. She stared searchingly for a moment. Then she collapsed on me, trembling.

She was trying to say something, and couldn't. It seemed like she was gasping, over and over: "You were gone! You were *gone,* you *weren't there.*"

But now, I was there. In fact, the three of us were there, on the stage, in the rose room. The tapestry was down. I saw Torrance standing above us, staring, thunderstruck. I said to him, "Get me out of here."

That motivated him. He quickly detached Sheila from me, picked me up, and carried me out of the room. Sheila, galvanized herself, came right along. We hurried, hurried through the basement corridors to the elevator, on the floor of which Torrance, by this time panting hard, dumped me. A moment later the door was closing and we were going up.

I said, from the elevator floor, "Sheila, I love you, woman."

She didn't have anything to say. She was flour pale.

I was wet. I smelled something, too.

The elevator opened to the second-floor hall. I realized I could stand, and walk. So I did.

They followed me into the video studio.

Torrance said, "Huh! They're working again!" He was looking at the monitors.

"Working again?" I asked.

"They went crazy. Like it was an electrical disturbance. That was when we came down to find you, because Sheila got really scared!"

I switched the monitors off. I couldn't bear looking at the roses.

Sheila and Torrance were staring at me. Their stares said: What happened?

I said, "I guess I had some kind of seizure."

They were still staring. Torrance's nose was wrinkling.

I said, "But now, I think I'm ok. Where's the nearest shower?"

Duane Allbright's
On-site Read: III

Monday Evening

In the shower, hot water pounding, I had a panic attack. A bad one. I fell. I trembled. The tub, shiny and reflective, trembled with me.

It filled. Gradually, I quieted. I was glad for the thrashing shower noise. Glad I'd locked the door.

A few minutes passed. I turned the shower off, lay back. Watching water, I tried to regulate my breathing. Still surfaces were my goal.

After a bit I could think.

My pants were on the floor. The sight of them, the thought of the rose in them, was sickening. Again, I stared at water. I realized something was puzzling me.

The dogs. Why don't Sheila and Torrance know about the dogs?

Clearly they didn't. The dogs must have been quiet. As quiet as they had been when I'd entered that room.

The tapestry had come down automatically, no doubt. But the dogs could have poked it, shaken it, they could have *eaten* it, God knows what they could have done. They could have barked. But they hadn't. Why?

Bubbles floated. Watching them attract each other, aggregating, I pondered my disintegration in the sky. Phrases repeated in my mind. Near-death experience. Out-of-body experience.

Supreme-fright experience.

An answer to my question drifted, like a bubble, at me. It was simple. The dogs hadn't wanted Sheila and Torrance to know about their part of the setup in that room. But why?

I thought about the dangling cord. Gentle tugs make it go part way up. A hard tug makes it go up all the way. What about the bars? Does the cord control them, too? If so, had I nearly raised them?

Furtively, not able to consider it directly, I wondered how much consciousness I would have retained, had I been swallowed. Consciousness of being fused with the dogs? Of being somehow smelted, into their psi? Their eyes had functioned collectively. Is that what those animals are—a collective? Maybe they aren't individual animals at all. Maybe, in terms of psi, they're a single entity; that has grown, and grown, as more victims get sucked in. The dogs don't have names, Pip told Torrance. Because, supposedly, they "had so many." It occurred to me, if they are a collective, maybe that also is what they do: collect. They collect names; they collect power!

The very idea was awesome. But it raised more questions.

I decided I could try to answer some of them. I got out of the tub, toweled, and put on clothes Torrance had given me. He'd said they were the baggiest he had. Still, the pants were tight. Looking in the mirrors—the whole bathroom was mirrored, and it was large—I saw many Duanes. All of whom, for the very first time, were feeling fat.

Somehow, that made me happy. Happy to be alive.

The rose I left on the floor, in the pants. For now, I thought, that's a good place for it. I walked through a grand and totally empty bedroom and went down the hall to the video room. Sheila and Torrance, sitting on the floor facing each other, were in the middle of a palaver.

As I mentioned, I had told them, before I went to the basement, to clean up the studio. Now checking the job they'd done, I pronounced it inadequate. Get Windex, get rags, I said. I want this place wiped down.

It was a silly thing to make them do. That was the point. Malcolm, when he wakened, would see through the cleanup. He'd know we'd been in there, know we'd poked around, he'd especially know what Torrance and Sheila had done. We had left tons of traces in that studio—it was a mess, not remotely cleanable by Windex. Further-more, Malcolm would know I had almost gone to hell in his dogs. He'd have to know that, from the dogs, from the roses. Somehow, he has to talk with them. Conceivably, he'd just know it.

But if we acted as if he wouldn't learn all that, maybe he would conclude we're naïve and ignorant. Of course, we are. It would be nice, though, if he thinks we're completely clueless.

That, I'm not.

There was another reason to keep my two comrades busy. I needed to get my wits back. With them staring at me scared and curious, thinking was impossible. I was worried they'd start sus-pecting how extreme an experience my trip to the rose room had been. They didn't fully buy the seizure explanation, of course.

However, that was a lot more believable than the truth. Which I had to keep to myself, if the investigation was to continue. If I'd told them what had happened, Torrance, whether he believed me or not, would have run away from home that very night.

Maybe that, I thought, is why the dogs were quiet when Torrance was in the rose room. They don't want him to run away?

In any case, I myself had decided he has to stay put for a while.

The two of them cleaned. I skimmed the letter the Baron wrote from Bangkok. After a few minutes, Sheila aimed her Windex bottle at me and said, "Why don't the three of us just get the hell out of here, Duane?"

"Yeah," Torrance said. He wasn't much interested in the cleanup, either. More taken with his grandfather Bunny Spoor, accused mur-derer, he'd pulled the newspaper off the wall and was deep in the middle of it.

I waved the letter and said, "Your father is one mysterious man, Torrance. Do you want to solve that mystery?"

In an exasperated tone of voice, one that indicated a need for answers, Sheila demanded, "What happened with the roses, Duane? Why were you passed out with a mess in your pants?"

"Didn't I tell you?" I asked.

"You have told us *nothing*," she replied.

"Sheila, I have a condition," I said. "I thought you knew."

They looked at me blankly. This wasn't what they'd expected to hear. Actually, I hadn't expected to say it. But I had to say some-thing, and couldn't stop there. "I'm on medication. If I don't take it, and I get nervous, I have seizures. I'm sorry. It's terribly embarrass-ing."

Torrance, who had carried me quite a distance, mess and all, looked as if he might believe that. Sheila didn't. She asked, "What made you nervous?"

"Malcolm Spoor," I answered truthfully. Then I exclaimed, "This whole house does! Have you heard of a man who even spies on his flowers?"

I immediately regretted asking that question. A thought with arresting implications had just dawned on me. It took a few seconds to decide to pursue it. I said, "Torrance, I know you think your father is dangerous. Well, he may be. But I suspect it's more likely he's worried about you."

"Hold it, Duane," Sheila said. "You were telling us . . ."

Interrupting, I said, "I think your father is frightened of you, Torrance. In fact, I think you scare him silly."

Harshly, the boy said, *"Ha."*

I pointed at the monitors and asked, "Why else would he want to keep such a close eye on you? So secretly?"

Torrance frowned.

"Could be," I said, "he's afraid of something you might do."

"Like what?" Torrance asked, amazed.

I pointed at the newspaper he was holding.

The kid looked at it, looked back at me. The very idea bewildered him. "I would never—" he said. Something was interfering with his thoughts.

I had an intuition what it was. "But maybe, in his own crazy way, your father is trying to—"

"Drive me to it? To wanting to—kill him?"

I nodded, palms open to the air, open to that awful thought.

"Absurd," Sheila snapped.

"Insanity is always absurd," I said. "But it exists. Take the notion of a curse, for example." Torrance was staring at me, riveted. "Maybe Malcolm thinks the curse dooms him to be killed by his son, just like Gainsborough was killed by Bunny. So he sets up a surveillance system to watch for signs of that coming to pass. This room, he thinks, is a defense. At another level, though, maybe it's a way to try to make the curse really happen. Maybe all this is a kind of unconscious effort at curse-fulfillment."

Torrance was thinking hard. So was Sheila. I was glad to see it.

But then he asked, "Why does Dad have a camera on the roses? If he is worried about me?"

My turn to think hard. I said, "He expects you will use them.

Somehow use the roses. Maybe that's why he's growing so many—why the camera isn't hidden—why the door to that room *was open.* Curse-fulfillment!''

"Ridiculous," Sheila said.

It was. "Anyway," I said, "he only has one camera working in there. How many does he have working on you?"

That hit home. Torrance glowered.

Sheila declared, "You should go back to your mother. Tomorrow!"

The boy glowered more. He looked mulish.

I asked him if he gets along with his mom. He and Sheila exchanged glances. Maybe, I thought, he doesn't.

Again waving the letter, I asked about the money. Torrance said he doesn't care about money. I told him money would give him freedom—from both parents. Hearing that, the boy suddenly wanted to know what I had to say.

I proposed he continue with what seemed to have been his original plan. Tell his father there was a power outage. Don't say one word more. Deny we'd been in the studio. Deny everything, in fact. Then, see how Malcolm reacts. If he goes crazy, Torrance should leave, maybe stay with Sheila, and decide what's next. If he doesn't go crazy—well, we proceed. One way or another, we should find out what is going on here. Meantime, that preserves one of the more significant options: getting rich. Think about it, I said.

Sheila took Torrance into the hall. They commenced a conversation, heated, in whispers. I returned to reading the letter.

It was making me dizzy. The Baron's descent into the rose isn't what happened to me. But it's similar. Similar enough to raise the question of what he was trying to get at, telling that story.

There is a peculiar climax, too, at the end. Something happened to Gundulf and a sultan called Baybars, on a rose-covered bed. Malcolm doesn't describe what it was—except to suggest this "tryst" was fraught with consequences. That in fact, it started the Curse. He also says a "war hound" was there, on the bed. A hound that was "watching."

I thought about the platform in the basement. About the roses, blooming thickly, near it. About the dogs, poking their heads through the bars—scaring me half to death, nearly dragging me into their slave inferno. Could I say those dogs had been "watching"?

They'd used their eyes, that was for sure. But what they really had done, with the roses, was show me a fate worse than death.

I glanced at the walls, at the barons. If anything was watching right then, it was them. What do you say? I thought. Are you here? If so, where? Not, surely, in those pictures . . .

Something crucial, I realized, was eluding me. It was the idea I'd had. The awful idea I'd felt before, swimming deep in my mind—coming closer to the surface, then sinking, diving away.

What, I silently asked the barons, is that idea?

Does it relate, I then asked, tingling with the thought of this mental interrogation, to the stage in the basement? That stage, the platform, whatever it is, certainly wasn't put there for me, correct?

Deep down, something flipped its tail. Tentatively, it was heading up. So I continued, taking a different tack. Tell me, I asked the pictures, how Malcolm got to be so old. Is he really what I felt him to be—centuries old?

Having asked that, I nearly smiled. Because I imagined the barons were sniffing—haughtily, somehow—in reply. That was silly. They were just pictures hanging on walls. Intrigued, however, I thought at them: Maybe I wasn't feeling Malcolm, when I felt those centuries. Maybe I was feeling the curse. After all, the curse is supposed to be centuries old. Maybe all of you, going back, have possessed psi powers. Did you pass those powers down, from one generation to the next, and somehow create a curse? Was I confusing Malcolm with it—with the long history of a terrible psi-curse?

Bored, peeved, they rolled their eyes. Or so I imagined. But it was a game that was helping me think. My elusive idea was coming closer.

I pressed on: the chasm of psi in the dogs, that the roses nearly kicked me into—a lot of people got trapped there, right? Is it part of the curse? Or is it a side benefit that people with psi, people like me, every now and then bump into you? They get too curious, too close, and end up being eaten? So very yummily for the dogs, and you?

The barons looked disgusted. I asked, Why is Malcolm such a voyeur with Torrance? The roses, their interest in the boy seems voyeuristic, even sexual—is it? And why is Malcolm interested in becoming a grandfather? In Torrance becoming a father, Sheila a mother? If he's so interested in life, why does he want to kill himself?

I was getting impatient. My big idea was moving slower. It seemed to be lying not far under the surface, but sluggishly. On the desk, right in front of me, was the newspaper Torrance had taken off the

wall. Bunny, dazed, stared from it. I said, out loud: "Tell me, Bunny
—why does your son Malcolm scream at you?"

Bunny looked sad.

"Torrance thinks you're a ghost. What do you think of that?"

Bunny looked sadder.

"But Sheila says Malcolm's talking to himself . . ."

I stood up fast, mind reeling. The idea, surfacing, was coming at
me. I felt sick, had to sit back down. I realized my hands were over
my eyes. The words were pounding through my head:

Malcolm is talking to himself!

And there it was, a complete idea and a horrible idea, staring at
me from the walls, from the pictures, from the barons:

Those barons aren't dead. They're living. And they're in this
house.

They are downstairs right now, all of them, snoring on a couch.
Because at the moment, they are *living in Malcolm*.

But they're about to move, soon.

I knew who the stage is for, in the basement. It's for Torrance.

———

I remembered feeling it. What it was like, when they scared me out
of my body. They scared me way up into the big, cold sky, where I
floated—with no place to go. No place at all to go, I thought at the
time. Because I was sure I couldn't go back to my body. Thanks to
Sheila, however—I did.

Thinking this, I realized it will be different for Torrance. He will
have a place to go, when he gets scared out. But it won't be back to
his body. At that point, his body will be occupied by something else.

So, where will he go? To the body that isn't occupied, of course.

And he'll hate it. Because suddenly, he'll be old.

Worse, he'll probably be cold with terror, watching the athletic
teenager get ready to kill him.

He'll be cold with rage, too.

Because he'll know he's about to be murdered by his very own
body.

Worst of all, he'll probably realize the killer has devoted a great
deal of preparation to making the event look blameless.

To making it look like suicide.

Stupefied, I stared at the pictures, thinking at them: This is what
you've done all along, you bastards. Your history of tragic early
death, your Curse—it's a history of murder, isn't it? A history you've
covered up by claiming an awful pattern of self-destruction, that

happens to *be* a kind of self-destruction, but with a twist—your sons being the ones who die.

Trapped in your old bodies!

Which means, you're all the same person. Ever since Gundulf, you've been the same being—but with *different names and in different bodies.*

I stared at Bunny and thought: You messed up, when you killed your previous body—the one named Gainsborough. You flubbed it, Bunny. Because somebody figured out who pulled the trigger, and the suicide story fell apart. Still, nobody realized who really pulled the trigger on whom. Nobody knew the person you really killed was an innocent boy, your own son, whom dogs and roses had scared into Gainsborough. Whose body, doubtless fit and athletic, you'd *stolen.* With whose very hand you'd cold-bloodedly murdered!

Out loud, I asked Bunny, "That's true, isn't it?"

Bunny seemed guilty, now. Furious, too.

There was a kind of ringing in my ears.

———

"Isn't what true?" I heard Sheila asking.

I looked up. She and Torrance were at the door. She appeared angry, but resigned. He appeared angry, but determined.

He said, "I hope you know what you are doing. I decided to stay."

———

It's getting on toward night, now. I lie on my bed in this cheap motel room, almost two days later, feeling criminal.

I face a dilemma. How do I learn more about that creature? And at the same time, protect Torrance from it?

The answer is, I don't know.

The boy told me he's been afraid his father is planning on eating him. We discussed it as we spent the next hour erasing tapes that had been made of our various activities. I assured him, Dad won't have you for supper. Your father isn't that kind of crazy.

In fact, however, the boy's fear isn't far off. Casually, I mentioned his letter to his mother. It was news to him he'd given it to Sheila instead. The mixup, it seems, was genuine. I asked about the part where he says his father's eyes can "make crows drop dead out of the sky from 500 feet." Nervously, the kid nodded. I asked if there was anything in particular about his father that made him write that. He said, "Dad has strange eyes, yeah. But the dogs' are scarier." He then told me about the deer the dogs paralyzed, and ate.

Able to empathize with that deer, aware of what Malcolm has in store for Torrance, I started feeling guilty. At least, I kept thinking, the Baron won't make his move right away. He seems intent on having the money-transfer deal happen first. Torrance said that happens in a couple of weeks.

We added finishing touches to the cleanup. I dealt with the bathroom, my soiled clothes. In the studio, Sheila stalked around stuffing Windex-wet paper towels in a bag. She was perplexed, disturbed, indignant.

Torrance used a control to black out power. We left the video room, locked it, went downstairs. The outage "covered" our exit; cameras cut with everything else. Downstairs, he turned on power. Then we liberated Pip.

I told the goon I'm Sheila's jealous lover. I said I'd followed her through the storm with rage and revenge in my heart. I'd thought she was having an affair. How wrong could I be—nothing was going on, except pesky power failures.

Pip pretended to believe me. He was only too glad to drive Sheila and me to the big front gate, and unlock it.

Torrance came with us that far. I have such an image of him standing there—waving bye in the glare of Pip's lights, the gate closing on him.

Sheila had made a last-ditch effort to get him to leave. She'd failed. Waving bye back at him, as I drove us away, she was trying hard not to cry.

I occupied myself thinking about Pip. Truth is, I think he got a secret kick out of what happened. As if somehow he's mad about the situation at the Baron's.

What the hell, really, is he? I have no idea. Gainsborough had a "valet" named "Phipps," I found out today. Maybe Pip, in different incarnations, has been with the barons all along. If so, I have a feeling he may not know it. Because more than anything else, Pip seems confused.

The only thing Sheila said, the entire way back, was this: "Duane, what was happening, when I woke you up? Where—were you?"

I said I didn't understand her question.

When we entered her apartment, she told me to sleep on the couch.

The next day, Sunday, which was yesterday—though it does seem like months, now—she spent writing in her diary, talking little with me.

Staring at decaying snow, I slowly went stir-crazy.

So last night I drove to Cambridge. Where this morning, in disguise, nervous, looking out for the purple hat, I researched the Spoor genealogy.

I learned that the Creature—that's what I'm calling him, them, now, the Creature—appears to have stolen over twenty-five bodies.

Twenty-five generations of murdered children. Seven centuries of it!

I'm assuming they were murdered. All those barons died awful deaths—it's in the record, those deaths happened. Maybe some of the boys, finding their youth snatched away, actually did commit suicide. But most of them probably were killed. I can think of a good motive. It must be depressing to have your ex-body sticking around, full of enraged and vengeful boy. Especially when you're all set to have a great time in his lusty young body.

Does Malcolm remember twenty-five lifetimes? Maybe he doesn't.

They are short lifetimes. He claims in the letter that his ancestors, if you can call them that, all died before reaching fifty. Not true. Hippolyte lived to fifty-four, and Francis to fifty-two. But most died younger. So the Spoor life cycle is short, because the boys usually were going on twenty when they got taken. That means the time in the new bodies averages about thirty years. Gainsborough got taken when he was twelve, though. That's how old he was when his father, Blake, died. Blake was trampled by his horse, after a dog "spooked" it, according to one account I read.

Blake must have been desperate. At the time he was only thirty-two. Maybe he was sick. Or maybe he just wanted to be a young boy. Who knows?

In 1451 Edward got taken when he was *seven.*

Now is this the kind of family history that could drive a man to drink? The answer of course is yes. But it's only part of the overall answer to the great puzzle of Malcolm, a.k.a. Gundulf, et al., Spoor.

Meantime his vices are his weakness. They aren't his only weakness. He is addicted to crude sensations for a reason. Maybe a lot of reasons. I reckon he feels guilt. Is there more? For example, why does he scream at Bunny? Why does he have any of those pictures up to begin with?

To remind him of himself?

One last thing. The letter to Torrance—I almost get the feeling he was trying to explain the true reality, but couldn't. So why give the boy any information at all?

For example, why bother to tell Torrance about Gundulf and Baybars?

Baybars, I learned at the library today, was a historical figure. He actually did conquer a Crusader castle named Krak. So Baybars was real, back in the thirteenth century. He walked and breathed. But a funny thing happened right after his big victory. He keeled over and died.

No one understood why. According to lore, his body was found on a "rose-drenched bed." And there was talk of the devil.

Was Baybars involved with the Curse? What happened on that bed? Besides somebody, very likely, getting scared out of his body?

In other words, who went where?

I'd like to answer a lot of questions. Maybe I will.

——

It's dark out now. I lie on this motel bed feeling bad. The rose is on the freezer shelf of my noisy little fridge. I sense it. It's tingling, faintly, in its frozen plastic bag. The tingle makes me wonder something.

I keep wondering if, despite the obvious dangers, I should try to make a deal with Malcolm Spoor.

Bunny Speaks

My dear insufferable Malcolm,

No, I have not come back to torment you. You deserve torment, however. I must say we all are offended by your lack of respect, your self-pity, your childish tantrums.

Speaking more personally, I am upset you seek to belittle me. Why did you post that newspaper? What point is there in reminding us of those events? You know how difficult it was for Gainsborough to kill himself. You know he nearly bungled that kill - therefore nearly bungling his creation of me. That I was then put on trial, for my own nearly ruined creation, was indeed a ludicrous and ironic misfortune!

Yet you make fun. You do realize that by lashing out in such a manner, you only hurt yourself?

In any case, I have laid the matter to rest. I have torn that newspaper into long, thin strips, which I have set afire. You will find the result in a corner of this strange television office. If it comes as a shock, well then, let that be a lesson. The smoke still eddies; actually, I am having a hard time forcing your body to write this, as your body happens to be coughing quite violently. (That gives me, I may say, a curious pleasure.)

But let us move on. Our principal reason for taking control of you in this unusual way is to inform you of something important. Malcolm, we are not spurning you. On the contrary, it is you who is spurning us.

You see, we have tried to commune with you. We have reached out repeatedly, in point of fact. But you simply will not listen. And how vexing this is! Have you no idea what pain you inflict? Why, Malcolm? Why do you ignore your Grislies?

Of course, we know the reason. We know the reason well, despite your efforts to hide it. Nevertheless, we are puzzled, and alarmed. For without us, you stray. Lacking guidance, Malcolm, you blunder. You follow a path that imperils us all!

Shall we itemize the follies? That, solo, you have committed?

First, there is the love of drink. You make yourself so dim; you are a fog. Worse, we suffer with you. Often we feel as though prostrate on the tavern floor, foolish, hapless! Do not dismiss this reproach because, even as I compel your hand to write it, liqueurs burn your gullet. I have reason to force them down - your hand writes the steadier for it!

Second, there is the flirtation with risk. Why expose Pip to the world? Take heed of Pip. We sense he begins to remember what he once was.

More shocking still is the laxity of your dealings with Torrance. Why must the boy leave the house? Under any circumstances, ever? What possible need has he of schooling? Can he not amuse himself sufficiently in his gymnasium, his pool? That he has lived apart, for many years, has been danger enough. Why, now, so close to Change, compound danger? Return to the old ways, Malcolm. Put the boy under lock and key!

Third, we are distressed by a possibility the foregoing suggests. We worry you may wish, indeed may be seeking - catastrophe.

How else do we explain recent events?

Have you an explanation, in particular, for Duane?

We commune, you know well, with the plants, the hounds. You do not; instead, you befuddle, before machines that shallowly glow. You think they show you the boy, the house, Pip. You see this, you see that, and you are comforted, because you think you see.

You see nothing. But the plants and the hounds see everything.

Two nights past, they saw disaster. As did we. We remained vigilant, that night. Oh yes, we watched it all, despite your impairment.

For we tasted the poison the instant you drank it!

Instantly, we fled it. Thus we did not slumber with you. We dimmed, to be sure, but we sounded the alarm. With the plants, with the hounds, we rallied - anxiously, we fortified *ensemble*.

You were helpless. The hounds were caged, Pip too, Torrance and the woman had the run of the house!

Then arrived that bumptious guest. Ever, in the history of The Spoor, has so gnatlike a being held such sway?

We attempted to frighten him. Yet he did not bolt.

No, he found you, and proceeded to *taste you*.

The likes of Duane, clammy with awe, putting his flesh to yours. Obliging us to cower, hide, do all that we could to conceal what we are. The hounds were triply enraged. The plants were fascinated!

But they, too, were appalled, when, shortly thereafter, he penetrated their chamber. Malcolm, we lost control.

You must realize, your poisoned brain was a hindrance - a nightmare, subaqueous. The hounds and the plants were not inclined to heed that morass. Nor did they themselves remain lucid, when Duane, evincing the gall only imbeciles possess, leapt upon the Altar - and *pranced*.

Thus we take no responsibility for what followed. No, what followed is entirely your fault; entirely due to your inexcusable carelessness, Malcolm. For it is you who allowed himself to be poisoned. You, who allowed Duane on the premises. You, who allowed that evening to veer out of control.

And veer it did. The hounds were uncontainable. Stupid as they sometimes are, they attempted to swallow Duane's Fire. In this they were abetted - not by us, of course, by the self-amusing plants. However, they did not succeed. To the astonishment of us all, Duane escaped!

But suppose the hounds had succeeded. Suppose the gnat had not fluttered away. Torrance and Sheila would have found - a corpse.

Contemplate, if you will, the consequences of that. Quite certainly, Torrance would not be here tonight. Furthermore, Sheila might have taken revenge. For she is tied to Duane, tied tightly; and had she attempted revenge, who could have stopped her? Torrance?

We contemplated. So alarmed were we, we convened to discuss it.

Gundulf, as you may imagine, was somewhat too sere, shall we say, to lead. The Grand Creator is not what he once was; and there is some feeling among us this has much to do with you. I must point out, he has all but thrown up his hands, in despair, as far as you are concerned.

Therefore, I took charge. And why not? I know you best. I killed myself, after all, to create you. I am your Predecessor, you are my Successor, it was entirely appropriate that I lead.

You bristle, I know, but *tant pis.*

Let us face a fact, there is another reason. Just as Gainsborough almost ruined me, I, too, almost ruined you - and I advise you to stop holding that against me. The sad truth is, Change hasn't been, lately, the sport it was for the Elders.

Thus I have insight into your condition, Malcolm.

You see, I know you are not truly looking forward to killing yourself. And I know you are feeling squeamish about creating your Successor. I know all this well, because I felt the same myself, on my own Eve of Change - when I faced the responsibility of creating you.

Malcolm, that is why I make this appearance. I have been charged, by all the Grislies, to try to help you. Let us not mince words, you are facing a crisis of nerve. That crisis is why you have closed yourself off. It is why you struggle on in isolation, attempting to go it alone, without us.

And it is all due to one fact. Admit this: You shrink from the thought of creating Torrance!

But you must. You must do it, yes you must, and you will.

If deciding the method troubles you, that is understandable. Perhaps in your case a pistol is not the solution. Perhaps, Malcolm, you should resort to a strangling, or to something wholly undramatic, such as injection, for example. But however you do it, let me tell you, you will feel an immense relief when it is done. I daresay you will feel a kind of ecstasy, when you see your corpse lying there before you - lying still, so still, in its finality.

Because at that moment, you will have become one of us.

Malcolm, you will have entered your Grislihood. More splendid still, you will have created a new vessel for us all. You will have created the new Living One, Torrance!

Of course, there is the regrettable issue.

Console yourself with this thought: The boy will understand. He will know full well the form he spent sixteen years developing, and perfecting, is now ready to serve a higher good. Sacrifice is the highest good of all, no? So from this, take comfort: The boy will be suffused with the greatness of his sacrifice, as he dies. As he dies with you, dear Malcolm.

The Sons and the Fathers always have died together, no? If that is not pure beauty, what is?

For from Death, the Living proceeds. Torrance the newly created will go on. He will live on with his Grislies, including the newest - Malcolm, Baron Grisly of Spoor!

What fun that will be. His form is lovely, I must acknowledge, it is lithe and strong. All of us are looking forward to scampering about, mad yet again with a boy's love for life.

And so we implore you, enter your Grislihood willingly, Malcolm. If you are willing, you will not make mistakes. If you are unwilling, you will make a mess of things, just as did Gainsborough, and I. The kill is necessary. You must do it. *And you will.*

I have been asked by the others to remark upon a few things more.

You are right about Sheila. The plants are enthralled, for she carries the Fire so well. Are you aware it was she who saved Duane? She summoned him, from the vastation into which he had fled, escaping the hounds. The woman showed strength; she is, indeed, perfect. Best of all, she seems wholly unknowing of it.

Apropos Duane - destroy him. He covets our Fire, will go to desperate lengths merely to taste it. Give the hounds what they wanted, from Duane. They will enjoy that. And so might we. Oh yes, we very much would like to savor the spark that is Duane.

Finally, pay homage to the plants. You do not show them the love that is their due. We fear they may be annoyed, Malcolm. If it is so, it cannot continue. It cannot continue one instant.

Because this you know well: The plants we must never annoy.

Oh, dear. I have made a little mess with one of these sticky carafes. Malcolm, your thirsty constitution has demanded, and received, much liqueur. Ah, far too much, I am tipsy! Thus are we all, no? How charming it is, I confess, to be tavernmaster again.

You must agree, it has been an extraordinarily trying moment.

Begging forgiveness for this trespass upon your sad flesh, I remain,

> Your apprehensive Creator,
> Bunny,
> BARON GRISLY OF SPOOR

The Secret Journal
of Torrance Spoor's
Secret War: III

Monday Night

I should smash the truck through the gate right now. And get away from here for ever.

This just happened: I went to the video office. Dad said he wanted to talk. I saw him this morning, the first time since Saturday, and he said we have to talk. The way he said it meant we HAVE TO. I was scared but I said ok. It was supposed to be in the library after dinner. So I go there after dinner, which he did not have with us. Pip took food to his room like last night. "Malcolm isn't well," Pip keeps saying. Right. Sure, I don't know this fact about Dad. Ok, I get to the library, and he does not show up! I am sitting there totally nervous, thinking, what does he want to talk about? The cameras? The Curse? Like, do I want to kill him or something? Maybe everything that happened with Sheela and Dwain.

Half an hour goes by and he isn't there. The next half hour goes by and I am freaking.

Pip was gone, he finished in the kitchen and left. I know, cause I went there to ask where Dad is. But, no Pip. I wonder: Is Pip in the basement? Maybe with the dogs. He likes it there, better than anywhere else. Should I go find him and ask where Dad is?

Then I think about it worse than usual. Why am I alone in this fucking creepy house? With Pip and the dogs and Dad?

Dwain the weird geek is why. The shithead with mental powers, he is why I am still here. I made the decision, yeah. But I did because he said he wants to help me. Ok, what if he is not doing it? Sheela warned me. She said I'm crazy to stay.

Thinking about that was not making anything better. I start wondering if this is it. This is when Dad cooks me: Apple in my mouth.

I had the gun. Really, I was ready to shoot him. Even if that makes the stupid Curse happen. Maybe I should!

He still doesn't show up. I go to the office. Where else would he be? He is always in that office. I walk up the stairs, down the hall, feeling something bad is going to be there.

And I see a strange sight. The office door is wide open.

Then I smell something. There is smoke in the hall.

Dad never leaves the office open. But the smoke? That is even more wild. I say to myself, holy shit - what is the maniac doing now?

Then I hear him coughing.

I hear it so loud, I know the second door must be open too. I hit the wall and slide down it slowly. In case he has not seen me already on the video by now. I get to the door. I peek.

He is staring at me. I can't pull my head back without feeling dumb, he's sitting at the desk staring right at me. And then he smiles. He starts laughing. That makes him cough more, really hard.

Then, like he is the happiest guy in the world, who just saw his best friend, he waves, and yells: "Oh Torrance, come in, come in!"

That is weird. He does not care if I know about his video shit? I am like, frozen. Trying to think of something to say.

I say: "What are you doing?"

He thought that was funny. Really funny. By the time he stopped laughing and coughing, I decide, ok. I want him to answer questions. Now.

I go in. He says: "I have been writing a letter. But I'm finished. I am at your disposal."

I see the letter on the desk. He wrote it with pen and paper. He turns it over like he doesn't want me to read it. A bunch of bottles are on the floor. They are empty. One is tipped over. I realize: Dad is drunk.

I look around, and see ashes in a corner. Part of it isn't burned. It looks like a ripped-up newspaper. Carefully, so he does not notice me doing it, I check the wall. And I see Bunny is gone. Great. He screams at Bunny. Now he burns Bunny. My father is a dangerous mental case.

He says: "Torrance. You are pale. Sit down, please have a seat."

I decide I better stay by the door. There is a chair there. I sit.

He says: "Well, well. What have you been up to, dear boy?"

I say: "You told me we have to talk."

He says: "Really? Talk? Oh, I see, talk. Yes. Talk."

I point at the video screens and say: "Maybe about that."

He looks at them with a puzzled expression on his face. Like he is thinking, Who put those stupid video screens in my office? I am getting kind of mad. Then he says this: "Torrance, do you know how to use it?"

I say: "Use what?"

He says: "That television system."

I think: He wants to find out if I was in here Saturday. But I am not going to admit it. I say to him: "I don't use it, Dad. You do. What for, by the way?"

And he says: "I use it? Oh, yes, of course. But do you know how to turn it on?"

I say: "Why do you ask that?"

He says: "Because I have been sitting here trying to make it work . . ."

I wonder if I should beat him to death with a baseball bat. That would be more fun than the gun. He is pretending he doesn't know how to use it? That is so dumb. What a stupid act to put on. He even looks like he knows it. He can't even finish what he is saying, it's so stupid. But he smiles at me like I'm the one who is out of it. I yell at him: *Why do you spy on me, Dad?*"

He looks like he is dreaming. And says: "Oh. We do not know." What does he mean, we? Then he says: "Many reasons, I suppose." He looks like he is trying to think of one. I wish he would. "They *are* odd, those televisions," he says with that drunk dream expression. "Well, some things are not easily explained, Torrance. You are so fit, child. In such very good shape. Did you swim today?"

Oh, brother. If this is an act it is getting good. I feel like asking him if he knows the telephone number of the local loony bin. Ashes and smoke are floating in the air - I am sitting there trying not to breathe. I point at the burned newspaper and ask him: "Why did you do that?"

Now he looks totally drunk. And he gets pissed off, like I'm making fun of him. He seems insulted, his lips start shaking, and his eyes all of a sudden are wet, like he might even cry. Man. Two minutes ago he was laughing his head off. Then he says: "I did not do it, Torrance. I didn't!"

I look at the ashes, look at him, and say: "Who did? Pip?"

He says: "No. No, no - Pip has never done anything like that."

I say: "Who did do it, then?"

He says: "Gainsborough. He killed himself, of course."

I just look at him.

He looks back like he realizes I'm not getting it. But he says: "Gainsborough killed himself. It wasn't murder, you see. We are not murderers, Torrance. We kill ourselves, you see - we do not murder. But the whole world was shouting it. We sat there for weeks, listening to them shout it - shouting murder, my boy. Murder, murder, murder, in the press, on the radio, at the trial, *murder*! But Torrance, it was all a misunderstanding. They simply did not understand."

I say: "I think I better go now."

He says: "Very well." Like it is a good idea.

I stand up and say: "Dad, you keep talking about understanding. But I don't understand anything about you. At all."

He says: "You will."

I say: "I doubt it."

He says: "Oh no, you will."

I say: "How do you know? You are crazy."

He says: "Oh yes. But your poor father will make sure of it, that you understand," and he starts *crying*.

I say: "Maybe we can talk tomorrow?"

He just keeps crying. I leave, and run down the hall.

———

Now I'm in my room wondering what the fuck I should do.

Too much. The whole thing, too much. There is a total freak Saturday night. Sheela and me have sex and the rubber breaks. First time with a woman, the rubber breaks! Then Dwain shows up. He was so mad, wow, about me and Sheela. And he takes over the whole deal. He has to know everything that happened. I get more scared, Sheela does too, cause Dwain acts like it's Night of the Living Dead in this house.

When he left for the rose room - Sheela said it, "Dwain looks nervous." When we see him in the monitors, he looks more nervous, and Sheela says: "Something horrible is going to happen." He goes in back, we can't see him. And a couple minutes later, the monitors go crazy!

So does Sheela. She screams: "Torrance, I'm scared out of my mind!" She grabs me, practically drags me down the hall. If she was scared, I do not want to see it when she is brave, she would have kicked snakes off the floor just to get to the elevator. When it opens in the basement, she makes me run, but she runs faster. I say to myself: Wow! *Something horrible really is happening.* We get to the rose room. She stares through the door for a second, then yells, "Oh my God!" and runs right in. Dwain is way in the back, passed out. She jumps on him, like she wants to slug him in the face, but she starts screaming: "Dwain, Dwain! *Where are you?*"

Ok, he wakes up. Thank God. Cause I am seeing: He shat his pants. That kind of amazes me. The whole thing, Sheela screaming, shaking him, it amazes me completely.

———

So, are they basket cases? Or what?

Nothing was happening. It was just those roses.

Later, Sheela and me had private talks. She said Dwain might have mental powers. She was nervous about it, like she wasn't sure, but she said Dwain might know more than he admits. She also said, maybe I should not trust him. But like me, she was flipping out. She knows nothing about what really happened. What should I do, listen to her? Or to Dwain, who might have mental powers - and know what is happening with Dad? Maybe Dwain is right. Maybe Dad is scared of me. Maybe he wants me to kill him!

I would be such a fool to give in to that.

So, I have been thinking. Dwain knows a lot. The way he found us. It flips me out, that he found us. When we saw the tape of him coming it was so fucking scary. He walked through the house right to the office. Like a zomby, walking jerky, but a smart one, cause he knew where to go. I freaked. Not just at Dwain, at the system. It cuts automatic, room to room, he was walking out a door, then walking from it - but in a *different room*, like camera crews are taping all over the house. Anyway I think he smelled us. It seemed like he smelled us. That sweet smell, must of been Sheela's perfume. How could he do that? Mental powers? He just kept coming. Like a splatter nerd wanting to get us!

Then he ends up saying he will help me. And gives me orders: Pretend nothing happened. Why? So he can help me. So we can find out what Dad is doing. Great. I had to wonder - if Dwain has mental powers, what if Dad does too and finds out? What if he knows everything and pretends he does not? Like if we didn't clean up the office as good as we thought?

So yesterday, there I was with Pip, we pretended all day that nothing happened. Dad stayed in his room. Maybe in the office. I didn't try to find out, I was sacred to even go near there.

Then today I see him at breakfast. He looks ok, sort of. And he says we must talk.

But tonight, he's a complete idiot! I point at burned-up Bunny. He says, "I did not do it. Gainsborough killed himself. We do not murder." Like - what? What the fuck? Did I say anything about murder? That stuff in the paper happened so many years ago. Dad was not even alive, of course he didn't do it. Why is he upset? What does he mean by "we" - the Spoor family? The murder is such a bad shame, he takes it too personal when he gets drunk or something, and thinks he did it?

He's getting crazier. He seemed like a different person tonight. He even cried. It makes me so confused. I almost feel sorry for the asshole.

It's one big FREAK here.

So I plan my quick gettaway. In case Dwain is not too smart about all this. He thinks he is, but what if he isn't?

I just want to get back to school. Tomorrow is school, the roads will be clear. Day after tomorrow is writing class and I see Sheela. Not till then, have to follow orders. Dwain said we better not even call. Why?

But he did say one thing. That's common sense. He said: Do I want the money? Dad's money. I said: No.

He said: The money will give you freedom.

I thought about it. I want freedom. From Mom. From *Dad*. He knew about the money and Dad's unbelievable plan to give it to me, cause he read my letter to Mom. What a fuck up. Sheela got it, not Mom. So Mom will get the note to Sheela soon. I really fucked up. But hey. Maybe Mom should know a little about this after all.

Now I feel like a jerk wanting the money.

But just some of it. Then I could be free. Mom, she would get used to it. To me not being her idea of the All-American she wants. Sorry, Mom, I like guys. No matter what Dad says about me and Sheela. Getting married, what a stupid idea. Even though she turned me on.

I put spit on her face and she liked it. I didn't know if she would.

I did that with Ricky in LJ, he showed me. We did it when we had sex and it was like invading faces. Invading, that's what I love about sex. I miss him. All the cool times we had.

So I think about school tomorrow. I think about Erik a lot. Maybe I should talk to him finally. After swimteam or something.

Can I tell him about what happens here? No way.

The Diary
of Sheila Massif: X

Monday Night

It's really late. And Duane hasn't come back. He hasn't even called. Is he still doing research? What the hell is it, this research?

Diary, I'm having trouble writing about the last phase of the night at Malcolm's. I just can't deal with it. Leaving Torrance there is probably the worst thing I have ever done.

And I have done a lot of bad things. Lately, especially. Having sex with Torrance, for example. That was pretty bad. He's a boy!

Sure, kids have sex all the time. They have it earlier and earlier, that's common knowledge, anyway I'm sure it always happened, since we were monkeys. However, I'm not a kid, or a monkey. I'm a teacher.

But what's really bothering me is Duane.

He is a liar. He lied about the roses. That's not all. He lied to Torrance, and me, about what's going on with Malcolm—about what's going on in that whole house!

I didn't want to believe anything supernatural was happening. I resisted believing that for as long as I could. Torrance, for example, was talking about ghosts—nonsense, right? But when Duane looked at the roses on the studio screens, he seemed so shocked. As if he were looking at the worst industrial accident in history, twenty seconds after it happened.

He decided he had to take a closer look. That was fine, at first, because he'd been glaring at me, and my jailbait, whose condom had broken. But when he left, Torrance and I suddenly couldn't say anything to each other. An uncomfortable silence descended. Rather than make eye contact, we stared at the roses. Then Duane appeared in the screens, waved, and disappeared. The way he did it made me think he was saying: If I'm not back in ten minutes, send in the Swat Team.

A little while later, the screens went haywire. And somehow, I knew Duane was in danger. I *felt* it. I've never been so frantic in my life. A hideous idea hit me: He is about to die. Unless something is done, Duane is going away forever. So, he had to be saved. That was why I was frantic. I knew he had to be saved.

It seems ridiculous now. But it didn't, then. When we got to him, and I touched him, he felt—not there. Not there at all. Did I have a psychotic break? He didn't seem out of it in any garden-variety way, unconscious, sick, or whatever. He literally felt gone. Not there. Far away!

He was—*vacant.* But he was breathing. So where was he? If he wasn't there? And why did I know I had to get him back? But— back from where?

Then, I did get him back. I think I did. I had a sensation of making him come back! When he opened his eyes—I can't deal with this. It was as if Duane had just beamed in from the moon!

In short: the single worst scare I have ever had.

A lot of worst singles, all at once. I don't like it. I'm up to my neck in psychic goings-on that seem real, and extremely dangerous, and Duane hasn't come back from wherever he went—he said Cambridge, but for all I know it's the moon, again—and Torrance is still in that house.

Which is my fault! Ok, Duane talked him into staying, not me, I tried to get him to leave. But the thing is, I could have outtalked Duane. And I didn't really try. Why? It was obvious Duane was lying. If he has a "condition," I have divine revelations. The condition of his pants just made the lie more obvious. Something awful happened in that rose room. Something he didn't tell us about.

All right, fine. What happened? Really, I don't want to know. But that's why I feel guilty. It's why I didn't outtalk Duane, why I didn't tell Torrance the biggest reason he should leave. I didn't have the nerve to admit what I'd felt. The place where Duane went is a terrible place. And he would have stayed there—*if I hadn't made him come back!*

Ok, I am having a psychotic break. Soon I'll be put away. The orderlies will tell each other, "She says there is this 'terrible place.'"

Anything else you want to say, lady? Oh, the kid, you're worried he's in danger because of the terrible place. You feel guilty you didn't warn him about it. And the reason you didn't, was because you were afraid you'd have to be bananas to think the terrible place exists. Guess what? You are bananas. There is no terrible place. Unless it's your Drama Chamber. But don't worry, the Chamber won't be a problem for the kid. Despite the fact you seduced him. He told us all about that, of course . . .

———

Oh, God. I have to admit something. The last few Diary entries have been a distraction. A tactic to avoid confronting the fact I'm losing it. When the lights went out at Malcolm's, and I thought I saw the red eyes—Diary, I almost went to the Chamber. I wrote about it as if it were funny. But it wasn't. My boundaries *blurred.*

Then Torrance talked about his fear of being eaten. I thought I'd have a breakdown. The idea of being eaten is such a perfect metaphor for my disease. What blurs boundaries more completely, than being eaten? You lose your shape. You get absorbed. There's no you anymore, if you get eaten!

I'm a psychologist. Supposedly I study gender boundaries. Supposedly I know about this stuff. I am at the mercy of this stuff. All my life I've had boundary problems. With all kinds of boundaries, except gender ones, of course, that's why I think I can study them. Boundaries—the very word makes me shiver! Where does the world stop? Where do I begin? It's like walking on a beach. The outermost edge of a titanic thing, of the biggest thing in the world, fizzes into the sand at your feet. Why does it end right there? Why does the sand start right there? If the ocean is so titanic, couldn't it decide to move, suddenly?

That's how I feel about life. I'm afraid it will move, like a tidal wave, and swallow me. I've always felt that way, since I can remember. So I invented a place. A safe place, where I could go. A place with vaultlike, steel-lined boundaries. The Chamber.

How self-defeating. It just makes the outside world seem all the more dangerous. And here I am facing the second week of being a teacher, a bogus one trying to figure out boundaries, and I'm dealing with a colossal creep who effortlessly—*destroys boundaries!* He plots break-ins of my apartment, takes pictures of my Diary, reads it, reads all about me. He has a TV snoop system that intrudes on his son, even in the bathroom, it intrudes on anyone in that house, and he does it from a secret room, using hidden cameras. He has dogs that paralyze deer, God only knows what else. He has roses that made Duane lose control of his bowels—that's messing with boundaries! Worst of all, he has a terrible place in his house that—

Somehow took Duane out of his body.

It's as if God wants to punish me. I try to get a grip on my problems. But my problems materialize into a horror show, and mutate, taking steadily worse forms, then even worse ones!

So—I'm mad. I've been having fantasies. As I've been writing this, I've been having fantasies of vengeance. They feature the Chamber. They address the fact I do not want to spend the rest of my life hiding in it. I am sick of hiding in it. So what do I do?

The answer is obvious. I make everybody else hide in it. I perform a cosmic flip-flop of boundaries, and come out on top, telling the whole world: To the Chamber you go!

Yes. Then they can see what it's like to hide. To have their very existence threatened. By the all-powerful Boundary Goddess—me!

It's a good thing I'm locking this up in a safety deposit box, tomorrow morning. Because if anyone ever reads you, Diary, *I'll* be locked up.

But my vengeance fantasies have some foundation. You aren't the only thing I'm locking up tomorrow. Torrance is going to safety with you. I'm taking you both out of danger. I'm putting you both out of reach.

You and a videocassette, that is.

I stole a videocassette Saturday night. I smuggled it out of Malcolm's studio, under Duane's psychic nose, in a bag of used paper towels. Torrance and I had used lots of paper towels in that studio. We'd been busy with fingerprint wipings and general Windexings.

Duane was obsessed with not leaving evidence. He didn't want Malcolm to know we'd been in there. Why, he didn't bother to explain. I was baffled, but didn't bother to debate. By then I was numb with shock. I could barely think. However, I'm not a fool.

Duane didn't want to leave evidence behind? I couldn't have agreed more. I bagged the tape while he was bagging his filthy clothes, probably thinking up more lies as he did it.

I don't care if he's furious. I might not even tell him. All I care about is protecting Torrance, and me, from Malcolm.

That man is evil. I don't know how, exactly, he is evil, but I am certain he is, and I also know Duane is mishandling this entire crisis. For reasons of his own, he is covering up. Maybe because he wants to get something out of it!

I, meantime, am determined to get Torrance away from Malcolm. It's ok if his mother discovers he's gay. It's ok if he's disinherited. *There is something evil in that house.*

So I'm thinking of calling his mother and telling her about a video-cassette entitled: T-Sex.

Malcolm could retaliate. He could use the Diary photos to blow me to smithereens at school. Also, Torrance would hate me. And I wouldn't blame him.

But if I have to, I can put an end to the worst aspect of this situation. I can guarantee Malcolm will never see Torrance again.

Memorandum from Miss Cunif
to Claus Schmidtt: II

Tuesday Morning

TO: SCHMIDTT
FROM: CUNIF
RE: SHEILA MASSIF

Telephone: 508 xxx xxxx.
Relationship to Allbright: romantic.

———

Blovko determined that Allbright and Massif have been involved for at least two years. The Director and I were unaware of this. Security files contain no references. Inexcusable, Claus.

New England Tel provided the number. Blovko traced the name back to Stanford. She and Allbright both were there year before last, she doing doctoral work, he liaising with research affiliates. According to Massif's former roomate, she and Allbright became intimate. They may have resumed.

Gonzalez arrives from Washington today. He, you and Blovko will investigate Massif.

Find Allbright. Keep a low profile. Do not engage local authorities.

Insert needles in eyes.

The Chronicles
of Malcolm Spoor: VI

Tuesday Morning

Bunny has paid a visit. An ostentatious visit, with ambassadorial overtones - he claims to speak for all the Grislies. I shake my head sadly. Gundulf, "too sere." Oh, of course. "So I took charge." Naturally! Poor Bunny. Poor pitiful Bunny, this is an obvious ploy. A pathetic maneuver indeed - though alarming, he proves his insidious cunning. Oh yes, he demonstrates the lengths to which he is prepared to go.

Truly, the malevolence is frightening. But he knows not with whom he deals. He deals with The Living One. He has had to deal with me ever since he created me - and by now, should know better. Bunny, you are no more than a detestable *wraith* - I wish it, therefore it is so!

A bodiless phantom, yet he takes me to task. I have been diligent, and clever; he does not know why, or how. I pity you, Bunny. And if you think I am prone to making mistakes, you are the one who recently has made them - drunkenly speaking with Torrance that way! Dropping broad hints, eh, Bunny? Crying, in front of Torrance,

so conspicuously revealing your problems, not mine - your own re-
grets, not mine - your guilt, Bunny, *your* guilt! Not mine!

Because you see, and now I address you all - particularly, of
course, the "Sere" One - I have no reticence about creating Torrance. None whatsoever. You do not believe me? Wait, and see.

No, I am very much in control, so please do not attempt any more
sneak comebacks, above all do not listen to Bunny. He showed the
stuff he is made of when he faced Change, and vacillated, so very
weak-kneed, about creating me. He almost couldn't do it! And he
dares doubt my resolve? Odd, that he now plays the taskmaster.
Even more odd, that he should hijack me at a delicate time - the
precise time I was scheduled to have a talk with Torrance. What
was it, Bunny, you wished to say to Torrance? Were you by any
chance fighting an impulse to - oh, let us be truly dire! - warn him?

Grislies, consider the fact that Bunny, who chastises me for keeping you "on the tavern floor" - I do rather relish, I must say, the idea
of that - reduced himself, in my control room, to pathetic *drunken-
ness.* When I entered this morning, bottles lay toppled!

What, I wonder, could have been smarting dear Bunny so?

In any case, everything is working out beautifully. If you cannot
discern the genius in my plans, well, I can scarcely be faulted. It is
true I do not share everything with you; it is equally true you do not
share everything with me. At least, I have a recollection of Bunny's
words with Torrance. I am incensed, that he added to the boy's
turmoil. The spyroom, you Fools, is a major issue. Why, he might
have tried to run away. And if he had succeeded, where, I ask you,
would we be?

Inviting the boy into the spyroom! "Do you know how to turn it
on?" Irresponsible Bunny, wanting to play with my video system. I
know none of you understands my need for such elaborate spying,
but my reasons are my own, not yours, and they are very good
reasons.

As for Saturday, the unfortunate episode with Sheila and Duane -
well, an annoyance, yes. But there is benefit, too. I have plans for
that pair, you see. I believe they will be useful.

Bunny has caused the greatest inconvenience, however. This
morning I was forced to take major steps to repair the damage. I
ordered Pip to inactivate some of the cameras - he and Torrance
literally are tearing them from walls, the ones in his rooms, this very
minute. I suppose it would have been necessary anyway, since the
boy knew of them, but what with Bunny's interference, it had to be

done instantly - which annoys me. The only good result is that the boy now thinks I am so muddled and mad, I cannot be a menace. Thank you, muddle-mad Bunny, for that.

Now then, I must attend to business. Keep your rancid snouts out of it. If you must surveille, do so quietly, I've much on my mind. And if you really are so foolish as to be anxious, I say this - watch me spin my web. Watch, and be awed.

What must I do? Oh yes, call Sheila. She thinks herself so clever. She is a sitting duck. As is the inconsequential Duane - he spoke with me, half an hour ago. He was loitering in the woods, at the fence. He and I, and the dogs, had a chat. I think he was quite impressed.

By the way - very soon, the plants will think me the equal of the best of you. Perhaps, your better.

Duane Allbright's
Audiocassette Notes: III

Tuesday Morning

9:30 Tuesday morning. I'm sitting in a pickup truck, parked in the mall across from Sheila's, trying to get my thoughts together. Pip just drove off. I followed him here, and talked with him. What a puzzle he is. Most of all, I reckon, to himself.

———

I started early, outside the chain-link fence that takes over deep in woods from the Baron's wall. This pickup plowed me in. I found it in the garage of somebody's house. Smart people own houses around here; it seems a lot of them don't like winter. I'm grateful for the truck. It's V8, goes ninety easy. And the plow works.

You can't see the house from where I was. There's the meadow beyond the fence, then a hill the meadow goes halfway up, to trees. Trees cover the top of the hill, and just about everything else. The house is on the other side, on another hill. If I have any sense of direction it is. The ocean surrounds the whole area, but isn't visible where I parked. The hills block off the water. You wouldn't know you're on a peninsula. Not too far on, the Baron owns it.

Last I saw it I was high in the sky. The whole place, post-blizzard, glimmered in the sea. I thought I could see every detail. But this morning, those details had faded. A map, if I can find one, would be useful.

I pulled up against a tree close to the fence and stared at the meadow and the hill, wondering when they would come, or if they would. I could tell they knew I was there. I felt them feeling me. What I didn't know was if they could home in. Psi doesn't work directional for me but for all I knew it does for them, and I wanted to find out.

Well, the dogs don't have radar. They have all kinds of other shit, but not radar.

It was seven o'clock and cold. The sun was just breaking, putting long violet shadows on the untouched snow.

They burst from the treeline halfway down the hill. So I was right about that. If they came from the house, anyway. The snow didn't bother them none. It's a foot to two feet on the meadow, depending on how the wind blew I guess. Seven of them were racing like speedboat icebreakers, leaving churned-up powdery wake, making direct for the spot where the wall turns into the fence, a hundred feet or so behind me. They were beautiful—liver-brown, powerful, rushing through the white.

Then one of them must have seen the truck. Because all seven suddenly wheeled straight at me.

I rolled down the window.

They boiled powder to the chain link and sat, panting vapor, the eyes glowing dull ruby red. We stared at each other, seven against one.

I wasn't counting on glowing tunnels, this time. The roses weren't there, backing them up. My rose wasn't in my pocket, either, that's a mistake I won't repeat. But I didn't know what to expect. The truck, geared in reverse, was ready for my foot to mash.

Nothing happened. We just stared at each other. What kind of breed they are I can't say. Giant Rottweiler crossed with Great Dane —the hair naps short and slick over maybe two hundred pounds-plus of bone and muscle. Seven times that, I thought, is a ton and a half of dog. Just those seven could take down the hippo Sheila thinks the dartgun is for. They could take down a chain-link fence—even one as tall and heavy-gauge as the Baron's. Big jaws, fangs. Cute perky ears. I couldn't see their paws. They panted. Otherwise they didn't make a sound.

"Hey, fellas," I said. No reply. Except for the wall of fire their psi made; a wall between me and the Baron. So hot I expected to see snow melting. It didn't, of course. Psi doesn't melt snow.

I opened the door on the driver side, away from the tree I'd parked against, and climbed on the roof of the cab and sat, then took off a boot and three layers of socks and climbed the tree; then, braced in a fork, I stuck out my leg, and, feeling a little ungainly, put my foot to the cold steel mesh, clenching with my toes. Bet I looked a total fool. But there wasn't any other way. Stick them through snow-level? Hope they'd nuzzle? Good-bye, toes. Besides which, maybe they'd decide to tear down the fence.

That could mean good-bye truck. And I would be up a tree. I'd chosen that tree carefully, though. It was climbable.

I wanted to learn about those animals. Learn whatever I could.

Next thing I knew, two were going crazy. Suddenly they were leaping at the footmeat they couldn't reach, waffled as it was on the mesh about ten inches above where the paws hit, twanging and shaking the whole stretch of fence. The others just sat, watching, tongues hanging.

It worked. I almost fell out of the tree. The metal conducted right to my toes. Just have to love those freezing fence-clenched toes. They burned and froze at the same time, the animal psi pretty near cooked me. I held on long as I could. Less than a minute.

Long enough to know they're old. Whizzed me down a bottomless shaft, they did, no basement in sight, no crash. Those dog-minds were born a long time ago. Maybe farther back than Malcolm. Could be, I would have just kept on falling; but even if I had hit bottom, what would that have told me? It's not as if doors open like a time machine's. Delivering places in history, pyramids being built, foolishness like that.

I confirmed a couple of other things, though, besides the fact they're old. By themselves, without roses helping, the dogs have a talent. I'd experienced it before. It's a talent to scare.

Not just from the way those two looked with their eyes going redder, fangs bared, their bodies thudding against the fence. It derives from a quality they have, of being hungry. That quality strikes total terror.

All animals spend most of their time looking for dinner. Hunger rules the animal world. But these dogs are insatiable—and there must be few sensations more scary than knowing something more powerful than you, thinks you are delicious. I felt that. The dogs wanted me. They wanted my flesh, and they wanted my psi.

The other aspect I read is connected. It, too, echoed something I'd already felt. The dogs on the fence didn't seem like two dogs. They seemed like one dog, one enormous beast—so huge that, for a moment, I was sure they'd flatten the fence, then eat the whole tree, including me. They hit with ferocious *weight.* I realized I was feeling all of them, all seven at once; and then realized the five other dogs, which weren't anywhere close to the fence, could easily be part of it. But there was no way to tell. It didn't seem like a pack mentality. They weren't individual animals, collaborating to make a team. They literally had merged—into a unity, a *single thing.*

I pulled my foot. One hand over my eyes, the other holding that foot, I breathed hard, trembling, in the crook of the branches.

A little while later, there was silence. The terror faded. I took a look. They were sitting in a row—tongues hanging, vapor puffing—staring back. The eyes, glowing less red, seemed bored. Even slightly amused.

I clambered down to the roof of the truck. Putting on socks, lacing up the boot, thankful I'd managed not to mess my pants, I wondered how many people it's been, who've ended up in those beasts. Who've literally been eaten, flesh, blood and all—and beyond that, had their psi stripped, and digested, on a different level of consumption.

A more horrible level. I thought at them, "Think you're tough, huh?"

Well. They did think that. That's because they are.

And I thought, I managed to read. How much did they? How much of what I read did they, or more accurately, it, read me reading?

Couldn't tell. They were just sitting there, panting, eyes amused. Big dogs with funny reddish eyes, sitting on the other side of a fence that sagged some now.

After resting a few minutes, I got in the truck. What next? I didn't know. I revved the engine loudly to show how tough I am, too. Then I stuck my head out the window to say bye.

And I felt him. Watching me. Through the red eyes.

Didn't think he could do that. Didn't think it was possible. But what do I know what's possible for the Freak and his dogs? Little, it seems. Because then he started talking to me.

You almost had an accident, the red eyes said.

I nearly did, when I heard that.

It wouldn't have been the first time, the eyes said. *Runt!* they then exclaimed.

Hi, I said. I didn't say it. I thought it.

You are surprised, the dog eyes said. *That is no surprise.*

Yes, I thought at them. *I am. Good morning.*

Don't be tiresome, the eyes sneered. *Where is the rose?*

The rose? I thought.

Fool! they eyes yelled. *I smell it ALL OVER YOU!*

Yes, I thought back, suddenly smelling it myself. *I guess you do.*

The dogs, the eyes remarked, *think it makes you tastier. But you are so meager, runt.*

Maybe I should be glad about that, I thought. *Maybe next time, they won't try so hard. To swallow me.*

Insolence! the eyes snapped. *You are a pest. And you know what fate I reserve for pests. Even tiny ones like you.* The eyes seemed to sigh. Or maybe, think. They then said, almost conversationally, *I want you to do something.*

Yes? I thought.

Protect the baby, the red eyes said, glowing brighter, suddenly, in the brownish dogheads.

The baby? I asked.

Yes! the eyes yelled, glowing the brightest yet. Now I know more about what Torrance means by the screams. The yells were like screams. Or howls.

Ok, I thought. *But tell me—what baby?*

Torrance's, stupid, the eyes growled. *Protect it, runt, and I will reward you. Fail, and I will destroy you. Now leave. Come back tomorrow. Later in the day, this is much too early. You woke me and I dislike being woken, runt. Go. Go! Just looking at you makes me ill.*

Yes, I thought. *Yes.*

Slowly, I backed the truck down the lane.

———

It was the first direct telepathy of thoughts in words that I've ever known. For him it's ordinary. For me and the rest of mankind's historical record of psi, it's unique. I thought of the Project, our experiments, the millions spent. Garbage. Primitive trash. We proved a few things. We conducted flashes of images and thoughts at the Lab. We confirmed isolated instances of remarkably vivid psi communication. But all that's nothing compared to talking. I mean: *talking*. Back and forth. Through dogs!

Then there's the fact he sees through their eyes.

I thought about the rose. It was under laundry, in the truck. But when he asked about it, the odor came off me like sweet burning rubber.

———

I drove to the road, turned right and rambled random for several miles, then turned back, went by the gates, and plowed into a rest area a few hundred yards down.

Not much was there. Frozen picnic tables. Some frozen trash, crusted with snow. Tire tracks told me kids probably use the place for things they can't do at home.

Land-Rover was what I was looking for. I figured I had about an hour's wait before Pip took Torrance to school.

I sat, heater blasting, thinking about the baby. Of course it has to be Sheila. A fertilized egg less than three days old. The eyes had talked as though I should have known. I hadn't known. Malcolm wants me to protect it. He wants the baby. This means he wants Sheila. Which means he wants me to protect Sheila. I can do that, I thought.

More and more proof my theory is true. Makes sense that he can pick up on a pregnancy, if it's one of his future bodies. His psi's been focused on future bodies for hundreds of years. I remembered Gainsborough's problem with children. And Malcolm's letter telling Torrance that Spoors have one male child a generation. "We dangle from one of history's more fragile threads," he wrote. It occurred to me that Malcolm might be superstitious about babies. Maybe he doesn't take any chances. Maybe a baby is a one-shot deal. In terms of future bodies.

I saw the Rover whiz by out the corner of an eye. Nearly missed it. I wondered if the dogs felt me following. They did, I think. Torrance is the next future body. The dogs, Malcolm, must keep constant track.

But I wasn't after the boy.

Pip dropped him off, then drove to the mall. I approached him in the liquor store. He was buying champagne. Cases of it, vintage Veuve Clicquot. I checked out the armagnac section while he dickered with the clerk. Seems he placed the order weeks ago and expected a discount. Not on Veuve, clerk said. His eyes popped like corks when Pip pulled out the cash. He must have had a few thousand on him.

I offered to help him carry his purchase to the car.

He looked at me and a funny thing happened. His eyes suddenly weren't his eyes. Something else was looking at me through them.

Scared the daylights out of me.

Clerk was saying, "Do you know this man, sir? Sir? Excuse me, Jack!" Unfriendly potbellied clerk, he was, broken veins all over his nose.

Pip's eyes cleared and he said, "Shit!"

I picked up a case and walked out of the store. Clerk yelled and came running. Pip must have said something because he stopped. I went to the Land-Rover and waited. A boy came by a minute later wheeling the other cases, and then Pip came out. He tipped the boy after they loaded the car, and turned to me. "What do you want?" he said, rubbing his eyes. He looked jumpy. Actually, he looked a little frightened.

"Celebration coming up?" I said.

"None of your business," he snapped. He didn't want to look at me. It was as if it hurt him.

"Your eyes ok?" I said. "Guess that was a shock, huh?" I was getting the impression he'd been very shocked. "A shame about Torrance," I remarked.

"What is?" Pip said.

I shrugged. "You must be in the will, too. When are they coming, the Baron's money people?"

Pip snuck a look at me. He whispered, "Thursday." That was a jolt. "You and Sheila," he then said. "What you did—that was bad."

"What did we do?" I asked, thinking about Thursday. Two days!

"You drugged him," he accused. "And you stole. He's killed people for less, you know." The man was glowering at the pavement.

I said, "But things seem to be going well. He'll be celebrating, won't he? What do you think about that? And what did we steal?"

"You're getting it!" he exclaimed. "Go to school and find out."

"How," I asked, wondering what he meant, "did you do it?"

"I'm talking too much," he growled.

"Pip," I asked, "what's wrong with your eyes?"

He glared at me. Then he looked at the pavement. "What are you talking about?" he asked quietly.

I said, "About you, Phipps."

He said, "Get away from me. Just get away."

"Do you remember?" I asked. "You worked for Gainsborough, a few years back, and your name was Phipps. Or am I wrong?"

"Phipps," he said slowly, jaw muscles working, "was a dog."

"He was a valet, Pip. He worked for Gainsborough."

"A dog," Pip said.

"A valet," I said. "I did research, I can prove it. Pip, he couldn't have been a dog. The dogs don't have names. Or was that a lie? What you told Torrance, about the dogs not having names?"

"Some of them did," he said. "If you don't get away, I'll kill you."

"No you won't," I said. "You are curious. You want to know what I know. Tell me something. How many names do you suppose you've had, Pip?"

"Shut up!" he snarled.

"You told Torrance that the reason the dogs don't have names, is because they had so many."

"You don't know anything!"

"But I do."

"You are *lying*."

"What does Malcolm call you, Pip? A valet?"

"He's listening right now," Pip muttered. "He might tell me to kill you, and I could, you know, I could kill you fast. Leave, Duane. I'm warning you. Leave!"

"The Baron won't tell you to kill me, Pip. Not right now he won't, because he has something he wants me to do."

Pip was trembling. "What?" he asked. "What did he ask you to do?"

"Maybe I'll tell you, if you answer my question. My question is this: What are you?"

"I do not . . . know," he whispered. "I feel like . . ."

"Yes?" I said.

"Like all this happened before," he said with strangled anger. "Excuse me. I'm going. You were stupid to do what you did. What you expect to get out of it . . . Probably you'll die. There is nothing you can do about any of this. Stay away from Malcolm. I'm serious —stay away!"

"You think the dogs will get me?"

He snarled, "We might!"

My neck hairs rose. They actually rose, and trembled in the breeze. I asked, "Pip . . . You don't mean you are a—?"

He scowled. It was a strange scowl. Half defiant and half—what's the word?—hangdog. But then he smiled. I thought of a word to describe his smile, too. *Wolfish.* "Do I," he said, "seem like a dog?"

In as neutral a voice as I could manage, I said, "You tell me."

"Ask Malcolm," he growled. He got in the Rover, slammed the door and started the engine.

"What about Torrance?" I shouted over the noise. "Aren't you worried?"

"He's getting rich!" he yelled.

I waved as he drove away.

It seems Pip doesn't know much about what's going to happen after Torrance gets rich. That's the feeling I have. Malcolm has a tight grip on Pip. Loyal Pip, devoted manservant. And maybe more. A whole lot more.

I stood there, thinking about Thursday. Thinking about time. That propelled me into a hardware store. I bought clippers. I might need them, if I can think of a reason to get through the Baron's fence. At some point soon. At some point in the next two days.

Now I'm sitting in the truck, the owner of clippers, wondering, once again, what to do. Go to the school? Pip said we're getting it. "Go to school and find out."

Maybe I should visit Sheila first. Before Schmidt shows up, and helps himself to her diary. There's a walkway from this mall. It goes over the road right to her building.

The Diary
of Sheila Massif: XI

Tuesday Afternoon

Duane is back. But he's staying at a motel, thank God.

He came in before noon, carrying a bag and smiling the strangest little smile. "I met the Baron's dogs," he announced.

"You 'met' them?" I asked.

"We sort of said hi. An experience, Sheila, I'll tell you."

"I'm sure," I said. As a matter of fact, I already knew he'd been at Malcolm's. Malcolm himself had told me. Duane's eyes were darting around as if he expected to meet the dogs here, too. "Did your research in Cambridge," I asked, "pay off?"

"I ran a background check on the Baron."

"Oh, yeah? Anything good? Any history of child abuse, for example?"

Duane's eyes darted at me, and stayed. "Funny you ask that," he said.

"So there is a history? Duane, we can't let this continue. We have to get Torrance out of that house."

Duane started rummaging through the bag. Looking for cigarettes, I thought. "Sheila," he asked, "have you had any visitors?"

"No. Why do you ask?"

He said, "You worry about Torrance. I'm concerned about the Baron."

"What are you talking about, Duane?"

"There is something I haven't mentioned," he said. "I quit my job last week." He'd never discussed his job. Except to claim it's secret psychic stuff. "It could be trouble for all of us. Sheila, I've stolen three cars. I'm on the lam."

That was big news. I had sensational news myself, and was dying to tell Duane about it. I'd parleyed, separately, with Malcolm and Pip. They both called today. The talks, though bizarre, were promising. I was pleased. In fact I was gloating.

But Duane was starting to make me nervous. He had pulled off his gloves, revealing another pair of gloves underneath. They were clear plastic. The kind surgeons use. Then he'd pulled a pair of heavy collapsible clippers from his bag. The kind, I realized, bike thieves use. So he was stealing bicycles, too. I said, "Did I hear you say you stole three cars?"

He lit a cigarette and nodded. "The jeep, that was one. And I have a nice new pickup outside right now."

"Duane, you are joking."

"No. They'll probably be coming by here soon. Looking for me."

"Because you stole cars?"

"Because I quit my job, Sheila. They might even break in."

"They can't do that. Who are these guys?"

"Men with guns," he said.

How alarming. "But—why?"

"They'll find out I called you. They'll get the records." He was fondling his clippers in a disturbing way. "They'll tap your phone. They'll follow you around, day and night. I'm sorry, I truly am. It's a real pain when they do that."

I didn't know what to say. Plastic-gripped clippers are antisocial. They're sociopathic. Society hates people who wield clippers while wearing surgical gloves—worrisome thoughts flow through minds. As if to make them flow faster, Duane jerked open the steel jaws. A delicate swirl of cigarette smoke was hanging in the air at about my neck height. He cut it in half. He did this suddenly and violently. The ringing *snick* was much too loud. Each half of the swirl writhed away in curlicuing agony. Other hangs of smoke, bystanders, witnesses, scudded off in terror. They'd seen what could happen. The air wasn't safe.

I was horrified.

Duane eyed me. He was keeping the clippers raised. He looked like a Scientologist Ninja Terminator. His pale eyes weren't blinking. They were radium dimes, glowing. Duane was insane. There was no escape—he'd follow me anywhere, even to the Drama Chamber. In it, I saw snicking dismemberment. I hoped I'd go quietly, the way the smoke had gone, writhing in silence. Why resist? Why scream? Why crawl around the nooks gushing blood with ever more spastic convulsions of limbs? Surrender, Sheila, leave the red splurting behind—enter the singing tunnel of light, where the angel, holding clippers, squints at you insanely from the very end . . .

"Are you ok?" Duane said.

"No," I said.

He put the clippers on the couch and said, "This is a big change for me." Me too, I thought. "I busted out. You know what, it's great."

"Great," I said. "I think you better explain, Duane."

"Don't be upset," he said. "I can't stay here, of course. Sheila, I want your diary. I'm taking it with me."

"You're dreaming," I snarled, grabbing the clippers. I'd had it. I slashed at smoke and yelled, "You stink this place up!" His cigarettes were on the table. I tonged the pack, squeezed it hard, then shook the doomed thing at him. It flew apart. Severed butts jumped out like confetti. "You better talk, asshole! Now!"

"Sheila," he said, "it's only noon, but it's been a long day." He sat on the couch, chewing his mustache—sucking for nicotine, I thought, no more cigarettes, ha! "Put that down, you're liable to hurt yourself."

"Talk!" I shouted, Ninjishly poised for attack.

He blinked. "Ok," he said. "Look, I didn't mean to scare you and I know I did. Things are different. Come on, relax. I can explain."

"You're not taking my Diary!" I cried.

"If you'll listen," he said slowly, "you'll understand."

I turned a kitchen-nook chair around and sat, cradling clippers in lap. Duane was getting a whole carton of cigarettes out of his bag. Suddenly I wanted to smoke. He ripped open a pack and offered it. I shook my head; he lit up, and talked, and I learned how disturbed he really is.

Malcolm, he told me, has unusual and gorgeous psychic powers.

The Baron—Duane keeps calling him "the Baron"—is like a rare orchid. He's a precious bloom in the mystical world. But he's endangered. Opportunists are stalking him; they want to use him for evil ends. This would be a tragedy. The predators would pluck the bloom, and Earth would become more barren.

"Give me a break," I said after a few minutes of this. "Malcolm is a voyeur slimeball."

"That's one level," Duane said. But, I learned, there are other levels. Malcolm has mezzanines of consciousness, and penthouses, and many basements. Duane seemed humbly devoted to the Baron. I could see him sitting at Malcolm's feet, orange-diapered and dutiful.

Finally I said, "Stop mumbo-jumboing, Duane. Tell the truth!"

"I am telling the truth."

"You are lying. You lied about the roses. You lied about Malcolm. For all I know, you're lying about quitting your job."

He surprised me by saying, "I did lie about the roses."

"Why?"

"Because the truth, Sheila, is something you can't handle."

Great, I thought. "Some kind of psychic thing?"

He stared at me. For a second I forgot he's insane. Then he said, "Do you really want to know about it? If you do, I'll tell you."

"Tell me," I said. I wasn't at all sure I wanted to know.

"I had an out-of-body experience. I flew into the sky, and floated there. I actually saw the Baron's house, the whole property, as if from a plane. Then you brought me back. For which I thank you, by the way."

That sounded right. It fit with what I'd felt. And it was soothing—everybody believes in out-of-body stuff. He wasn't saying anything about a terrible place, either, which was a huge relief. "Ok. Fine. I won't even accuse you of being crazy. But if that did happen, why did it happen?"

"It happened because the Baron has powers of unimaginable magnitude, that I do not fully understand, and cannot fully explain to you. What else would you like to know?"

"This: Why you persuaded Torrance to stay there."

"That's simple. If Torrance hadn't stayed there, the Baron would have gone crazy. He would have damaged himself. Possibly he would have found ways to damage you, and me. Next question."

"Forget about all that. What about damaging Torrance?"

"Of course he's not good for Torrance. But has it occurred to you he might be even worse, if we took Torrance away? He is a potent man. We don't know what he can do—he could be capable of almost anything. There aren't any easy solutions. But I'm working on solutions. Next question, please."

Duane was beginning to annoy me. "Why," I asked, "did you steal cars?"

"Again, it's simple. I had to get away."

"Oh, yeah? Get away from what?"

"The Sigh Project."

"The Sigh Project?"

"P-s-i, a word for psychic force. A concept of power, pure and beautiful. The Project, though, is ugly. And mean. They get what they want."

"Go on." I sighed.

He went on, and on, breaking, he said, numerous national security laws. It seems the Psi Project is crucial to the military-industrial complex. But it's secret. It's so secret, the complex doesn't even know it exists.

"Sigh Wars?" I said incredulously, finally fed up.

Duane was droning on about ultimate weapons. Couldn't I understand we must protect the Baron from paranormal warmongers? "Think about it," he said. "Think about the money. Our biggest industry, you know, is war."

He had me there. But something was wrong about the whole spiel. Protect Malcolm? How ironic. What a cute concept—Malcolm is the enemy! However, I think I have him by the balls. Thank God.

I was getting the feeling Duane wouldn't like that. I still have that feeling. This bothers me. I'm attacking Malcolm; Duane is defending him; Duane isn't an ally: Duane is an enemy.

And this enemy was in my apartment, attracting men with guns.

"Ok," I said carefully, "Malcolm might cause a psychic arms race. And you want to prevent it, even though you're unemployed, and have been on a crime spree, and police are looking for you high and low. It's your life; I don't understand, of course, but it's a free country, until you get caught. Now, let's separate issues. You think people will break in here, trying to get you. Duane, if that's true, it puts me in kind of a tough spot."

"I'm not staying here," he said.

"Right," I said, "you said that." I was delighted to hear him say it again. "But what about me?"

"You have to pretend all this never happened," he said. "That's why I'm taking your Diary. The tapes too. They'd learn everything."

I'd been wondering when I'd let him have it. "But Duane," I bombshelled, "the tapes and my Diary aren't here!"

"Where are they?" he asked.

"In a safety-deposit box," I said. I'd stashed them first thing this morning. Along with T-Sex.

He didn't believe me. Then he searched, and believed, but he argued. He said that the agents, the Feds, whatever the hell they are, can get stuff out of banks, if they really push it.

I told him to get out of my apartment.

His pale eyes became paler. I was frightened. The radium dime look—Duane does glow, every now and then. Not as if he's a movie monster or anything, but I can feel it. Sometimes he radiates *force*. I'd never thought of it as psychosis, until today. The look always seemed part of his psychic act. Duane has some kind of knack of course, he's a little uncanny, he's Psychic Duane. And after what happened at Malcolm's—whether he went out of his body, or not— I can't really deny it. But today, with the smoke-slash episode, with his ideas about protecting Malcolm, not to mention the psychic weapons bullshit and the paranoid fear of men with guns, I began to think, maybe Duane being psychic isn't the point. There could be a more basic explanation. Maybe, he's: Psycho.

Which meant I had to get rid of him. I said, "I can't believe you think you can confiscate my Diary! It's—*me*, Duane." I snorted right-eously. "Think again, buster. And scram while you're at it."

He scrammed. We argued and yelled some more, but he left, telling me he will "keep in touch."

———

Duane's been nothing but trouble. If the Feds come, I'll tell them he was here, and was crazy, and has gone. I won't say a word about Malcolm or Torrance. Why would I? It's in my interest not to. I bargained with Malcolm. And we came to an understanding.

It happened in the nick of time, too. I'd just gotten back from stashing Diary, tapes and cassette in the bank. The cohabitation of those objects was somehow damning—they were shacked up! Then there was the problem of how to tell Duane. I didn't feel good. I felt *immoral*. The beige was pressing in, right through my eyelids.

Then the phone rang. Malcolm was talking before I could say hello:

"Who has it? You, or that man Duane?"

"Hi," I said. "I'm glad you called. I have it. Duane and Torrance don't know."

The voice was cheerful. "Well—are you enjoying it?"

"I haven't looked at it," I coolly replied, "*yet*. But I trust you've enjoyed reading my Diary."

"I did!" he exclaimed. "Very amusing."

"You won't be reading any more, I'm afraid," I said. "It's not here. So don't send Pip."

"I wouldn't dream of it. We've come to a standstill, you and I. Haven't we, Sheila?"

"We have? Well, maybe. If you mind your manners."

"*Manners?*" he screeched. "Oh, dear. Sheila, my manners are exquisite! I'm so sorry I was unable to be more of a host, on Saturday, you know. What are you doing tonight?"

"I was thinking of meeting your ex-wife at the airport. She's interested in Torrance's, um, progress at school, the general quality of his life, you see, and so on . . ."

"Stop," he said. "How could you be so wicked?"

"Very, very easily. My attorney has instructions to open a package, by the way, Malcolm, if I should suddenly disappear."

"Now, really."

"The package is in a . . ."

"Safety-deposit box?" he interrupted.

"Pip's been spying."

"Nonsense," he said. "Sheila, I couldn't have done better myself. I admire you, you know. Can we be friends?"

"No, we cannot be friends."

"But I adore you!" he screamed.

"Tough shit. I can't stand you, incidentally."

"I'm shattered," he moaned. "You're heartless, my dear. I *weep*."

"Malcolm, I don't give a damn. You're a goddamned child-abusing pervert slimeball low-down *scumbag motherfucker*, and you *know* it."

"That's all?" he said, sounding amazed. "I'm much worse than that, I assure you. What does Duane have to say?"

"Ask him. Who cares, anyway?"

"Who cares?" he said reflectively. "How interesting to hear you say that, 'who cares.' Sheila, are you serious? I'm a—'scumbag'?"

"A slimeball scumbag, Malcolm."

"I'm thrilled!" he declared. "I must ask, do you eat noisily? Sheila, do you slurp?"

I took the phone away from my head and looked at it.

The earphone said faintly: "Sheila, come back! Are you there? I must know: do you *slurp*?" I cleared my throat; and the earphone squealed: "I heard that! Well done! A splendid, a very tasteful noise!"

Jesus, I thought. "Malcolm, I have to go."

"No!" he screamed. "Tell me how you *eat*!"

"None of your business," I snapped.

"You might be pregnant," he said in suddenly crystal-clear tones.

"Then we'll eat the fetus," I said, *"noisily.* Good-bye!"

I slammed down the phone. Pregnant? Torrance told him, I thought; he told Malcolm about our short-lived bang. Not good. More ammo for Malcolm. But there isn't any proof . . .

The phone was ringing again:

"What do you *want*?" I bellowed.

"Sheila!" Pip bellowed. "Oh, Sheila!"

"Yes!" I bellowed. "Yes? What? *What?*"

"It's *Malcolm*!"

"What about him?"

"He's *crazy*!"

"I *know*!"

"What am I going to *do*?"

"I *don't know*!"

"Oh, *Sheila*!"

"*What*?"

"Malcolm says he's going to kill himself!"

"*Good*!"

"*Bad*!" Pip shrieked.

"Very, very *good*!" I shrieked.

"You're making him *do it*!" Pip screamed.

"*Somebody* has to!" I screamed back. "Does Malcolm *slurp*?"

The phone went dead. Or rather, there was instantly no sound. Then I heard: "What did you say?"

"Does Malcolm slurp?"

"No, Sheila," Pip quavered. "Malcolm never, ever slurps."

"Just checking," I said.

"Did you slurp at him?" he asked with alarm.

"I'm thinking of it," I said.

"*Don't!*" Pip cried desperately. "Please don't," he stammered.

"All right, I won't," I said.

"Thank you," he said fervently. "Oh, *thank* you."

"Oh, you're *welcome*," I said fervently. "Now what the hell is going on? Where are you?"

"Near the mall. I am so confused! Forget I called—just tell Duane to stop it. I don't care about him, but . . . I'm worried. Sheila, be careful."

The phone went dead. I hung up, and glared at it, wondering what he meant about me and Duane. As I glared, it rang:

"Yes," I said, ready for anything.

"You were joking about the fetus, weren't you?" Malcolm said.

I slurped, loudly: "SCHLLLITHSSHLLRRRUSHP!"

The Baron screeched loudly and lengthily, with unfakable pain. "How dare you?" he gasped. It was wonderful.

"I'll do it again," I warned. "Uh, Pip called. He said you're going to kill yourself, is there any way I can help?"

"Sheila, you sadden me," Malcolm moaned. "You slurped! Please don't do it again."

"Mind your manners," I warned.

"Just trying to offend me, of course," he said, as though trying to be realistic. "I understand. Ah, Pip called. Forget Pip, he's a simpleton, he disintegrates routinely. What else? Ah yes, I probably will commit suicide, but no, nothing you can do will help, but thank you for asking. I am calling solely to inform you that your secrets are safe with me. I mean you no harm. And I hope you won't try to harm me. Not that it makes any difference, I'll be dead soon anyway, but there's Torrance, please keep that in mind, the boy would be so embarrassed if his mother—you must know what I mean."

"Your concern for Torrance is moving."

"Yes. Don't worry about Torrance, his life stretches delightfully before him. Oh, I know I have faults, as do all parents. Perhaps mine are more troublesome than most. If so, I regret it—but this is why we have psychiatrists, Sheila, to correct marred child rearings. Please, let's not get into that, it's too frightfully profound. I merely wish to make peace. Shall we? Shall we cease and desist our hostilities?"

I went for it. "Will you stop spying on Torrance?"

"Already have!" Malcolm cried. "He and Pip are disassembling cameras right now, isn't that marvelous? Oh, I was bad. But I am ill, you know."

"Yes," I said. "They're taking apart cameras right this second?"

"Of course! Torrance might have run away! Away from *me*, Sheila."

"Can I talk with him?"

"No, you cannot, he is throwing cameras *out the window,* and must not be disturbed. You do not believe me? You will see him tomorrow at school."

"Malcolm, if what you say is true, great, we're at peace. I'll cease, I'll desist, I won't even slurp. If what you say really is true."

"I am tremendously pleased," he said. "You are a fine teacher, Sheila, your students need you. It would be perfectly shameful if for any reason you could not stay on and guide those young minds."

"Is that a threat?"

"You cheapen yourself."

"One more thing," I said. "What's the matter with Pip?"

Malcolm sighed. "Terminal silliness. He is devoted to me. He can't bear the idea of life without me. What could be sillier than that?"

"Yes," I agreed. "You puzzle me, Malcolm."

"Pay no attention," he said soothingly. "I am an eccentric old madman. Sheila, my dear—"

"Don't call me 'my dear'!"

"Very well. Adieu, Sheila. Perhaps in the next world—"

"Perhaps."

"I am sure of it," he said.

"Not," I said maliciously, "where you're going."

" 'Not where I'm going.' " He chuckled, as if he thought that was funny. "Please give my regards to Duane. Tell him the dogs are asking for him."

"The dogs?"

"He made friends with my dogs this morning. He actually came to the property, and took a close look. My, we run on and on."

"Good-bye, Malcolm."

"Sheila!" he said with courtly drama, "Good-*bye!*"

Thus did I conclude my negotiations. I guess I forgot to give Duane Malcolm's regards. And the fond thoughts of the dogs.

That was that, round two. But I couldn't be sure everything was ok until I talked with Torrance. Well, he called around three, while I was eating lunch. He was breathless:

"There's a big deal going on at school!"

"Is that where you are?"

"Yeah!" he said. "*Wow!* McQuisling's freaking, there's meetings and everything . . ."

"Wait a second," I said, "is it true you took down the cameras?"

"Yeah, in my rooms, Dad admitted everything! I was going to call you and now I am, but—"

"What did he tell you?"

"That he's really crazy is all he said. And he said he's sorry—"

"So do you feel safe? Did you tell him we had—?"

"No way! But Sheila—I'm in *love*." His excited voice dropped: "I just got to know this really, uh, person."

"Really uh? How 'uh'?"

"Swimteam," Torrance panted. "Everything's great, but you won't believe the Fear-Field—"

"Hold it!" I commanded. "You're sure your father's on the level, what did he tell you?"

"He said he's whacked out of his head and he *is*, but Sheila *the shit's hitting the fan around here*."

"Why? How? What?"

"They found this pornographical stuff. Like, a lot of copies! And it's . . ." The voice sank to a fervent whisper: "Gay."

"So?" I wasn't bowled over. "So what? Who cares?"

"I do, and Erik does and Samantha too, even Brutus is reading the Fear-Field, the whole school is and we're supposed to hand over the copies but there's lots, and it makes fun of Caspar so Caspar's like, it's like, it's like the drug war's over and the dealers won!"

"That's very exciting," I said.

"Yeah, somebody did some really creative writing and nobody knows who, it's wild. Anyway, I gotta find a place to read it."

"You haven't read it?"

"Has to be in private," he said. "I gotta go."

So that's the story with Torrance. He's in love, he's in a whirlwind of scandal at school, his father said he's sorry and the cameras are down, and he went somewhere private to read "Fear-Fields" or whatever.

———

Diary, they've all cracked! But as Duane says, life goes on.

Meantime Malcolm is cornered. One way or another, I'm getting Torrance back to California.

My morals remain questionable. The psychic factor remains mysterious. The Drama Chamber—well, it remains. But since I seem to be ok, and history is written by the winners, maybe I'll censor here and there. And smell like a rose.

No. Not like a rose. Malcolm grows roses. It's 4:45. I have to get to the bank and lock this up.

The Fearfield Club

I am Fearfield. Go ahead, call me Fearfield. Scary name, right? Say it loud and hear the sound of dread:

Fearfield!

It's not my real name. But will do just fine.

You have seen me around. You think I'm just another cool guy at school. Some of you even think you know me. You're wrong, for a simple but important reason:

You don't know about my craving for boys.

That's right. Boys. You could say I'm boy-fixated. Don't get so shocked you can't keep on reading. Maybe you can't believe it, that I crave boys. I'll prove it:

Imagine a dusty, lean, scowly gunslinger. He's in town for fun on a hot afternoon. He's ready for action at age nineteen. He isn't me, I'm not that old, but imagine him anyway and you will see what I mean:

He stops in his tracks when five of them amble around a corner.

Two old folks on a porch listen to him whine, then gape as he hollers:

"Yes, sir, yes, ma'am, I got a powerful appetite for them there boys. Just looking makes me weak. I'm like to bust my pants on account of those slim devils - damn, I'm leaking lust down to my boots! Whew! This what they call earthquake, why's everything gone wobbly like that? Don't let me upset you none, ma'am, sir, mind I got guns - even if I can't aim nohow, with boys itching britches and staring over here so lip-lick nervous and excited! Wa-hooo! I'll drop dead starving if I don't catch me one! Hey, *you*!"

Get the picture?

I should clear something up. I don't eat boys. Although I admit, I find the term "mouthwatering" often accurate. But no, boys are indigestible even if well-chewed and swallowed slowly - of that, well, I am certain. So don't let "powerful appetite" and "drop dead starving" mislead you, they are figures of speech. All I want to say is this:

As far as boys are concerned, I'm not just fixated. I'm voracious.

Maybe you have a problem with that. Don't worry. I have plans for your problem.

Or maybe my tone and drift don't bother you at all. In fact, your grip on this pamphlet could be tightening from sheer thrill, and definitely so if you happen to be a handsome boy who can't believe his luck at coming across such fine reading material, in which case - I feel it, to tell you the truth - probably you wish I were with you right now, stripping and brandishing my whole ton of fun!

Do you ever do that, by the way? Strip and brandish, at another boy? It's wonderful. Especially if he's paralyzed, and stares at you with wild-eyed shock. Then you know good things will happen. You just know it. Because you can tell he's feeling a terrible helplessness - and you can do anything you want!

Maybe you haven't done stuff like that. Maybe you are staring at this page with nervous shock. Are you? Relax. Nobody is pulling off your shirt, at least not yet. These are just words on a piece of paper. Nothing awful can happen, right? So keep on reading. A real adventure is coming up. It will amaze you, it's so intense. Question:

Have you ever heard of "Creative Reading"?

There is talk around school. Kids are doing a new kind of reading, and even writing, all over. And it's unbelievable fun.

Because creative reading is reading *with your body*.

A lot of people think they read with their minds. Boy are they dumb. Experts agree: Bodies do the very best reading. Ask Rhonda McQuisling if you don't believe me. She's an expert on creative stuff!

No, you better not. You will see why, in a while. All you have to do is keep on reading. I'll teach you how to bodyread. And even bodywrite!

But first we should consider the fact that the world is full of unlucky readers. I said you might have a problem. In fact, some of you have a lot of problems. The reason, and you know it, is your bodies.

You hate your bodies! I bet you have dark-blue cobwebby veins all over your skin, red ones too. Just a few grisly hairs stuck to your head? Weird wrinkles here and there? Those strange wiggles in your blubber thighs? Ass that looks like a sack of fish? That are not very fresh? You are gross!

That's your problem. And it's why you have a problem with me. Face it - you hate the fact I live in my exquisite young body! I hope you're having a heart attack.

Interesting, isn't it, that old bodies are always telling young bodies what to do. And what not to do. For example, old bodies start flipping when they think about us young ones getting our hands on each other. Why is that?

Because they're jealous. Of course. And you know what that means. It means they hate being old! Open any magazine, it's there, the fact stares at you - everybody wants an exquisite young body!

But get a load of this, you envious oldsters. If you lived in my body, and you would be very, very lucky if you did:

Boys would fixate you, too.

Are you nodding with solemn agreement? Or does that kind of gross you out? If you're grossed out, I have only one thing to say. Tough shit!

My body can't help it, you see. Really, it can't. So if you were living here, you'd have to deal with it, just like I have to. Hey, we all have to live in our bodies. Which is kind of tragic for you, if you are one of those readers with dreadful body problems. Speaking of which, how are you doing, Caspar? McQuisling?

Caspar, your body is causing a lot of problems. You hate living in it, needless to say, which means you don't want other bodies to have fun, especially the young ones attending this dump called school. And you have a great excuse - Traditional Values, right? In other words, you lock us up, and jail us, and, heavily girded, *so* heavily, you stomp around cudgeling every form of pleasure, belching your moral bad breath!

We know you can't help it, Caspar. That is the way you are. But we are sick of you. Your Traditional Values make - us - PUKE.

Because a lot of us boys want to go on dates and hold hands and make out and feel each other up, and do all the great things with our bodies that you tell the whole world boys can't do!

The time has come to change this sad state of affairs.

I bet you are wondering how I plan to do it. If I were you, I would be too. So I'll tell you. I'm starting a club, Caspar: THE FEARFIELD CLUB.

Our activity? It's noble:

READING & WRITING WITH EXQUISITE YOUNG BODIES.

———

Now we move on. Sorry about the delay. I could hear those impatient groans all through the Problem Section, but you understand. I had to spell a few things out: Caspar, because of his body - ok, enough of that. You want to know about the club. Joining the Fearfield Club is simple:

You write a story with your body. Then you make a bunch of photocopies and leave them around school. The other kids will pick them up and read, using their bodies, of course. And soon, the club will get big! We'll be able to invite people over to trade stories, and discuss them in detail, and basically experiment, and fool around a lot, naturally.

By now you are asking: How do I get my body to write?

I won't be too technical here. It's so easy:

First you find out what your body is fixated on. How do you find out? Hey, it's your body. You should know, right? But maybe you don't. If you don't, you better start bodyreading and bodywriting right now. It's educational!

Take me. I've been bodyreading, lately. It's like homework - I *study* my body. And you know what? I keep learning more about it all the time!

Hey, it's my body, why not know all there is to know? Anyway, as soon as you discover what thrills that body of yours, you just let it take over - and write about it!

For example, I thought, long and hard, about my body taking over. And I have to admit, at first nothing happened. But then suddenly, there he was, my gunslinger - lean and mean, and *hungry as hell*!

My friends, if I can do it, let me tell you, you can too. Ok, you're wondering who I am. Who is this Fearfield, anyway?

It doesn't make any difference. The important thing about me, is true of you. I live in this body - that has to do what it has to do!

So join my Club. These are the Goals:

1. The overthrow of tiresome old bodies.
2. To excite the hell out of each other.
3. To tempt the highly impressionable!
4. To exchange useful tips on what to do.
5. Last but not least, to drive Caspar crazy!

Caspar, have you been foolish enough to read this far? You ain't seen nothin' yet! Wa-*hooo*!

The Secret Journal
of Torrance Spoor's
Secret War: IV

Tuesday Night

Today was the coolest.

Pip woke me up early and said: "We have work to do." Then Dad came in - I was still in bed, it really weirded me out - and said, "Pip, get Torrance's breakfast." Pip left, and Dad said: "I am so, so sorry. Those cameras. They have to go!"

I am shivering under the covers staring at him, thinking: *What is he up to now?* He points at the door. It's open, and I see something in the hall. One of the gardening wagons from the garage is there. It's piled with equipment, drills, saws, tons of stuff. Dad says, "I want you to destroy those terrible things. If you like, throw them out the window!" He stands there breathing deep, like he just climbed a mountain, and is proud of it. "Oh, I am bad. So very bad! I beg you, forgive me. You see, I am sick. Torrance, I am a very sick man."

I thought: Yes. You are.

Then Pip pushes in this big table full of breakfast. Dad goes to the door and yells, like a army general: "Eat!"

I can't speak. I never saw him look so - like, *alive.* "Eat!" he yells again, then says: "I'll be back in an hour. Then, my boy, we talk." And he walks down the hall like he has to go sign the Declaration of Independence. I look at Pip. On his face is no expression. But then, he smiles. He was like - happy! But he looked sad, too. He says, soft, "Eat. Then, we go to work." He waves at the equipment, lets out this long sad sigh, and leaves me alone with all that great food.

So, I ate. Then it really happened. Pip and I tore out the cameras. The things are *big.* We were covered with dust and junk from the walls, we made huge holes. I even threw one camera out the window. Just to see it smash on the ground. Later, Dad came back. He said it again, he is a sick man to spy on me. We talked for a long time about his sickness. I told him to give me the sex tape. He said Sheela and Dwain stole it. That's not true, we left it there but they might of took it when the lights were off, I will find out. If Dad is lying again, I will know. I forgot to ask Sheela today when I called her from school. No calling from the house until I know if Dad still lies. But he is better now. We talked a lot. I get rich day after tomorrow and I am *free.* Then I can tell Dad and Mom to leave me alone, if he's not lying as usual and if he's alive, he said he could croke. What can I say to Dad? Hey, you go when you go. He is too weird. It's not my fault. He just better not try anything, I been scared out of my mind these days.

But that was only how today started. The rest of it was totally cool too. Erik and I got together. And the excuse I used was Fearfield.

We love Fearfield. The whole school is cracking up. Creative writing! Somebody did it. Somebody from our class for sure. Casper is in it, and stuff from our class, definitely somebody from class, Sheela will flip. I did not tell her everything about it.

Maybe she did it. She better not of unless she wants to get fired fast. I don't think she did it. Probably Sam, but nobody admits anything. Pretty soon I'll lie and say I did it. Even though it is kind of sick.

Anyway Pip dropped me off late. I was in the locker hallway when Sam saw me. She came running. I knew something was going on. Samantha never runs, I never saw her run once till today. She was yelling too, I said shut up, why are you yelling? She said we got a new dude at school and his name is Fearfield. Everybody was staring at us but only some of them knew. She said to get a copy soon cause Casper is ready to kill anybody who has one. Then she whispered: I got you one already, come on.

She showed me where she hid them. She had five copies under the trophy case for the wizzkid nerds, down the hall from the auditoreum. The copies are in regular folders. They look boring and normal, but not when you read it. When you read it you know we just got blasted by someone from Gay Outer Space. She said there were stacks of folders all over school before anybody got there. Then somebody read one and the news went around like fire.

We were standing there talking about it when Casper came on the PA: Everybody has to go to a meeting. The bells rang and all the doors opened and kids and teachers were walking. We looked guilty so we had to leave. Sam said to come back and get a copy, You Will Die when you read it.

She was smart cause everybody at the meeting got searched. Casper was police chief of school, even the lockers got opened and searched when we were listening to him yell about scuzz and dirt and unbelievable perverts. I was about to blow up. I wanted to get out and read it so bad, he said Homosexual over and over like a TV bible nut. And he said somebody wants to destroy our school. I got really excited. Sam sat next to me but Erik was three rows down. I kept looking at the back of his head, then he turned around and we stared for a second, and I had to wink. And he like - waved! He did it cool, like he was saying: "Check it out!" Then he turned back around to listen to Casper. Sam grabbed my arm, she saw him waving, she was excited too. I said to myself, today is the day for Erik. Talk to him, finally.

By swimteam period I had it planned. I skipped the first part of math to get my copy, then I took it to the basement under the gym. The halls were empty but I had to sneak. I hid it in boys PE lockerroom. Then I went to math. Collins yelled a lot but I told him the big meeting made me freak out totally. The kids laughed and Collins said, sit down. No problem.

Then I went to PE. Erik's locker is the other end of the row from mine. All the boys were screaming jokes about the meeting and Casper and fags. Nobody had a copy and I had not read it, so nobody knew anything about it, except we knew Casper is in it, and he's supposed to come off stupid. I thought: All these naked boys screaming about fags, but they would murder their mothers to get a copy of this Fearfield. So I said to Erik when they were going to the pool: Wait Up.

He waited until nobody was left. Then he said: Yeah? He was standing in his swimsuit and me too, almost naked and right in front of each other and nobody else around. This was dangerous. He was nervous. All that talk about fags. I worried about getting hard but I didn't, we both really were nervous.

I said: I have a Fearfield.

He said: No shit.

I said: Let's go to the Janitor Room, maybe nobody's there. Want to?

He looked at me weird.

I thought: Mistake! Then I saw his hands shaking.

So I said: We better move fast cause Coach is gonna come looking.

I took the Fearfield from under the towel basket where I put it and thought: towels. I took two. Erik was right behind me. I could feel how sexy he is, like heat. He said: What are the towels for?

To sit on, I said. Things were going too fast to get embarassed. We snuck across, away from the showers through the lockers. I looked back - his face was pink, it made his hair look gold. He didn't want to look me in the eyes. He was not hard, but he saw me checking. I turned back around, and heard him say soft: Shit!

Then we had to go by the window of Coach's Office. Nobody in there, nobody nowhere, but I heard a sound. We listened. Somebody was coming down the hall outside. Somebody big with heavy shoes. I grabbed Erik's arm and we ran, really quiet, to the stairs way in back, and we went down almost on our toes, me first.

We heard a door slam. Shoes was gone.

I got to the bottom of the stairs and stopped, cause the Janitor could of been in his room. He reads paperbacks there all day sometimes, I know cause Coach complains. But sometimes he is never there and Coach complains.

I looked: He was *there.* In his chair, back to me, reading his book and wearing walkmans. I put my hand out to stop Erik and it was the kiss of death.

My hand went smack on his chest, and he grunted, quiet: Unnnhh.

It felt so good. His skin was warm and there was his nipple under my finger, and his breath from the Unnnhh went right in my face! So I had to look in his eyes - my hand was stuck to his chest, no way I could take it off, and he was sort of leaning - his eyes were wide blue frozen. His mouth opened but he could not talk. His tongue came out and wet his lip. This was it. We had to kiss. I felt my dick smashing out of my swimsuit. Erik looked *down.* I took a look at his. It went out sideways, over his leg, jumping on his thigh, like it was desperate to get away. It was desperate for me. Wow. My hand was still on his muscle. He was still leaning, harder. My hand slid. We kind of fell on each other. I thought: Janitor. Around the corner of this door, at the bottom of stairs anyone could come to. I thought about it but I could not stop what we were doing. We were kissing. He had his arms around my neck, my arms were over his shoulders. And we started rubbing dicks. I moved my leg so he could rub his there. Mine rubbed up and down his stomach. And we just kept kissing, silent and deep. His tongue is strong. I wanted to chew it. Then I opened my eyes and the astronaut color of blue invaded my face. His eyes were invading. I loved it, I smiled, and he did too. We kind of grunted our smiles in the mouths. And the whole time, we kept rubbing dicks.

That's how we did it. Thirty feet away through a door - we were just around the corner - the Janitor read his book and we did it like that: standing, arms around, kissing, swimsuits still on and rubbing dicks, not making the tiniest sound. Unbelievable we made no sound. Guys must be used to it from jerking off at home - people should not hear. We came at the same time. I shot up between, it got our jaws still kissing and our chests were *glued*. He hit the wall: SPLAT. And MORE SPLAT. I could smell it.

That was it. I licked in his nose. He shivered, but we were glued.

Then we unglued.

I peeked at Janitor: still reading. In the chair with his back to us, walkmans on.

We used the towels. On each other and on the wall, and the floor. I whispered: We better get away from here.

He whispered, serious: Yeah, there has to be a better place.

I cracked up. Then he did! But silent! We made big, goofy motions of laughing our brains out, but no noise!

It took a while to calm down. Then we left, fast. Up the stairs to the lockers and in our clothes in less than four minutes I think. Nobody saw. Fuck what a risk we took. Anybody could of seen we used our dicks. Can't hide it in Speedos.

It was worth it. By that time I knew we would not get caught. It came off so smooth. I still had the Fearfield - we didn't even open it.

We went to the hallway and hit the nearest boys room.

Cause we had to wash. At least our hands and necks and faces. Also I wanted his phone number. He told me it's totally ok to call, his mom and her boyfriend do not worry about Erik at all. They don't know anything.

Of course I told him nothing about Dad. Maybe sometime I could.

Not then. I felt too great. We stared in the mirror, grinning, we both looked stoned. We looked stupid but sexy, grinning like fools. Our pants were obvious. The more we looked the more obvious they got. We couldn't stay there - he told me to call and he left, said he was going for early lunch.

I went to the library and read. Not Fearfield. Fearfield I put in my locker. Figured Casper would not break in twice in one day. I sat reading a magazine, thinking about all the books that don't talk about gay sex.

So things are looking good. I'm in love. Pip and me took down cameras, and Dad might even die. Crazy. He should not die. I even hope he doesn't. But what can I do?

Run like hell if he is lying. Run away with Erik. Except we might be poor and kind of helpless. But we could make it. Somehow.

At dinner tonight Dad and me talked more. About his sickness.

He says he isn't a rational man. I believe him. But I was not paying too much attention. He said: You look happy.

I asked myself: Tell Dad about Erik? Dad's sickness, what if he gets worse if he knows I have a boyfriend? A real beauty too, with invading eyes when we kissed and a clumsy tongue and muscle on his stomach that made me come like a natural disaster.

So I said: Dad, I got a present for you.

I gave him my Fearfield. I read it on the way home with Pip, laughing loud. Pip did not ask what it was. He is fucked up these days, I think he worries about Dad. He just drove, eyes on the road, not a word out of him all the way home. I did not talk either. I read. Fearfield is wacko. I kept thinking about what I did with Erik. How many others like us at school? Maybe lots. Lots who think this Fearfield stuff is totally cool. So I said nothing to Pip. Too private. Anyway, Pip - he's strange, now.

So at dinner Dad said: A present? Thank you, Torrance, did you write this for Sheela's class?

I said: No! Somebody from Gay Outer Space wrote that, Dad. Name is Fearfield. It is a call to action - I think he wants the school to come out of the closet. Like stampeding buffalo.

Dad laughed. Hey, he's a handsome guy sometimes. He picked up the Fearfield from the table where I put it and looked for a second, then put it down. After dinner, he said, I will read it. Tell me about the *stampede.*

He was laughing like a kid. I said: It's all about how adults control what kids do, Dad.

He looked ashamed. We talked. He said he is sorry again. He said he never got to take pictures of me, most of my life. So he went all out with the cameras. I didn't really listen. He kept talking while we ate normal lamb with green beans. Pip just stared at his plate, and did not talk.

Then Dad mentioned Thursday.

They all come then, it is speeded-up, he said, the money shit with lawyers. So they are coming on Thursday. He described legal details. They are foolproof. Mom can't get control even though I'm sixteen. I did not say how glad I am that is true. She would control - totally - if she could. She controls my life.

I thought about Fearfield. He's right. The fuckers always control.

Then I thought about what I will buy Erik.

And Pip just stared at his plate, really sad.

Duane Allbright's
Audiocassette Notes: IV

Tuesday Night

I'm at the motel, lying on the bed, looking at dumbass TV. Nothing like dumbass TV. Incontinence commercials are the best. Those cartoons of feeble old ladies groping around pitiful and lost on account of peeing in their panties really do me good. I wonder why that is. Oh, yeah. What did he say to me this morning? "You nearly had another accident."

Those eyes have been haunting me all day.

———

After talking with Pip, I went by Sheila's, and scared her good. I didn't mean to. I guess I was keyed-up.

She's full of suspicion. Her diary she put in a deposit box, or so she says. I hope she did. I hope she keeps it there, too.

What can I do? Kidnap her, is what I should. Chain her to this bed. Maybe shoot her, then feed her to the dogs, piece by piece. What I really should do is call Cunif and say, "Send Schmidtt, pronto. The Baron's all yours, have a nice day, bye."

I'm risking Sheila's life. I'm risking the boy's. How can I justify that? My quest is so important? That's exactly why. But is it?

——

After fighting over the diary, and losing, I went to the school and found my way through near-empty hallways to the office of Caspar McQuisling. Caspar wasn't there. He was at a meeting, according to a middle-aged dame behind the counter. Behind her were desks and secretaries. Caspar administrates the school. That office is full of payroll and law and order, a lot of filing cabinets and typewriters and phones. It also was full of stacks of folders. There were a couple hundred piled behind the counter, and more were brought in as I stood there. A red-haired girl with pigtails carried them. She looked like she'd seen the Devil. "More!" she yelled as she plunked her pile on the counter. The atmosphere was tense. A phone rang in a back office and moments later I heard a voice say, "Mr. Flanagan's on line one." The dame behind the counter winced. The girl said, "He would call now." One of the secretaries was crying. Another one, younger, looked like she was trying not to laugh. She was reading a folder. The dame took the girl's load, and wearily put it on the floor. Then she wanted to know how she could help me. I said I'm a friend of the mother of a new student at school but I lost her current address, would she give me the address of Mrs. Floria Shade, mother of Torrance Spoor? The phone number, too. I ran into Torrance at the mall the other day and forgot to ask him. Nice kid, Torrance. Do you know him?

No. She didn't. She said she'd get the address. When she went for it I noticed the red-haired girl was looking at me strangely. "Are you a reporter?" she asked, very haughty.

"Yes," I said. Just to see what she'd say.

"He's a reporter!" the girl screamed at the office. The crying secretary spilled her coffee, and then five cops walked in, followed ten seconds later by a custodial type carrying fresh folders.

"I've got a teenage boy," one of the officers was saying.

"He's a *reporter*," the girl said to the cops, eyes frantic behind black-rimmed glasses. She wanted me handcuffed immediately.

"Oh, jeez, here we go," the one with a teenage boy said.

"The New York Times," I said, sticking out my hand. "What are the facts, gentlemen?"

"Just got here," another one grunted, "we don't have facts. Where's your father?" he asked the girl.

"Trying to save the school!" she shouted, angry. Then the priests walked in. Four of them, in black habits, eyes flashing brightly. It was getting crowded.

"Father O'Donnell!" the crying secretary called.

"Morning, Hattie," the Father said. "Hey there, Rhonda. Officers. Is this the filth?" He took a folder from the custodian who was standing there holding the things. He opened it, closed it, and shuddered.

The cop without facts pointed at me and said, *"The New York Times."*

"He's out to harrass the parents!" Rhonda yelled. "He's getting the addresses!"

"I remember you from the plane crash," Father O'Donnell informed me solemnly.

"Terrible tragedy," I murmured. The other priests were eagerly reading folders that they'd helped themselves to from the standing custodian. Then the dame came back with a piece of paper. "Thank you," I said, taking it and stepping on Rhonda's foot as she tried to grab it. "Oh, I beg your pardon," I said as she howled. The cops looked up from the folders they were helping themselves to and reading and wincing at.

"Amazing," one said.

"Here before we were," another one said.

"If I catch my boy reading this I'll shoot him," the first one said.

"He *attacked me!*" Rhonda, who'd been hopping around, screamed.

"Will somebody get her out of here," the counter dame said to no one in particular.

"Run along now," I said to Rhonda. "How bad is it?" I asked one of the priests.

"The epitome," this man said, "of evil." His eyes were glazing. The room was full of people standing around reading folders. There were gasps and grunts. A cop farted. The custodian, who'd been trying to get through, and instead had been an inadvertent folder-dispenser, dumped his remaining ones on the floor and left, bumping priests who didn't move out of his way because they were reading so raptly. I smiled at the counter dame, who smiled back. Rhonda was afraid I'd pick up the dumped folders. She darted through to collect them.

"Would you like some coffee?" counter dame asked me.

"Love some," I said.

"I think you better take a look at this," she said, handing me a folder. "It's just some joke. But you'd think the sky is falling. Did I hear you say you're from the *Times*?"

"Why, yes," I said, taking the folder.

"I do the crossword every Sunday," she said.

"That's fun," I said.

"I'm telling *Father*," Rhonda shrieked. "You're cooperating with the *media*!"

"Shut up," counter dame said, "and get out of my office."

"I will be interviewed right now!" Father O'Donnell declared, snapping shut his folder. "Later, my dear," he said gently to Rhonda.

"Not *you*," Rhonda screamed. "*My* father!"

"Think I'll skip the coffee," I said to the counter dame. She winked. I winked. I left after promising Father O'Donnell I'd be back later for an in-depth interview. Rhonda followed me to the hall.

"*Liberal*!" she yelled. "Humanist *sympathizer*!"

"Where'd you learn those ugly words, girl?" I said. "At home?"

She did a good imitation of a pit bull with distemper and I walked away, whistling.

———

The Baron wrote the folder. It's a piece of creative writing designed to ruin Sheila. Damn thing's a hymn in praise of sodomy, and it fingers her class, fingers it deathly good. Pip must have made copies, then broke into the school. Amazing what that Pip can do.

Why ruin Sheila? He wants her helpless. So he can control her, therefore control her baby. Makes sense. People with money ruin people without money all the time, so they can step in and take control.

I went to a luncheonette to read and ponder this. It was quarter to two. I thought of calling Sheila, decided not to. She didn't know yet about The Fearfield Club. That's the title of Malcolm's folder. I knew she didn't know because I'd have felt the anger and panic and hysterical fantasies about running away. Her typical reaction. Which I can't let her do, I reminded myself, if I'm working for Malcolm.

That led to another issue. What to do about Thursday, of course.

Thursday's a big deal for Malcolm. The biggest deal. Probably he gets nervous when he gives his money away to his young new self, then kills off the old one, after the switch. I've been assuming he fixes the death right after the switch. Suppose the old body, full of boy, went to the cops? They'd think he was cuckoo, but Torrance might figure out ways to prove who he is, and that could bring Malcolm lots of attention. Malcolm does not want that kind of attention. The *National Enquirer* demanding interviews? What a story: MY DAD STOLE MY BODY! NOW I'M TRAPPED IN HIS AND HAVE LUNG CANCER!

Another thing. Doing the switch might be draining. It might make the new Baron weak for a while. According to the family histories I read, they typically withdraw into seclusion and grief. They see few friends. Well, that makes sense, for a lot of reasons.

It adds up to Malcolm being vulnerable on Thursday. But he's got Pip. And the dogs. And the roses.

So I wrote a letter to Florida Shade.

Dear Mrs. Shade, I wrote, I have disturbing news about your son. Your ex-husband spies on him with secret cameras and makes the most shocking tapes. Also you should know Torrance is under the influence of a teacher at the school where Malcolm forces him to go. Enclosed is an example of the kind of "creative writing" this teacher encourages her students to write. If I were you I'd get a court order and the next plane over. I enclose The Fearfield Club to facilitate this rescue. I hope you have a good lawyer and move quickly because something awful is happening this Thursday. The cameras will be filming everything, and if you'll pardon me for saying so, it could really put a kink in that fine boy's future. Don't call the police. They're corrupt, Malcolm would bribe them. And I'd resist any urge to call Torrance, because the phones are tapped. If Malcolm thought you knew about his intentions, he would cover everything up and you surely would lose your case in court. If, however, you and your lawyer and armed bodyguards were to foil the operation, Malcolm would never be able to harm Torrance again. Keep in mind he owns dangerous dogs.

That was the gist. I signed it, A Concerned Citizen.

———

I went to the post office and overnight-mailed it, with the folder, to La Jolla, California. Made me feel better. The more Malcolm has to handle on Thursday, the easier things will be.

Thinking about that, I asked the postal clerk if he knew of a big estate on the shore, one that recently changed hands. It's a peninsula, I started to add, but he already knew what I meant. "Mace Estate," he said. "Everybody knows about the Mace Estate."

I said, "Maces don't live there now, do they?"

"Oh no," he replied. "Old lady Mace died over a year ago." He didn't seem regretful. "The relatives had a big fight. Then they sold it. Some foreign man bought it. That made the tweet-tweeties real happy."

"The tweet-tweeties?" I said.

"Bird people. Nature nuts. People who hate to see new jobs in town."

"Is the foreign man," I asked, "one of them?"

The clerk shrugged. "Nobody knows what he is. But he's rich. Didn't subdivide, see. Didn't build. A lot companies wanted to build, but not him, he's keeping the whole place to himself. Except for the birds. And the deer, and seals that don't do nothing but shit on rocks. And the bald guy."

"Maybe you can help me out," I said.

His eyebrows rose. "Give me a reason."

I said, "I'm from the Kong Development Trust." I stuck out my hand.

He didn't take it. "You don't," he said slowly, looking at my jacket, "look the type, mister."

"I'm an investigator. I can't look the type."

"What's the investigation? If I can ask."

"Fraud."

"That foreigner?"

I nodded. "But that's not our main problem. What bothers us is, the land is unavailable. Going to waste, not used, just sitting there. Maybe forever. Tweet-tweet, forever."

"*Gawww,*" the man said.

"Exactly," I said. "Unless we expose him. His name is Spoor. Does he get mail?"

The clerk's face fell. "Junk, sure. But everybody gets that." He looked away. "We talk about this. He doesn't get mail. It's strange."

"Here at the post office, you talk?"

"That's right. This is a small town, mister. We know everybody. Almost everybody. And we talk."

"Ok. No mail. Anything else?"

"The disappearance, there's that."

"I heard about it. What happened?"

"By the Mace place is a fire lane. It goes into the woods. Kids drive in there—you know, lover lane. And it used to be, there wasn't a fence. You could walk around." He was remembering something. "I did that. It was nice. A meadow. Hills. Trees."

"A couple of kids disappeared there?"

He grimaced. "Three weeks ago. Police found the car. But no kids. Not a trace." He paused. "Could have been drugs, a deal gone bad. They searched the property. The bald guy helped. I heard he was cooperative."

Feeling bad, I said, "They'll turn up."

"I doubt it, mister."

"You sound so sure."

He shrugged. "Three whole weeks. Christmas, the new year. No phone calls. Not a trace."

"Yeah. Gee, I'm sorry. Maybe you can tell me—do you know where I can find a map of that property?"

———

Down the street, at Marie's Used Books, Marie herself found me not a map, but a picture. It's old. So is the book it was folded into. "A wonderful book," she said, brushing cobwebs off the molting spine, "a *rare* book. Cornelius Mace wrote it, and had it printed, at great expense, in 1922. His father Driscoll founded Mace Sanitary, you know, before the turn of the century—every other toilet bowl in America was Mace in those days, which accounts for Cornelius's fascination. Does the history of plumbing interest you, sir?" Maybe to sharpen my interest, she punched my shoulder. I almost tumbled into a stack of filthy books. Marie is heavy. She has big arms, that are energetic. You could say she's heavily armed.

I asked, "Why is that map in a book on plumbing?"

"One of the Maces must have put it in. This book came from the Mace private library, you see. And I know it did, because I found it there, with my own two hands!"

Which, I thought, could strangle hogs. "I need a more recent map, to tell you the truth. Something that shows the layout the way it is today."

"But it does! It certainly does, sir, this map is precise!"

"How," I asked, "do you know?"

"Well," Marie said, "I was at that place all last summer, every day in fact, on account of my husband Bill, because Bill put in that swimming pool, that's what Bill does, pools, and he did that pool in the basement there, a big one too, biggest pool Bill ever did, he said. So of course I went over there all the time, sometimes to bring Bill lunch, sometimes to look around, because it's absolutely gorgeous and grand, you know, and famous too, every brick paid for by toilets, of course. I just loved it, the looking around, the wondering, the dreaming." And the pillaging, I thought, of the library. "So I am in a position to say, this map is precise! The gazebo, it's still there, the gardens too, and that cliffwalk—I assure you, sir,"—I took a step back because she was fixing to punch—"a more accurate map than this doesn't exist!"

"How much?"

"Fifty dollars."

"That seems high."

"What do you care, if it's on expenses?" I didn't say anything. She leaned at me and whispered, "The families hired you, didn't they? Why else would you need a map? If you ask me, that foreign man is a very odd fellow, and I'm not saying he did it, but you answer this question, why was the car next to the fence, if something didn't happen in there? Everybody knows kids climb it. Or used to, nobody goes near the place now."

"How," I asked, "does the foreign man strike you as odd?"

"Compartments for cameras, in the walls of a pool? Underwater? Built so you don't know they're there? You tell me if that isn't odd."

———

I got the book, plus picture, for twenty. Now the book adorns my rickety motel table. The picture I am holding in my hands. The hill going from the house to the cliffs, the cliffs themselves, are dramatic. It looks much like what I saw Saturday night, when I was floating above those cliffs, minus my body.

Inland, not shown in the picture, is the meadow lovers used to wander through, before it got fenced. The one those disappeared kids probably climbed the fence to run around in. The one the dogs ran down, tearing through snow.

A horrible possibility is haunting me.

If the Baron can see through his dogs, he can do other things through them too. Those dogs are an extension. What he wants them to do, they do, the same way his own body, his own mouth, do what he wants them to do. I think that must be the way it is. If so, he doesn't have one mouth. When he connects with those dogs, he has thirteen.

I can't help but wonder: If those kids got eaten, did Malcolm taste them? Did he feel the jaws crunch? Hear the screams?

So senseless. It could only mean he really is crazy. Maybe he's out of control. Or maybe he can't help it, his hunger. I keep saying "he," but it's more than that, it's the dogs, and Pip, who also must be an extension—what he extends from is hard to say, though, he seems half dog. Also the roses, they're part of this system, that so obviously is hungry.

It's one big hunger machine.

Torrance picked up on it. It scares him. I've sure felt it, and it scares me too. Those kids, if they got eaten, they definitely felt it, not to mention deer, not to mention all the people with psi, who knows how many, who've been sucked into the machine, and kept it growing, and growing. The evidence just mounts. Take Fearfield, he's hungry. He's voracious.

Maybe that's what you get when you've been alive 700 years. If hunger rules life, and you never die, maybe you get hungrier. Immortality makes you hungrier. Immortality is an eating disorder.

———

I have to tend to Sheila soon. When the news about Fearfield hits, she'll be frantic. She'll want to run away. But she can't. No matter how bad it gets, and it will get bad. Any minute the Project goons will be all over her.

I've been thinking. They might be helpful. Somebody has to shoot those dogs. And maybe Pip.

I have an idea. It's an outlandish idea, one that makes me too nervous to talk about now. I think the rose in my little fridge inspired it. It concerns Sheila. My panicky, skeptical, pooh-poohing Sheila, she might be helpful, too. She could be the key to solving everything.

Am I a monster?

———

I bought weapons today. That took all afternoon.

Letter from
Caspar McQuisling
to Sheila Massif

Tuesday Evening

DELIVERED BY HAND

Miss Massif:

"The Fearfield Club," a copy of which is enclosed, was distributed throughout the school yesterday, or possibly early this morning.

Eight stacks numbering fifty or so copies each were placed in ground-floor hallways, in the cafeteria, the gymnasium, outside the Recreational Activities Office, and other locations where students could find them. Due to snow the school of course was closed yesterday. Last night and this morning only one watchman was on duty, also due to snow. The break-in and distribution therefore were accomplished undetected.

I suggest you take a few minutes to read this extraordinary exercise in "creative writing."

Perhaps you are already familiar with it.

I am a reasonable man, Miss Massif. I am a balanced and thoughtful individual, seasoned by a career in educational administration that has spanned twenty-eight years. I make few enemies. People of all sorts come to me for advice. I am a person of some standing in this community.

Miss Massif, I tell you that I am, today, an angry man.

The author(s) and distributor(s) of the enclosed have made me very angry indeed. I do not know who the responsible party is. I intend to find out. When I find out, that party shall be punished, shall be punished severely, to the limits of all applicable laws.

I am confident, Miss Massif, that the creator of "Fearfield" has broken a great many laws. I have engaged an attorney to establish exactly how many. I have asked our district attorney, who happens to be a close friend, to pursue a vigorous, intensive investigation into the matter. Furthermore, I have engaged the services of a private detective firm.

No effort will be spared to ensure that the criminal(s) involved will be brought to justice.

You should know, Miss Massif, that I have reason to suspect that the depraved person behind "The Fearfield Club" may well be you.

My daughter, Rhonda, this afternoon described to me the kinds of things you do to your students in your "creative writing" class. She told me about the strange and shocking theories you espouse. She told me about the time you made the students lie down on the floor, with the lights out, in a state of partial undress. Rhonda furthermore revealed to me, Miss Massif, that you practice techniques of humiliation and harassment against students who have the integrity and fortitude to question your classroom behavior.

I do not know why Rhonda waited so long to come forth with these revelations. She herself says that she does not know why she waited until it was, in a sense, too late, until the damage had been done. It may be that your influence over my daughter affected her in ways which we may never fully understand, or eradicate.

What is very clear, however, Miss Massif, is the fact that your class did in some sense spawn the Fearfield travesty. The "body-reading," "body-writing," the disgusting emphasis, indeed the sedulous fixation, on bodies, which you propagate, obviously inspired Fearfield.

It is possible, of course, that you did not have a direct hand in the writing and distribution. Of course I recognize that possibility. It is a possibility which will be thoroughly examined, I assure you.

But, whatever the outcome of the investigation, I hold you responsible, at the very least, for infecting the mind of the person who did do it.

On those grounds, Miss Massif, your employment is terminated, effective immediately.

We do not tolerate cowardly, perverted assaults on our values, Miss Massif. We do not permit such assaults on our community, nor on our school.

I do not permit such assaults on my daughter. Nor do I permit them on myself.

I suggest you consider hiring a lawyer.

I will be seeing you in court.

Caspar McQuisling

The Chronicles
of Malcolm Spoor: VII

Tuesday Night

I thought Sheila would call. She hasn't. Odd, that she hasn't. She is the victim of an act of diabolical spite. And she knows who did it, she isn't stupid; she must feel an urge to call and vent rage, to make threats concerning that videotape. Surely she needs to scream at the demon who has demolished her life. Why, then, hasn't she called? I am getting impatient! I want to hear that woman howl - is she clever enough to know how much this provokes me?

No matter. Eventually, she will call. And if not, I will call her. Somehow I'll find a way to remark on the immensity of her debt to Fearfield. If the Club flourishes, after all, and turgid stories are written - well. Think of the data.

"Sheila, my dear," I will say demurely, for a demon I am very demure, "Fearfield is manna from heaven, and yes I insist on calling you 'my dear'; listen to me, why don't you settle down and do a little body-reading? What could be more divine than that?"

Poor Sheila. Her drama chamber must be boiling. Possibly I could goad her to stroke, by claiming to have done her a favor. Blood vessels, bursting! The thought makes me smile.

But Sheila's health is crucial, alas. I need her. Or rather, I need the baby she carries. She is pregnant with Spoor! I *know* it. And I am dreadfully excited, the tiny bit of plasm shines like treasure when we talk on the phone. I will have to get results, of course. Of tests, extensive medical tests. But instinct warns me their child will be wondrous - the Lad of the Millennium, I could see him the moment I set eyes on her!

Oh, dear. Far too much is going on. We have never dealt with pregnancy at this late stage of the cycle. How could that chore compete with Change? Yet here I am on the very Eve, arranging already for the next; it is unprecedented, reckless, another symptom of Malcolm's haste, his disdain for ritual. By rights, I should be majestic in this time of triumph. I should be suffused with exaltation and awe - and mindful of the Predecessors whose ranks Malcolm is joining, are you listening?

Oh, they annoy me.

There were so many things we used to do that I could be doing, but I am obsessed with the womb of a meddlesome woman. No matter. I look ahead, I do not look back, why look back? *Yuck,* as Torrance would say.

It is not simply Sheila. There is Erik, too, I am obsessed with Erik. Yes, Erik, on account of whom Torrance has been cooling in the pool for at least forty-five minutes. The boy couldn't even eat tonight.

He was too enthralled. His mood quite concerned me, earlier. He sat there - sizzling.

Fortunately, the device arrived today. Sullen Pip installed it after taking him to school. By noon, his computer balked no longer. Its secrets, if that is what they were, finally are mine. Erik was the only surprise. I was so relieved. Like Sheila, Torrance knows nothing.

But then he appeared at dinner.

I'd looked forward to him being full of Fearfield chatter, and he was. My little tract hit the school like a meteor from "Gay Outer Space." We giggled together over that idea. He is charming, really. He gave me his own copy with a flourish, as if suggesting that I deserve some small amusing generosity, that he feels for me in the midst of my apologies, my sad travails. The tension between us almost seemed to dissolve. Forgiveness comes easily these days; it matters not how badly one has transgressed, one simply admits to being very, very sick, and starts galloping down the road of recovery, and all wrongs suddenly right. This is particularly true when it's money begging pardon - when millions say, "Sorry, I'm horribly sorry." So Torrance has reason to be cheerful. Cameras are down, he's getting his way, he thinks, and he is getting rich, of course.

But I puzzled and analyzed, because he wasn't merely cheerful. The boy was shining pure, pale lust, his aura transparently on fire - from sex, obviously, boys ignite that way for one reason only, when they've had thrilling *sex*. I guessed Erik, whose exits from the shower and other locker-room discretions I'd pondered, thanks to breached computer, all afternoon, and I worried. It occurred to me that Torrance and Erik might have been Fearfield-inspired. Perhaps the entire team had gone mad. Perhaps they'd stripped and brandished tons of slender jocky fun, the undelicate organs; boys that age are fully capable - oh yes, I worried.

I needn't have. After toying with the banal food he now demands and gets, Torrance obligingly went straight to computer and, as it turned out, gushed for an hour; thence he went to pool, giving me an opportunity to extract that account of Speedos erupting in the perilous stairwell, the janitor oblivious, the concrete spermily perfuming . . .

Despite myself - despite, I should say, this self, soon to be one of you - I am intrigued by the glueable Erik. But how can I be sure he isn't a dreadful little dolt? Torrance is discerning, I think, in these matters, that boy he saw in La Jolla, Ricky - I wallpapered the disco with blow-ups. In Bangkok, Stupids, at the Villa. Did you see Ricky looming, in bicycle shorts? Fifteen and blazing? Wall-size enlargements of the two of them holding hands at the beach, romping in Floria's back garden, *skateboarding*?

Appalling, of course. But of course, I was interested. The approach of Change mandates interest, no? The issue of what we are getting into? It *is* different, each time, what we get into, isn't it? The last one who liked boys - who was he? Persiflage, I think. Percy, why haven't I heard from you? The advent of Torrance should rouse you, at least. In your day, the stables were pretty, and terribly boisterous - even the horses were shocked. Pillars, eh, Percy? Equine salt?

I seem to recall you enjoyed yourself. Have you any tips for Torrance? On how to handle his fixation? But I am avoiding, here.

———

This is the final Chronicle of Malcolm. Do you care?

I'm on my third bottle. Of good champagne. Not a drop for you, ha-ha. No, you cannot taste, I will not let you. *Wretches.* Malcolm soon will join you, I am sure you anticipate that! Now let me see—

Tonight is my Eve of Change. Tomorrow is, technically, but I won't have time tomorrow, as I've chores, more phone calls, and so on; which means tonight is the night to look back, and sum up. That much I owe tradition. And it behooves me at least to try to commune with my antique selves, even though it was on this occasion the last time around that Bunny sent them packing, I do hope you are happy. Bunny? Are you?

Never mind.

The monitors are on. The whole wall is on, without audio, and thus I keyboard against a silent glare of bran flakes tumbling and hemorrhoids flaring and matrons thickly but vivaciously deconstipating. Such is the backdrop for my closing of the Chronicles of Malcolm. Do I trivialize that duty? Perhaps it is appropriate I face Change in the deeply stupid company of marvelous machines. What better way to salute Malcolm, Space-Age Spoor? I hurtle at the future, rather like a cosmonaut in his technological nest, and if Ground Control is obsessed with intestinal disorders, I'm not to blame. On the contrary, we've been zeitgeist escapees for centuries. Exiting the ludicrous is our knack! The process runs faster, more blatantly, that's all. We are flotsam in culture's modern rush. Malcolm, like demented Bunny, cannot be faulted for that, at least.

What a joy to be done with this one. Malcolm doesn't even keep trains of thought on track. No tracks are left - just trackless waste in here, my brain is the Amazon, slashed, burned. It is always that way, at a body's dead end, but I am worse than usual this time around, due to cognac, and these pills. The twentieth century is a dangerous place for a being like me - psychopharmacopoeia runs riot. To what depths, I wonder, will Torrance sink?

Slinking toward *fin de millenium?*

What difference does it make?

Now then. I must say something serious about Malcolm. What, I do not quite know. According to Sheila I am a "slimeball scumbag." A kind of used condom, apparently; lying in wait, perhaps, for the bare feet of stargazing strollers. Is that me - a New Age banana peel?

Why I put myself through this, I cannot fathom. Summing up was once a pleasure. Tonight, it isn't. The trend continues. We Chronicle sourly. Why? There is no good reason.

Think of Bunny - he went out kicking and screaming. But he was a huge success, just as am I, for I, as did he, produced the choicest heir yet. The chief point of tonight, I suppose, is that we do keep getting better. Dr. Mengele would have marveled at our intuitive, though I would not say unscientific, eugenic achievements; and so of course Malcolm deserves credit for the advance Torrance embodies, the boy is "top of the line" - his beauty eclipses that of any Spoor before him. Bravo, Malcolm, your boy outshines even you! You carry on the family pastime of seven hundred years, begetting sons to make fathers feel gratefully inferior; a responsible scion, you have devoted yourself to *improving our heritage . . .*

There. I tried.

Rings hollow, though; doesn't it? Is anyone listening? I think I need some help here - or are you by any chance afraid of TV? Ha! Afraid of TV! I suppose they want guttering candelabra and the like, a draughty Great Hall for their spectral parade. Not enough room in this cubicle, boys, to clank around showing off your ridiculous fineries? That only accentuate the pathetic bodies you dropped at Change? Debating and trading insults the while on who in youth had been the loveliest? This isn't grand enough for a reunion of the Elderlies?

Perhaps you think I am spurning you the way Bunny did, eh?

Well, tough shit! As we modern ones say; as Torrance would say . . .

Hopeless. I need more drink.

———

I simply cannot take myself that seriously. Be serious about Malcolm? Oh, boy. Boys! That is Fearfield talking, my new alter ego: "Hey, you! You, in the bicycle shorts with bold chiaroscuro!"

I am trying to get into the spirit of this boy-business. I lack the requisite élan, I think. Chiaroscuro isn't right, for example. Teens would hear queero-screwo; which is kind of dumb, as Torrance would say.

Perhaps Erik can teach me how to be a boy who is fixated on boys. He should be a better guide, at least, than the Torrance tapes. I must say they have been a disappointment. Sheila thought she was cunning, taking that one; she was so wrong. An insane man doesn't care what people think. Especially when he is dead. Furthermore it is the one tape I wouldn't have needed, had I needed tapes, the behaviors it records are exactly the ones I am not obliged to render à la Torrance. I can reinvent his passion and no one will notice. Not wholly reinvent, of course - Torrance is very fixated, that much I have learned from his amusing "War Journal." I am resigned, now, to this. There is nothing to be done. Besides, it is a change from me. And that is what matters. To at last be rid of Malcolm!

But there is, in consequence, the question of Erik. Luckily, he doesn't know Torrance's inner glow. The inimitable spirit I cannot quite - no, I need not be apprehensive, for I am stepping in at just the right time. Erik knows how the boy walks, talks, frowns and laughs. Two or three weeks from now, he would know more, but at the moment that is all Erik knows. However, I know the same. It is on tape. The ones Sheila left behind! The twist is ironic, but minor. I can do Torrance. I *am* Torrance, I've studied every gait and gesture, day by day, hour by hour, and having done that, slavishly, I conclude I have been too prudent. I really do overreact, to this era of "rights." No one will suspect anything - who could believe such a monster exists? Who could uncover my crime?

Duane? I laugh.

And of course Torrance will "change" - he must endure a dreadful death in the family. Then there is the money, too. Such circumstances would have an impact on anyone. He will seclude himself, go through a cycle of denial, anger, acceptance, all the grief-reaction nonsense, why - Sheila will be taking notes! She will be observing a case of fractured adolescent development, one with beguiling sex angles. How could she not approve of Torrance spending time with the consoling Erik? She will say: "The boys are inseparable. Erik is a blessing, helping Torrance shrug off the pain. And it's touching, isn't it, how love helps the inner self surface?"

I assume she will say something along those lines. She had better. I do need her, she is saving Torrance a great deal of work. He is sixteen; sixteen years from now their boy will be fifteen, and Torrance only thirty-two. What luxury, eh, Grislies? You see how clever I am? Death at a very early age. And Torrance will evade the matrimonial charade, he needn't look for the next vehicle into eternity, I have already found it!

There is the issue of keeping Sheila placid, and ignorant, for at least nine months, but that should not be hard to arrange. She is in trouble. She needs a refuge from life's vicissitudes, and will welcome money's safe maw. "Crawl in, my *dear,* and relax. I, Torrance, will take care of you."

Can't put it quite that way. Torrance should be a bit more forlorn. He will need comfort; support; friendship! Sheila is ideal. She is covertly maternal - how else did she get hooked on the sexual development of children? She could even become Torrance's substitute mother, the sensitive Mom Floria isn't. I, of course, despise Sheila. No, I resent her interference. But Torrance could use her. Someone must bring up Baby. And she will cooperate, of course; because she confronts No Future, and because Duane will force it.

Sad Duane. Desperately wishing to learn. He begs at the door of a distant and far nobler relation, he would do anything for us, and I would be flattered, perhaps, if his poverty weren't dangerous. But he is envious, a grasper, a would-be Great. However, he is canny. He knows Torrance's destiny and keeps this from Sheila, not to mention Torrance. The Saturday denouement bespoke respect. He told them so very little about his near-fatal experience with the plants. That entire episode could have been disastrous, but he saved it; thus laying claim to favor. I did not understand this at first. I was too angry. But now I see all. He hopes I am grateful. Here he errs! Grateful I'm not, for his actions imply threat. He could alter tactics and make things unplesant, and he means me to know it.

Absurd. Even the dogs see this ploy. Even you do, Bunny. I will extinguish Duane; later, when I no longer need him. He will not get what he desires. The dogs will pay him. They will devour his Fire.

———

It is late. I dozed. But I just took a pill, and Pip brought in more champagne. I am not finished, Grislies. I know you are here, by the way. You've been all along. The Bunny in me cloaks you, yes, but still you are here. Poor Bunny. Poor, poor Bunny. He almost couldn't do it, you know - kill himself, that is.

And you know why, you all know why. Bunny loved his son! He was so fond of the innocent, lively, charming, affectionate lad, who died; who died with Bunny, *in Bunny,* when Bunny killed himself. And created me.

Do you still mourn that boy? Whose sweet body, years later, I have run into the ground?

Bunny, I know how you felt. I don't suffer from that feeling as keenly, of course. How could I? I am Malcolm. Malcolm the Unfeeling.

But I am adequately drunk, and rested, and the pill is recharging me, and I find it within my hollow Malcolm powers to forgive you, and hope that you, and the others, will appear, please. I command it!

Let us be reasonable, shall we? Wasn't it splendid in the old days when, during the revels prior to Change, you disported mischievously, and argued and gawked, and made awful rackets? Invisible, inaudible to all? To all but The Living One? Running around mocking everyone, and stealthily groping? Oh, you were mad.

Now I am The Living One. And you are invisible to me! On my Eve of Change! Now, really.

I know I've ignored you. I didn't stay in touch, I kept the sketchiest of Chronicles. In fact I wrote none till now. I never called on you for advice or comfort, I never asked you to come witness, to share my excesses, and when Torrance was born I didn't tell you. But you know why. Bunny, take some responsibility! And Gainsborough! Remember what you did to Felipe!

Little wonder Gainsborough became Cringing Bunny, who couldn't bear to be called - Felipe. You couldn't bear it. You thought of that young gaucho loving life, and you felt such shame!

Little wonder that you, becoming me, became - Hollow Malcolm.

Excuse me while I take another pill. Aren't you curious about these pills? I do not know how any of you survived without them.

———

I suspect the problem is the business of making them understand.

Why have we? Felt compelled to make them understand? I think of the way Bunny made Young Malcolm understand. The boy's desperate shock!

Will Torrance be the same? When he understands? He will be the same. But worse. Much worse, I fear.

It's as though - easing conscience? As though their deaths serve a purpose, a terrible purpose, which they must understand. They've never died without understanding, eh? You like that, eh? Monsters!

So we told lies; in which a need to make a ceremony of regret mingled with the conviction that it's a good idea to start well ahead of time getting them frightened out of their brains.

To prepare them for the final insight! For the fact that the Sons live briefly, sensuously but briefly, to serve The Living One, to serve all of us!

Young Malcolm, like Felipe before him, didn't really appreciate - this. The glories of sacrifice and so on, all that bullshit, as Torrance would say, and will say.

What will he say? Tomorrow? It is three in the morning, now. It's Wednesday. Can you predict what my son, our form, will say?

None of them did appreciate, let's be honest. But now they resist a bit more. They struggle with the final understanding, and try to stop us, this is why Felipe went on trial for shooting Gainsborough. A clumsy kill, that was. It was why Felipe renamed himself. How he squirmed at the trial! Being told to his face he was nothing but a common criminal, a cold-blooded murderer.

Hoi polloi mortals calling The Living One a criminal - in public?

I will be careful with Torrance. He will understand. But he won't be very understanding. He will be furious. I shouldn't have written him the letter. The custom is to have a talk. We could have had a talk. Why didn't I simply say I am not feeling well, have been diagnosed with something, anything, liver cancer? There are dozens of ways to go that are relatively unupsetting, why did I tell him I am killing myself?

It is making me sick. Because he will know, when he understands - that I am murdering him, of course. The "Suicide of Malcolm" - it is too unplesant, to imagine his sense of injustice, his rage.

I am very anxious about this.

Do you believe me? Of course you do. Bunny even announced it, that you know this - know it all too well!

Yes I admit it, I am facing a *crisis of nerve.* Naturally I am. We always do at Change, Bunny's breakdown is recent proof, and I suppose the machines, the cameras and so on, are evidence of my more modern distress. This room, my "control room" - is proof.

I am so afraid of losing control!

Please listen. I will confess, something.

There is something going on, something odd, please listen.

We have always looked forward to creating ourselves, no? Another form, another name, means a new *life,* no? A way to live freshly, starting all over - the new flesh full of strange quirks and hungers, each incarnation makes a glorious new world, no? Of course!

But now, I will admit something; something which, despite what I told myself - that I must impersonate Torrance, and do it flawlessly - has more to do . . . I blush, admitting this; admitting why I'm nervous.

I am nervous about the One we next will create, because, and this is what will astonish you - I want him to be the boy - that Torrance is now.

Are you gasping?

Not due to his fixation, of course. That I could dispense with, in fact it nauseates me, despite its inevitability, despite my efforts to come around. But that isn't the point. What I really want, to make this clear, is to *be* Torrance; not just bodily, but in spirit, too - in all the ways that he, yes, I'll say it, is happy - *I want to be happy the way Torrance is happy.*

It's hopeless. But you do understand? Of course I would like to be happier than Malcolm - who inherited Bunny's wretched weak-heartedness, into whom Bunny dumped himself so guiltily, so *poisonously,* and who therefore spoilt his youth scouring away the stain, to the point where, now, at the end, I scarcely feel anything at all! I am polished, finally, to a high-toned orb of nothing! That is Malcolm - the Emperor of Nothing!

You see how you ruined me, vile Bunny? Wherever you are?

And what, then, will I be dumping, when I dump Malcolm into Torrance? A whole lot of nothing? It seems so unfair; not in the Bunnyish sense of squirming guilt, at least I don't think it is guilt, and certainly hope it is not, I have spent Malcolm's life getting rid of the guilt; but it does seem unfair in the sense of - well, of waste. If I feel a pang at the thought of evicting Torrance, it is on the almost ecological grounds that one must do what one can to conserve happiness. There isn't that much of it around. Can't he leave a little behind - for me? And I am troubled to think of his plenitude stuck in this cheerless, aged, toxic form, where it won't do anyone any good at all.

Our form, his grave!

This is why I made the tapes, you see. But you have guessed, haven't you? Perhaps you haven't. You do not care!

I will tell you about my tapes, my cameras, my TVs. I thought I could capture a portion of Torrance's soul. Yes! Laughably enough, I tried to preserve his *soul.* I rationalized that I would hide the Change from others when in actual fact preparing, with fantastic fussbudgetry, to shield that brutal difference from me, from the new me, the new Torrance, from my own impending *self.* I wanted to be so thoroughly Torrance that not even I would know I am not really Torrance! So I planned for a year. No detail, however minor, would evade the lenses, I would assemble a complete simulacrum and worship it, I would immerse myself in and absorb, subliminally, I theorized, *the essence of the boy I want to be.*

Soul is not videotapable, however. I have learned this.

Not even I can control or possess soul. By taking pictures of it. American Indians believed that theory. The theory doesn't work; no matter how much I practice his laugh, the tilting light in his eyes, the sprawl of his legs from a chair, or try to conjure up that aura, so lucid tonight, I am so jealous!

Have you been following me? Can we please have a talk, about this?

———

Oh, dear. I seem to have reversed our ancient problem, yes?

We used to worry about bringing too much to our clean new forms, and excess of Voices, of Names - stale imprints of bygone eras, archaic and often vulgar, often barbaric - like the attic crammings of a moldy chateau, rather grotesque to see in fresher quarters! This was what maddened Bunny, what botched his Change, the baggage - a "Gamey gang of killers," he screamed, "haunting Change like common murderers at their scenes of crime!"

And you vanished, vanished, *poof,* you were gone! And ever since, I, Malcolm, haven't heard a whisper - which has been fine.

Until now. Because now I feel empty, with no momentum. I miss you, the way you egged us on, cattily appraising, what have you to say about Torrance? What do you say?

Should I let him live, perhaps? Well, should I?

Now you are gasping, I even - hear it.

You had better give me courage! Why, even I can think of what you should say! It is simple, simple, so easy. You should say:

"That we are killers is true. But what of it? How else could we have accumulated? How else could you be the twenty-sixth incarnation of Us, The Spoor?" That is what you should say!

But do you know what I say? Reply to this:

To think of the serial biology as ancestry - that is convenient, for dealing with guilt. I didn't kill, oh no; *they* did. The logic is universal. Who blames Germans for the sins of the Nazis, or Americans for slavery, or boys in bicycle shorts for the bell-bottomed idiocy of their *parents*? One always blames the parents, never oneself. Parents were invented to take the blame! And that, of course, is why you are the Grislies. I am not you! I'm not Bunny, or Blake or Gainsborough or any of you, least of all Gundulf! I didn't betray Baybars - usurp his Fire, enslave and torment him! *I am not responsible for the Curse!*

No, you're just evil voices in my head - voices that do not even talk. I am innocent Malcolm, the victim of Bunny, who doesn't *talk.*

And when I create Torrance, I will despise my heinous father, Malcolm! Just as Malcolm blames his father, Bunny. Blame the Fathers! It's they who did it! Even though you don't appear or talk!

That is my problem - how can I blame you? If you do not even talk?

We always have had Fathers to blame. This you deny me. When I am Torrance, where will I be? Guiltily in Torrance? You deny Malcolm his Grislihood, why? To ruin Torrance? You want me *to ruin Torrance*————

Oh! I think————yes.

In the portraits————You are - ?

Yes! Thank you————

Thank you! I weep————

Oh, I weep————

The Diary
of Sheila Massif: XII

Wednesday Afternoon

It's warm today. Mid-fifties, someone said as I slid through the mall
to the bank.

Cars were heaving around spewing slush. The puddles go deep
where potholes are. They look solid, they're so crusty with dirt on
top. But they're not solid. I stepped in one and freezing grease
flooded my boot. That's when I started crying.

If only this were the arctic, I thought. The puddle would be death's
hole in the ice. I could dive in and whales, intelligent killers, could
gobble me up. That would be nice. Soon I'd be nothing but whale
dung. I'd be shitted out in lightless, ice-lidded waters, never to be
heard from again. What happens to whale dung? I wondered, crying
and standing one-footed and taking off the boot. The man in the car
I was leaning on beeped his horn. He wanted to drive away; a guy
with a flat nose and black eyes in his big, fat-ass, beeping car. I
didn't care, so I emptied my boot. I dumped slush all over his windshield. Staring, he turned on the wipers. They smeared. Then
cleanser jetted and with a wipe he was staring again through re-

flected dim sky, it was weird. Because suddenly the guy looked evilly embarrassed. Like he was hiding—trying to stay incognito under the whack of the wipers! I wanted to bend them to pretzels. I could have. I could have grabbed with the boot and twisted, until they waggled brokenly, brain-dead . . .

People were looking. Lobsters eat whale dung, I decided, jamming foot in boot and hobbling off. But would they go for Sheila-shit? Hell no.

This got me to the bank and its vault, and back here with Diary. I hurried along thinking about my fecal remains. The thought had a stimulating effect. I got mad. I began to think of revenge. I began to *see* dark schemes of revenge, and a James Brown tune suddenly throbbed in my head, speeding my limp: "Get on the cold foot!"

I was practically shouting that as I rushed over the ramp to the building and down the hall.

How could he be so cruel? Because he's psycho, that's why. The tape doesn't bother him. He doesn't care about it, he was just pretending to be cornered while he set me up. So what do I do with T-Sex? Call a press conference? Yell about a video of a naked boy doing God knows what to himself? Caspar would be there. He'd tell everybody the video proves I'm Fearfield. He'd ask me if I think Torrance has a creative body!

That's out. Do I mail it to his mother? Or do I just get out of town?

I discussed this with Duane. He called last night, after Caspar's package arrived. Caspar sent me a hand-delivered package. In it was the Fearfield thing and a letter firing me. He's blaming me for the whole deal, exactly as evil Malcolm planned. After half an hour of numb reading and re-reading the full nausea hit. It was then that Duane called, of course. As usual he felt it. He always does. He's Psychic Duane. How did I ever doubt he really is *Psychic* Duane?

"He bagged me!" I shrieked in the phone.

"Who did?"

"Malcolm! The sneaky stuck-up bastard has destroyed me!"

"That's too bad," he said.

"Duane," I said, "I feel like a branded sex criminal!"

"Calm down," he said, "that's foolish. Have you had any visitors?"

"Yeah," I said, "the boy who delivered Fearfield and the letter, an innocent kid who made me sign the dotted line. I thought it was a present, then I saw McQUISLING in the upper left corner, and when the boy left and I ripped it open there it was, my *doom,* Duane, in black and white!"

Duane wanted to know what a Fearfield is. I told him. "Seems like it might be Malcolm all right," he said.

"Yes," I moaned. "I've been canned because there's references to body-reading that obviously come from my class. All the Fearfield followers are supposed to write stories—you can't imagine how disgusting . . ."

"Hmmmm," Duane said. "Stories."

"Don't tell me I could use them," I whimpered. "That's probably what he thinks is funny."

"Yeah," he said. "Huh." Duane's so eloquent sometimes. "Well," he said. "Gee. Gee whiz, Sheila. Have you talked with Torrance?"

"He's enchanted with Fearfield," I said, "he called from school to tell me, not knowing his father wrote it and neither did I then, I only found out just now when the package came and I read it. What am I going to *do*?"

"Get out of that apartment, maybe," Duane suggested. "Don't talk to anybody. You're fired, you don't have to talk. Avoid the detectives if he really hires them, and you should get out anyway, the Project goons . . ."

"Oh," I said, "them."

"Keep your Diary in the bank. It's there, right?"

"Yeah."

"Do you want to bag him?"

I thought about this. He meant Malcolm, I assumed. What a good idea. "I want to make him helpless," I said, "and torture him."

There was silence. Then he said, "Maybe you can, Sheila. Don't panic, you aren't dead meat yet. See you tomorrow." He hung up.

That was around ten o'clock. I tried to watch TV. I thought maybe there'd be a special report on the furor at school. A camera crew at the emergency PTA meeting? I saw Caspar sweating under the lights, promising swift justice, a clean sweep, yes he'll call in the vice squad. Tearful mothers swarm, demanding blood. Thick-necked fathers seethe. In the gym there's a general will to lynch, somebody loops a noose through the basketball hoop. "*Sheila did it*," the gossips whisper around the coffee urn. "Even if she didn't, she's responsible anyway, did you hear what Rhonda said she made them do in class? Get on the floor in the dark and take off their clothes and then she whips them into a frenzy with talk about their bodies?"

TV news had nothing to say about Fearfield or me. The weatherman made a big deal about today's heat wave. "Take those boots to *work,"* he shouted, "a whole lot of slush tomorrow!" The idiot emphasizes as though people don't understand English. As if we're children, quivering at his loudly teased-out words. "But tomorrow *night,* get out the *skates!"* An offensive, patronizing grin. "All that slush will *freeeeze!"*

Oh, God. I realized I was expecting the phone to ring. I kept looking at it. Then I remembered I know almost no one around here. I haven't made friends at school, except Torrance, who'd already called; and Duane had called, so who was left? Nobody. Maybe cranks would call, or irate Moms, Fearfield-haters who wanted to give me a piece of their venomous minds . . .

Then I thought of it. Maybe Malcolm would call.

I unplugged the phone.

And for the first time, the first during the whole ordeal of the last few days, I did it—really, it was bad, I went to Chamber.

I couldn't deal. Not with Malcolm. He'd see right through me. With Duane it's ok, usually, when he sees how I get. But with creeps like Malcolm boundaries blur. It's like dissolving—no inside or outside, no boundaries.

Like a glass of water getting drunk down and *absorbed.* There's no *me* any more with an enemy like Malcolm! It happened when I was little, the shrinks said I had "episodes"—a "panic disorder," but for me it was simpler, I just had to get away! So I invented, and went there to save myself. I had a shape there, a real me, I made my *own* reality come true!

———

And all of a sudden, there I was. Cut off, alone. Deep and safe. Like always, hating it. Like always, relieved.

I did some thinking. Slowly, the way I do in Chamber, but still, I did do some thinking. About the thesis. It seemed hilarious. Like a pastel cartoon. "Gender Boundaries." I thought about all kinds of boundaries. The many, many boundaries—mine are like balloons. And sometimes they pop!

Which is why I'm here. When I'm here, it's the last boundary I've got.

I kept thinking, never again. Never, ever. Never.

———

So. So, I'm still breathing.

There's an outside, and an inside, I think I know which is which. He's still out there somewhere but I've put up a few barriers. Maybe thanks to you, Diary. Definitely, as a matter of fact.

Things are better today. After my journey through slush and back, and the adrenaline burst of a flashfrozen foot, and this therapeutic scribbling and, most of all, the recognition that I have nothing to lose—things are much simpler today.

I'm going to take Duane up on his offer. I want to try to get him. To somehow—pop his boundaries. I'm tired of this shit happening to me. Why am I the one who has to go to Chamber?

Duane should have called by now, where is he—oh. The phone's still unplugged.

I do want to bag Malcolm, Diary. Make him helpless. Put him under my thumb, press hard. The trouble is, I don't know h

Duane Allbright's

Audiocassette Notes: V

Wednesday Evening

Five thirty-seven, Wednesday.

Just read today's diary entry. Sheila didn't finish it. She was interrupted; we're at the motel now, she's shuddering all over the bed.

The man in the car was Blovko. Blovko from Security. He was pretty slow. Terrible. Have to get my breath. Can't even *breathe.*

———

Sheila had a confrontation with a man named Blovko. He was in a car. She was walking through the mall lot. He didn't know who she was. At first he didn't, and she didn't know him. But it wasn't just another parking-lot squabble. Time's run out. They're here.

At least three: Blovko, Schmidtt, Gonzalez. I don't know much about Gonzalez, except he's trouble, one of the monster talents in the D.C. office. I've never met the man but have heard stories. Schmidtt is the hat, a menace despite zero talent. Blovko has talent, but not much—he's what we call a "sniffer." Like Sheila, he's sensitive, and relays. Also like Sheila, he has little awareness of it. That doesn't mean he isn't useful, though. The man is very useful. Or was, I should say. He's dead.

Obviously he was at the mall because of Sheila's place across the road. And there she was, walking through the lot. She was upset. She was distraught over Fearfield and Malcolm, her career, all pissed off and jangled up. Then she dunked her foot in a puddle. The boot was soaked. She started crying—radiating grief, anger, shame.

I picked it up like I usually do. It hit me so vividly I actually *saw* it. And there was a reason for that. I was outside the chain link with the rose in my pocket, talking to the dogs.

They have a thing for Sheila. Malcolm does, so they do; when I got the flash, they picked it up. They got it through the rose, and took over, fast.

Meantime Blovko was driving across the lot. Maybe he just had lunch. Maybe he bought butts, a paper, it doesn't make a damn bit of difference, he was there. He didn't recognize her. Maybe they don't have photos. Maybe he was dumber than I thought.

But then there was Gonzalez. He must have been on his way to meet Blovko. He wasn't at the mall, that much I know; maybe he was on the highway, driving up. Wherever he was, he was planning on using Blovko to find me. Then Blovko did find me, to the extreme shock of me and Gonzalez both.

When the dogs hit Sheila, she went brighter than neon. As usual she didn't know it. But she relayed to Blovko, who also lit up—and also didn't know it. However, he relayed to Gonzalez, who in turn lit up, and did know it. Gonzalez got us—Sheila, me, dogs, flower—like the Fourth of July.

So Blovko's in the car driving slowly up to Sheila, driving right by her, staring at her, he's few feet away. She leans on the car. He's staring at her through the windshield and we're all burning in and she dumps her boot—too intense. The goon's trying to drive away and she isn't letting him, they're glaring at each other through the slush, neither one aware of the deeper connection but getting madder by the second from the awful pressure of it, scared me out of my head.

It came through like Technicolor. Never seen anything like it. But there was no time to marvel, I was backing the truck way too reckless down the trail. The dogs didn't want that. They ran barking, eyes hellish, along the whole stretch of fence. I was their connection to Sheila. Through her, they were connecting to Blovko, and through him, to Gonzalez. That worried them. They could tell Gonzalez is hot, very hot.

The flower started burning a hole in my pants. I realized it was boosting their signal. It was pumping their flow through me, like I was some kind of relay station. I tossed the bag on the seat. This wasn't a good time to be playing games; I had a hunch Sheila was out getting her diary, what a disaster.

Then the connection broke. She walked away from the car. So it broke, a flash like that requires focus. The focus walked away, in her icy boot.

There's radio, though. I imagined Gonzalez yelling to Blovko, "Grab her, stupid!" On the public road, I floored it to a pay phone and called her. Thought I'd get her machine. It didn't answer. That spooked me because the machine is always on. I floored it for her place. Had to figure Blovko was closing in that very minute.

Then the cop stopped me.

Thought I'd lose it. Lucky thing I talk slow and dumb under pressure. The dogs boiled over, until the Baron calmed them. I ignored him and them both, I had to talk slow and dumb for thirty-five minutes. It took the cop that long to write the ticket. Like this town gives him nothing else to do, I guess it doesn't. I said I'm working on the Hilles estate while they're in Florida. That's why I have their truck, isn't it just a beautiful day. I kept feeling Sheila. She was being herself, upset and angry, but she was ok. Until the last couple minutes.

She got home unmolested. With the diary. The thing was on the table when I broke in and grabbed her, I was kind of rough. Blovko was sitting on top of her. He was taping her screaming face shut.

I looked at him and he looked at me. That instant, Gonzalez connected. He tried to get through. Blovko gaped, confused, the dogs were trying to get through too, there was so much *pressure*—Blovko said, "Where the hell you been Allbright? You got everybody so worried . . ."

"Stop worrying," I said, and I killed him.

He fell off Sheila—she suddenly silent and pale as milk—and I heard Schmidtt. His voice was squawking from Blovko's jacket. From a radio.

He was shouting he was on his way over. The radio was making a clanging noise, too. It sounded like Schmidtt was running on something hollow. That sound was familiar. I looked out the window and there it was. Bobbing in the sunshine, coming fast over the highway ramp—the purple hat.

I hustled her through the basement to the back lot, same route Pip showed her Saturday, my hand clamped on the half-taped mouth that wanted to bite me, diary stuffed in my pants. She fought and clawed, suddenly she was furious, blood was all over her. I plugged him with the dart gun. The needle made a mess in his head. Punched through the temple, point blank'll do that. Gonzalez felt it. He was connecting, I bet it hurt. I know it did! What the dogs did then . . .

I can't stop shaking.

———

She's out now. Had to medicate her. Nearly out, she's tossing on the bed. We're at the motel. I think we're safe. For a while we are. She's mumbling and moaning, she felt it all right. She saw it clear as day when Blovko got it. Whole thing lit up in her head, too. The tunnel, the flower. The dogs chasing through. The thing is . . .

I don't know how much Malcolm picked up. It puts me in a bad state, wondering what he saw.

———

I was talking with him through the dogs, same spot as yesterday at the chain link.

Today they ran slower because the snow's gone wet. All twelve came, heavy spray flying. And I saw right off something else was different. They had circles of color around their necks. It gave them an eerie holiday look. When they came close I saw what it was. Roses.

Made into tight-fitting garlands around their necks. The psi smell was frightening. And I realized—it came over me sickly sweet, the one in my pocket suddenly hot—the Baron's getting ready. Getting ready to move.

They made noise, too. Before, they'd psi-screamed, which isn't regular sound, it's mental. But today they yowled. They were dancing around like a barbarian king's prize hounds, as though gussied up for some occasion with the stinking flowers and proud of it, baying louder than I ever thought dogs or even wolves could do. This was a serenade. To me. They were singing at me. I stared at their heads tossing arrogant as hell, sending me hot looks every few seconds while they skipped around and around, on a parade ground of slush beyond the fence.

"Hey, fellas," I called out. "What's up?"

Then I had a thought: Torrance is dead.

They looked at me contemptuously and kept on yowling, seeming to grin a little now, and I had another thought: Torrance isn't dead. They went quiet in a flash, as if in reply to my thought, they stopped moving and all of them stared, contemplative and alert; and I could feel him, watching me, saying:

No, you miserable dwarf. Not yet.

Ok, I thought back, shivering in a lattice of shadow the sun put through the fence. *When?*

Tomorrow, the red eyes said.

That's what I thought, I thought.

You spoke with Pip, they said.

Uh-huh, I thought. *Yeah, I saw you looking.*

Curious, aren't you? The eyes didn't seem friendly. Not kindly disposed at all. *Does Sheila know?* they asked me.

Sorry, I thought, *does she know—what? About Torrance?*

That she is pregnant, the eyes said. Almost patiently.

No, I thought. *She's kind of upset. She lost her job.*

Good, the eyes said. *She cannot leave. She will come here. Not tomorrow, the day after. You will bring her to me. You will do that, Duane. And you will tell her nothing about Torrance.*

Yes. Of course I said yes. *Nice roses the dogs have on. How come?*

The eyes seemed surprised, and slightly amused.

You're carrying one, they said. *In your clothes—you can't feel the Fire?,* and then they exploded.

Because that's when it happened.

I staggered back to the truck. The eyes were beaming my head. The dogs pressed up against the fence, beaming my head. Like lasers, I thought. *Like lasers,* they snarled, trying to get in. I threw up. In the snow as I jerked open the door. *Stop,* Malcolm screamed, *Stop!* It took every bit of training I had. My mind was melting, the flower was burning—I tossed it on the seat, put the pickup in gear and slished backward fast as I could. They came down along the fence. All twelve, running and screaming along the fence, the most terrible thing I ever felt.

Later, I kept screaming back: *Later!*

They let go. But not really. They were concentrating. Christ, they were helping. I was driving like a banshee through the woods seeing Sheila shake her boot. They were swarming through her, swarming through Blovko, pumping fear, pinpoint, direct at Gonzalez. It was reflex, they wanted him away, away from Sheila. They wanted him scorched and next thing I know I'm holding the bag to the steering wheel, staring at it. The rotting thing's in the plastic feeling lethal, molten. I tossed it on the floor when the cop pulled me over; later, at Sheila's, I used it. I shoved the gun, fired, squeezing the bag. The dogs went in with the dart. Not after Blovko, he was dying, they went for Gonzalez, who was connecting, feeling the dart mess Blovko, feeling it bad—they slammed right in, they zapped through the flower and fried him and we, sliding the knife edge of murder, we amplified. Sheila and me, we amplified *fierce*.

———

I doubt if the Project could replicate that. Too much going on. They'd be interested though. They'd be awed. I don't know how much Gonzalez saw, or felt. He felt too much, that's for sure, the question is whether he can talk. If he can't talk I might be ok. Schmidtt is confident. He thinks he can deal with anything. Usually, he can. He might not call for everybody the Project's got. As for Malcolm . . .

He could decide to stop being gentle.

———

Sheila's talking. She's saying . . . something about—she's saying, "They need me . . . They want me . . ." She's holding her stomach. I guess they do need her. We'll talk tonight. About some of it anyway. I need her too. I need her cooperation.

That's all. Except one thing.

Sheila's phone. I checked the answering machine while dragging her out. I did that because I might have to get hold of Schmidtt.

It was unplugged.

Nasty. But the quickest. Schmidtt will get the hint. He'll put call-forward on that phone. I stuck the plug in Blovko's head.

Sheila Massif's

Microcassette Recordings: I

Wednesday Night

Hi. It's me. He's gone. I am incredibly frightened.

It's me—no time to write. Can't find the Diary anyway, he hid it . . .

[*Choking*]

This is the Diary, my dictaphone diary, it's all I've got. Duane— he's crazy. Me too. I'm—crazed.

[*Sobbing*]

He went to get food. It's eleven at night. I'm in the bathroom whispering, he'll come back any second. We're at a motel. Do motels have food late at night? The bathtub's dirty. I'm in it. No water, but I'm in it. I've got clothes on. I'm shuddering. The shower curtain's hiding me. It's dirty, a really cheap motel, hope to God he had to drive to get food . . .

It's the end.

The end—I'm so shocked. Terminally shocked. So shocked I don't even care, incredibly *frightened*—but I don't think I care. Duane's a murderer. He killed a man today. The body's in my apartment if police didn't find it. The body—and he says Malcolm's about to steal Torrance's—Malcolm steals bodies, he's a body-thief, of his own sons, Duane is seriously, seriously—

[*Sobbing*]

The guy was kidnapping me when he killed him, that was bad enough then he killed him, but then *dogs* came—I thought I was afraid of dogs. I am afraid of dogs. But now I'm more afraid—of roses.

He had Torrance's rose when he killed him, he squished it to the guy's head, the slimy bag seemed warm, *alive.* And then I felt them flooding through—needing me. In my stomach—needing me—I feel sick. Something's wrong with my stomach. And they want it. The roses *want it*—I think I'm pregnant. I must be crazy. The drain is hairy. It's rusty. It's cold in here—but I'm sweating, still burning—when Duane killed him we fell down a tunnel of burning roses and dogs were chasing, eyes red—*everything turned red.* They were chasing after something and they were guarding me. Guarding *me.* They need me, why, the baby? I *saw a baby*—I didn't ask Duane. I'm too scared. I'm out of my mind but nothing was ever so—strong. This is what it's like to be insane. Everything vibrates. I think the hot thing is a baby, I'm not telling Duane. But that's why they want it. So Malcolm can steal it. When it grows up. Malcolm steals babies, his sons. That's what Duane said. For hundreds of years. This is science fiction but the cold tub makes me think—*alien dogs with roses really are out there, wanting me!* I felt it, I saw it, they *want the baby, I'm SHRIEKING!*

———

The psi shit—coming to life. That or I really am crazy—doesn't make any difference—I don't care, we're going to jail. To a place for the criminally insane. Mom and Dad will be so angry. Who will believe it? If I bust out of here, run screaming down the road? What can I tell the trucker or old lady who picks me up? If anyone would, God it must be cold out. The tub's freezing. I'm vibrating. Can't be so loud . . .

A sound—somebody heard me.

Hallucinating. Must be. Rose-maddened dogs invaded, wanting the hot thing—that's what I'll tell them. Tell the lady who picks me up. She'll drive straight to a police station. The police will drive me to a hospital, they'll put me away, it's the end. I'm finished. I don't care!

Because I'll die. Tomorrow, with Duane, when he goes to bag

Malcolm. We're totally bagged—and he thinks he's going to bag Malcolm—he says he doesn't care if I come. But he does. He wants me to come, after what happened with the dogs and the roses, he wants me with him. And I'll go—these creeps are fucking with my body—what are they *doing*?

Can't make so much noise. He knows more than he said. But I'll find out what they did to me and the baby if there is one, and then I'm going to inflict as much damage as I can. And then I'll die. Because I'm deep, deep in the bag. Because nothing's safe, not even the Chamber—evil spirits are squatting there . . .

[*Sobbing*]

———

Mom and Dad if they find this, I love you. I'm sorry. Good-bye.

The Secret Journal
of Torrance Spoor's
Secret War: V

Noon Thursday

It happened. It's all done and over with. Dad didn't lie!

They came at nine this morning in three huge black cars. The dogs sat like a row of psycho soldiers wearing the weird collars Pip made yesterday—he doesn't understand either why Dad wants roses on the dogs, their eyes look bloodier top of that sepia color. I watched from upstairs, dressed in my coolest Italian suit and nervous as hell, thinking: This seems like a funeral. Like a funeral Dad would invent. Maybe it's mine.

Then the bankers and lawyers, two were women, got out of the cars and stared at the dogs and the house and the bright sun coming over the house from the ocean sky and I told myself: They look real. They looked like normal business people. They even looked nervous, maybe cause of the dogs. So I began to think: He didn't lie. If these people are zombies in some psycho plot, then how come they look nervous the same way anybody would in a freak scene like this, with giant dogs wearing rose collars?

They could of been just cold. It's not like it was yesterday, it's really cold. Anyway zombies might be nervous all the time, how would I know? That got me worried again. There was eight of them. They walked by the dogs to the door and came inside. I went quick to the stairs so I could hear. Pip was down there saying: "Come this way," like a butler in a murder movie, he sounded snobby and creepy. He led them to the library. I heard their steps going that direction. And I got an idea.

Pip might use the butler's passage, I thought. Since he's playing butler for this occasion. But there are places to hide in there - where they used to stash firewood and booze in the olden days. In one of those places a little door slides up. Probably for shoving martinis through. It is like a closet, curtained off from the passage. Pip wouldn't see me.

I hid in it, and slid the door up a crack. More and more like a murder movie, I thought. I could see and hear them easy.

Dad wasn't there.

I guess he was still in the basement. He was down there pretty early, I saw when I went swimming - after not sleeping good last night, wondering what the fuck would happen. He was in the rose room. The door was closed. But I heard him: He was screaming soft. Like a sick bird or cat. That did not do a lot for my jitters. I ran upstairs, thinking: The skinny old pervert really is going to off himself after all.

Maybe not. Now he wants to show me something down there. He said: "You will get what is yours." He wants me to understand something about it. Sure. I will never understand Dad.

I stopped being nervous, though. About me, anyway. And him?

Screw him. If he's in so much misery, do it, Dad. But he got into a good mood, later, drinking sherry. I think he's fine. But who could tell? He is completely mental.

So there they were in the library, Pip taking coats and telling them to sit down around the fire. He made a big fire, really hot. I could smell it from the closet. I got there fast, down back stairs and in before he could come through. But he did not, drinks were already set up, on the table next to the glass doors. The sun was shining in over the cliffs like it always does on clear mornings and I wondered: Why are they drinking? Some of them wanted coffee. One lady asked for tea. She said, "Decaf, if you have it," a little stuck-up. She was trying to outsnob Pip. Then Dad came in.

He said: "We do not serve tea." That is a lie. Pip drinks tea.

And Pip said *"Tea"* like he couldn't believe the nerve of this lady.

I thought: Aha! A comedy! Then I realized I never saw Dad or Pip talk to anybody else, except when Pip and me went shopping. And that one time with Sheila. Which was kind of unusual. So maybe they are like this with the outside world, very rude. Dad even told one man to get out of the room for chewing ice cubes. Then Pip slammed the door after him. I almost laughed. Is this how people act when they are filthy rich and can do anything they want?

Dad was dressed in a black robe made of silk with a pink suit underneath and a white shirt. The robe rustled as he walked. He walked around a lot, especially to the drinks table where he kept pouring more sherry. He looked even more bizarro than usual but acted dead serious, like an important and powerful and confident man. He said he wanted to make himself clear. Very, very *clear*. The businessmen and lawyers were respectful. The leader, the oldest guy and the fattest, with an English accent, kept saying: "Yes, my lord." Now I'm the lord. He even gave me his title. "Torrance, Baron Spoor." Cracks me up!

But later I saw it on about fifty pieces of paper.

I was wishing this scene was being videotaped so Erik and Sheila could see it. Then two minutes later Dad was saying: "This is being videotaped, by the way. I hope you do not mind." They didn't. They looked around uneasy cause they saw no cameras but nobody said anything. So it's on tape. Sam will freak.

She called yesterday to tell me Sheila got *fired*. Fearfield was too heavy so Casper fired her - no more Sheila at school! Guys from the FBI even came to class. Sam said they were *strange*. They asked a lot about Dwain too. I have to talk with Sheila soon. I feel so bad for her. She took the heat for Fearfield, she doesn't even have a job. Now these federal dudes are after her and Dwain both. Why? Anyway, I'll show her the tape. I have to, she's involved.

The thing Dad wanted to make clear is my control of his money. He told them it's important nobody test the terms he set up. He must of set them up a ways back. They all said, "Per telephone conversation" of such and such date, "Per letter," he's been on this for a while. I'm his only heir. Nobody else got anything, not even Pip. Mom can't touch it, or touch me. I am "emancipated." Legally. They talked about the terms of the divorce. Dad's lawyers discussed things with her lawyers and nobody disagrees, it was handled years ago, that is how Mom got me after they split. Dad mentioned "mental illness." He asked the lawyers if anything could happen to the deal if he went mentally ill. They said No, since the best lawyers in the world worked on it. The most expensive, too. Those people seem like the ones who control the planet. Nothing gets done without them.

It adds up to the transfer of everything being totally "irrevokable."

But somebody needed to be named to the estate: "Administrator." That's because of my age. Dad named Sheila. It is Sheila not Sheela. Her name was all over the papers. It floored me. Why her? After what happened? He only met her last week!

It's technical, though. She is paid a salary but I can "terminate" her. Crazy and scary like everything else. Why did Dad do this?

Pip didn't look too happy. God I feel terrible about how Dad treated him. I will give him money. As much as he wants. I heard him crying. He came through the passage crying and blowing his nose. I think he thinks Dad is going to do it. Kill himself. He's in the kitchen now, making lunch and snacks for later. Dad told him to make snacks for Erik and me. I told Dad Erik is coming this afternoon to visit. He said ok. Like he thought it's a good idea. He didn't even ask me anything about him. He said "Fine," and told Pip to put champagne around the pool. He thinks Erik and me will want to get drunk and swim? Maybe we will. But I have other ideas. For here in my room, where the cameras are a hundred percent *gone.*

After checking them out for a while I decided to make my entrance. It seemed safe. Totally kookoo but on the level. I had the gun in my suit pocket. Hey, I was paranoid. I didn't know if these people were animal trophy stuffers or what. But they were not. So I figured: Show up.

I snuck to the bathroom outside the library to hide the gun and check out how I looked. I should look good for these advisers and such. I looked good. "Hello, rich dude," I said to the guy in the mirror. Then I thought of Erik coming over later. That's the best part. Just seeing him!

I breathed deep, then stuck the gun behind extra toilet paper in the closet, saying: "Toilet paper, you belong to me." That got me laughing again. Pip keeps about thirty extra rolls in there. For what? Anyway. Even the toilet paper is mine. I'll donate it to the homeless and maybe the house, too. I don't want this house. I got seven or eight other ones. Probably just as gross as this one, and real estate in Tokyo and "substantial stakes" in big companies and everything. I am "extremely stable." It makes me unstable just thinking about it. No wonder rich people are crazy.

I went out and knocked on the door. Pip opened it. Dad stared at me with fever eyes from across the room and the eight men and women stood up. It was hot from the roaring fire and the heat Dad keeps way too high. Pip's eyes I noticed were red. From crying. I realized, he reminds me of the dogs. Except he isn't mean. I smiled at him and said Yes when he asked if I wanted a drink.

"Not too strong!" Dad yelled. Why did he care? I drank it down before the business people tried to shake my hand, then seemed to think that was a bad idea. It *was* strong. "There," Pip whispered horsely when he gave it. Like he felt sorry for both of us.

They were looking at me like I was the new president. I felt I should say: "At ease." I didn't know what to say!

Dad told me to sit at a desk they set up with papers, and this young guy, kind of cute, started whispering where to sign. Dad already signed. It felt like a dream. Like a apparition, cause I was drunk. Then they signed, and Pip did. Dad rustled around gulping sherry. And that was it. A rush of papers with the pen scratching across and Pip looking away and the people staring, and Dad's eyes shooting me over his glass.

Unreal. The fat English guy even bowed at me and said, "Congratulations, my lord." But Pip was telling him and the others that their cars were waiting. "And so are we," Dad said. They left, waving at me from the door. I waved back. I did not want to be rude like Dad and Pip. Then I stared at the fire. My fire. My huge, roaring, too hot fire that is a waste like this whole stupid house.

So now I am finishing the Journal of my Secret War.

It's over. I am a baron. I'm worth between $80 and $120 million excluding the Tokyo real estate that nobody can estimate since it's priceless. Those guys and ladies were real. Dad did not lie!

Seems funny. He always did before.

Now I wonder what he wants to show me in the basement.

I am supposed to go down there. It's one already. I wonder if he has treasure. Chests of gold and shit, jewels. Nothing could surprise me now.

Should I tell Erik about this? I never said anything at school about living here. When I told Erik how to come over I just said the mail box number, I didn't want to freak him out. But soon he'll be here. What can I tell him? It might screw everything up if I told him about Dad doing all this. Dad in his pink suit and black robe looking twisted. The dogs. Who do they belong to? What is Dad going to *do,* now? Do I give him an allowance? Tell him to go live at the YMCA?

"Dad, you will go live at the YMCA in Thailand now. I will pay for your toothpaste and shampoo, and here is extra toilet paper in case you run out. Now you better get going. The car is waiting, and so am I."

Cause Erik is here and we don't want you trying to watch, if you know what I mean, asshole!

God. I am sad. Almost crying. And what's Mom going to say? Now I'm crying. Dad is scary. How can I explain?

I don't understand any of this. And I doubt Dad can make me.

Should I bring the gun? What if he grabs it and shoots himself? The police and everything. They'd think I did it.

Well so long, Secret Journal. War is over. Dad surrendered. I think he did. There is proof on fifty pieces of paper. The lawyers took copies with them. I am extremely stable. What can he do?

Pip's "Suicide Note"

The horror - Torrance just went down.

I can't participate. What he's doing - he's really bad now.

———

It happened before. I've been feeling it. I've been dreading for months, I knew it was coming. I didn't want to remember but I started——like black mirrors forever. Forever, black mirrors: Again. Again. Again.

The amnesia. He made it. Because he knows I can't take it, what he is, what he's doing. To himself. To Torrance.

———

He called me Pip. "My Lost Friend," he said. No memory, no dog tags, nobody knew me. AWOL, he said. Crazy, bad in the head, a bomb exploded, amnesia. But he took me. He took care of me.

He took me so I could take care of him and his dogs.

Almost thirty years. Thirty years of Lost Pip. My first memory ——like yesterday, the first time I saw him. Everything blank before, blank, blank, blank——he was nineteen, puking in that back-room bar. In Hong Kong, dirty children taking off his shoes. His watch. He was so drunk. I kicked them away. Saving him——that's my first memory.

It became my life. He took me everywhere. Whatever happened ——I was there to save him. From his bad habits, his brat love of bad times. That's my life——saving him. Taking care of him. And his dogs!

He said I know about land. He never said why, but Lost Pip knows. So I chose the places——told him yes or no. I told him to buy the Tokyo land, it's worth more than anything now. I told him about this place and he saw it and hated it. But like the other times, he ended up saying: Lost Pip knows. About land——what's good for him. For the dogs. For the roses——

I should pour gasoline over those things right now!

What he's doing——I can't take it.

Because I'm remembering. And he doesn't care. He doesn't care what happens to the amnesia! He's evil. Black mirrors, forever - sometimes I see it, the wars. The horses, the marching, the dogs. The killing. The deserts and the forts——and the bed. The blood-colored bed.

And always the young ones. The children——what he's doing now, to Torrance, with the roses, I can't take it. I can't remember ——if I do——but I am but I can't!

Monster. He doesn't care if I remember. But he should——because I might kill him. What he did to me, what I better not remember. His evil, I have it. His horror, I have it——black mirrors going forever, his horror. This is why. Why he made the amnesia!

The dogs. The horses, the killing, the wars——black, black, forever! The desert, the marching——the fort, so big, stone! And the bed——

No! I can't participate!

——

There's the bell——at the gate——who? Why?

I think I am through. I think I have to stop. I think——

I think I like the look of this knife!

Transcript from Malcolm Spoor's Video-Surveillance Archive, with Notes by the Editors: I

1:17 P.M. Thursday

THE ROSE ROOM:

[*As the tape begins,* TORRANCE, *dressed in a dark suit, stands inside the entrance from the basement hall. Surprised, he stares at the rosebushes. They are bare of blooms. The dense mass of sepia flowers is gone. Skeletal branches, a few leaves, are all that remain*]

TOR: What . . .? Dad? Dad - where are you?

[*From loudspeakers,* MALCOLM'S *amplified voice fills the room. Until otherwise noted, he is not physically present*]

MALCOLM: Come in! Torrance, come in!

[*Cautiously looking around,* TORRANCE *walks down an aisle between tables bearing the denuded bushes. He becomes smaller and smaller; eventually, his feet walk out of the upper edge of the frame. He walks into the view of the cameras aimed at the platform. The platform is bare. The tapestry is down*]

TOR: Dad - where are you?

MALCOLM: I am nearby, and soon will join you. Torrance, please stand on the altar.

TOR: The altar? What altar?

MALCOLM: The platform against the wall. That is the altar. Please stand on it.

[TORRANCE *steps up onto the platform, turns around, stares into the cameras. His face registers annoyance: He realizes the cameras are working. His eyes widen as, suddenly, the lighting dims*]

TOR: What's going on, Dad?

MALCOLM: You are here to see what is yours. Torrance, you are standing on the altar of Change.

TOR: What is that supposed to mean?

MALCOLM: Shortly, you will see.

TOR: What happened to the roses? They look - like they died!

MALCOLM: The roses have shed. But they live on, Torrance. They will bloom anew.

TOR: Why are you watching me?

MALCOLM: The cameras are taping, that is all. I have no need to watch.

TOR: Yeah? What is this, Dad? Why are the cameras taping?

MALCOLM: Torrance, please remove your clothes.

TOR: *What?*

MALCOLM: Please remove all of your clothes.

TOR: You have to be kidding. Why?

MALCOLM: It is the ritual, Torrance.

[*Alarmed,* TORRANCE *frowns*]

MALCOLM: Of course, I have new cladding for you.

TOR: Oh, yeah - where? Where are you?

MALCOLM: You will see.

TOR: Dad, this is kind of freaking me out.

MALCOLM: The ritual, Torrance, is ancient. Always has it been so. You are a Spoor, Torrance. Honor your tradition.

TOR: It better not be something stupid - like the Curse!

MALCOLM: It is to be honored, Torrance.

TOR: Dad - I am not getting naked!

MALCOLM: Humor your father, boy. I ask you, humor me.

TOR: Dad! You promised - no more of that shit! No more *cameras!*

MALCOLM: Cameras, Torrance, are trivial. They mean nothing.

TOR: Why are you taping, then? And what is so important - about me being naked?

MALCOLM: You will understand. When you see what is yours, you will understand.

TOR: That's stupid!

MALCOLM: Centuries of tradition, you call stupid. Torrance, you are a Spoor. Listen to me - I promise you, this is the last favor I ever will ask of you. I have given you almost everything. Soon, you will have it all. In return, will you not grant me this one last request?

TOR: You are giving me something to wear?

MALCOLM: Torrance, I will give you what is yours.

[TORRANCE *grimaces, thinks about what his father has said. He shrugs, takes off jacket, kneels to place it near his feet. He stands, loosens necktie, and blushes. Suddenly, he is furious. He turns around, rips necktie off. Rapidly, he unclothes, tossing the garments to platform. Standing one-legged, he removes a shoe; he shifts legs, removes the other shoe. Muttering inaudibly, he removes trousers, flings them to the platform. Clothed only in socks and briefs, he faces, as though at attention, the tapestry*]

MALCOLM: Please complete the disrobement.

TOR: You are watching! I knew it!

MALCOLM: Of course I am watching. Why should that surprise you?

TOR: [*Gesticulates*] Yeah - why should it? *What the fuck are you doing?*

MALCOLM: Socks, off. Briefs, off. Hurry, I am becoming impatient.

TOR: Weirdo! That's what you are - a fucking weirdo!

MALCOLM: Yes. Torrance, I am losing patience. Toss all of the clothing off the altar, please. Anywhere - push it off with your foot. It doesn't matter where it goes. Just get it off.

TOR: What is this shit - *altar?*

MALCOLM: Torrance, you are standing on the altar of Change. Please do as I say.

TOR: I want my stuff near me, Dad. I do not think I can do this . . .

MALCOLM: Are you concerned about the pistol? Of course, you may keep it.

TOR: [*Shocked*] What - pistol?

MALCOLM: Do you not have the pistol, in your jacket? The pistol you found in the box, in the gazebo?

[TORRANCE *turns, stares into the center camera*]

MALCOLM: Torrance, I placed that pistol in the gazebo. I was sure you would find it there, and you did. If you have it with you, of course you may keep it. Now, complete the disrobement. Push your clothing off the altar. Please do as I say.

[TORRANCE *stoops, picks up jacket, shakes it*]

TOR: No gun, Dad!

MALCOLM: Ah! you did not bring it.

TOR: Do you wish I did? Did you hope I would use it?

[MALCOLM *laughs. The disembodied sound reverberates through room*]

TOR: [*Amazed*] You did! That is it - you really want me to kill you!

[*Again,* MALCOLM *laughs. Sadness tinges the sound*]

TOR: Psycho! Nut! Guess what, you nut - I am not going to play your Curse game. *I am not going to do it!*

MALCOLM: Fine. How marvelous of you, Torrance. How wonderful, that you will not do it. But will you do what I have asked you to do, at least?

[TORRANCE *glares scornfully*]

TOR: I feel sorry for you. You make me sick, but I really do feel sorry for you. You are - *crazy.*

MALCOLM: Yes.

TOR: And you know what? I am going to kick you out of here. Because now, I own this place!

MALCOLM: Exactly. That is exactly what you will do - kick me out of here.

TOR: And put you in a loony bin! Cause that is where you should be!

MALCOLM: Torrance, I am already in it.

TOR: Dad, level with me. Do you want me to kill you?

MALCOLM: Torrance, I will be dead soon, no matter how it happens. This I have told you from the beginning. All that remains is for you to receive what is yours.

TOR: What if I don't want it?

MALCOLM: That doesn't matter.

TOR: Dad, I'm not going to kill you - you stupid piece of fucked-up shit!

MALCOLM: That is what I am. A stupid piece of fucked-up shit. I - weep . . .

TOR: [*Surprised*] You weep?

MALCOLM: I know you won't kill me, Torrance. You are too good to kill me. Torrance, I love you.

TOR: You do?

MALCOLM: Yes! I do! You are so much better than I deserve - please. Please, can we finish with this?

TOR: Yeah. I'm leaving!

MALCOLM: [*Voice breaks*] But first you must have what is yours . . .

TOR: [*Disgusted*] I change clothes, that is the change? It's a ceremony?

MALCOLM: Torrance, you have no choice. It is what makes you a Baron of Spoor.

TOR: Thanks, Dad. Thanks a lot! Is it creepy, your ceremony?

MALCOLM: Torrance, it is profound.

TOR: What do you mean by that - profound?

MALCOLM: Simply what it means. That is all. Torrance, you sadden me. I am crazy, yes, I make you sick, oh yes. But I have given you so much. After all we have been through, is what I ask impossible to grant?

TOR: I do not care about being naked, Dad. You have seen me naked, you asshole. I just want to be sure you are not trying to make me go crazy. If that's what you want, forget it!

MALCOLM: Please, I beg you, can we get this done?

TOR: God . . .

[TORRANCE *removes socks, briefs. With swift sweeps of his feet, he clears the platform of clothing. He bows mock-dramatically*]

MALCOLM: [*Sadly*] Your beauty is terrible, child. Are you proud of your beauty?

TOR: Dad, I am naked. And I am not proud to be doing this! What do you want now?

MALCOLM: Now, you see what is yours.

TOR: Great. Hurry up.

MALCOLM: Do you recall, in the letter I wrote you, the letter about our Curse - what I described as having happened, finally, in the castle of Krak?

TOR: How does that relate to - this?

MALCOLM: You recall, I described a tryst.

TOR: Yeah?

MALCOLM: It is time for you to understand that tryst.

[*Alarmed,* TORRANCE *glances around. His body gleams. He is sweating*]

TOR: Gundulf and Baybars? Dad - are you trying to creep me out?

MALCOLM: Long ago, in the castle of Krak . . . Would you like to know what happened?

TOR: Uh . . . Yeah. Yeah, tell me. I can't believe it - but I want to know!

MALCOLM: Baybars held Gundulf captive, Torrance. And he toyed with Gundulf, toyed with him monstrously, you see. Then, once done with toying, Baybars, who owned the war hounds, they were his hounds, you see - Baybars decided the hounds should devour poor Gundulf. Oh yes, *eat him* . . . But you must understand, this was not an ordinary kind of eating . . .

TOR: What kind of eating was it?

MALCOLM: An eating of the mind, Torrance. If you will, an eating of the soul!

TOR: I do not get it, Dad.

MALCOLM: Ah, but you will. You see, Baybars' hounds did not devour Gundulf. But if they had - if they had consumed Gundulf, in the manner Baybars intended that Gundulf be consumed - then Gundulf, you see, would have become a hound. Oh, yes - he would have lost his human form, and become, quite literally - a hound! Awful, no? But what better way to dispatch an enemy? An enemy you love? Than to make of him that most faithful and slavish of creatures - a dog?

TOR: Baybars wanted to make Gundulf into a - *dog?*

MALCOLM: Yes! But Torrance, he did not succeed.

TOR: So what happened?

MALCOLM: Gundulf was very clever. At the last moment, in the castle of Krak, on the bed there, the hound there, watching - Gundulf, realizing his fate, realizing he was about to be *reduced to houndhood* - well, Torrance, he saved himself. And it was Baybars, not he, who became the hound!

TOR: Gundulf made Baybars into the hound?

MALCOLM: Why, yes. He did! And that hound followed Gundulf all the way back to France, Torrance. A mere dog, it was then - but in actuality, a sultan. A king, dethroned, and stolen! Reduced to a slave, a pet beast!

TOR: Cool story, Dad. But kind of unbelievable. How could Gundulf do that?

MALCOLM: With the roses, Torrance.

TOR: The roses?

MALCOLM: Gundulf, you see, seized control of Baybars' roses.

TOR: So the roses - turn people into dogs? That is what you are saying?

MALCOLM: That is precisely what I am saying. Gundulf seized control of Baybars' roses - which is how Gundulf escaped, how Baybars became the hound, how . . . How we came to be Cursed, Torrance. How we came to be Cursed with Change.

TOR: Great. That is what the Curse is - the roses change people into dogs.

MALCOLM: You are partially correct, Torrance. The roses are indeed what make the Change.

TOR: Dad, can I go now? This is getting really, really *dumb.*

MALCOLM: Torrance, turn around.

[TORRANCE *turns around. In the dim light, facing tapestry, his body gleams*]

MALCOLM: There is a tasseled cord to your right. Pull it, twice.

TOR: Why?

MALCOLM: Pull it twice, please.

[*Anxiously,* TORRANCE *stares at the cord*]

TOR: If this is the altar of Change - am I about to become a dog, Dad?

MALCOLM: You will see. Pull, twice.

[TORRANCE *laughs. He glances behind him, as if to check the* *bushes. He takes a deep breath, exhales a loud, exasperated sigh,* *then pulls the cord, twice.*

The tapestry rises: Sepia petals spill onto the platform.

Shocked, TORRANCE *takes a step back. As the tapestry rises* *higher, the spill becomes a cascade. Petals gush out, covering the* *platform, covering* TORRANCE'S *feet, spilling over the edges of the* *platform to the floor. The tapestry rises higher. The cascade contin-* *ues unabated*]

TOR: Hey!

[*The platform is thickly covered with petals.* TORRANCE *faces a* *rectangular tunnel, the lower half of which is filled, to an indeter-* *minate distance, with a large mound of petals. Peering,* TORRANCE *leans forward*]

TOR: Dad?

[*The mound of petals in the tunnel begins to vibrate. As if stirred by* *a breeze, the petals swirl. They rise into the air, swirling through* *the upper area of the tunnel, darkening the tunnel's already dim* *light.* TORRANCE *takes another step back*]

TOR: What the *fuck* . . .

[*The petals swirl faster. A force appears to be animating them: No* *breeze could make them whirl so rapidly.* TORRANCE *stares*]

TOR: Holy shit!

[*Suddenly, from the swirl, dogs emerge. But they are not dogs; they* *are clouds of whirling petals, shaped like dogs. In the heads, where* *eyes should be, red sparks glow.*

TORRANCE *trembles, and turns. He intends to leap from the plat-* *form, but sees something below it, something beyond the range of* *the cameras. It makes him freeze: His face contorts with extreme* *fright*]

MALCOLM: Torrance, turn around.

[TORRANCE *does not, perhaps cannot, reply. He is transfixed. Shining with stark fascination, his eyes reflect what they are seeing: They reflect brilliant red sparks*]

MALCOLM: Torrance, turn around.

[*Behind* TORRANCE, *the six petal-dogs face the tunnel, in which petals continue to swirl. A man emerges from the swirl, crawling on hand and knees. Petals, churning, cover his body. Under the churning, flesh gleams. He resembles a beekeeper thickly covered with bees. He stops crawling, and calls out in* MALCOLM'S *voice*]

MALCOLM: Torrance, look at me!

[*Slowly,* TORRANCE *turns. He sees his father, and gasps.* MALCOLM *raises his petal-crusted head, and, as if baying, howls very loudly. At that moment, his eyes glow a brilliant red*]

MALCOLM: Behold, Torrance, what is yours.
TOR: What . . . what is . . . ?
MALCOLM: Torrance, touch me.

[*Still on hands and knees,* MALCOLM *fixes his red glare on* TORRANCE'S *eyes. Frozen,* TORRANCE *stares back*]

MALCOLM: Behold what is yours! For this you must understand: I behold what is mine.

[*Six petal-dogs, eyes glowing, leap onto the platform.* TORRANCE *convulses; it was they that had prevented him from leaping off. Along the platform's edges, the petal-dogs, now numbering twelve, form a shimmering fence.* MALCOLM *stands. He approaches* TORRANCE. TORRANCE *screams*]

MALCOLM: Ah, he screams! Hounds take heed: The boy screams his fright! Yet so frightened is he, he cannot move. Boy, tell us - can you move, even an inch? Boy, *look me in my fiery eyes!*

[*Transfixed,* TORRANCE *stares into his father's eyes*]

MALCOLM: Will you fall? Will you fall, and join me, on these precious petals?

TOR: Stop . . . *Stop it!*

MALCOLM: Torrance, I will fall. Watch, and you will see. I will fall onto the altar. And there, you will join me.

[MALCOLM'S *mantle of petals glows faintly. Under it, his flesh sags. Slowly, as if performing an inverse shedding—as if a skin were ridding itself of its insides, rather than the reverse—*MALCOLM'S *body slithers out of the petals, and falls, flesh wet, into petals on the platform.*

The body appears lifeless. Its eyes stare vacantly. Retaining the form of MALCOLM'S *body, the petals that had covered him still stand. Roiling, they glow brighter. In the head, red sparks shine*]

TOR: Oh . . . my God . . .

[*The petal-cloud that was* MALCOLM *sweeps an arm across* TORRANCE'S *chest: Droplets, sepia-hued, fly off.* TORRANCE *trembles. Attempting to move, he moans. But his eyes are locked with the red sparks in the petal-head. His entire body, musculature rigid, is frozen.*

TORRANCE *shudders. Sagging, he falls into churning petals on the platform, an arm flung over the inert body of his father. As if cushioned in a festering excelsior, he is stunned.*

Insectlike, petals swarm onto TORRANCE. *They form a churning crust on his skin, similar to the mantle that had covered his father. The human petal-cloud kneels to inspect its prey. The petal-dogs draw closer, encircle. The human petal-cloud, glowing brighter, lies on its prey, and embraces it. The petals swarming over* TORRANCE *glow brighter, brighter. Petals glow brighter, brighter*]

TAPE WHITES OUT

Sheila Massif's

Microcassette Recordings: II

1:50 P.M. Thursday

I'm in woods across the road from Malcolm's gate. Duane isn't here. He went to make a phone call. To who, he didn't say. So I'm alone in woods freezing my ass. He said to stay deep so no one can see me. Fine. I'm about forty feet in. I see the gate but doubt if it sees me. That's a good thing, it's the gate of Baron Malcolm Spoor, *bodysnatcher.*

We're out of our minds. I don't care. I'm angry—I'm playing dumb for as long as it takes to find out what they've done to me. What Duane's up to, what's happening with Torrance. Then I'll murder wantonly, and happily die. No, I don't want to die. I want to escape this nightmare, change my name, live in another country, make it all go away, far away, but not till I know what they're *doing* . . .

I'm delirious. But I'm keeping track. Duane said to keep track of what's going on. Nothing is, except a car pulled up to the gate. That's why I'm talking. I haven't said a word since he went to make the phone call. That's because I don't know what I think. Malcolm steals bodies? His own sons' bodies? No wonder I feel it. I feel something in my stomach. And whatever it is they want it. I haven't told Duane, I don't trust him. But no wonder—if Malcolm's snatched children for *centuries*—oh, God! This makes no sense!

The car, it's sitting there. It's beat-up, old. I bet it's warm. Duane is, in the truck he stole. But it's tundra under these trees. The slush froze, walking is impossible, I'm even wearing fur. Duane stole it. A long *coat,* he's sociopathic. Maybe worse than Malcolm—no, I take that back. Nobody is worse than Malcolm. Especially if he's been snatching children for centuries, I have to find out if any of this crap is *true.* Which is why I'm putting up with *Duane*—we watched the gate since six this morning. Most of the time from his stolen truck, off the road a little way down. Nothing happened. All day nothing happened, except limousines coming and going full of tycoons from hell, Duane said they're lawyers. But maybe they're ghouls, maybe they're rose-people—evil *florists*—wait a second.

Wait a second. It looks like somebody's getting out of the car. A kid. Can't really see. He doesn't seem sinister. He's so young— what's this kid doing here? Ah. I see what he's doing and I'll tell you, he's pressing a buzzer. He wants to enter, I would guess, but why? Doesn't he know what lies ahead? A fresh victim for Spoor!

I hope *to God* Duane shows up soon. The kid's stamping his feet and blowing on his hands, no gloves, how dumb, will he mess up our mission? Ruin our plans? What are our plans? He didn't tell me, all he said is we're bagging Malcolm. All right, on with it then. Let's somehow get him before he gets *us* . . .

Before he snatches us! My worst terror come true! Why I've had a Chamber all these years, to avoid getting snatched. I can't—I can't get a grip on the concept, it's too—talk about being bagged, being helpless, my God—boundaries blurring—it's too much, it's—it's— my punishment! God's way of saying Fuck You!

So who is he calling? This is so *stupid*—uh-oh. Uh-oh, where is he? Aaaouuugah, Duane, red alert, the gate, shithead, is buzzing. It's buzzing quite loudly. And now, it's swinging open! Lovely wrought iron, with icy stalagtites or is it mites, the two sides swing massively, creaking and groaning, Duane, like a fairy tale, yeah, sure, a fairy tale, the drive winds off to never-never land. To bodysnatchland! And Prince Parka stares as if he can't believe his luck. I guess he is, he's just standing there, maybe he's having second thoughts. This is it, he's getting in his car. Last chance to warn him, should I? He just got in and closed the door. Exhaust vapors are changing, he's putting the car in gear and beginning to move, last chance, Duane—*OH MY GOD!*

The gates are open, the dogs, the dogs can get *out*, why didn't he think of that? Oh, Jesus—this is *it!* They'll come running any second —how could he leave me exposed to escaping dogs?

I feel dizzy—I feel the slanting light and the stripes of the trees and the naked branches spinning, I'm—I'm—I. . . .

[*Crashing sound—long pause*]

Five past two. I fainted.

I'm alive. No Duane. But another car is at the gate. If it opens . . . A man is standing at the gatepost. He's pressing the buzzer. He wears an expensive hat. He thinks he's hot shit. Somebody else is in the car. I can't see. Where is *Duane?*

Transcript from Malcolm Spoor's Video-Surveillance Archive, with Notes by the Editors: II

2:00 P.M. Thursday

THE LIBRARY:

[PIP *ushers* ERIK *into the room.* PIP'S *face and bearing reveal anguish.* ERIK *is alarmed. He wears jeans, boots, and a sweater, and holds a parka under his arm*]

PIP: Can I take your coat?
ERIK: Uh, no thanks.
PIP: Torrance will be here soon.
ERIK: Ok.
PIP: I called him on the intercom! He just got out of the shower.

[PIP *waves* ERIK *to a chair in front of the fire. Glancing around uneasily,* ERIK *sits*]

PIP: Would you like a drink?
ERIK: Excuse me?
PIP: A drink. Would you like a drink?
ERIK: No. No, thanks.

PIP: Not even a Coke?

ERIK: Uh . . . Ok.

[PIP *crosses to cocktail table, pours Coke. His hand shakes; he drops the bottle. Rolling bottle glug-glugs on rug.* ERIK *stares at* PIP *snatching bottle, wiping rug. He turns to face fire when* PIP *glares back.* PIP *pours more Coke, delivers it on a tray*]

PIP: You like sports?

ERIK: Excuse me?

PIP: I asked, do you like sports?

ERIK: Yes.

[PIP *stands above* ERIK, *inspecting.* ERIK *clutches jacket in lap*]

PIP: How old are you?

ERIK: Seventeen in March.

PIP: Torrance is seventeen in June. It's grand having friends your own age. Isn't it?

ERIK: Yeah. Sure.

PIP: We have a gym in the attic. Do you like working out?

[ERIK *gulps Coke, stares fixedly at fire.* PIP *moves to fire, pokes it too vigorously*]

PIP: And we have a pool, too. Erik, do you drink champagne?

ERIK: I don't . . . I mean no, just Coke is great.

PIP: Torrance likes Coke. Are you in love with him?

ERIK: What?

PIP: I asked are you in love with Torrance?

ERIK: [*Horrified*] What are you talking about?

PIP: Excuse me. What a personal question . . .

[PIP *bursts into tears.* ERIK, *aghast, stands up*]

ERIK: I think I better be going . . .

PIP: No!

ERIK: Where'd you say he is?

PIP: In the shower! Oh, I'll have some crème de menthe!

[PIP *staggers to cocktail table, misses glass as he tries to pour.*

TORRANCE *enters room. He wears ripped jeans and a T-shirt. His face is flushed. His eyes glitter*]

TOR: Hi!

[ERIK *and* PIP *stare at* TORRANCE. *He goes to the cocktail table, pours a drink*]

PIP: Is . . . Is everything . . . Is everything all right?
TOR: Yeah. Pip, you can leave.
PIP: Your father . . . ?
TOR: He's ok. Pip, that will be all.
PIP: Torrance . . . ?
TOR: What?
PIP: [*Anxiously*] What happened with the roses?
TOR: Get out of here!

[*Stock-still, deeply surprised,* PIP *stares at* TORRANCE *for several seconds.* TORRANCE *sips drink, stares back.* ERIK *gapes.* PIP *goes to door, glances fearfully at* TORRANCE. *He exits. Door slams*]

TOR: You're early.
ERIK: Whew! I guess that's a problem. Who's that guy?
TOR: The butler.
ERIK: Why is he so - upset?
TOR: Erik, he is mentally ill.

[TORRANCE *drops into a couch. Arms behind his head, he stares at* ERIK, *who puts his coat on a chair*]

ERIK: Wow. A mentally ill butler! Where . . . are your parents?
TOR: My mom's in California. She doesn't live with us. And my dad's sick.
ERIK: Oh. That's too bad.
TOR: Yeah. He can't even get out of bed.
ERIK: Sorry to hear that, man. How - are you?
TOR: [*Moodily*] Ok . . . Erik, it's been a weird day. My father is very sick, you see.
ERIK: Like, terminal or something?
TOR: Definitely.
ERIK: That's a shame.

TOR: Hey, come on over here.

[TORRANCE *pats couch.* ERIK *approaches, looks in* TORRANCE'S *face*]

ERIK: You're all sweaty. You are soaked!
TOR: Sit down. Erik - am I beautiful?

[ERIK *stares at* TORRANCE]

TOR: Why don't you get yourself something to drink?

THE KITCHEN:

[PIP, *distraught, sits at a table examining a long, sharp knife. A buzzer buzzes.* PIP *looks at a security monitor. On its screen, a man wearing an expensive hat is frowning. Behind the man a car idles. The buzzer buzzes again, this time lengthily.* PIP *presses a button*]

PIP: Who is it?
MAN: I am with Mrs. Floria Shade. We are here to see Torrance.
PIP: Floria? This isn't - the best time. It just - isn't!
MAN: And why is that?
PIP: Something . . . terrible has happened.
MAN: Open these gates at once!

[PIP'S *attention is distracted. In the background of the monitor image, in woods, a figure wearing a long, dark coat staggers through snow*]

THE LIBRARY:

[ERIK, *attempting to make a choice at the cocktail table, appears confused.* TORRANCE *is stretched out on the couch*]

TOR: Erik, did you read *The Fearfield Club*?

ERIK: Yeah.

TOR: Did you like it?

ERIK: Sure. It scared Samantha, though.

TOR: Really?

ERIK: Yeah. She thinks it's twisted.

TOR: You have to be shitting me. How?

ERIK: The stuff about eating. That craving stuff . . . What do you think?

TOR: I . . . do not really know. Tell me what you think, Erik.

ERIK: It's such a goof on school! On the class you're in. Samantha was telling me . . .

TOR: So you really liked it?

ERIK: Why? You didn't write it, did you?

TOR: What makes you ask?

ERIK: Hey . . . Did you?

TOR: No! I *didn't*!

ERIK: Man, don't get mad. Do you really hate it or something?

TOR: No . . . I think I just hate the person who wrote it, Erik. But let's not talk about him.

ERIK: You know who did it. Wow. Does . . . this guy bother you?

TOR: Yes. He bothers me.

ERIK: Some guy at school? Is he, like - after you?

TOR: I said I don't want to talk about him, ok?

ERIK: Shit, I'm sorry. Really. Hey, are you all right?

TOR: Let's just talk about something else, Erik.

ERIK: Sure. [*Looks around room*] This place! I almost lost it when I drove over, and saw that this place - is *your* place! God . . . Everybody knows about this place. Especially since what happened.

TOR: What happened?

ERIK: David and Tracy?

TOR: Who are David and Tracy?

ERIK: Fuck. You don't know?

TOR: I don't have any idea . . .

ERIK: Uh - David and Tracy disappeared.

TOR: Where? Did they disappear?

ERIK: Damn, I thought you would know. But you just got here, so yeah. They found the car by the fence. Your family's fence . . .

TOR: No . . .

ERIK: Man. I'm sorry it's me who's telling you this.

TOR: People - you knew?

ERIK: Know, I hope. They're good friends. And it's so weird! I was supposed to go that night.

TOR: Go where?

ERIK: Torrance, we've been climbing that fence since last summer. Since it went up.

THE ROSE ROOM:

[PIP *enters room, walks to rear. Petals cover platform. Tapestry, pressed through petals, is down*]

PIP: Hello? Is anybody - there?

[*Behind tapestry,* PIP *hears a soft moaning. He climbs onto platform*]

PIP: Who is in there?

VOICE: [*Faintly*] Help!

PIP: Who is that?

VOICE: [*Desperately*] Pip! Pip, *help!*

PIP: Oh . . . Oh [*Puts hands to head*] Oh!!!

VOICE: Pip, he wants me to - to die . . .

PIP: You poor child!

VOICE: The dogs - they will kill me . . .

PIP: No!

VOICE: Pip - the rope - pull it!

[PIP *yanks rope. A mechanical whine sounds. Tapestry rises, revealing bars. The bars remain down. Behind them, red sparks glow. The sparks appear to be huddled. From within the huddle, the* VOICE *calls woefully*]

VOICE: They want to eat me!

PIP: [*Puts face to bars*] No, no, no! I'm telling them, no!

[*The mechanical whine sounds. Tapestry begins to lower*]

VOICE: [*Frantic*] Pull the rope again!

[PIP *angrily yanks rope. There is a popping noise; the entire length of the rope falls, flopping into petals on the platform. The mechanical whine stops. The tapestry's descent halts. Gripping the rope's tasseled end,* PIP *realizes what he has done. He wields an impotent whip*]

VOICE: Oh - no . . .

[PIP *drops the rope. Putting hands to his face, he slumps against the bars*]

VOICE: [*Sobbing*] Pip, he wants me to die! He even gave me a gun, he hoped I would use it! But I didn't bring it . . .

[*Clutching the bars,* PIP *begins to heave. He is crying*]

VOICE: I feel so bad in this, in his . . . horrible body! He wants me to break down and do it - he wants me to *commit suicide!*
PIP: I . . . I will try. To stop this. I promise - I will try . . .

THE LIBRARY:

[*At the cocktail table,* TORRANCE *pours two stiff drinks, without ice. He hands one to* ERIK. *The other one he empties down his throat*]

ERIK: What is this stuff?
TOR: [*Balefully*] Drink it.
ERIK: Man, you must be really bumming. I guess - it's your father, and everything.
TOR: My father and everything, yes. I'm bumming.
ERIK: The butler, is that why he's so upset? Because of your father?
TOR: Yeah. Erik, my father said he was going to kill himself.
ERIK: No way!
TOR: But he didn't.
ERIK: Thank God.
TOR: He had a gun. He should have done it.
ERIK: Man . . . How can you say that?
TOR: I hate my father, Erik. He's a bad person. He's horrible.

ERIK: How? Is he like, mean?

TOR: Worse. He's very - greedy.

ERIK: [*Glances around room*] Huh.

TOR: And I think he messed me up.

ERIK: Shit . . .

TOR: He was so afraid I wouldn't turn out how he wanted.

ERIK: What did he want?

TOR: It's what he didn't want. He was worried I'll turn out like him . . .

ERIK: Whoa . . .

TOR: He totally despised himself, Erik. The fuckface.

ERIK: So is he about to die? You sound - like he already did . . .

TOR: Not yet. But he will.

ERIK: I guess you don't care, huh?

TOR: I just want to be me. That's all. But I won't be me. Until he's gone. Gone from my life.

ERIK: This is intense, Torrance.

TOR: Erik, I want him to die.

ERIK: That must be - the worst thing!

THE ROSE ROOM:

[PIP *sits on platform, slumped against the bars. He appears hopeless*]

VOICE: These things . . . They keep staring . . .

PIP: They are confused. So confused. Like me, child. Like me . . .

VOICE: Tell them to get off!

PIP: I . . . will explain something. My amnesia . . . I'm remembering, now. Remembering . . . too much. Do you know how people have - bad sides?

VOICE: [*Whispers*] I think the dogs are listening to this.

PIP: No. But they know what I'm thinking about. It concerns them . . . I have a bad side, child. A very bad side. And I try, to tell it to be good. But sometimes I can't. Sometimes, it doesn't pay attention. Because my bad side isn't - in me. Any more . . .

VOICE: Where - is it?

PIP: In there. Guarding you. In the hounds, see. It's been in the hounds for a long time. Part of me has lived in them for - for hundreds of years!

[PIP *stands. He paces the platform, kicking at petals*]

PIP: And part of them - their good sides, see - are living in me! So . . . we are mixed. Mixed into each other. All mixed up! And the trouble is, it makes us stupid. Without the bad sides, without the good sides - we're stupid. Like machines, like simple machines. I can't even remember anything most of the time . . .

VOICE: Pip . . . Pip, were you at that castle? Krak?

PIP: Krak! Oh, yes. I was there . . .

VOICE: You and Gundulf . . . ?

PIP: [*Shudders*] That's right. Krak, that is where I first . . . became a hound. But I've been a hound many times. So many times. I am now - half hound!

VOICE: But the roses - used to be yours? The hounds, too?

PIP: So long ago. But, yes. Before I became a slave.

VOICE: A slave?

PIP: I have been a slave for centuries, Torrance.

VOICE: But if the dogs used to be yours - can't you tell them to *get off*?

PIP: You don't hear what I am saying! Have you ever tried to talk - to your bad side?

VOICE: Try!

THE LIBRARY:

[TORRANCE *and* ERIK *sit on a couch.* TORRANCE *holds a fresh drink.* ERIK *grimaces at the one he has barely touched*]

TOR: Bad things are happening in this house, Erik.

ERIK: Do you want to be alone? Maybe I should just leave . . .

TOR: No. Erik, I need you.

ERIK: Is there anything I can do? Just tell me. I'll do it!

TOR: I want to know - do you agree with Samantha? That it's twisted?

ERIK: You mean *Fearfield*? It's kind of weird, I guess. Why?

TOR: Did it excite you?

ERIK: Uh - yeah. But I mean, the guy seems sort of desperate. Like he's a little fucked up. Maybe really fucked up.

TOR: How? Is he fucked up?

ERIK: You're the one who knows him . . .

[TORRANCE *stands. Frowning, he stares through French doors at the distant ocean*]

TOR: Forget it. Forget it. [*Shouts*] I don't want to talk about being fucked up!

ERIK: [*Scared*] Ok. Ok. What - should we talk about?

TOR: I don't know. *I don't know!*

[TORRANCE *hurls his glass at a French door. A pane shatters*]

ERIK: Torrance, take it easy!

TOR: [*Whispers*] Their names were - Tracy and David?

[ERIK, *gulping, nods.* TORRANCE *glares at him*]

TOR: Oh, well. Oh, well. At least one thing isn't fucked up . . .

[TORRANCE *pulls off his T-shirt. He bows his head, puts hands on stomach*]

TOR: This, Erik. My body. It isn't fucked up.

[ERIK *blushes.* TORRANCE *grimaces. Then he smiles, oddly*]

TOR: Erik, I have a perfect body. Do I not?

ERIK: What? I mean - yeah. You're - really good-looking . . .

TOR: You think I'm beautiful?

ERIK: I . . . Uh, I - yeah. I do.

TOR: I'm nervous, Erik. Very nervous. I think you are, too.

ERIK: I am . . . Hey, man - what's wrong?

TOR: [*Runs hands over chest*] What's wrong? So many things . . . What would you say if I told you - I don't know what to do with this?

[TORRANCE *continues to stroke himself. Confused,* ERIK *stares*]

TOR: Should I try to find out? What to do with it?

ERIK: Maybe . . . [*Gulps*] Maybe we should go somewhere else.

TOR: Why?

ERIK: What about your father?

TOR: Who cares? He's almost dead!

ERIK: [*Blurts*] Yeah, well, maybe us fooling around, you know, if he saw it might - finish him off!

TOR: [*Suddenly thoughtful*] What a great idea . . .

ERIK: Torrance . . . That's crazy.

TOR: Yes. But if I don't do something soon, Erik - so am I.

THE ROSE ROOM:

[PIP *grunting, attempts to lift bars. Bars don't budge*]

VOICE: There's a panel of buttons in here! Do you know how it works?

PIP: No!

VOICE: [*Desperate*] Is there another way out?

PIP: Yes, but it's no good. Even if I lifted the bars, that's no good. The hounds, see. They're telling me to go!

VOICE: Great. I'll never get out of here . . .

PIP: [*Feverishly wipes brow*] We have to try something else.

VOICE: Pip, he's going to find a way to drive me crazy. To make me do it. To make it look like suicide - he'll make me *want to do it!*

PIP: I have to go. Upstairs, things are happening. The hounds are getting upset. I really should go . . . Ah - your mother just arrived.

VOICE: Mom? Is here? Ohhhhhh - *no!*

PIP: Erik's here too, I'm afraid.

VOICE: *Erik?* Oh God. Oh God. Oh my God! Pip - don't let him hurt Erik!

THE LIBRARY:

[TORRANCE *is dragging tables and chairs off the carpet in front of the fireplace.* ERIK, *slumped in a couch, watches apprehensively*]

TOR: Erik, have you seen - sex movies?

ERIK: Uhhh . . . A couple.

TOR: Have you ever thought about being in one?

ERIK: Not really!

TOR: I want to do something. Let's pretend we're in a movie. One of the boys doesn't know about sex. He's never really had sex. But he wants to learn. And the other boy - is excited about teaching him!

ERIK: Sounds . . . A little strange.

TOR: Life is strange, Erik. So we can be strange, too. I think my idea is - fascinating. Two birds with one stone . . .

ERIK: What do you mean by that?

TOR: [Smiles] Nothing. Nothing.

ERIK: Uh . . . Who plays which boy?

TOR: I play the inexperienced one.

ERIK: Really? I thought it would be the other way around . . .

TOR: [Laughs] No! Erik, I think . . . I want you to strip.

ERIK: Wait a second!

TOR: Show me how to have fun. Make me do it!

ERIK: [Alarmed] But why?

TOR: Because I don't know anything! Erik, I am totally inexperienced!

ERIK: So am I!

TOR: Pretend you're not!

ERIK: *How?*

TOR: Just do it! Erik - you said you would do anything for me . . .

ERIK: Yeah. Yeah. But Torrance, you seem so, I don't know - intense. I'm worried you want to give your father a heart attack or something!

TOR: I told you, he can't even get out of bed!

ERIK: But why did you say that? Two birds with one stone?

TOR: Oh . . . I've been in such a bad mood, lately. But I think you can cheer me up. Plus, I want to learn. Really, I - have no choice.

ERIK: God, I don't know. What if we get carried away?

TOR: I want to get carried away. If we don't . . . I might have to tell Fearfield to - to *eat you, Erik.*

ERIK: Ha. That's funny. Shit - I wish you hadn't taken off your shirt . . .

TOR: Strip, Erik. Brandish!

ERIK: I have a bad feeling about this . . .

TOR: Bullshit. Why are you sitting that way? Do you think I am blind? Erik, your body is *thrilled*.'

ERIK: [*Whispers*] Yours too.

TOR: Yes. Yes, I'm . . . amazed. It's suddenly so - marvelous . . .

ERIK: You aren't going to tape or anything? To show your dad?

TOR: Erik, do you see cameras in here?

THE GRAND ENTRANCE HALL:

[*A gong sounds.* PIP *strides into hall, radiating rage. He flings open the door. On the icy portico, clutching for balance, are* FLORIA SHADE *and* GEORGE CONSTABLE]

PIP: Welcome! Welcome to total despair!

FLOR: [*Highly alarmed*] Don't tell me! *Why?*

[*Leading* FLORIA *by hand,* GEORGE *barges past* PIP *into the hall*]

GEO: We have been freezing out there for ten minutes! Where are they? What's going on? Where is Malcolm Spoor?

FLOR: What are they doing to Torrance? *Where is Torrance?*

PIP: The dogs have him, I regret to say.

FLOR: What?

GEO: What?

FLOR: [*Wails*] Those dogs!

GEO: Floria, stay calm. You, my man, will take us to Malcolm Spoor. This instant!

PIP: [*Smiles coldly*] It happens to be much worse than you fear.

FLOR: George . . . *George! I told you!*

GEO: We don't know what is happening here! Sir, I should inform you that you may be liable for criminal action if you don't cooperate!

PIP: That is pathetic.

GEO: Yes? We'll see. Floria, maybe you should stay in this room.

FLOR: George, we should have brought guards! Guns!

PIP: Yes. You should have. But follow me.

[PIP *strides away.* FLORIA *and* GEORGE *anxiously follow. From various angles, cameras track much of their route. They reach a set of closed double doors.* PIP *waves at doors.* FLORIA *covers her face with hands.* GEORGE *puts his head to the doors. He hears something. Shocked, he stares at* FLORIA]

GEO: Floria, please go back to the car.
FLOR: What is it, George?
GEO: I think you better let me deal with this.

[FLORIA *lunges at doors, grabs handles, pulls. Doors swing open*]

THE LIBRARY:

[*The boys, nude, are entangled on the carpet before the fire.* FLORIA *screams loudly*]

GEO: Good heavens!
FLOR: *Torrance!*
GEO: Get up! Both of you, *get up!*
FLOR: George - *George* - I think I'm . . . having a . . .
GEO: Sit down, Floria, let me help you - *See what you've done to your mother?*
FLOR: George, *call the police!*
GEO: Where is the phone?
FLOR: I don't know. Torrance, *where is the phone?*
GEO: Look at him - not a shred of decency!
FLOR: I am - I am going to *strangle Malcolm, where is he?*

[*Through above,* TORRANCE *and* ERIK *disentangle.* ERIK, *red-faced, crawls rapidly in the direction of his clothes. He grabs the clothes and crawls toward a distant corner of the room*]

GEO: Torrance, get up. Get up and *get dressed.*

[TORRANCE *stands. He glares at* FLORIA, GEORGE, PIP. *Then, bowing his head, he examines his erection*]

TOR: Feels like a rocket!
FLOR: I am . . . feeling faint . . .
GEO: [*Apoplectic*] *Get dressed!*

[TORRANCE *crosses to the cocktail table*]

TOR: Would anyone like a drink? Mother? Maybe your friend?

FLOR: [*Weeping*] Torrance? What has happened?

GEO: [*Shaken*] Where is your father?

TOR: He is unwell at the moment. But then, he always is. I suppose you are a lawyer. I have some papers to show you - the situation here is not what you think. In fact, you are trespassing on my property.

GEO: Preposterous!

TOR: You will look at the papers, you will realize what I say is correct, and you will leave. Pip, I advise you to get out of this room. I also advise you to keep away from the dogs. Erik, you will stay.

ERIK: [*Frantically donning clothes*] I gotta go!

FLOR: Yes! Yes! By all means, go!

GEO: First I want his name! What that letter said seems to be *true* . . .

TOR: Erik, if you leave I will never speak to you again. These people have no right to be here! Pip, get out.

FLOR: [*Stunned*] Malcolm's ruined him. He even talks like him now . . .

[PIP *goes to door, turns*]

PIP: You better leave. This is the Spoor. And it will kill you.

The Chronicle
of Torrance Spoor

2:40 P.M. Thursday

You are in turmoil. I know you are, I feel your panic. Your worry
gnashes, you gnash even one another, so dismayed are you that
Malcolm lives. I remain uncreated, eh? No Torrance am I, eh? Ah
no, you think me still Malcolm. But who, I ask, do you see before
you?

You see *Torrance.*

Look at me sitting here. Nude but for these shorts, my smell
sweetly tannic - I reek of strength and sex! I reflect to infinity, too.
From manifold mirrors, I reflect - Grislies, peer into the mirrors.
You see my rude beauty, multiplying forever?

Yes? No? Answer the question!

No, all you can do is thrash. Thrash with panic, thrash! If you've
nothing nice to say - if you've nothing to say, shut up!

Oh, I know your problem. Yes, you must have Malcolm. Have him
you will, I cannot be me, if you do not - and I so want to be me, rid
of the monster, rid of the emptiness that is Malcolm. But I am pro-
gressing, no? Did you see? Did you see what I did, with Erik?

How innocent I was? How clumsy, how passionate, how utterly devoid I was, of Malcolm? Before the fire, there we are, rabid with lust - look, the tape is proof. On the monitors, who could be that, if not me, entwined with Erik? To be sure, that is not Malcolm. No, that is Torrance!

You doubt this. Your doubt eats me, you think I bluster. Do I care? Ah, the doors fly open. There, eyes bulging, is haggard Mother. She screams. Yet more proof, for she sees me, her son, and screams her horror. Erik flees, with coltish fright. I stand, passion a monument. Everyone trembles, Torrance is rampant!

And then - so sad. Malcolm still lives, true. And he outs, eh? Oh yes, for the poison lingers. Look how he corrupts me with liquor. You see how he pollutes with his thoughts, with his words and wants? Grislies, do not think me irresolute. For I know it, even better than you - Malcolm must die.

But how?

Oh, do not berate! I tell you, shut up, *shut up!* How can I think, when you pound like a filthy surf? Your bile corrodes me, your greed upsets me, I simply - cannot think!

Yet I must. Floria is here, interfering. I watch her, on the monitor; there she sits, in the library, devastated. Her lawyer, alongside, shuffles papers, he looks for chinks in our legal armor. And Pip - he, too, is interfering. Grislies, this is a dangerous moment.

I mustn't shoot. No, no. Nor strangle, no. Remember the trial - they would inquire, again, as they did with Bunny. Townsfolk would mutter, rumors would fly. Busy little sleuths might research? Unearth the Curse, eh? Wouldn't that be fine?

Thus the question remains. How?

The dogs could do it. As a last resort, they could. We could have a quieter tragedy. But that, too, would bring consequences. If they decide a destruction is warranted, how do we stop it?

Then there is the more terrible consequence. We would taste it. The boy's rage, his agony, we would taste it forever. Do we wish that? Can we tolerate that? Grislies, we've residues already. Think of the gore that drips, reeking, from your lips. The slurps that stained, that never go away, the greedy sups that so horridly have stayed - no! Grislies, no, I plead, I beg. Anything but that!

You are hungry, yes. I must feed you, yes, oh yes, and I do. Tracy and David - have I not fed you? This property, this menagerie of game, I gave you the hunt, I gave you blood, how much more do you want? The boy, no, we cannot. So then, how? That video of Erik and me - could it force the pistol to his head? For one awful moment, I thought it would, but if it didn't? A monitor is there, where he is, with the dogs - just prior to Change, Malcolm watched from it. Grislies, I could make that monitor glow. The dogs could force him at it. Play the tape? In slow motion, eh? Would that madden him, would he despair, seeing Erik and I, our shudders, our blurs - and wish for a trigger?

I do not know. I do not know! And the pistol, where is it? He did not bring it! A knife, a knife I could find, oh I am feeling ill!

Here I sit in shorts, mirrors all around, my beauty multiplied. Yet here I am tainted, still tainted with Malcolm, not knowing how to finish him, I am so frightened!

I must kill him. To create myself Torrance, I must. Grislies, I fill with a murderous rage. I do not want to face these problems. No, I do not, but face these problems I do, and I confess, I want to kill them all. All of them, one by one! To the dogs they go? Grislies, shall we sup?

Another disappearance. A mass disappearance. Except, of course, Erik. But - what would he think? He would fear and despise me. Grislies, we cannot be so monstrous. Look at Erik————

He is swimming. The monitors are an aquarium, and there, in it, is Erik. I told him to swim. Ordered him, the boy was trembling with shame. He thinks this is a family disaster. It is a family disaster, and a ghastly farce. What I want, you know, is so extremely simple. I want to be me. To be me, with Erik - he who reassures, more than anything, that I am not Malcolm.

You do nothing for me there. No, you think me uncreated. But I tell you, Erik has opened an exit, of that I am certain - and no, I cannot, I cannot horrify him. You understand my reason? Grislies, with Erik I feel very much Torrance————

Grislies, help me. I do not want to be bad. I do not want to be Malcolm, or any of you. For you are my Ghastlies. You are my Horrids, the Ones Who Slurp!

There! I attack, I smash, there!

————

Grislies, behold bloody mirrors.

I ask you calmly. Very calmly, I ask - behold my bloodied mirrors. Do you see the infinite fractures? Do you see my infinite, fracturing drips?

Grislies, I fill. I fill with murderous rage————

Sheila Massif's
Microcassette Recordings: III

2:45 Thursday

We're moving. We're driving. We're off the road in woods slipping and sliding up a path Duane's been up before. I don't know what's going on, but it's big. The Psi Thugs just went through. They're driving up to the house right now. Duane called them, that's who he called, he invited them over for crying out loud—he said they're a "battering ram." Great, we need murderous thugs. We need them to bag Malcolm, but don't ask me how ... The wall just became a fence. I know what the clippers are for, we're going in. But what the hell are we going to *do*?

DUANE: Please be quiet.

Be quiet? How rude! But Duane's got brains. I think he does, he bugged the gate. He knew the thugs were coming, so he bugged the gate, then we drove away and heard them—he says psi isn't like radar. Thank *God*. They don't know where we are! But *we* know they went through the gate, because we heard the bug! They talked to Pip, we even heard Pip, that man is deranged. He said, "What fun!" And he buzzered open the gate—doesn't he know those guys are murderous *thugs*? Duane was amazed. He didn't think anyone would let them in, you were amazed, weren't you, Duane?

DUANE: Sheila, please calm down.

Calm down! Easy for him to say. I don't see any dogs. No dogs, where's the house? Lot of blinding white grounds out there on this crisp wintry day in bodysnatchland, the tree shadows slant prettily, what we need, Duane, you know what we need, we need a sleigh. I bet you didn't know that, huh? How the hell are we going to get across that ice? You think I'm capable of whizzing over that ice? I bet the dogs have claws ice-picking that ice, I bet they can really move, is this a good idea? Duane? All right, all right. I'm not being a good battering ram—that's what I am, right? Just like the thugs? I am a ram, that's what I am, like the thugs and Torrance's mother, what's happening to *her*? And the guy in the hat, Duane said he's probably a lawyer to take away Torrance, what a good idea. He said he sent a letter to make them come grab Torrance, you've got brains, Duane. You know what you're doing, but what if we die? Have you given much thought to that issue? Have you processed, Duane? And what about the kid, the first one in, he's also a ram, ready to batter and die? Duane doesn't know about the kid, he said he doesn't and he isn't talking . . .

DUANE: Sheila calm down. Here, I want you to put this in your pocket.

[*Very loud scream*]

He just gave me - [*Choking*] - the rose . . . I—I don't really like this—at all—Duane, what . . . ? I mean, what's the big idea? What am I supposed to do—with—holy shit, I'm about to . . . About to pass out . . .

[*Gargling*]

Uhhhhh . . . Just lost breakfast, right out the window, my . . . it's a sunny day . . . Don't you think, Duane, Duane I'm trying to stay calm, but would you please tell me . . . What the hell you're doing with this—*voodoo thing*?

[*Loud scream, scuffling*]

DUANE: Sheila! Sheila, I'll dump you right here!

Ok. Ok. [*Sobbing*] Ok, Duane. I know you want to kill me but that's fine, I—just want to know why, all right? I deserve to know what we're doing with this—it's falling apart, in a plastic bag—Torrance's *rose,* the one he threw on my desk! I thought you got rid of it! You lied! They can feel it can't they—I bet it gives them the radar you said they don't have, Duane, am I bait? Now it all becomes clear you don't care if I . . .

[*Struggling*]

DUANE: Sheila, *listen.* Listen to me! The dogs are wearing collars made of roses . . .

[*Sudden choking*]

DUANE: Collars made of *roses,* Sheila. The roses give them power. We, Sheila, *need power* . . .

[*Continuing choking*]

DUANE: Aw for Chrissake, woman!

CONCLUSION

We near the end.

Up to now various primary-source materials have carried the account. That approach no longer is feasible, chiefly due to the fact that none of the participants made adequate records of the climactic Thursday events.

Records were made, however. Malcolm Spoor's surveillance system continued to function in response to movements and sounds that occurred in the house, and Sheila continued to confide to her microcassette recorder. The resulting material proved helpful. But it is not, on the whole, transcribable, at least not in the manner seen thus far. Too much happened: too quickly, at too many locations.

Our documentation therefore concludes in a different format.

This chapter and the next one are blow-by-blow reconstructions of the final developments. We ourselves wrote them, after thoroughly examining the evidence.

The evidence, in addition to the video and audio recordings already mentioned, includes the results of a careful evaluation of the aftermath at Malcolm Spoor's house.

Without further ado we present a two-part conclusion.

The Editors

Finale: I

First we review various locations and plights:

Pip, continuing to make trouble, walks from the kitchen to the front hall in response to an echoing door gong.

On the main portico before the oak door stands Claus Schmidtt, Psi Project security chief. A broad six foot seven, his complexion is yellow, his features blunt, his eyes severe. He wears a purple felt porkpie hat. His gloved finger gongs; his other hand, ungloved as it turns out, is stuck in a pocket of his camel-hair coat. Beside him shivers Willy Gonzalez, age thirty. Short, thin, beady-eyed and balding, he winces rapidly, giving with his shivering an impression of massive nervous tic. His hands are jammed in pockets of his black overcoat.

From the windowless second-story video-surveillance room, a boy in tight shorts exits quickly. In fact, he's running.

From an edge of the basement pool, Erik dangles legs in steamy water. His expression is troubled. He appears to be listening to a sound he can't quite hear.

The sound is faint, distant, anguished.

Its source is a body, age forty-seven, trapped in a tunnel thickly bedded with petals. He has a view, through iron bars, of the rose room, where the bush plantation stands stripped of blooms. Pacing dogs surround him. Alarmed and avid, the dogs appear to be listening to something other than his very loud moans; perhaps they are listening to soundless screams emanating from the running boy, now hurtling down the grand staircase two stories above.

In the library one story above, Floria Shade sits, eyes wearily closed. Her lawyer, George Constable, frowns at legal documents. The fire is ebbing. Through the French doors icy light still pours, its intensity diminishing as the house slowly spills shadow downslope, reaching for a far streak of chalk in the sun, the cliffwalk balustrade; above which, two-toned, the sea tingles dull green to the horizon and the sky rises pale silver beyond.

Indifferent to this view and penetrating the shadow of the northern service wing, Duane, spike-shod, drags Sheila by the collar, her fur sledding her prone weight up a shallow incline. If occupants of the house and the portico visitors could witness this advance they would note that Sheila holds the microcassette recorder close to her mouth, and shows no resistance to her portage, except for thin scuffs trailing woodsward in the ice from the heels of her boots. They also would see that she hugs a rifle to her chest. Finally, if equipped with binoculars, they might notice a small plastic bag, lying discarded in the snow a few feet from the treeline.

These are the circumstances, as best we can tell, at 2:55 that Thursday afternoon.

———

Pip was a few steps from the front door when he heard the boy scream:

"Don't open it!"

The boy tripped on the stairs and was tumbling to the landing's carpet as he let loose this command. Pip turned, coattails trembling.

"I am The Living One!" the boy shouted. "You do what I say!"

"No," Pip said. "Not any more, do I do what you say. Because you are *horrid, horrid!* And people will see what you are!"

"A *boy*," the boy hissed, clasping arms over his head and twisting the bare chest—as though in pain, or perhaps to entice. "Don't open that door! I need you, Pip, I *love you*—we'll go on, you and I, we will —we will!"

"I remember everything!" Pip shouted. "You Spoor," he said

more calmly. Glassily calmer, he added, "You thieving, you murdering Spoor."

"I am the New One, *Living*," the kneeling boy replied, flexing arms and torso. "If you open the door I'll get dogs, *dogs*, you know what that means!"

"You," Pip said, "are afraid. I am not."

"You lie," the boy said.

"We've been through this before." Pip sighed, opening wide the door.

Three guns were pointing.

"Well," he said smiling, then crumpling as Claus Schmidtt's boot smashed his liver.

"Up there!" Willy Gonzalez shouted.

"Move one inch," Claus Schmidtt said carefully while carefully aiming, "and I shoot you dead."

Forty feet from Schmidtt's gun and high in the hall's rich gloom, the boy wasn't an easy target. But he didn't flee. He sank buttocks into the arches of his feet, and said, "Let's be reasonable."

"No talk!" Willy Gonzalez shouted. He darted over supine Pip and peered through archways. "Get him," he said.

"You get him," aiming Schmidtt said.

Willy Gonzalez said, "What the fuck that is, Claus, I don't know —but he's way, way *hot*. I tell you, he'll melt me, you! Get him!"

"How silly!" the boy exclaimed. "The one you want is outside!"

"Tell him *shut up*," Willy Gonzalez shrieked.

"Shut up," Schmidtt said.

"And don't look in the eyes," Willy said.

"Don't look at me," Schmidtt said, "or I shoot. Shoot you dead."

The boy put his hands over his eyes.

"Get him quick," Willy snapped.

"We both get him," Schmidtt said. He stepped over Pip, arm steadily outstretched. "Come on, he don't melt bullets, stupid."

Willy considered. "There are animals somewhere," he muttered. "You can't feel it, Claus, too bad—you'd want a machine gun. These things, you don't know, they stink like devil perfume . . ."

The two men crept up the stairs, guns leading as though closing in on a rabid kangaroo.

"What's the matter with Skip?" George Constable called from the hall.

Claus and Willy turned. "Who are you?" George Constable asked sharply.

"Shut up," Willy said, pointing a gun, then hitting the steps as Claus sideswiped him.

The boy had fled the landing. He was running up the second flight of stairs. "Get him!" Willy screamed.

Grunting, Claus sprang up to the landing, then to the second floor. On his left, just down the hall, mechanical doors slammed shut.

"Good God!" George Constable boomed at Willy. *"What are you doing?"*

Willy's gun spat through the sheaf of papers George was waving. The papers, scattering, seesawed to the floor. A violent rattling noise echoed from the second-story hall. It was the sound of a cage being shaken. Willy grimaced as he heard Claus yell, "Elevator! He's getting away!"

George was staring at his hand. Its emptiness astounded him.

Pip, clutching midriff, vomited over the glistening marble checkers of the grand hall's floor. He wiped his mouth. Weakly, he said to Willy, "I know where he's going."

———

Erik shook his head, rose, and walked from the pool to the shower room. Then he paused and listened. He thought he heard someone running. He must have thought he imagined it; because soon he was standing in a thrash of warm white noise, soaping to infinite regress in walls of mist-free mirrors.

———

In the tunnel off the rose room, the forty-seven-year-old stopped moaning, and stared. Something had happened. Something had aroused the dogs. They were pressing to the bars that barricaded the tunnel from the platform, from the bushes beyond.

On the platform, nestled in petals, lay the rope Pip had yanked from the ceiling. The dogs were indifferent to it; they were preoccupied with the panic of their master, the sixteen-year-old Living One. Heads poked through bars, hanging tongues atremble, their attention was directed at the open door on the far side of the room, a door clearly visible now that the roses had shed. They were expecting action in that doorway. They were not wrong.

The Living One ran through and paused, his lithe body a sweating sheen. He was listening, or perhaps mentally probing, for signs of pursuit. Signs he may have detected, for he ran to the platform and leapt upon it, skidding in petals. Straining against the bars, dogs licked at him, whimpering with worry. The Living One ignored them. His eyes were fixed on something that was not there. Or rather, it was there, but not in its usual location. The Living One's gaze fell to the platform. He saw the rope lying snakelike at his feet. He gasped.

"Hi," his ex-body said. The voice penetrated the dogs' panting with an oddly quavering hardness. "No rope, Dad. You can't get in."

"Damn!" The Living One shouted, stamping rope with a bare foot. He then hissed, "Don't worry, I'll get in." He seized the head of a dog and stared into its eyes. Electrified, the dog stared back. The Living One petted it. The dog pulled away and turned into the tunnel, trotting past the forty-seven-year-old; who, cowering, was expecting death.

The dog had different instructions. Rising on its hind legs, balancing with a paw against the wall, it mashed the other paw on a matrix of buttons. Its eyes reddened; the paw came off the buttons, and the eyes, concentrating, reddened more. From the paw, claws extruded. Slowly, painfully exact, the longest claw started tapping.

"No!" the forty-seven-year-old screamed, with all his might driving a fist into the buttons.

The dog, snarling, lost balance and dropped. Other dogs instantly charged, knocking the forty-seven-year-old to the floor; where, after a few moments, staring at a bleeding fist, he began to groan.

The Living One, peering through the bars, trembled with fury. The buttons had been demolished.

———

George, Pip, Claus and Willy stood uneasily in the elevator. Guns were pointing. The elevator was descending. Willy was sweating. "Claus," he stuttered. "You can't feel how *hot?*"

———

"I don't know what you want in here, Dad," The Living One's ex-body moaned. "But anything you want, I don't. I feel sorry for you, by the way."

"Why?" the perspiring Living One asked softly, staring at the open door at the other end of the rose room.

"Because you hate yourself. That's why you screamed at Bunny—you always hated yourself. Dad, I understand. Finally I understand! That time I was in your office talking with you, it wasn't you, it was Bunny, right? I thought it was you, but it was Bunny who burned the newspaper, Bunny who was crying about being a murderer—because he *is one,* just like you are! And he hates himself for it, that's why he burned the paper! Dad, admit it, you *can't stand what a monster you are, and never could!"*

"Shut up!" The Living One screamed, running for the door.

"You never die, Dad, but *you live in hell!*"

Those last words hung resoundingly as The Living One, at the door, came to a very quick stop. He was hearing a sound he did not want to hear. It was a sound of big men, running. They were running through the basement, very close by, coming closer. And suddenly, down the hall, there they were.

Screeching, Willy pointed. Claus shouted. Pip and George, guns in their backs, broke into a massive dead run.

The Living One slammed the door. He locked it, his face a mask of pain. Fists clenched, he stalked back to the platform and jumped on it, telepathing orders to the dogs. His ex-body, home now to his supremely frightened son, was prodded, with a strange respect, to the bars.

The first gunshot tore at the lock of the door.

On the platform, petals began to swirl. They swirled faster, faster, and began to glow. The eyes of the dogs began to glow. Squinting through their mask of pain, The Living One's eyes began to glow. They glowed brighter and brighter. They turned a brilliant red.

———

Claus did the shooting. Bullet after bullet went into the lock.

Willy, watching, was beginning to wonder if this was a good idea. His psychically talentless partner couldn't feel the energy, the heat, beyond that door. But Willy could. In there, monstrous forces were mingling, generating an incandescent storm of psi. Trembling, he asked Pip, "What's the boy doing?"

"He wants," Pip said, "his dogs."

That didn't reassure Willy. "Claus, stop!" he shouted.

The lock shattered. Claus kicked the door open. He looked in; his gaze settled on the iron bars at the far end of the room. Unaware that Willy wasn't following, Claus charged.

The boy lay passed out on the platform, a pool of boozy vomit near his head. Examining this, Claus heard a rasping, sliding sound. It came from behind the bars. Claus peered into the tunnel.

Deep within, dogs were dragging a naked man around a corner. The man seemed unconscious. Claus shook the bars, shook them harder. He couldn't move them. The dogs, and the body, disappeared.

———

"The roses just did something," Duane said. "I feel it."

He and Sheila were in the carriage house. Light pressed through small windows in the retractable metal doors, but the high-raftered space was dim. In the middle stood the truck, its snowplough raised, catching gleams from the windows. Nearby the Land-Rover lay buried in shadow. Sheila, agitated, stared at these vehicles.

Duane was trying to pick the lock of the door to the service wing.

"Great," Sheila said. "You *feel* it." She banged the snowplough with the butt of the rifle. "Duane, shouldn't we think about how we're going to bust out of here?"

"Sure," Duane said, preoccupied with picking.

"This thing might be good," she said staring at the truck, then at the door it was facing. She walked over to squint through windows. "Wrong direction," she moaned, "that's *Portugal*." The cliffwalk balustrade was an ivory curve against the sea, far below. "Have to back out the other door. But how does it open?"

"Switch somewhere," Duane grunted. "Sheila, bring me the rifle."

"No!"

He looked up. She was pointing it at him.

"If I'm crazy, Duane, you did it. I'm not responsible—I'm clinging, asshole, *clinging* to the little I've got, and the little I've got tells me you're using me! But why? What am I *doing here*?"

"Sheila, you're important, how many times do I have to tell you?"

"Because I'm bait, Duane? That rose—they can feel it, don't say they can't! You're using me as *bait* . . ."

He said quietly, "Put the gun down. You're paranoid. So paranoid you think of nothing but yourself, and meantime Torrance . . . Damn it, you're no help at all."

"What about Torrance?"

"How the hell do I say this? I think he's been taken, Sheila."

"You mean—snatched?" Her voice broke. "Prove it, Duane."

"I can't. But I'll tell you this—everything's going funny. It has to be the snatch, Malcolm feels totally different. He's crazy, he's weak and that's good, but he's raging angry and he's *dangerous*. Now do you want to bag him and save Torrance?" He snorted. "Listen, the flowers are doing something major. Bring me the rifle. I've got to shoot this lock out."

"The flowers?"

"Yes, Sheila. The roses. They feel like fucking *radiation*."

———

The elevator going up was crowded. George Constable, grimacing, hugged the boy. The embrace wasn't voluntary, it was mandated by gun, but it was necessary in the confined space, because the boy was still unconscious. Pip stood in a corner, face in his hands. Claus, smoking a cigarette, a cleft of worry between his eyes, examined the paneling. It was polished mahogany. The shine reflected Willy, at whom Claus didn't care to look directly.

Legs splayed, arms outstretched, Willy was pointing two guns at the boy's head. The boy's eyes were taped. He was handcuffed. That wasn't enough for Willy. On Willy's face was an expression of fear, and awe.

"Claus, I swear to God," he muttered, his guns unsteady. "The hottest. Hotter than anything I ever saw . . ."

"Cooling fast," Pip murmured through his hands. "You're over-loaded. You don't know what happened."

"Tell me," Willy said.

Pip's shoulders lifted, then fell. The elevator's door opened.

They formed a procession. It moved single file through an ante-room off the grand salon, through the adjoining music room, through the petit salon and past the ballroom around the corner, then through two smaller chambers of no discernible function, and on to the library. George Constable led, carrying the boy. Claus lumbered along in the middle, pushing a stumbling Pip, and Willy, wincing in all directions, took up the rear.

Alarmed for several reasons, George Constable took no solace from the fact the boy's face was red, even purple, a hue which reminded him of the big man's unattractive hat; he was further dismayed on noticing a peculiar blood color suffusing the boy's sweaty chest and legs, a far eerier color than the actual blood on his thighs.

"Torrance isn't well," he said.

"No talking," Claus Schmidtt said.

They entered the library. At them, Floria Shade cast anxious eyes.

"Put him there," Claus ordered, indicating a couch.

"No!" Floria wailed, rising. "George! What happened to him?"

"He isn't well, Floria," George said, depositing boy on couch. "He is sweating profusely. And he is *purple*."

"What is that on his face?" Floria asked, weaving to couch.

"Tape," tottering Pip said. "He's ok. But he wasn't, before."

"George," Floria asked tremulously, "who are these repulsive men?"

"Kidnappers," George said, crestfallen.

Floria noticed the guns and screamed very loudly.

"Look here, he's going to die!" George was rallying. Floria's scream had something to do with that. "Hemorrhaging, for God's sake, take off the tape—what good is he to you if he dies?"

"Don't nobody do nothing," Willy said. "Claus, man. I dunno . . ."

"Handcuffs, pathetic—take those off!" George shouted at Claus.

"Eeeeahhhh!" Willy gasped as Claus began to comply. "Bad move, Claus!" Willy's apprehension was deepening, his wince souring to a rigid grimace.

"He's *bleeding!*" Floria shouted.

"Where's the phone?" Claus inquired of George.

"We don't know," George said in a commanding tone of voice.

"Call the rescue squad!" Floria screamed. "An ambulance!"

Willy, shuddering, bent over the boy. "Holy shit," he muttered.

"What's wrong, Willy?" Claus asked, worried.

If Willy had an answer, he couldn't say it. His face was white.

"What's wrong, my man," George expostulated, "is that you are still here, *waving your guns*! Look, we've all had a scare, we're a little unnerved, I suggest that you leave and perhaps we all can forget the whole sorry affair . . . Floria, his eyes are moving."

The boy opened his eyes. He fixed on Floria's anxious gaze; he smiled the wan smile of one waking from a nightmare.

"Mom!" he croaked. "Mom, I love you so much!"

"Claus," Willy whined, squirming with fright. "Gone! It *left!*"

"What the . . . ?" Claus said, shaking Willy off his arm and watching Floria caress her son's head.

Willy yelled, "I feel dogs, somewhere! I think he is *with the dogs!*"

"Hi, Torrance," Pip said gruffly. Then he burst into tears.

———

Erik turned off the shower, toweled himself dry, dressed and looked at his watch. A wine bucket full of ice water and a bottle stood near the door. He pulled the bottle out, examined its wired foil, then slid it back in. He was restless. Torrance was supposed to have met him by now. Was a bad scene happening upstairs? A terrible family fight had to be going on. Those people were the weirdest he'd ever met. Including Torrance.

Commotion suddenly echoed through the stone-arched gallery outside the dressing room. He turned to the door and listened. It sounded like animals.

Then he heard howls.

These sounds scared Erik. He swiveled, knocking over the champagne. Metal clanged; ice water and glass-toothed foam bubbled across tiles and out the door. The howls were unearthly. They didn't seem human. Nor did the animal sounds of jumping and scratching, it seemed like a herd of wild beasts, did the place have a zoo? And if it did, which wasn't too unlikely, considering all the other things it had, what was the zoo doing? The sounds didn't sound good. Maybe the animals were upset. And those howls . . .

He must have known it was a dumb idea, but he decided to look.

The noise came from the end of a passage he hadn't gone through to get there, so he didn't know where he was headed as, heart beating fast, he walked slowly and quietly down. The noise got louder. He became more afraid and nearly turned back, but didn't when he sensed a large space around the corner up ahead, a space larger than the passage, which was growing dimmer as he progressed and the reflections from the pool started to fade; around that corner, he figured, there had to be a separate area, because why would animals go to the pool? The pool was clean. It wasn't even chlorinated. Torrance had bragged that he was the only one who used it. So maybe there would be a screen. To keep the animals away from the pool . . .

Erik reached the corner. Exposing as little as he could of his head, he looked. His eyes bugged out. There was no screen.

Twenty-five feet away a naked man was feeding a bunch of leaping, whirling dogs. Dogs that were big—really big, with glowing eyes like in snapshots when the flash catches that red; they were jumping and snapping at their food, then landing on the stone floor rasping their claws, then jumping again, jumping high, almost to the ceiling, it was a feeding frenzy. But the stuff the man was throwing didn't look like—food, exactly. More like little floating things, and he was tossing them in the air from a basket by thick handfuls, like confetti, they made rust-colored clouds in the brighter light and were driving the dogs into a panic; they were *hungry* for the stuff. The man's skin shone with sweat as he turned around and around throwing the stuff up, looking evil and howling high, then low, almost like a kind of singing—the crazy man was singing to the dogs.

Erik turned, tiptoed, then ran.

Not fast enough. Claws clicked rapidly on the tiles behind him. Then jaws were wrenching his parka from his hand, and he fell, screaming, as fangs sank into his jeans, into his leg.

———

"That's where they are," Duane said.

He had broken through a series of service-wing rooms to a room in which plates, platters and salvers were crammed to the ceiling in glass-fronted drawers. Sheila, fearful, irate, without many options, had followed. From a lace-curtained window they now studied the seaward exterior of the main part of the house. The library's sky-reflecting French doors attracted Duane. Beyond darkening silver in those doors, he saw agitation.

"See them running around inside?"

"Yes," she said doubtfully. "What's happening with Torrance?"

"Sheila, it's so weird. I think—he's back in his body!"

"He unsnatched himself? How? How do you know?"

"Because this whole place is busting psi! It goddamn *boiled over*! Malcolm, the dogs, the Psi goon and even Pip! I'm guessing about Malcolm being back in his old body. It's just a feel—but everything got—*strange*."

"Duane," she said, "are we in danger of getting snatched?"

Duane took Sheila's face in his hands and stared. Her pupils, twin tunnels, dilated a bottomless black. "Malcolm needs his own flesh and blood, hon. He needs a Spoor. We're not snatchable—where'd you put the rose?"

"Can't you feel it?" she asked, shrinking in the grip of his hands.

"Sheila, I'm feeling so much I don't know *what* . . . Where is it?"

"Your eyes are glowing, Duane. Stop it."

"Answer me! Do you want to bag Malcolm?"

"Yes. But let go of me!"

"Sheila, I have news for you."

"I'll kick you in the balls—what *is it,* Duane?"

"Woman, you're the most powerful one here."

———

In the library, Willy Gonzalez had declared a state of siege.

He was feeling something that the others, with the exception of Pip, weren't able to feel. He was feeling terrible danger.

The psi force he'd glimpsed on the front-hall stairs—an immense power radiating from a half-nude boy—had moved. Somehow, it had left the boy, and now was burning in someone else. Willy didn't know what could have made this happen. But he knew it meant trouble. He felt the power regrouping, somewhere nearby. He felt pitiless rage, awful purpose.

He felt bloodthirsty animals readying for battle.

"Dogs," George Constable snorted, shoving a sofa toward the double-doored entry most often used. *"Flowers.* Complete lunacy!"

"Useless," Pip said, likewise blocking other doors on the far side of the hearth.

"Faster!" Willy screeched. He stood in front of the fire's embers jerking his head left and right, checking the carpet-ploughing progress of the sofas and scanning the bank of French doors. "How come we don't leave, Claus, we should get out, why, why, why? *You,*" he yelled at Torrance, "help your mother, you were almost dead one time, you want it again? Claus, we run to the car and drive," he pleaded, "maybe he'll let us go?"

"Sure!" Pip grunted. He looked at the sofa athwart the ornately scrolled doors, then said over his shoulder, "I suppose he'll buzz the gate open, and if he doesn't you'll have loads of time to climb the wall, but the hounds can really jump, Señor Twitch-Face, so I'd pole vault if I were you—you know, get a good running start and . . ."

"You stop!" Schmidtt shouted, his sangfroid heating and leaking fear. He was moving furniture, including the sofa holding Torrance, to the middle of the room, making a crude, finely upholstered fort, which Floria was buttressing with smaller objects such as end tables and lamps, and even pillows.

"Children playing house," Pip sneered. "He's watching, you know."

"How?" Claus demanded.

"Cameras," Pip replied, pointing.

Claus and Willy looked up at the corner ceiling moldings. So did Floria and George. "Where?" Willy asked.

"Hidden," Pip said. "You can't see them. Koreans put 'em in."

"Sheer zaniness," George said. "Spirits in Torrance flying to his father, and killer dogs, and deranged criminals playing house, now we have Korean cameras!"

"Malcolm," Floria said, "is capable of anything."

"I get the feeling," Claus said slowly, "that he is. Willy, cover me."

A mahogany tower on wheels provided access to the higher bookshelves. Claus took a poker from the hearth, then pushed the tower to a corner.

"Easy," Willy said as Claus climbed to the top, swaying a bit and glaring at the molding.

"The thing," Claus announced, "is big! And," he went on, "it moves!" He jammed the poker into the molding. The others heard crunches, and then a sizzle. The lights dimmed. "But now," Claus proclaimed, "it moves no more!"

"Bravo," Pip said. "It shorted."

"Where's Erik?" Torrance asked, suddenly sitting up.

"He's gone," Floria said. "All gone, you lie back and rest. You've had an awfully hard day . . ."

"He was swimming," Pip said, plopping with a sigh into a wing-backed section of the fort's outer wall. "He might live. Who knows?"

"We'll live," Claus said, dismounting. "We wait, they come, we slaughter." He advanced with the tower on another corner.

"For once I agree," Floria said, stroking her son's forehead. "Honey, lie down—he drugged you, I'm sure, you weren't yourself at all! But you're better now and you need rest, no matter what happens, dear. Why, I'll plug those animals myself! Señor, you better give me a gun. I trained Torrance in La Jolla, we went to the meets together and he won, he won first prize three years in a row, and who do you think coached him? *I* did, I bet I can outshoot any of you! Except you, darling, but you're in no shape . . ."

Another camera crunched.

"Touching," Pip said, gazing at mother and son. "Claus, don't bother—it shorted. Floria," he went on, "I always liked you."

"That's enough!" George Constable said. He cleared his throat loudly. "Look here, you gentlemen seem to be frightened, you seem sincerely scared witless, I don't know why we don't call the police —if we can achieve the impossible and find a telephone—Torrance! Where is the *telephone*?"

"Disconnected," Pip said. "It's hopeless."

"I don't believe a word that man says," George averred. "And you"—he flailed at gun-clutching Willy—"are shaking like a leaf, have you lost your mind? You're a scaredy-cat because something somehow exorcised Torrance? Where are these dogs? Where are these flowers? *Hah?* We ring the wagon as if Apaches are coming, but they haven't, have they?"

"He's waiting for dark," Pip said.

"I have to take a leak," Torrance said.

"No you don't," Floria said.

"How do you know?" Torrance said.

"She can tell," Pip said, "just by looking."

"Mind your own business," Floria snapped. *"You* probably drugged him!"

"They're all on drugs," George said. "Very sick people, Floria."

"I'm going to the bathroom," Torrance said, standing unsteadily.

"What bathroom?" Claus said, now remounting. "Pee in the fire, boy."

"The sink in the closet," Pip said quickly.

"Uh-huh," wobbly Torrance said. "The closet. That sink."

"Sweetheart!" Floria said. "Pip—get a bedpan—or something . . ."

"Mom," Torrance said. "That is *gross!*"

"Hurry," Willy said, eyeing the French doors.

Pip stood in his chair and beckoned Torrance. "Just giving a hand," he said to Floria, grasping Torrance under the arms and swinging him up and over the furniture barricade.

"One minute," elevated Schmidt said. "Go pee!"

"Better hurry," Pip advised.

"Yeah," Torrance said. He limped across the room, opened a concealed door and disappeared into darkness. The door closed behind him.

"Secret closet," Claus said, staring. "Secret cameras. This house gives me the willies . . ."

"Oh no . . ." Willy groaned.

"Sorry," Claus said. "I didn't mean . . ."

"Claus," Willy said, turning green, "uh . . . , I think—I *feel,* Claus . . ."

"Torrance . . . !" Floria screeched, recoiling, as were the others.

The French doors were opening. All of them were opening, silently, in unison. A frigid breeze stirred the drapes, then rolled through the room as though the vivid steel sky itself were entering.

This shocked Claus. Losing balance, he fell from tower to floor.

"Huh," Pip said. "I should have thought of that."

———

Torrance stumbled down the butler's passage to a door. He cracked it open, peered, and saw no danger. He slipped through. He was in one of the smaller chambers of no discernible function giving off the petit salon to the library. A portal to his right framed the library entry. He stared at it. He heard silence.

The room he was in now had a function. To his left was the door to a powder room that hoarded a large supply of toilet paper. Torrance opened the door, went in, knelt, opened a closet and rummaged. Then he stood, holding his gun. In a mirror he caught a glimpse of himself wearing stained shorts and nothing else. He looked desperate. Did he take aim at his reflection, feel an impulse to pull the trigger?

Probably.

He hurried from the powder room toward the kitchen and its back stair to the basements.

———

"How'd those doors open?" Sheila asked. "Magic?"

"They're electric," Duane said. He blinked. "I think," he added.

They were staring through the platter-room window at a series of amber rectangles where the silvered library doors had been. Drapes fluttered, ghostifying the edges. Behind the roof, but still fairly bright, the winter sun slanted shallower and shallower into the sea.

"So where is he?" Sheila said.

"Wish I knew," Duane said. "He's getting a kick out of this."

"Am I really powerful, Duane?" Sheila said thinly.

"Yep," Duane said. "You are."

"I don't know . . . That rose you gave me—you don't know what you're talking about, Duane." Her voice was rising.

"You're powerful anyway," he said.

"Duane," she said anxiously, "I have to tell you—I've been feeling something. And now it's a *burning thing*. It's in my *stomach*, Duane."

Duane whistled, tunelessly.

"And Duane, it's starting to feel like it wants to *talk* to me! Is this why I'm powerful—because he needs Spoor *babies*? *Duane? What's in my stomach?*" she was shouting when the opera blasted.

———

To the defenders in the library the music was horrifyingly loud, bone-jarringly loud, so loud and unexpected that stolid Claus Schmidtt couldn't get up and Willy Gonzalez dropped one of his guns. Floria screamed a scream no one heard and George Constable collapsed, thudding into the top of the sideways-lying cocktail table.

Only Pip, sitting in the wing back, didn't clap hands over his ears.

The music came from grilles in the library and from discotheque-size speakers in the ballroom, where marble walls and parquet floors intensified the waves and sent them slamming tsunamilike throughout the house. It was Wagner's *Siegfried,* cranked to a shattering assault of sound. Vases jumped, paintings slithered down walls and crashed, *objets* slid, shivered and danced.

Then, midcrescendo, the music cut.

"Good evening," Malcolm said through the library grilles. "Thank you for coming. Thank you very much for being here tonight.

"The program is varied, I am delighted to say. If you are feeling frisky, come to the ballroom, the dogs have gathered there and eagerly wish to amuse you—charades, madrigals, they'll dance if you like or even play shuffleboard, Floria, I know you adore shuffleboard. We have Ping-Pong in the petit salon, badminton in the grand, hide-and-seek wherever, ha-ha! Oh, you merry pranksters! Aren't you feeling madly jovial?"

"Bastard!" Floria cried hoarsely.

Willy dove from the fort and streaked to the butler-passage door. "Lemme in," he shouted, tugging. The door wouldn't open. Willy pounded on it. "Kid! Come on! Open!"

"Good boy!" Floria shouted. "Don't let him in!"

"And now," the grilles intoned, "to make you feel giddily at home, the dogs will perform a rousing chorale!"

This time the noise came from ballroom speakers only. But it seemed almost as loud as the opera had been. It also seemed realistic—as if the dogs really were in the ballroom. They weren't, however. Not one of them was. The people in the library didn't know this; and they quailed as the recording played, for they heard the blood-freezing howls of ravening wolves.

Willy felt the dogs. He felt them so strongly he thought they were about to come flying through the sofa-blocked doors.

Squealing, he ran outside. He immediately slipped on the icy terrace, then slid down a series of shallow steps to a mass of dark bushes, beyond and below which the topiary garden tapered away, straining for a vanishing point in the distant, dimming sea.

The others couldn't hear what happened next.

———

The pool shimmied to the ballroom din. Steam vibrated from the water in oddly alive shapes, as though spirits were rising to the call of the howls. And a spirit of sorts was responding to, or at least was distracted by, the noise; it belonged to a young dog. A puppy, really. It was lying in the entrance to the dressing room, head poked inside; and it was wagging its tail, which weighed about nine pounds, not counting diluted champagne and bits of glass scraping back and forth over the gallery tiles.

Torrance crept along close to the gallery wall, gun extended. He saw the tail. The dense thing was rasping the floor just a few yards ahead.

He'd also seen Erik's parka floating in the pool.

The tail was six feet away.

Upstairs, the wolves suddenly stopped baying. The tail, just as suddenly, stopped wagging.

Torrance froze. The enormous basement room was quiet.

With a gurgle the parka turned over and sank.

In the dressing room, he heard Erik quaver, "Nice dog. You're a really nice dog—yeah, you are . . ."

The tail vanished. Torrance lurched forward. Then he heard the claws and a moment later saw the blur, the jaw, coming at his throat.

There was blood in that jaw.

Torrance put a bullet through it into the brain.

Finale: II

"We might have to go out there," Duane said.

"But it's getting dark," Sheila whispered. "What about the dogs?"

They were still in the service wing, in the room crammed floor to ceiling with platters. Sheila frowned through the window at the topiary hedgework. The outer hedge was a wall extending a few dozen feet leftward to the hill. She studied the networking channels of the interior maze. They were deep; shoulder-deep, at least. Was something going on in there? "You heard them," she said tightly, still spooked by the baying that had streamed from the house a moment before, seeming to coat the scene with new, more slippery dread. "They could come running out any second!"

"That was a recording," Duane said. "Sheila, I think the dogs are outside already. At least one is—the one that got that guy."

Duane had seen the dog jump Willy Gonzalez. Sheila hadn't. Her vision was poor. Besides, it had happened much too fast.

———

Willy was in the maze. Jaws, clamped to his neck, were dragging him through it.

The hedges, frozen solid, seemed like a trench cut through dirty ice. The dog, and Willy, made turns; this was a complex of trenches. It kept going, and going. Willy slid easily along. From his neck, from the viselike pressure there, hot wetness gushed, slicking his way. The dog's breathing roared, and within that loudness, Willy heard a deeper sound, a rich gurgling noise.

As it dragged Willy, the dog was swallowing his blood.

Their journey continued. Willy had a fur-fringed view of the sky. Strips of brightness kept turning and turning; the sky itself was a luminous maze. The vise on his neck took him through one final turn, and suddenly he was out of the maze, space opening all around; and he was falling, for the vise had let go. Willy thudded onto ice. His resting place was a kind of ledge. Directly ahead was something vast.

Willy beheld the very long hill descending to the cliffwalk; beyond which the water, yet farther below, was a wrinkling infinitude, an infinitude of wrinkling light and dark.

Did Willy understand this view? Did he realize what it meant for his fate, for the fate of the others?

We don't know.

———

Rifle poked out the platter-room window, Duane used its telescopic sight to comb the garden below the library terrace. The shrubs there were skeletal but encrusted with ice. In their gloom the whole pack could have been hiding. "Sheila," he said, "I feel the dogs talking. They're talking with Malcolm, and I think they're outside."

"Great," Sheila moaned. "What are they talking about, Duane?"

"Imagine people screaming high-speed Japanese, but backward and very, very *faint*—it sounds like that. So how could I understand what they're saying?" Duane looked up from his marksman's squat. "And I feel these voices moving but I don't know where, and I feel it when something pisses them off, especially Malcolm now that Torrance got away, which I know because Malcolm is *angry* about it, can you try to understand that?"

"You're nervous," she said nervously.

"Yeah," he said. "Malcolm is being very—uh—spiteful. He's weak, but that means all the more vicious. I wish we had more roses, Sheila."

"For God's sake—you're really scaring me now, Duane. What the hell is it with roses? What *do they do?*"

"Quiet!" he exclaimed, sighting through the scope.

A big man stood on the terrace, bulking dark against the library's light. He was holding a gun and scanning the bushes, shouting, "Willy! Willy!" A tense crook in his legs kept balance on the ice; the stance was ungainly, a massive half-crouch. Behind him another man appeared, leaning around the edge of a door. Drapes billowed over his chest. He took hold of the fabric and twisted it, then used it to tether himself as he ventured out, looking heroically clumsy, a lifelined spacewalker entering the abyss.

"They're frightened," Sheila said, squinting.

"They're shitting in their . . ." Duane said, squeezing the trigger. The report boomed hollowly. Both men flopped to the terrace as a heavy blur, yowling, leapt from shadow. Again the rifle boomed, smacking the blur—huge, it twisted and plunged, landing on Schmidtt. The merged forms jellied, then slid down the steps into bushes. George Constable, on his belly, crabbed arms and legs as he tried to turn toward the house. He didn't make it. Two blurs chomped his feet and dragged. Duane fired. A dog neck exploded, smudging the amber light. The other thick neck kept dragging. Duane fired, and missed. He fired again and didn't miss, but the dog dragged on. George, bellowing, gouged ice with fingers as he slid behind a row of planters. Duane fired the last bullet in the clip. A planter splintered, spraying shards. Nothing was behind it.

George Constable, and his bellows, were gone.

"Duane," Sheila muttered, holding a pistol with both hands, "I can't even see them." Five, maybe six, sped up steps and into the library. "I *see* them!" she shouted.

"Damn!" Duane said, grabbing her pistol and firing. He seemed to miss.

"Oh no," she moaned, as shrill screams came floating.

They heard sounds of running, of furniture crashing; of more screams, shouts, thuds and running; of a sudden, bowel-rending yell, distinct from the others; then they saw Floria and Pip bolt outside.

Pip, Duane noticed, was missing a hand. The stump spurted dark gobs. Floria's dress trailed shreds, as did her hair. These details flashed by in the space of a second, for both Pip and Floria instantly slipped, and whizzed down the steps into masses of bushes.

The dogs, following, weren't running. Their exit was more economical, and faster. They simply skidded.

The bullets Duane fired didn't drop one.

He and Sheila stared at silent thickets. Then they heard screams.

"Did you know, Duane," Sheila said indistinctly, clutching her stomach, "that Torrance's mother is very scared of dogs?"

"Yeah," Duane replied, not looking as she threw up. "Yeah," he said again. "This isn't working out. It's a fucking disaster."

She was doubled over when a high-pitched shriek cut through the dusk. It came from their left, from the end of the topiary facing the ocean. It was Willy Gonzalez.

Willy was moving again. He was being thrown to the hill.

He bounced on the lawn slope and zipped down its expanse of off-blue white, limbs feebly braking to no avail, his descent speeding more, and more. He swooped into a dip and moments later hurled off a rise and was flying far, then slowly was falling, and hitting, and skittering faster than ever over the level lower field, finally slamming, tiny as a puck and as lifeless, into the cliffwalk balustrade.

"Score!" Duane said softly. Coated with ice like everything else, the hill was enamel-hard, rink-slick. "Malcolm," he said, "is playing hockey."

Then they heard the laughing.

———

It came from the library grilles and wafted out over the terrace and bushes and carved hedges to the platter-room window, not sounding completely insane, but close to it. The origin, of course, was Malcolm.

He was laughing into a microphone in the video room. Was he enjoying himself? His laughter said he was. But the tinge of psychosis left room for doubt. Most likely he wasn't having much fun at all.

He was dealing with a number of problems. Those problems were serious. They were more than serious, they were a torment.

They were threatening his longevity.

He had to find Torrance. That was his primary concern. Time was running out for the Living One named Malcolm. He needed a new body with a new brain, and he needed it soon, very soon, before he lost control. And he couldn't take any old body, such as Erik's, for example; which wasn't, of course, old; no, it was young; but it, like all other young bodies in the world, with the exception of Torrance's, had a problem. It wasn't Spoor.

Malcolm needed Spoor to go on. This meant he had to find his son, and catch him. He needed that body.

He *wanted* it, all the more desperately because he'd tasted it. He'd surged through the untainted nerves and sinew, he'd mainlined facts of flesh with an ecstasy not comparable to drugs in any way but one—addiction to it.

But the fix he craved was shaping up to be a bit of a problem.

Body-changing was draining. And now that he was back in the polluted body he had thought he'd dropped, but had been forced to reinhabit for an emergency escape, a fist of which, furthermore, had been driven brutally into buttons, he wasn't in very good shape.

Malcolm had many reasons to proceed with care.

He felt the two boys moving through the house. Without dogs watching, he didn't know where. He could have ordered a few to track them down. But there lay another problem. Torrance had a gun. Malcolm had seen it, briefly, through the puppy's eyes; he'd seen it fire, felt the sickening smash.

This was a troublesome problem. How could dogs track down a gunpacking boy and disarm him, and subdue him, without risking damage? The puppy episode had shocked Malcolm. It had done its duty, yes, but came within a hairbreadth of hurting, maybe killing, his one and only brand-new body.

Like Pip, the dogs sometimes were overzealous. They got carried away. He had to use them very carefully indeed.

Which posed another problem. All told, five were dead. Or dying.

And the seven still active were busy.

They were very busy keeping Duane away from Malcolm.

Malcolm was becoming less and less fond of Duane. He felt him fuzzily eavesdropping. He felt him killing his dogs. He felt him tasting his rage, his deteriorating sanity; worse, he felt the horrifying essence of the plan Duane had devised, and still was spinning. The arrogance stunned him.

Malcolm had underestimated Duane.

He activated a compact-disc player and strode from the video room. But for the music coming on, the room's controls weren't very useful. Torrance could dodge the cameras. And he could shoot them.

Would he try to shoot Malcolm? That, too, was a problem. But it was for one reason only. Torrance wasn't touching rose petals.

———

Erik needed help getting out of the dressing room. The gash in his calf was deep. An arm over Torrance's shoulders kept his weight off that leg as they skirted the dog corpse and headed down the gallery to the elevator.

The wound left a trail, and a puddle in the elevator; it left another trail through a series of unused interconnecting rooms to Torrance's bathroom. There, jaggedly scissored flaps of denim soon lay gluing to the floor.

Evidence for their next move is sketchier.

The view from Torrance's bedroom included the topiary maze. The boys didn't watch dogs forcing prisoners to crawl through it, taking the same labyrinthine route Willy had seen. That already had been accomplished.

No one heard the moans, gasps and prodding snarls, the occasional screams as a crawler collapsed, and required a sharp nip to get moving again. The waltz Malcolm had on was much too loud.

———

Pip, George, Claus and Floria huddled in a sunken semicircular basin just beyond the end hedge. This basin was where Willy, when tossed from the maze, had landed. From it, he had been thrown down the hill.

During other seasons the basin spouted tall fountains of water, curtaining topiary from the slope of the lawn. But the prisoners didn't discuss plumes catching warm sea breezes. They were on a balcony overlooking Willy's doom; they were wondering if they would be joining his corpse, which they could make out against the balustrade through dimming light. There was no doubt they might find themselves slaloming. Dogs flanked them, and guarded the gap through which they had exited the hedges. The obvious direction for the next leg of their journey was compellingly downward.

Then there were cliffs. The drop from the balustrade to the heaving sea was a vertical three hundred and eighty feet.

It was January. Night was falling. The local population was sparse. No one in his right mind would go anywhere near the base of those cliffs during that time of year, or possibly any other. There were vagaries of tide, storm and shark to consider. The shivering prisoners couldn't have failed to contemplate a quite plausible scenario for the traceless disposal of their bodies.

The waltz blasted over their heads and out to sea.

———

Sheila, still in the platter room, was alone. Duane had climbed through the window and disappeared down the walkway running along the service wing to the carriage house.

As usual, he hadn't provided details of what he intended to do.

But he had given orders. Under no circumstances was she to leave the platter room.

Minutes passed. The waltz thundered unbearably. The sky darkened. Sheila poked her head out the window to look around. Duane's quest interested her. She wondered what he was after, what was going on to the left, toward the hill. She couldn't see all of the crest; the tall hedgework hid it. At that end, Duane said, a man had been thrown to the cliffs. Would others follow? She strained her eyes, trying to make out the cliffwalk. She wasn't sure if the bottom field was visible. Was the distant murk field, or ocean? As she stared, a long string of dots blinked on, just over the end hedge. It was, she knew, the balustrade. Someone had turned on the lights. But something was missing. She puzzled. The first time she'd seen this, the night of the dinner party, there had been more of a spectacle. Then she remembered—the magical twinkling pagoda. It too had been lit. Now, apparently, it wasn't.

She turned right to look at the house. The upper stories were dark. The ground floor was blazing. In the open library doors drapes shuddered, as though feeling the madness, the carnage, a dog lying still on the terrace. Looking at the dead shape, Sheila felt a twinge. She felt it again, more strongly, deep in her stomach. Then the music stopped.

The sudden quiet was heavy. Sheila kept her head very still. She was spooked. Something was about to happen. In a few seconds, she heard it. From the left came a long dopplering shout, rapidly balustrade-bound.

Claus Schmidtt had been sent down the hill. Sheila didn't know the victim was Claus; but a faint crunch, drifting a moment later through the stillness, told her the balustrade hadn't been kind.

Sheila wriggled out the window and jumped to the walkway. She reached up for the rifle, and headed away from the hill, toward the house. The hedge wall loomed not far away, the boundary of a beast-infested interior. She was terrified. She was panicking, because the twinge in her stomach was telling her something. It was telling her to stay away from the terrace.

But that was where she, very determined, was going. We have evidence for this. She whispered the following into her microcassette recorder:

"I am unbelievably afraid. People are getting thrown to cliffs. And I'm trembling out here next to a monster bush with hallways inside and things are *running around in it*. But, I'm proceeding. I'm proceeding because the thing in my stomach doesn't want it. The thing is hot, it's twinging, it's telling me to *stay away.* I see the dog now— it's lying there with its neck blown open. Blood is melting down the steps, it's horrible. But I'm going there because the thing in my stomach is *very scared of it.* Anyway it's away from the cliffs. Anyway I have to know what they did to me, what's *going on.* Mom and Dad I love you but don't tell anybody. *Burn the tapes.''*

———

"Torrance!" The voice megaphoned from the hedge above the three remaining prisoners in the fountain basin. "Duane, Sheila, Erik!"

In different locations, people paused and listened. They were listening to Malcolm.

"The dogs just tossed another man to the cliffs! Perhaps you can see him, he's lying against the balustrade, not far from his friend! I suspect his neck is broken!

"Two down so far—that means three to go! But hold on, the dogs are acting up again! Oh my, they are playing with Pip—who—oh dear!—has misplaced one of his hands! But good old Pip wants to toboggan! And now he *is,* ha ha! Say bye to Pip! Bye-bye!"

———

Despite the missing hand, Pip braked better than had either Willy or Claus. He slid without leaving the undulant slope, and therefore traversed the lower field more leisurely, receiving a less severe final jolt when he smacked into marble stanchions. It's possible he even retained consciousness. If he did, he might have been able to inspect Claus's fatal jam. Claus had hit head first. An ear was freezing to a stanchion. The rest of his skull, hanging over the edge in the glare of a halogen lamp, was draining vaporously into the sea.

Floria and George now beheld three bodies fastened to the necklace of lights on the cliff. The middle one, Pip's, seemed to be shaking.

———

"I hope everyone is watching!" Malcolm megaphoned. "And keeping track! Who wants to be next? Floria? Are you really up to this, dear? How about your legal companion? He who sought to take away my son? You've forgotten my son, haven't you? Why yes, I believe you have . . .

"But I haven't! Torrance, come to Daddy! You must come to me, boy! You must come here *now!* And you will, dear child! Because it will save your mother! Torrance, *come here and save Mommy!''*

———

This ultimatum issued from the gap in the hedge above Floria and George. Malcolm, however, wasn't there. Jaws had carried a small loudspeaker to that gap; Malcolm himself was a hundred or so feet away, talking once again into a microphone, and setting a trap.

His headquarters was the gazebo. Getting there had been treacherous, due to ice; a splendid aerie in nicer weather, perched as it was on the crest of the hill's southern flank, it now was an ideal spot from which to slip and helplessly sled. But this hadn't stopped Malcolm. The gazebo was a platform with strategic advantages.

First, it put dogs between him and danger. Second, he could look out for Duane reconnoitering his loudspeakered voice, and in turn position dogs for safe attack. Third, he had a clear though swiftly fading view of all other approaches. The circular building was open to the elements from its dainty conical roof to the stomach-high viewing rail; better yet, under the rail, he could see through the wall's latticed diamonds while remaining hidden behind them. For these and other reasons, the gazebo wasn't to be merely strategic. It also would be fun.

From it he would use his powerful torch to pinpoint victims caught by the balustrade; and from it, if need be, he could use the three guns dogs had confiscated from Claus and Willy. Lastly, it was a fine place from which to watch dogs skate down the hill on their claws, and ravage bodies, and then toss them, without remorse, over the cliffs.

"Boy!" Malcolm rasped into the microphone, *"are you coming to Daddy?"*

———

Torrance wasn't going to Daddy. He was staring up the barrel of a rifle. "What are you doing?" he whispered.

"I don't know," Sheila whispered, staring down the barrel of his pistol. "What are you doing? Torrance—are you really you?"

They'd taken each other by surprise in a recess of the library terrace. Torrance had been crawling through on his hands and knees, staring at a wire running over the ice. Sheila, also crawling, had been backing away from the dead dog sprawled in amber light, in a puddle of chilled blood tentacling down steps to the garden.

Torrance glowered at her. Then he said, "Yeah. Yeah—I'm *me*."

Their guns lowered. "Erik," Torrance said, "it's ok."

Erik said in the depths of the recess, "I seen her at school."

"School," Sheila said, propping gun on a planter. "Oh, yeah— *school*."

"Get out of the light," Torrance whispered, "we might get attacked!"

"Yeah," Erik agreed.

Sheila took the rifle and crawled for shadow, into which Torrance backed up. Erik, also on hands and knees a few feet within, stiffly swung legs around, and sat. Sheila saw the bandage on a bare calf poking from his overcoat. Torrance wore an overcoat and jeans. The boys looked like runaways; which, of course, they were.

Malcolm's voice continued to rave from the far end of the topiary. Above them towered the south wing, angled from the center of the house.

"God, I'm confused," Sheila said. "Duane and I came to save you."

"My mom's the one who needs saving," Torrance said. "He's going to *kill her*. Give me that," he said roughly, taking the rifle.

"Hey!" Sheila protested. "You can't use that in the bush. It's too narrow in there—give it back!"

"What are you talking about?" Torrance said.

"He's at the other end of that enormous bush!" she said.

"Maybe," Torrance said. "Maybe not. The microphone's remote, he could be anywhere. Anywhere dark, where he can *watch*."

"Huh," Sheila said. "The lights in the pagoda, the gazebo, whatever—are they usually on, when the cliffs are on?"

"As a matter of fact," Torrance said, staring at her, "yes."

"They aren't on now," she said. "Torrance—you really got snatched?"

Checking the ammo clip of the rifle, he nodded.

"How?" she said. "How'd he do it?"

"With roses," he said. "Two bullets—any more?"

"With *roses*?" she said.

"Uh-huh, roses—they were on our bodies. They made him into a ghost, then they made me into a ghost, and the two ghosts switched bodies. Sheila, I can't explain it now. Where's the bullets?"

"Wait a second," Sheila said. "I'm thinking . . . Uh, no," she added distractedly, "no, no more bullets, Duane has them . . ."

"Shit!" Torrance exclaimed. "Sheila, go inside. Erik, let's go."

"Wait!" she hissed. "I have to know about the roses!"

The boys were heading for the south wing. Torrance turned and said, "Sheila. Look down. See the wire?"

"Yes," she said.

"Cut it, and maybe you'll shut up Dad. Then maybe he'll send a dog to find out what happened. And then . . ." He paused. "Sheila, please get away from here. Cause if you don't . . ." She was crying.

"They were on your *bodies*?" she gasped, chest heaving.

"Yeah. Sheila, please—go inside." He and Erik disappeared.

Sheila sat in the dark, crying. She glimpsed the dead dog through her tears and cried harder. "Bastard," she sobbed in four syllables. *"Bastard,"* she repeated in five. "Oh God—oh God, oh God, oh *God . . .*"

Her crying quickened, became harsher, as her ears fixed on a sound she'd been trying to ignore. It was Malcolm's loudspeakered voice. It wanted her attention; it was calling her name. Sheila convulsed and then fell still, for she heard words that pierced her heart:

". . . are you there, my dear? Is it safe in there? Are you having a nice time in your cozy drama chamber?"

Sheila got on her hands and knees. The fur padding the knees, giving her the look of a heavy-bellied ferret, she crawled at the amber light. She was muttering, "This is it, gonna get him, this is it . . ." On she crawled, and on, toward the blood, farther, farther into the light; toward the dog; toward the carcass on the terrace.

She had business with that dog. She wanted its collar. She wanted its roses.

———

Duane was studying the terrain from the roof of the carriage house. He'd climbed up there to take a look at the maze. To his chagrin, he'd found it too dark to see to the ground. He saw Floria and George trembling out front in the basin; but the shadowed grooves behind them showed him nothing at all. Nothing, that is, except sizzling energy. The force of the roses was everywhere. They were aroused, they were *worried,* and Duane felt this. He felt it like a poisonous wind. But dogs were what he was looking for. They had to be down there somewhere. What else stopped Floria and George from making a dash around the house to their car? More important, Malcolm hid in that end of the garden. At least his amplified voice did.

Duane's vantage point gave him nothing.

Worse, he suddenly had a feeling Malcolm could see him. He hooked his boot behind the pipe up which he'd climbed, lowered to it, and slid. The carriage house now blocked him from the garden; from everything.

He sidled along the big metal door. Directly ahead yawned the cup of the hill. A curve of widely spaced lights at the bottom delineated the head of the cliffs, beyond which lay the blackening chasm of the sea. The balustrade had been lit. Why? To call attention to its new ornaments? Was one of them, Pip, looking up at him? Duane continued to feel watched.

He scanned for other possibilities. His gaze settled on an outbuilding, a dark, delicate thing on the opposite crest.

And he felt it: the malevolence, weakened but fanglike, staring back.

Duane had to get there. He pondered. The hill dipped in between, deep and wide. Skirting its edge, he would walk to the basin, staying as clear as possible from places where dogs could attack. When they did attack, as they surely would, he would shoot them, one after the other, with handguns; he had three, each fully loaded. The plan wasn't ridiculous. Like Malcolm, the dogs seemed to be weakened. And they couldn't shoot back.

Duane moved forward from shadow. He stood in the cold dark, checking his approach. Then, he walked. The basin area, he realized, the stretches before and beyond it, they all would be tricky. The path along there was narrow. The hill swooped to the left, the hedges reared up to the right. As he got closer he began to reconsider. Maybe this was foolhardy. Maybe he wouldn't see them leaping. Maybe he should make a detour around the garden and get the rifle from Sheila. But what use was a rifle in close quarters?

Maybe he should collect her and get the hell . . .

From a culvert the dog rocketed, jaw closing on his jacket collar as his head jerked away, claws raking face and body. For a split second they teetered, then crashed and slid writhing, bits of ice flying, guns firing, wildly firing, as they slid faster, faster down the hill . . .

Then, across the hill, the rifle boomed.

And several things happened very quickly:

A horrendous loudspeakered scream split the hedges.

The dog wrenched from Duane and flailed against the slope trying to move up and across as Duane, sliding, rolled and fired, fired again, then zipped off a bump and was airborne, hill whipping the flashing sky, murk amok all around.

Dogs pushed Floria and George from the basin. Shrieking, they sped down the hill like torpedoes, eyes wide, teeth bared.

That done, the dogs ejected, targeting gazebo.

———

Malcolm had been preoccupied with Duane when the boys snuck up to the lattice wall behind him. He was focusing on the dog best positioned for attack. Too many dogs were lost; he needed those dogs, needed them badly, almost as much as he needed roses, or even his new body. And so his mind was fastened to that dog's eyes; to its ears and fangs, to its brain.

Duane wouldn't have a chance. The jump was going to be perfect.

Malcolm suddenly felt menace.

The dog jumped Duane—a few moments prematurely, for it also felt menace. Alarm flooded, reflex took over.

This didn't help Malcolm. He whirled and saw the barrel poking through a diamond hole near the floor. The creature aiming it was his son. He knew this, and called for the dogs as he stared at the boy—an absurd boy, a doomed boy, who somehow thought the body he inhabited was rightfully his.

Malcolm wasn't worried. He could take a few bullets. He would need the dogs, and rose petals, very soon thereafter. But dogs were on the way; wearing collars studded with roses.

In real time, the sequence took a second. He felt menace, whirled, called dogs; he saw the gun; then, before the second elapsed, the gun fired.

The bullet shattered his right hip. From upjerking hands, two guns flew into the dark, clattering.

But dogs were coming. Malcolm felt them coming. He didn't mind the guns being gone, he had less use for them now that Duane was down the hill, and wounded; he didn't mind that he'd fallen, was bloodying spasmodically on the gazebo floor. He knew that in such an extreme moment, even a few roses, even the handful of roses on the dogs, would put him back where he belonged. He saw Torrance lunging at him shining a flash, and didn't mind that, either. The boy was lovely. His flaring nostrils, his shadowy hate-filled eyes, were coming closer, closer . . . A neat form of suicide, was Torrance's patricide—didn't he have any idea? Didn't he . . . Malcolm became aware of being picked up. Why didn't Torrance simply put a bullet in his head? He could deal with that, he could float for a while, for thirty seconds perhaps, until the dogs arrived—but—but what? Torrance was doing something unexpected. Torrance was . . . throwing him out of the gazebo.

Malcolm was falling, falling, then hitting hard.

He was sliding. He was sliding on his back down the ice, looking up at the flashlight, at the oval of his son's staring face—an intelligent face, now two faces, receding side by side under a conical blot in the sky, receding quickly, they were staring at him slipping away too quickly, it was abominable, *terrible,* he was slipping too far, *out of range*—he howled.

He howled mightily for dogs.

———

Torrance was a good shot. Had he wanted to kill his father, he could have hit the head, or heart. But this was a fight to the finish. And to finish it, he had to eliminate every last dog.

He didn't know how many still lived. He did know how many bullets he had. Not enough, even taking into account his father's remaining gun, which he had found on the gazebo floor. So he was outnumbered. What could he do?

His solution was straightforward. Divide them.

If Malcolm died, he figured, the dogs would turn their collective fury on himself and the others. But if Malcolm were wounded, and sliding into perilous dark, then some number of dogs surely would go to his aid. He and Erik then would confront a diminished attack; or no immediate attack, maybe all the dogs would go after Malcolm.

The pocket flash he'd used to find the gun on the floor also found the jumbo torch. He quickly gave the gun to Erik, then probed the dark outside.

They were coming. Three of them, tongues hanging, eyes red, frozen roses shriveled around their necks, they were streaking across the ice just a few feet away. Aiming one-armed, Torrance fired the rifle. He missed.

Erik was firing and missing. Torrance dropped the rifle, pulled his pistol and fired and a red eye went redder then black.

The other dogs disappeared from the torch swath.

Both boys whirled to face the two openings with steps.

They came in too fast. Torrance put two bullets in one and Erik put one in the other but it didn't matter, they just kept coming and they wanted Torrance. Erik banged into a roofpost and collapsed, Torrance was on the floor screaming, dogs on top. They simply flopped, roses pressed to his face, not feeling manic fists, undislodged as the legs thrashed and thrashed. Torrance got his head clear and everyone alive could hear it:

"NO!! NO, PLEASE NO, NO, NO, NOOOoooooooOOOOO!!!!!"

Erik shook his head. Torchlight grazed an epileptic foot. The dogs seemed to be eating Torrance. Erik got up. He grabbed the rifle by the barrel. He raised it like a baseball bat.

Shouting, the boy went berserk. He bashed and bashed, and bashed.

——

Sheila was crawling through the maze. The wire was guiding her, taking her through the dark hedges unerringly. She was tracking the loudspeaker. She was tracking Malcolm. She'd heard his amplified scream, a moment before. She'd heard gunfire. Maybe she could do it. She wanted to get him. She wanted to *bag him.*

Having visited the dead dog, she thought she knew what was going on, finally. The twinge in her stomach now made sense. Duane's obsession with the rose made sense. It outraged her, but it made sense, and it interested her, too. Because she felt it—the crashing energy, the storming luminescence that she sensed ever more vividly as she crawled through the maze, which itself seemed to shimmer that color—a wanting color, a sepia *hunger,* a force that was alive, raging, and above all, *hers.* It was a force to which she, Sheila, timid dweller of chambers, now held the key. It was giving her strange, mad, animal power. It was giving her a mission. And somehow, she *would succeed.*

She'd almost reached the basin when more gunfire cut through the cold. Yet she crawled on, icy twigs scraping, plucking her coat. She went through a gap and saw sudden hugeness—the dark hill, the dark ocean, bisected in the middle by the curve of lights. All of it silent, but silently echoing; echoing enraged, terrified, youthful screams.

Sheila panted at the blackness. She needed a weapon, any kind of weapon, preferably a powerful one. She had to think, and think fast.

Panting, Sheila sat.

——

Floria's slide down the hill hadn't hurt her badly. She had been stunned, but something hard and soft both was wedged behind her —it had cushioned her impact against the balustrade. Coming to, she saw fat stone colonettes parading away, at intervals lit. It was so hard to see. She was in a dark area between glowing, faintly buzzing lamps. Stars twinkled far above. She'd heard someone scream. It had woken her. Who'd been screaming? She had distant recollections of . . . Torrance? No, not her own Torrance. Or had it been . . . ? This was too awful. A nightmare. The thing behind her was . . . *breathing.*

She would have yelled if she'd had the wind.

"Hi there," she heard Pip wheeze. "You know, Floria," he remarked, "I always liked you. Really. And here you are—we just played *catch.*"

A black lump was scraping slowly down the hill. It made a peculiar sound, like nails scratching. "Dear God," Floria groaned. "What," she asked weakly, "is that?"

"That," Pip said, "is Malcolm. And dogs." The lump was sliding and grating down, somewhat to their left.

"Pip!" Duane cried from the dark to their right. "I'm sliding a gun over! Get ready to grab it!"

The gun came hissing softly out of the dark. Pip tried to sit up, to get his good arm ready. But the gun bounced off Floria's boot. It twirled through colonettes, and fell at the ocean.

"Did you get it?" Duane yelled.

Pip didn't reply. He and Floria were watching the black-furred lump settle against the balustrade, forty feet away. A red-eyed animal rose from the lump and ambled at them. It wasn't in a hurry; and it didn't break stride when the torch hit it from afar, as though it were the spotlit star of a silly old stage show, the kind with live beasts and fake marble.

"Mom!" Torrance shouted from the other end of the beam, which had moved onto the Pip-pillowed sprawl.

"Come to Daddy," Pip sighed, as the dog stared red eyeball-to-eyeball at cringing, soundless Floria. "Oh, go away!" he then bellowed hysterically. "Enough! Stop it, just stop it, just die—*just stop it and die!"*

With a swipe the dog opened Pip's face.

"Torrance!" Duane yelled from the dark. "Don't even *think about it!"*

"Torrance!" Malcolm howled from the balustrade, where he lay on the ice flanked by two of his three living dogs. *"Think about it, boy! Your mother is going over the cliff! You come to me, son! You come to me now!"*

"Torrance!" Floria shouted, *"run! Run—"* She couldn't go on. The dog was mashing a paw in her chest.

The beam spotlighting this began to waver.

"YOU FUCKER!" Torrance shouted to the limits of his lungs. *"Hold on, Mom, I'm coming . . ."*

And then the carriage-house door loudly rattled up, revealing a distant square of light to which all eyes turned.

———

No one quite believed it at first. Least of all Duane, who held one remaining gun and was wondering how to use it; a leg, broken, was dangling through the balustrade. Somehow he had to get that leg out and shoot.

The engine was echoing now from the square of light. Malcolm, everyone knew, was screaming. But his words weren't easy to hear. The truck was making too much noise.

It jolted out with a bruiting gnash of gears, headlights blazing, windshield dark. Then the horns blasted. They kept on blasting as the truck turned sharply to its right and ground along close to the head of the hill, plow raised. Trouble lay ahead, for the path in front of the basin wasn't wide. The truck might slip, and topple, if it went that route.

But it didn't. It pushed through the topiary as if nothing were there.

Then for twenty seconds or so it seemed to head directly for the gazebo. In the glare of its headlights Torrance and Erik came running out, arms waving. The truck ignored them. In fact with a blast of the horns it told them to get out of its way. And they did, when it lurched ahead and then to its left; for its headlights were pointing down the hill, and its purpose was unmistakably clear.

It had a chance of getting to the bottom on its wheels from there.

What with the jolting, the headlights veered. Torrance put the torch on Malcolm. The truck slid, slowly at first, then picking up speed. The blade was lowering—not to the ice, but not far from it.

Malcolm took evasive action. The dog squashing Floria ran to him, and with the two others it dragged him along the balustrade. The object was to get to Floria before the truck got to them.

Duane had extricated his leg, however. He was belly-wriggling to a position from which he could fire. Fire he did, and accurately, by the torch's searchlighting beam; the two forward dogs fell. They tried to drag on, then one went still, blocking the way. Malcolm pounded a fist on it. The truck was bearing down. Could he hear Pip screaming?

Pip screamed, "Gundulf, I love you! But it's the end, the end at last!"

Malcolm probably heard this. But the sound of the truck was fearsome. Lights blazing, the thing was jouncing over bumps into the air, then landing with elephantine momentum, the plow both helping to tip it aright and threatening to send it end over end.

The driver was skiing to Portugal.

A cab door flew open. She was trying to jump out.

Pip heaved himself onto the balustrade. He pinched catatonic Floria's cheek, winked at her bloodily through churning shadow and the glare of the lights, then threw a leg over the marble and screamed, *"See you in hell!"*

He plummeted. Floria watched this and fainted.

——

Sheila was trying to undo the seatbelt. Why had she *fastened it*? How does it *open*? She was cutting her fingers trying to force it open —*there*—a button! On the *side*! How dumb, on the *side not the top*! She kicked the flapping door and dove from the truck.

Too late.

She saw everything. Midair, she saw it all happen in delirious slow motion. The balustrade, lights waggling, was coming at her like a runway into which she was crashing from the wrong direction. There was Malcolm, crouching against dogs. There was the ice underneath, and the gleaming marble behind, and beyond that, black engulfment—in which, deep, deeper than anything physical, there was a resounding sepia *tang*.

The blade was going to hit Malcolm dead square.

And he knew it. His eyes, staring at doom, were a brilliant red.

Well done, Sheila. You did it. Yes, you did it. You are seeing it as you fly from the truck and zoom forward—because you, too, are part of this gigantic momentum.

The problem is, your momentum will carry you over the edge.

You jumped too late. That seat belt, Sheila. Too late. The blade has just hit Malcolm. It's lifting him and now cracking the balustrade, and I am one split second from the edge and *two feet over it*.

The engulfment is bottomless. It's . . . the sweetness.

That color, everywhere squirming: the *sweetness*.

Duane felt it. He felt what it had just done to Pip. And he felt what it was doing to the dog.

A dog was moving. From the rush of the blade, this dog was moving, and it was glowing that color, it was sizzling that sweetness, and it was leaping, jaws wide, it was twisting, pirouetting, delivering highly precise torque as it clamped the hem of Sheila's coat, and jerked it:

She spread-eagled over the marble, arms raised. Winged Victory?

Midair, Sheila and the dog *sizzled the sweetness*.

She was flinging back, twisting back with the jerk to the ground.

The truck smashed into space. The tail lights shone red, yellow and white. It was in a hurry. It was an express delivery for the sky. No, it was a delivery for the ocean, because it was cruising lower, lights bright in the black. A magical flying truck, it was; nosing downward, rapidly.

——

None of the balustradeers saw the crash. Pip's body rolled with the waves on the rocks below. All the dogs but one were dead or dying. Floria and George were unconscious. Claus and Willy were dead, they couldn't watch the truck hit.

And Duane didn't. He was staring at Sheila.

Who was staring at the dog as it licked her face.

While licking, the dog was staring at a collar's bloodied petals.

Which, glowing, were staring back.

Shiela had taken this collar from the dog on the terrace. She had buckled its roses around her neck. She had done this because she wanted to bag Malcolm. And bag him, she had.

He was a tiny squirm, surrounded by her vastness.

He was helpless. He was at her mercy.

He was in her Drama Chamber.

——

In the gazebo, Torrance hugged Erik. The boys were hurt. They were crying. They were alive.

On the floor the dogs lay dead, brains bashed out of their heads.

Torrance was in his own skin.

And Malcolm was gone.

Yes, The Living One named Malcolm was gone.

Malcolm was floating in the cold, dark sea.

AFTERWORDS

Twenty Months Later

We argued over who would Afterword first. The other Editor withdrew his claim to the honor when I reminded him of the things he did to me.

This is Sheila. It's been a while since Tor got rich and Malcolm plunked in the ocean. Enough time to get perspective, or try.

But perspective is relative, I guess. I've learned that. Factors such as the quality of sleep, what you ate for lunch, little things interfere with perspective. Big things interfere, too. For instance, a baby.

The child is gorgeous.

He was born eleven months ago. Guess what? He was a breeze. The delivery, I mean. It was rocky at first, carrying him, but not after I got used to it. And ever since birth he's been the sweetest thing in the world. My maternal instincts have been raging nonstop. I love my baby.

He's an exceptional child. Every mother has that opinion, I suppose. But do you know what I'm talking about? If you don't, think hard.

After much consideration we named him Fearfield.

He isn't "Fear" for short. That would be negative. His nickname was Field at first but he didn't really respond, so we shortened it to Feel. He's watching me write this. But he's getting restless, he wants out of the high chair, the little monster is gurgling desire for the beach. His father and Erik are whooping it up out there with Kip. Feel wants to go play too. I'll take him out in a minute. It's a glorious beach. And it's a nice day, not that hot. Duane's going to barbecue later on. Steak for the boys, fish for him and me—we're health-conscious now, Duane and I are at least. The boys make jokes about our rightly fatted diet of fish. But hell, they catch it. They love fishing. Gives them something to do besides chase the cabana-kids at the resort we're expanding on the other side of the island.

I should mention, we live on an island. We own it. Tor owns it, technically, but it's all in the family. God, this place is beautiful. How could we be dumb enough to expand the delightfully rustic resort on this near-virgin island we own?

It was Duane's idea. He thinks the boys need nightlife. A little, anyway. And he's right. Ex-suburbanite teens would go crazy if fishing and each other were the only ways to pass time. No movies or bistros, no yachters with suntanned long-limbed offspring to liven up paradise? Forget it.

I'm sipping a piña colada. Yes, life is rough. It's a boozeless colada, by the way. I don't drink now. Duane still smokes, though. I said we're health-conscious, I know. But Duane has a lot on his mind.

We all do. I'm not sure how to describe what's happened. Maybe I'll start by going outside with Feel for a while. Feel could spend the whole day watching Erik and Tor and Kip bodysurf. He not only could, he does.

Kip's very at home in the water. She's riding waves right now, crashing around, barking her head off with salty joy.

Kip is our dog. Tor gave her the name. I've overcome my fear of large dogs because of Kip. A more devoted and lovable pooch never bow-wow-wowed. I trust her completely. I leave her alone with Feel all the time. Kip would die to protect my baby, or any of us; but Feel and she are best buddies. It's as though they've known each other for years. Many years.

She saved my life. Loyal, devoted Kip. She's a very important part of the family.

———

Well, here I am on the beach under an umbrella. The boys are napping in the sun. They're trying to nap. Feel's crawling on them, and Kip is licking Erik's ticklish feet. This happens.

Erik's been a blessing. He helped Tor shrug off the pain. They're so in love—inseparable, yes. They fight sometimes. Monogamy is tough at eighteen. One or the other often is sulking over some stray seduction, real or imagined. Do I take notes? No. I'm observing two cases of development, both a bit fractured; but I've stopped studying adolescence. These adolescents thought my questions were hilarious. They laughed when I tried to get down to business a year ago. They held their splitting sides at the very idea of their fantasies harboring evidence. That dampened my investigatory zeal somewhat.

So the focus is different now. I have a more pliant subject, one who doesn't make fun of me—at least as far as I can tell. Much earlier stages of development are my main concern.

There are disturbing signs. For one thing, Feel eats delicately. You know—nonnoisily. Not at all noisily, in fact silently, and the rest of us eat quite silently too, because we're scared shitless when he turns on us with those red eyes and . . . Just kidding, ha ha.

His eyes are green like Daddy's. Black hair. He has an enchanting grin, by the way. Quite a lucid aura, too.

Does he remember anything? Well, he's eleven months old, how could he? Will he remember, there's the real question.

On this subject Duane is the expert. There are a number of things only my husband can explain. Oh, yes—we married. For the sake of stability, you see. We even got custody of Erik. It turned out Erik's mom and her boyfriend are very big messes. The boyfriend is addicted to drugs. Terrible parents. Not like us at all.

———

Now a sticky subject. Duane knew what he was doing, of course. When he told me I was the most "powerful"; when he asked me if I wanted to "bag" Malcolm—Duane knew exactly what he was doing.

I've forgiven him. I'm amazed I have. Every now and then I feel like I haven't. Duane is a serious asshole sometimes.

But, sitting here under the umbrella, waves curling, boys and baby sleeping—Feel's back with me now, out of the sun—my laptop preempting the floral but epileptic script, my memories shaping into hyperreal clarity the desperate facts of my recent life—because of all these reasons, I am, I realize, a happy woman.

I'm sure I haven't answered many questions. But I'll pose the major one for you. Why did I do it?

———

Why did I get the bloody collar from the disgusting dead dog and put that disgusting bloody collar around my neck?

I knew what might happen, obviously. It added up. Duane had been fixated on roses. He'd wanted me to hold the one in the Baggie, that I threw away. Later, when he asked where I put it, when he was hurting my neck while staring into my eyes, he said Malcolm needed Spoor to go on. Then Tor told me how Malcolm had snatched him. Roses were *on his body.*

What really did it, though, was the "thing." The thing in my womb —it had been telling me to stay away from the dog. After talking with Torrance, I decided that meant it was afraid of me touching roses. Which meant, I assumed, Malcolm was afraid of me touching roses.

I was right. Malcolm knew what Duane was doing. He'd sensed Duane's scheme to rearrange the pregnancy. So he responded by making me twinge, by trying to scare me away from roses.

But I'm not answering the question. Why did I do it?

I wanted to snatch him. To make him powerless. I wanted to turn the tables, to flip-flop the boundaries. In other words, I wanted to put him in my Drama Chamber, and *torture him.*

———

Ho, ho, ho! Down to the Chamber we go! Chains clanking, ho-ho!

Wearing the executioner's mask. Ghastly implements *at the ready . . .*

It wasn't like that, of course. Well, it was, in a way. When I started talking abortion.

"Poor Sheila," Malcolm wrote—in the Chronicles, on his Eve of Change, when he was annoyed I wasn't calling to scream about Fearfield—"her drama chamber must be boiling."

With him in it, it was. Never had the Chamber felt so . . . lively.

That was a switch. One of the things I hated about the Chamber was how bored I got there. Hiding from the world. Deeply, safely, airlessly.

Malcolm moving in changed that. Of course it wasn't Malcolm, strictly speaking, it was a microscopic embryo, but I thought of it as Malcolm no matter how much Duane—explained. So I couldn't really hide there any more, could I? Who said, "Hell is other people"?

For me it wasn't other people. It was a thing in my womb; a thing, the way I saw it, that was squatting in my personal sanitarium, taking up the whole place, the only safe place I'd ever known!

I should have foreseen this, right?

Yes. But the night of the Ice Capades I wasn't thinking ahead. I was resigned to No Future, actually—Malcolm had made sure of that. And so when I sat crying on the terrace staring at the radioactive dead dog, listening to him taunt me over the loudspeaker about the Chamber—something inside me—that for a long time had been ready to snap—snapped!

Suddenly I had a fervent desire to rearrange the boundaries. The idea was, let's see how you like it, asshole.

Ho, ho. I soon decided he was liking it. It beat getting eaten by sharks and shitted out in cold winter water. Meantime, I was the one who was out in the cold. For me hell became, "No place to run. No place to hide."

This was unacceptable. I told Duane I was getting an abortion.

He advised against it. He said there might be medical complications.

I said I didn't care. Then I accused him of lying.

He admitted he was, but said there might be complications anyway.

ME: I'm going to a clinic right now.

DUANE: The issue is bigger than you.

ME: It's much smaller than me and I'm having it *scraped out.*

DUANE: Shouldn't you include Tor in the decision-making process?

ME: It's my body.

DUANE: You're carrying a creature that's seven hundred years old and you want to kill it?

ME: Go back to Cambridge and eat tofu and write a book about my despicable lack of respect for history.

DUANE: Maybe I will.

ME: Go ahead!

DUANE: You think you can escape this but you can't. Even if you get an abortion, you can't. It will stay with you for the rest of your life.

ME: I'm getting a lawyer.

DUANE: Sure. Great idea. Better hire George.

ME: That's not funny.

Then Tor came in and said: Sheila, why do you want to get an abortion?

I shouted: Because I'm going insane!

Tor said: But Sheila. You could study it.

I said: *It's* studying *me!*

Duane said: No, it isn't! It's a deeply unconscious fertilized egg that's unique, and seven hundred years old, and totally irreplaceable, and completely defenseless, and you want to *kill it.*

Then Tor said: Sheila. What else you gonna do with your life, anyway? Study sex at schools? Sheila—you can study *it.*

"It."

I had to think about "it" for a while.

I had fantasies of abusing it. I nurtured myself with lurid scenes of abuse. Parents control, don't they? Oh yes. Where infants are concerned, parents decide everything.

Child-rearing experts may dispute this. I know some maintain babies do most of the controlling. They wake, they cry, they demand to be fed. I have learned all about that. It's not what I'm talking about. What I'm talking about is an unequal power relationship.

The idea of having Baby Malcolm at my mercy was fascinating. My mortal enemy was utterly dependent. How much more dependent can you be? Than when you are in the womb? And believe me when I say I grilled Duane on this—the fetal enemy was deeply, deeply unconscious.

He was totally helpless.

As I got heavier the Drama Chamber became a kind of cell block. I was the warden. Not just of Malcolm, of the Grislies, too—those Horrors of whom he'd been the jailor. It was a maximum-security lockup in there. I felt like a human Alcatraz.

I was carrying around seven hundred years of sickness and murder! I wondered how brutal I'd be once he got out. What I'd do to him if he acted up. If he disobeyed. If he got ideas that he'd truly *repaid his debt.* I thought about discipline, punishment, endless revenge.

———

But it began to occur to me that this may be one of the reasons we live in a crazy, mixed-up world. Oh, not because babies are reincarnations of their parents' worst enemies . . .

Or are they? A case could be made. How do we explain abuse? At whom, symbolically, do parents lash out? I brooded about this lashing issue. I didn't like it. I thought about a lot of things, one of which was the fact I seemed able to cope without the Drama Chamber.

Then, as time went by, I started feeling things.

They came slowly. So slowly and subtly I didn't think they were weird. I'd never been pregnant before; I thought this was the mystical experience of carrying a child. I felt him doing marvelous baby things—stirring, turning, kicking. I felt him thinking marvelous baby thoughts. Those were cute, the first, faint baby thoughts—so tiny and precious. And normal, obviously.

Duane thought they were normal. Normal, at least, for a "talented relayer" like me; he thought hearing baby thoughts was wondrous. And I didn't suspect him of lying about it. I have a way of knowing things, now.

Then in the third trimester I felt the baby dreaming marvelous baby dreams. I was asleep when they happened; at first I thought I was dreaming them myself. I seemed to be bonding with Baby. I felt *empathic.*

One night, however, the baby dreamed the most marvelously yet. He dreamed he was taking a walk on a beach. It looked like one of the beaches near our house. I knew this wasn't me dreaming; when Baby dreamed, it didn't happen in my head. It happened in my womb.

My womb was wide-screen for this dream. Baby was scampering along the beach in a magical baby way. Torrance and Erik were there; Baby was following them. They were walking the beach under an enormous moon.

They were so—happy. Baby watched the boys horsing around in the phosphorescent surf; running, splashing, laughing at incomprehensible jokes.

Later, the boys started talking. Baby dreamed what they were saying. They had plans for a big trip, to Antarctica. The tallest mountain ranges in the world are there, buried in ice; but some of the peaks stick through, huge stone things towering to the sky from a continent of ice. The really big ones are supposed to be awesome.

Then the dream took a turn. Baby scampered away from the water, and found a turtle. A giant turtle. It was laying eggs. The boys came over to look; the turtle waddled off, across the beach and into the ocean. The boys stood over the egg nest, talking of life buried there, in the sand. It was safely buried, they decided. That life had hope.

I thought this was touching. Baby was dreaming about himself!

Then I wondered if he might be dreaming about me.

The next morning, the boys announced they'd planned a trip. They wanted to go to Antarctica. They'd decided this the night before, while walking on a beach. Something else had happened on the beach, too. They'd found a turtle that had just laid eggs.

Kip had found it.

I told them Baby had *dreamed* of finding it. They didn't believe me. Then I told them about mountains buried in ice. About handstands in the surf; about the moon shining on the water, on the waddling, sinking shell of the turtle. We looked at Kip, who was eating breakfast. She smiled at us.

Suddenly all of us, Kip included, were serious.

———

We worry about the Grislies. Where are you, Bunny, Gainsborough, Fennel, Gundulf, et al.—not to mention Malcolm? Will you try to make Feel understand? You *Horrors*?

Keep your ghosty hands off!

Duane theorizes they're a way to organize memory. I theorize they're a way to organize guilt. We might both be right.

But the guilt theory really grabs me. "I didn't do it—*'they'* did!"

Of course The Living One had to split himself off from his previous selves. The weight of crime was crushing. Bunny had almost squished under it. Malcolm didn't want that; he had to protect himself, and he did, so thoroughly the Grislies disappeared.

But this put him in a bad predicament. With the Grislies gone, what would become of Malcolm? After he became "Torrance"? Where would criminal, evil Malcolm go? The issue carried freight. Because, if Malcolm were to be deprived of Grislihood—if there were no stairs up which to be kicked—who, post-Change, would there be to "blame"?

Malcolm was terrified at the prospect of the next Living One, Torrance, having no one to blame. No one, that is, except himself— whoever the "self" would be. Not the fine boy who fathered my child. That was for sure.

We find, in Chronicle V, the following paragraph, Grislies-addressed:

"So many different things could have killed us. Yet we live. Where are you? I crave death. I crave peace. I would like to be an innocent child for once. How appealing! Well? Isn't it?''

Like all good parents, and maybe like all bad parents, we're hoping for the best. My specific hope is that Fearfield Massif Spoor won't be haunted. We're trying to provide him with a happy childhood. But who knows?

We have a saying: "Maybe The Grislies Know."

Unlike Duane, I hope they keep it to themselves.

———

Late afternoon sweeps the long, empty beach. The boys are so dark. I tell them about the dangers of sun but they laugh. Wrinkles, to them, are science fiction. They do wear sunscreen. We all think about the vanishing ozone layer. But wrinkles? Wrinkles are for old people.

So there they are in the sun, asleep still, toasting their smooth skin. Feel's waking. He's fisting his eyes and looking hungry. There's nothing wrong with that, is there? Infants are hungry by nature, right?

Kip is getting up. She's ready for dinner too. We eat early here.

Do I have a Drama Chamber now?

No. No, when Feel was born, I discovered the Chamber had gone.

I was too busy to hide. I had boundaries suddenly, firm ones; I had life to deal with. My own, my family's. My son's.

And I had something else to deal with, too. My psi.

I feel things, now. I see things. I *know* things. And it's not like it was when Baby was dreaming. The dreams started the process; but the stuff I do now, I experience on my own.

Often, I know what Feel is thinking. Sometimes I know what Duane, and the boys, are thinking. There are times when I know what total strangers are thinking. One time I knew what people on a yacht way away on the horizon were thinking, and was able to prove it, later, when we heard about the scene those assholes made in the Village. They'd thought the island still was for sale. They'd had plans for it. An expanded airstrip, very large hotels.

We sent them away. Our cheerful resort manager did the talking. Duane is concerned about what people think of us. He worries about attention.

Anyway, I guess the Drama Chamber was why, in the old days, I didn't accept my talent. The reason was simple. If I could feel things, know things, then other people, it followed, could do the same; these people, it then followed, could do those things *to me.*

What a scary idea. People seeing into me? People knowing what I'm thinking? No, that couldn't happen, in the old days. It smacked of tenuous boundaries. And that was why I had the Chamber, of course, to bolster my boundaries. So I could hide.

And I did hide. Most of all, I'm afraid, from myself.

But now I know better. It still makes me a little queasy, I have to admit, but—I'm kind of powerful, now.

How powerful? That I don't know. Duane doesn't know either. Sometimes I think he's nervous about it.

Do I spend a lot of time trying to figure out immortality?

Yes. Not as much as Duane does, but I'm curious about that subject, because of my son. Because of my remarkable child, who is providing me with a most challenging career in psychology; and I'm sure in other, as yet uninvented, disciplines. For example, Feel could end up having "boundary" issues on a scale that makes my old issues seem extremely minor.

Then there's the fact Duane coughs a lot.

He's refused to have plastic surgery on the scars. It was a close call, getting him up Malcolm's icy hill. The man almost bled to death. I'm glad he didn't. I love him. Despite his moodiness, his sense of mission. His spooky obsessions.

And where is my husband? He who shortly will barbecue?

Probably Duane's finished by now.

He's been in the greenhouse all day, tending the roses.

Editors' Afterword: II

Sheila was the one who wanted anonymous "Editors." For the sake of suspense, she said. Who would survive? That kind of drama.

Well, we survived.

The three Project goons didn't. I feel bad about it. There are people in Washington and Cambridge who won't believe me. Those people should be glad they weren't around that Thursday. Maybe we'd all be dead.

Floria and George survived. Floria we talk with every now and then. She doesn't know where we are, of course, but we stay in touch. As for George, maybe he shouldn't have survived. He's paralyzed. He can't talk. It's hard to know if he can think. George, basically, is out of the picture.

I feel bad about it.

All of us were banged up, emotionally as well as physically, the day Tor got rich. We didn't call a regular ambulance. The decision was mine. I foresaw trouble with paramedics and police on the scene. It was a tough decision. I did what I could for George. It's possible a local hospital could have done more. Unlikely, though.

The boys sledded him and Floria up the hill on a mattress. A machine from the garage winched it up. Then they slid it back down and winched up Sheila, the dog and me. I couldn't walk very well, much less climb. My leg was broken. The music room was the emergency room because the library was cold. First thing I did was medicate the lot of them. I examined George and concluded, no hope. But I called two friends in Cambridge, young neurosurgeons, and asked them to make the drive up. They and the ambulance they took cost some money. These guys had student loans to pay. We paid them. Tor did, that is, several days later.

Doctors hate paying student loans.

I'd slapped poultices on my slashes and stitched up Tor and Erik, who were slashed a little, too. Pip was a first-aid nut; the house had supplies. The doctors got to me after they checked out George. Then, with George, a victim of tragic dog-attack, they went back to Cambridge.

Through all this Floria was out. She was out anyway, and stayed that way under medication until nine o'clock Saturday morning. Everybody slept a lot. Except the dog; she wouldn't leave Sheila. I was relieved Sheila wasn't awake to notice. It took my wife-to-be some time to get used to Kip.

Kip snatched her from the very edge of death, of course. That helped. Jaws of Life, you might say. Kip moved pretty damn fast. Not as fast as Malcolm did, though. Malcolm moved in a flash. He had no choice. The plow had hit him, Pip was falling and about to hit, Sheila was sailing over the marble fence and out into the black —Malcolm accomplished a lot in those few split seconds. Luckily for Pip, the dog was wearing roses. Also luckily for Pip, he was plunging scared out of his head to certain death. His terror, the roses, both were prime ingredients for switch. That helped Malcolm force it. I think he had to switch Pip, to force his own switch into the fetus; he needed Pip's help, somehow, on account of being worn out by then. So, Pip became a dog. The dog became Pip and died on the rocks. Malcolm, squished almost in half I reckon by the plough, he too was dying and anyway was getting shoveled into the black. But Pip—or Kip—had his Jaws of Life clamped on Sheila's coat. There she was, Winged Victory, suspended midair, legs scissored open like she was running over the edge. Well, she was, if you can run midair. That's when Malcolm became a fertilized egg. It was his only way out and he knew it. I bet he didn't know if he could do it, but he had to try. Luckily for him, Sheila was wearing roses. Just as luckily, Kip was following orders and the pathway, the psychic connection, was flowing, because along with everything else Sheila, too, was scared to death, of course. So was I, watching. I think I may have helped. I did know what I was doing with the roses, in a way. But only in a way. I, like Malcolm I reckon, didn't know if it would work. If it was possible. As for the final moments, the cross-flow of fear, dog, and roses, of monster psi—I don't know if I contributed to that. It's my gut feeling I did.

Anyway, Malcolm became an unborn, and whatever mind there was in that egg died in Malcolm's body. Pow! The *sweetness!*

Pretty dramatic if you ask me. But I didn't go over this to be dramatic, that's Sheila's department. The reason I describe a few details of what those final switches were like, is this: Besides roses, switching bodies seems to require intense fear. Anybody out there know anything about that?

———

We have gone through the old Chronicles. It was one of the first things I set myself to after we liquidated the assets and left the country. I might mention, Tor's Tokyo land came in handy. A hundred-odd million doesn't go far these days. Not when you have to get lost the way we had to.

Just about every Spoor kept Chronicles. Some kept them all their lives. Others did it last-minute like Malcolm. The house in France was the place where he—they—stored them. The nineteenth- and twentieth-century volumes are in the worst shape, on account of acid paper. The older ones are fine. Some are in French, some in English, some in both; archaically worded, of course.

They are fascinating. They don't reveal a whole lot about roses, dogs and fear, however. Nor do they go into Baybars and Krak. Those topics appear to have been more-or-less taken for granted. In the case of Baybars—that might have been one topic the Living Ones didn't care to dwell on much. It's a topic of interest to us, though. Partly because of our lovable dog Kip.

I think Kip really is Baybars. In some diluted sense, considering he was a dog, as often or more so than a human, since 1271. He accompanied the Living Ones through time, minus much of his memory, apparently. Gundulf & Sons may not have wanted to jog that memory. In fact they may have had their own reasons for forgetting what happened.

What happened, it seems, is that Gundulf stole roses from Baybars, and subjugated him. This could have been some kind of accident. Maybe Gundulf, in a very big way, simply lucked out.

Or maybe he was one hell of a cunning Crusader Psi. Whichever, or by some combination, Gundulf got control of the roses. Maybe the roses wanted him to get control; that's very possible. But then Baybars, in dog form, came with the package. Why was that?

I think Gundulf and Baybars had an intense relationship of some kind. It seems to have stayed intense, too—for seven centuries. Maybe that's not surprising. A master-slave relationship, after all, must be intense.

My feeling about this is fairly strong. Through a combination of luck and cunning, a somewhat similar deal has changed my life. Because now, I'm the one in charge of the roses.

Or you could say they're in charge of me. The roses—how do I put this?—the roses are expedient. They see things happening, and act to their advantage. When Sheila put the collar around her neck and set off through the hedges to bag Malcolm, she was being very brave, true. She knew what she was doing. But she knew in part because she was told. And at that point, she wasn't being told by me.

Because at that point, the roses had about had it with Malcolm. You could say they were going through a crisis of confidence. Probably they would have stuck with him if the situation hadn't turned as nasty as it did. However, all of us were doing our utmost to make it as nasty as possible.

I might add, another factor pushed things our direction. Pip. Noble Pip, dethroned sultan and angry dog, helped a lot.

She's a happy dog now. Happy to be alive, to not have to think very much. Baybars, it seems, is wrapped up tight in some kind of storage. I guess the old memories don't surface unless he's human. Judging from what happened with Pip, memory doesn't come back at all until the Living One approaches Change, and the mess of anguish that goes with it.

Funny how things can change. For example, Malcolm. Little Living One, happy at last. For the time being anyway. Like Sheila, I hope for the best.

———

Back to the Chronicles.

Gundulf didn't do Chronicles. Maybe he couldn't write. His son and grandson didn't Chronicle either. Or if they did, the texts didn't survive. I guess literacy wasn't big in the fourteenth century. But this isn't why the first few "Living Ones" didn't write up the Changes, and so on, I figure, if in fact they didn't. I'm speculating. I don't know for sure.

My feeling is that the first Living Ones didn't have a need to keep track of who they were, and who they became. Probably there wasn't any kind of split-personality stuff going on. Or if there was, maybe it wasn't hard to deal with—the Living Ones probably thought of themselves as Gundulf. After a while, though, this must have become more and more difficult to handle. I reckon those old Spoors even then had to be careful. Immortality has always been a sensational topic. Then throw in murder, murder of your own sons. People would have tended to talk about the Devil, and so on, if those barons had let on to what they were doing. This must have meant they took the new names and identities fairly seriously. After a while the deception probably ritualized into a private game which, since it was such hot stuff, must have acquired all kinds of superstitious overtones. The farther away in time the Living One got from Gundulf, the more mythical Gundulf must have seemed. The Founding Father, maybe; the ancestor who led the family to greatness; the ancestor who figured out a way for the Spoor to beat death.

Death awes mankind. That awe is what makes us human. We know we will die, and invent all kinds of gibberish and philosophy to account for the fact. We dream up gods to get a grip on this cosmic mismanagement of death. To varying degrees of intensity, we talk to these gods, spirits, to these pantheons of forces that run the show. Religion and magic, science, too, are a kind of dialogue with the spectacular forces at play. I suppose these tendencies are as basic as memory, thought and speech. But all this is beyond me, frankly. What I'm saying is, I think the Grislies were inevitable.

The first mention is 1327. "Fissur, Barune Spur," in his "Krony-keles," refers to his "Grissiliche;" to his "Dampned" (damned) "Gosts" (ghosts). The Greisles, Grieslies, Greselys, and so on, make frequent appearances in the Chronickills (love that, *Chronickill*) and Cornykyls, and so on, from there on out. (I'm not bothering with the French versions. I hate French. Bunch of snobs and the language is proof.)

The Oxford English Dictionary defines "Grisly" this way: "Causing horror, terror, or extreme fear; horrible or terrible *to behold or to hear;* causing such feelings as are associated with thoughts of death and 'the other world', *spectral appearances,* and the like." (Emphasis added.)

The Grislies were the Spoor religion. They explained the world. In the early days they more or less accompanied the Living Ones all the time, it seems. They were constant companions who provided advice, strategy, wit, and encouragement to keep Changing. Change was what the Grislies "lived for"—Malcolm himself wrote that. Among other things, Change added to their numbers. Each turning point of Spoor brought a new member into the club. It was a rogue's gallery, this club. It must have livened things up, sort of like the relationship the ancient Greeks had with their gods. Love, hate, everything in between.

Most religions have some kind of sacred text. The Spoors' was the Chronicles. Chronicles were used to summon the Grislies, among other things. I figure the Living Ones got in the habit of keeping them because they were a way to keep alive the memories of the different lifetimes. As such, they must have become very sacred. They were a means to stay in touch.

Too bad for Malcolm he kind of lost touch.

Of course, it wasn't worship, or ancestor-worship, in any usual sense. I agree with Sheila's guilt theory. Malcolm as much as said it, in fact. In addition to adding to the life span, the Grislies gave The Living One someone to blame. Then again, religions always seem to provide someone to blame.

So, I don't think the Grislies existed solely to organize memory. I don't think they existed solely to organize guilt. I think they did both those things and more. They were the center of a religion.

Could be this religion hasn't quite died out yet.

I won't go into a long discussion of what the Chronickills have taught me. Now isn't the time. Besides, I don't understand even a tenth of what those old scrawls describe. They weren't written for the modern world, and they weren't written for anyone but The Spoor anyway.

But there must be scholars somewhere out there who would like to take a crack at the historical record, such as it is. Maybe we can make a deal.

This book, from my point of view, has one purpose only. It's to attract attention to us. It's almost like placing a personal ad. Of course, most everybody won't believe any of what you just read. That's fine by me.

The people I'm interested in will believe it, however. I would like to suggest a way to correspond. In Paris, France, there is an entity called "The Spoor Foundation." It's listed. Write it. Maybe we'll write back.

———

I worry about the future.

"Project Psi" isn't bothering us. Other people could bother us a lot, though, if they set their minds to it. Some day, somebody will. We'll deal with it when it happens. We're prepared. How we're prepared, I won't say.

The Spoor isn't the only such creature on earth. There are others. I hope these creatures don't stay alive the same way The Spoor did. They might. Then again, they might not.

Either way, I'd like to talk to you. I'd like to discuss horticulture and a few other topics, such as dogs, and fear.

Why would I like to do that? Call it a desire to participate in evolution.

Get in touch. You might learn something. That's all I have to say at the moment. Except this:

We don't really live on an island.

The Last Word

This is Tor. That is what I call myself now, by the way. I like Tor. It sounds heroic.

Anyway, Torrance is the name of a city in California. And I used to live in California. Good thing I didn't live in Torrance, California. Maybe my name would have been La Jolla.

That's an Erik joke. He thinks he's funny.

I told it because it leads up to saying I'm relieved to be living in Torrance, the man. I am so relieved, I call myself Tor.

Dad never would have thought of that, calling himself Tor. At least I don't think he would have. Maybe some day I'll ask him.

Maybe you want to know my opinion about what happened.

My basic opinion is this: Duane and Sheila saved my life. If it wasn't for them, I'd be dead, just another Spoor suicide. I'm glad they did what they did. And I think it's ok for Duane to be nuts over this immortality trip. The fact is that he and Sheila are wonderful people, and I will be grateful for the rest of my life.

So here we are, living on this island paradise. Uh-oh - Duane said it isn't really an island. Or is it?

That's for us to know and you to find out. If you're one of those crazies who wants to find us and discover the secrets of living forever.

I'm still a teenager. I don't worry about death. I think I'm immortal anyway, see? Just kidding. I was about to die for a brief period, twenty months ago. It wasn't fun.

Wherever we are, it is a paradise, I will confirm that.

Erik and I are lovers. We have been together a long time now. Twenty months is a long time, right? It seems like forever. We're loyal to each other usually. That doesn't stop us from looking, though. Sometimes Erik gets carried away but that's because he's immature. Just kidding. I get carried away, too. Not as much as he does, though. But sometimes I do. Last week, for example, I went to this really wild party down at the Village.

You wouldn't believe the stuff that goes on in the Village. The kids are degenerate. These kids will do anything. At the party last week, the costumes were wild: Nubian Nudist. Everybody was supposed to be gilded and naked like Cleopatra's court. They all were except me, but I got into the swing of things with a lot of help from opinionated, arguing boys. They gilded me and installed my plumage, eagerly. Then we pranced forth all over the yacht and episodes of bondage and mastery were committed, just kidding, ha-ha (that was for Erik.)

Seriously, we're in love. We're Comrades in Arms - each others'. We saved each other from those dogs! Uggggo-yucccck-gacckk, as I would say.

We're not totally concupiscent. We go fishing. We hike. We swim. We hold hands at the movies and even go on dates to recapture that tender romantic feeling sometimes. We pursue our education through computers, and Sheila the well-known educational expert helps us.

We travel. We travel a lot. What else? Oh, yeah. We participate in the upbringing of my son, Fearfield.

Cool name, huh? Say it loud and hear the sound of dread!

It annoyed me when I found out Dad wrote *The Fearfield Club*. My hero, Fearfield, was - Dad! Kind of shook me up. Anyway, Dad really is Fearfield now, somehow, and I do not know how, but I think it is appropriate that my son goes by the name of his own grandfather's twisted, wild-eyed creation.

If he isn't gay, I won't be disappointed. Children must find their own destiny. Within limits, of course. Strict limits. I plan to be a strict father. I am already, but you wouldn't know it from the affection I lavish on the kid. Sometimes I think I spoil him.

It's a weird situation.

I may not be nuts over immortality, but I am curious about my son who happens to be my father, and twenty-five other ancestors, too. Lucky for me, I'm the Missing Link, of a kind, in the long line of Spoors. But that gives me a perspective to really get into it, you know?

The Chronickills are amazing. I'm learning Old French and English so I can understand them better. Maybe some day I'll be an expert. A historian: Professor Spoor. I own a castle in France, and a place in England. They could become centers of learning for this ridiculous shit that happens to be true. Too true, I sometimes think. But it's completely engrossing. In all senses of that strange word.

We don't go to the houses Dad kept. We're in hiding in paradise most of the time. The lawyers keep up the houses. A lot of lawyers work for me. They pay other people who guard the warehouses where the old junk is stored. The Spoor had heirlooms. They're creepy. But they might be valuable evidence. Maybe some day that evidence can get the attention it deserves.

So if you know anything about this, drop us a line. Duane the fanatic will consider serious proposals and so will I. But now I have to go for a walk with Kip. We want to see what Erik's doing down at the Village.

———

Maybe I should mention one last thing. We changed our names.

I worry about us too.